CURSE OF MAGIC

The Fairy Tale Enchantress Book 2

K. M. SHEA

CURSE OF MAGIC
Copyright © 2019 by K. M. Shea

Cover Art by Deranged Doctor Design
Edited by Jeri Larsen

All rights reserved. No part of this book may be used or reproduced in any number whatsoever without written permission of the author, except in the case of quotations embodied in articles and reviews.

This is a work of fiction. Names, characters, places, and incidents are either the product of the author's imagination, or are used fictitiously. Any resemblance to actual persons, living or dead, or historic events is entirely coincidental.

www.kmshea.com

ISBN: 978-1-950635-04-7

For Meg, Myrrhlynn, Jeri, and my Mom.
You guys make up the best team an author could have.
Thank you for encouraging me through the painful creation of this series.

MAP OF THE CONTINENT

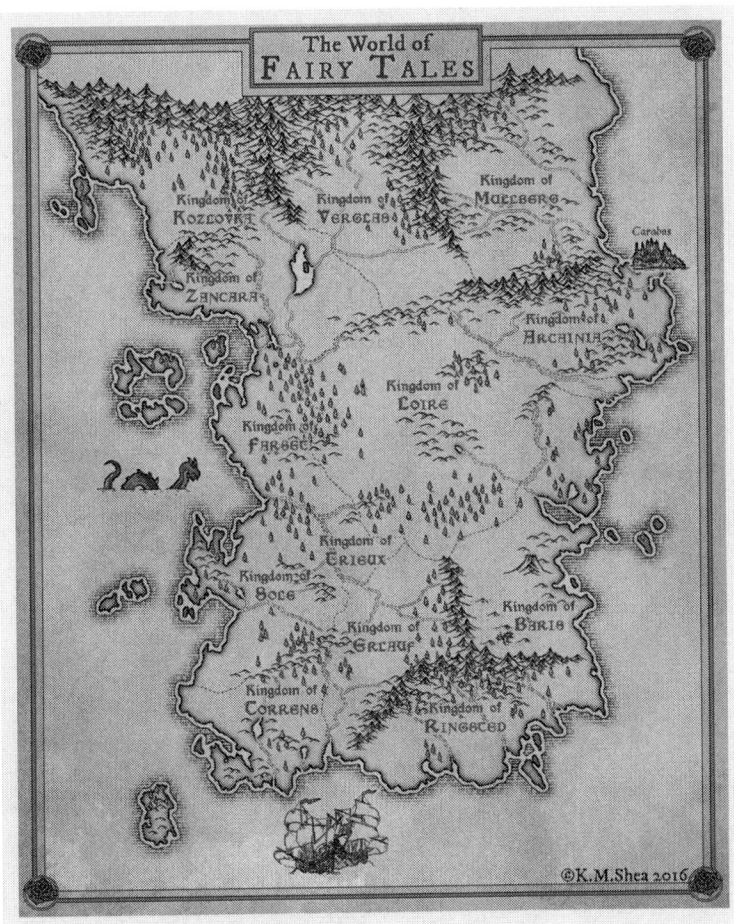

CHAPTER 1

My first task without any sort of supervision, and I'm plotting how to bluff my way into a royal palace. That certainly bodes well for my future as an enchantress who stands for all things good and righteous.

Angelique squinted at the white walls that surrounded the glittering royal palace of Loire. It was separated from the rest of the city, and even above the walls, she could see the ornate eyesore that was the palace. (Whether the royal family was trying to flaunt their wealth, or they really had such poor taste in architecture and decorating, she didn't know. Regardless, Angelique suspected one should not have more than a dozen statues of naked baby cherubs decorating a single wall.)

Even though I'm only an Enchantress-in-Training, I'm fairly certain they'll let me inside. But I'll need a believable story for why I want to see the royal family's enchanted mirror.

She couldn't tell them the *truth*. If word got back to the Veneno Conclave—the organization to which all good mages, fairy godmothers, and enchanters belonged—she'd be sent back to her empty home.

No, she'd have to trick her way into the mirror.

No doubt any other mage would gasp at the idea of lying—no, *bluffing*...that sounded a little less morally...wrong—but Angelique was backed into a corner.

Her master—the youngest Lord Enchanter in history, who had taken her on as an apprentice to keep her from being sealed for possessing dangerous magic—had been captured by black mages, and it was all her fault.

The Veneno Conclave was making an effort to find him...if by "effort" one meant creating a committee that was investigating all black mage reports over the last 50 years.

It would be years before the committee would be able to find him, if not decades. And Angelique wasn't going to leave him in the clutches of black magic for that long.

I need to get to that mirror to see if I can verify his location. There were other mirrors, of course, but they were all owned by other magic users—no one who would be willing to help her: the Veneno Conclave's barely tolerated *monster*.

Angelique shook her head. *Focus. What story can I peddle that will get me inside and give me access to that mirror without stirring suspicions?*

She tapped her chin as she flicked her gaze from the wall to the guards standing at the gateway. There were more of them than usual; at least two dozen were present. *I'm not confident in my ability to cast an invisibility spell strong enough to get me into the palace and to the mirror. I don't even know where they are storing it these days. I can't very well sneak in like some kind of spy—I'd probably break my neck climbing the wall. Yes, a bluff is the easiest method. If that is the case, then, I better fit the role.*

Angelique checked her dress—a purple gown covered with iridescent gauze—and rearranged her face into a bright smile.

While traveling with Evariste as his student, Angelique usually adopted the personality of a cheerful—if not slightly vapid—young lady. But now, without Evariste present and adding an automatic air of awe, she'd need to add a flavor of competency to her presence (because if anyone got even a hint of her true, sarcastic nature, they'd think her even more morally gray than originally believed and seal her magic so fast her head would spin).

Angelique tipped her head as she thought of the beautiful and awe-inspiring elves of Alabaster Forest. *Yes, that will be the sort of front I need now.*

She made her smile slighter—and more serene—and twitched off the hood of her cloak. A quick, ladylike pat assured her that her long brunette tresses were still mounded on her head with jeweled pins, and a twitch of magic confirmed the presence of the illusion spell she used to color her eerie silver eyes to a blue hue. She was properly dressed for the role.

Then let's begin.

Angelique approached the gateway, noting the way the guards' hands were settled on their swords or spears. The handful of them that had crossbows already had bolts loaded, but they seemed to be paying closer attention to the palace that stretched behind them, not the city street before them.

That is rather odd.

She didn't let her confusion show on her face, but when she drew close enough to see the beads of sweat that lined their upper lips despite the cool evening air, she doubted the intelligence of her plan. *If they are this nervous, perhaps this is not the best time to attempt a break-in.*

She considered turning back, but it was too late. Several of the guards had already noticed her presence and stood at attention.

Fabulous.

Angelique kept her smile slight as she offered them a tilt of her head. "Good evening. I am Enchantress-in-Training Angelique—"

"Thank the stars!" one of the soldiers gasped in relief, his shoulders drooping. "Maybe you can stop 'im!"

Angelique blinked. "I beg your pardon?"

The guards' tight expressions thawed, but she could still see the crinkle of worry in the eyes of those closest to her.

"This way, Lady Enchantress." A guard wearing some sort of armband gestured for her to follow him down the white lane that led into the palace grounds.

Angelique reluctantly trailed after him, fighting to keep calm when three soldiers fell in line behind her. *Well, I'm inside. But I suspect it's not because of my dazzling greeting.* "I'm afraid there might be a mistake, for I am not a Lady Enchantress but only an Enchantress-in-Training."

"In-training or not, you're the only one who might be able to do something—before we have a real tragedy," the lead guard said grimly.

That delightful statement made the hair on the back of Angelique's neck prickle. "I don't understand." It took her quite a bit of effort to keep her voice serene as they veered off the lane and took a stone pathway that snaked around the side of the glittering palace.

"He's gone mad," the lead soldier explained as he passed by a flowering rosebush. "And he's transformed into some kind of animal!"

Angelique clenched her teeth, still struggling to understand. "Who?"

"Prince Severin," a guard behind her said.

Severin? Angelique briefly strained her memory before she recalled the name. Severin was King Rèmy's illegitimate son that Queen Nicole had officially welcomed into the family when he was a child.

And now he had transformed into an animal? *But...how?*

There was a roar that cut off into an animalistic snarl. It sounded like the source was just a bit past the bushes.

The lead soldier glanced back at Angelique, his face white. "That would be His Highness," he said, his voice strangled.

They rounded a bend in the path and almost rammed into the

wall of soldiers lined up around a garden that was already half enclosed by rose bushes that were blooming unseasonably early.

"This way...Prince Lucien will want to speak with you first." Angelique's guide strode around the edge of the wall of soldiers, leading away from the snarls that clawed their way out of the enclosed garden.

Angelique inclined her head, trying to peer over the men, but she couldn't see anything as the purple haze of dusk settled over the garden.

A man shouted in pain, and there was the roar of a wild cat.

"Your Highness, you *must* retreat to a safer place."

Angelique snapped her attention forward.

Soldiers and medics dressed in white were clumped around a blond-haired man who was dressed in the height of Loire fashion —an emerald green coat with jewel buttons, white breeches, and black, buckled shoes. Though dressed like a fashionable dandy, the young man's face was twisted in the rather *un*-dandy-like expression of anger, and a hint of fear showed in the way his hands shook.

"I'm not leaving him," the young man spat. "The second I do, you're going to kill him!"

"Your Highness, we are doing our best to contain him," another soldier said. "But if we cannot take any measure to subdue the beast—"

"He's my *brother*, not a mindless monster!" he shouted. "And if you harm him, I'll have you thrown in the dungeon myself!"

"Prince Lucien!" Angelique's guide shouted. "I brought help."

Prince Lucien—who was, if Angelique recalled correctly, the crown prince of Loire—eyed the guard, though he stopped breathing when he looked over Angelique from head to toe. "Who are you?" he finally asked.

"My name is Angelique, I am an Enchantress-in-Training—"

Lucien knocked over five guards as he lurched to Angelique, snatching up her hands.

Angelique jerked her head back in surprise, her unease growing as Lucien stared into her eyes as if she had made the world.

"Can you help my brother?" he asked.

"I don't know," Angelique said honestly. "What happened to him?"

Lucien dropped her hands and strode away, beckoning for her to follow after him. "No one is sure. He had just droned on at me for no less than an hour about our country's cavalry. When the meeting finished, he headed out to the rose gardens. Shortly after, this happened." Lucien climbed onto the lip of a fountain and pointed into the garden.

Angelique hesitated, then joined him, the new vantage point giving her the extra height she needed to see.

A *beast* prowled in the rose garden. A creature that was an eerie union of feline and canine with the head of a black cat, unnaturally broad shoulders, and the hind legs of a dog. The tattered remains of what had probably been a white shirt and navy trousers hung from the animal's fur-covered frame, which was matted with blood—not his, judging by the bloodied claws that jutted from his fingertips.

The beast snarled as it stalked through the garden, stepping over inert bodies of soldiers strewn around the gardens. Its slitted, amber eyes seemed to glow brighter and brighter as night fell, and the garden was lit only by the light of the moon and a few flickering torches.

"That is Prince Severin?" Angelique asked, unable to keep the disbelief from her voice.

"It is," Prince Lucien said with more certainty than the situation warranted. "Those are his clothes he's wearing. When the guards first heard him roar, they entered the gardens just in time to spy a witch fleeing. Assumedly, she did this to him—and when I find her, she's going to pay *dearly* for doing so. Can you help him?"

Angelique took a breath as she reached for a wisp of her magic.

It flooded her with too much enthusiasm, and she barely had time to smother the automatic cringe.

Up until recently, Angelique had kept her magic as cut off from her as possible. She had done it because there was no denying that her core magic—the ability to control anything with a sharp edge—was dangerous. But it was the practice of keeping herself isolated from her magic that had cost Evariste. If she had reacted faster...

Angelique shook her head as she manipulated her magic, letting it flow through her before she looked back at the prowling beast.

She barely held in her hiss.

A spell, signified by the blood-red chains of symbols and magic script, wrapped around the prince-turned-beast.

The letters and symbols glowed like angry, red-hot coals, and as Angelique watched, they sank deeper and deeper into the prince. A red haze surrounded him, but most of the fingers of dark magic hovered around his head.

As she watched, the transformed prince loped at the eastern wall of soldiers, his clawed fingertips extended.

The men held their spears out and steeled their shields in preparation.

Prince Severin—or rather the beast that used to be Prince Severin—lunged. He raked his fingers across the surface of a shield, leaving jagged claw marks behind. The guard holding the shield stumbled backwards, but the soldiers standing behind him steadied him.

Several other guards crowded forward with the spears, jabbing them at the prince.

"Don't hurt him!" Lucien shouted, ripping at his fine blond hair with his hands. He tried to approach the gardens, but three soldiers held him back.

A swipe of Prince Severin's claws, and he chopped the end of a spear off, but another soldier thumped him in the side with a sturdy staff, making the beastly prince retreat.

Prince Severin was spelled for certain, but it seemed like something...more. There was something about the spell that reminded Angelique of the tiny Princess Rosalinda of Sole who had been cursed as a babe.

It took her a few moments to pick apart the pieces of the spell before she was certain. "Prince Severin has been cursed," she said, "to take on the body and mind of a beast." She frowned as she read another strand of magic. "And those belonging in his household have been cursed to wane away with him."

"What does that mean?" Prince Lucien impatiently shifted next to her.

"It means all of the prince's personal servants are going to disappear, and Prince Severin will be a wild animal," Angelique said.

"Can you undo it?" Lucien demanded.

"No one can simply *undo* a curse," Angelique barely kept herself from growling. "We can modify it, perhaps change it so it can be broken, but curses aren't easy to dismantle."

"Yes, but can you save him?" Lucien asked.

Angelique slowly shook her head as she watched the spell settle deeper and deeper into the prince. The curse was too quick and too powerful—whoever cast it had as much power as an enchanter or enchantress, and with her limited knowledge of curses, Angelique couldn't stop it.

Lucien grabbed her by the shoulders, making her look at him. "I'll give you anything you desire—money, lands—just, *please*, save him!" The crown prince knelt before her in desperation.

Angelique shook her head and glanced back at the transformed prince when he roared and ran at another group of soldiers.

She wanted to scream in frustration. This is what she was

supposed to be trained for—to save people! Evariste had spent over a decade teaching her to help those in need, and the first person she encountered without him, she was incapable of helping.

Her heart heavy, she continued, "I'm sorry, but—" Her apologies died in her throat when she studied the cursed prince again.

As she watched the blood-red script of the curse that surrounded Severin, she realized the curse wasn't one solid spell, but rather cast in two pieces. There was a line of script cursing the prince to have the body of a beast and dooming his household, and a separate line giving him the mind of an animal.

And as she watched, she spotted a few symbols in the latter two pieces that were weakened by the pulsating magic that powered the spell. *I think I can cut off the bit that makes him mentally an animal, and if I insert my modification correctly, I think I can stop his servants' curse, too, though I can't reverse whatever damage has already been done. But to insert the modification, I need to give him a way to break his curse.*

The line of the spell that cursed Severin into the form of an animal was undoubtedly the strongest. It seemed to spit sparks of magic, and it swirled around his body at a much faster rate.

That part is tied to his appearance...and what better way to defeat a spell based on appearance than romantic love? I can use the power unleashed by love when he falls in love with a girl and she with him! A lucky thing given that not all curses are structured to be defeated by romantic love, when romantic love is the only modification I know how to cast.

It would be risky—curse modification was an advanced magic she hadn't learned much about. But though Evariste was who-knew-where, Angelique could almost *feel* him prodding her.

The danger didn't matter—she had to save him.

"I've got it," Angelique said. "I can save him—or his mind and servants at least."

"Do it!" Lucien commanded.

Not so fast, Mr. Impatient—I can't afford any misunderstandings as long as I'm wandering around without a master. "There's nothing I can do to dismantle the curse of his physical appearance," she warned him. "But I can give him a chance to do it himself by harnessing romantic love. He'll be able to reverse whatever effects the spell has already inflicted on his household as well."

"Whatever is necessary, I don't care. Just *save him*!" Lucien growled, sounding a little like the animal prowling the rose garden.

Angelique nodded and made her way to the enclosure. Lucien tried to follow her, but based on his complaints, his men were holding him back.

"Excuse me," Angelique murmured when she reached the wall of soldiers.

The guards bowed their heads in respect as they parted, letting Angelique edge her way through.

Angelique's heart throbbed in her chest as she stepped into the garden, leaving the protection of the guards. The metallic scent of blood and the fragrant smell of blooming roses created a gut-wrenching combination that made her feel a little ill.

Prince Severin didn't notice her right away—he was harassing a soldier on the far side of the garden, blood flecking his white teeth.

She held in a shiver. *No fear—I haven't any room for it right now. Besides, in comparing abilities to kill, I crush him with my war magic.*

She eyed the spellwork twining around him again, confirming her observations about the formation of his curse.

He roared when a soldier jabbed him in the chest with the butt of a spear, and he swiped, his claws grazing the guard's bicep.

Angelique pushed her shoulders back. She had better get started, or he would attack her before she could stop him.

Hesitantly, Angelique reached for her magic. This time, instead of taking in the smallest wisp, she let it flood her.

She hissed as her cold, sharp magic enfolded her. Her mind

felt clearer, but it was the heady weight of *power* that made her nervous. It ran from her itchy palms to the soles of her feet, an intoxicating sensation that made her clench her teeth.

Enough!

She widened her stance and stopped her magic from further invading her senses, then slightly shook her head in wonder.

If this is how it felt for other enchanters and enchantresses, no wonder Evariste had always been after her to let her magic go free. It was so much easier to wield, but it was also dangerously *intoxicating*.

Prince Severin's amber eyes yanked Angelique back to the present. He was watching her.

Whispering under her breath, she started crafting two spells at once—one that would stop the prince if he tried to jump her, and another that would serve as the modification to his curse.

Silvery puffs of mist started to ebb around Angelique as she built her spells, and soon her hands glowed silver as well.

Prince Severin growled, a noise so loud Angelique felt it in her belly, and his triangular ears twitched, but he didn't attempt to approach her.

Wise move, kitty-cat, Angelique thought as she sucked on her teeth. *I'm not even half as confident as I appear to be, and a wrong move might make all the guards' weapons turn on us.*

She was confident in her defensive spell to be sure, but the modification? No. Curse modification required a precise and calculated use of magic—something she didn't exactly have time for at the moment.

But I have to try to save him. If Evariste were here, he would make me attempt it, even if it is dangerous...

Angelique cut her thoughts off before she could start mentally despairing her wretched powers—now, with a prince covered in blood and fur, was *not* the time for a tea party of pity.

Prince Severin snarled and took a step towards her, crushing a fallen rose beneath his foot (or rather his paw, considering his state).

She hurriedly heaped her magic, forging the modification to the spell and preparing to forcibly insert it. (That was where the real danger was: trying to squeeze her work into the curse.) There was a perfect spot for it—a piece in the chain of the curse that was clearly weakened.

Still, if she blundered her spell and snipped the wrong part, she'd kill him. *Of course, if I lose control of the defensive spell, I'd likely kill everyone in the garden, so perhaps inserting the modification is not so risky after all.*

She grimaced, more aware of her station as a mere student than she ever had been before.

There were so many ways this could go wrong. *I'm overreaching. Only fourteen years of practice is barely a grain of sand to an enchantress with the lifespan of an elf. There's no way I can do this!*

Angelique double-checked her modification as Prince Severin began stalking in her direction.

Hurry, hurry, HURRY!

She swallowed a yelp when he leaped at her, his claws extended, and his eyes gleaming yellow in the moonlight. He snarled, and one of his claws brushed the fabric of her skirts before she thrust her left hand forward, hitting him with her defensive spell.

Her magic surged, and the cursed prince was thrown backwards with such force that his snarl was cut off into a gurgle. He smashed deep into a rose bush and was still for a moment, dazed most likely. (He would have plowed into the wall of guards far across the garden if he hadn't taken the dive into the thorny bush.)

Too much magic in that spell. Probably.

Angelique didn't allow a flicker of fear to show but instead kept her expression impassive even though internally she was not nearly so calm.

Cripes, that was close! I have never been so near to shrieking in my life!

Though she dearly wanted to run away screaming, Angelique remained motionless. If she let on just how inexperienced she was, if anyone realized she really shouldn't be wandering around without supervision, her plans to find Evariste would be sunk before they even began.

Don't move, don't move, don't move. Angelique hurriedly finished her modification spell, hesitating as she looked it over one last time.

I have no idea if I've done this right. If Evariste were here, he would assure me and coax me along but...

Angelique only allowed herself to blink when the cursed prince began rustling in the bush, growling his displeasure.

Roland, however, would tell me I am horrible at this, but that I need to fake it anyway. Perhaps, in this case, he is right.

Her heart pounding in her throat, Angelique waited until Prince Severin stumbled out of the rose bush—which had made an even bigger mess of his clothes.

When he looked in her direction and his lips peeled back, revealing his blood-covered teeth, she struck.

Angelique flung the spell at him, every muscle in her body stiff with worry. She held her breath as she watched her modification hit him.

It was supposed to make a precise cut to the curse that gave Prince Severin the mind of a beast, making it dissipate.

Instead, Angelique watched with horror as her silvery spell briefly bumped against the angry red script before swallowing it.

Her silver magic swirled up and down the chain, devouring it with an inescapable hunger. A sound not unlike a thousand blades pulling free from a thousand scabbards filled the air as her spell *ate* the last part of the curse.

Silver mist pooled around Prince Severin's feet—paws?—as her spell then began encircling the second piece of the curse—the part that doomed his household to fade away and gave him the form of a beast.

In a blink-and-miss-it move, her modification sliced through the chain of spellwork. Her magic surrounded the loosened link of the curse, smothering it within a moment.

Prince Severin made a confused-sounding mewl before collapsing on the ground in a heap.

Angelique tried not to gape in horror. *What just happened?*

The combination of her magic modifying—or *eating*—the curse gave her a rush of information. Angelique blinked as she tried to process what her powers told her—that Severin's servants had started to fade away, beginning with their faces and voices. Just as her magic now padded his body—which would help shatter his curse once he broke it himself—she was vaguely aware of her magic slipping from her and forming face masks for Severin's servants.

Angelique barely managed to keep her eyes from bugging. *Advanced magic—like curse modification—is entirely different from simple things like illusions and alteration spells. Evariste either drastically overestimated me or lost his last bit of sanity if he thought I was ready to take my vows as an enchantress!*

Her head held high, Angelique waltzed across the garden and elegantly crouched in front of Severin, appearing calm when, really, she was holding her breath, praying she had not just killed the illegitimate prince.

Please be alive!

She relaxed slightly when she saw he still breathed. *I can't tell if it worked yet, but at least I didn't kill him.*

A quick scrutiny of the new spellwork revealed everything was working as it should be. His curse to have the body of a beast and the bit about his servants was still present, but her modification was now a silver line in a chain of angry red script.

The cursed prince groaned—sounding more human than animal, which was a very promising sign. She tugged on her magic and prepped another spell that would drive him back into the bushes if he still lacked his human mind.

Angelique pressed her lips together as the prince peeled his head off the grass and peered up at her. "Prince Severin, can you hear me?" she asked. (She thought her voice sounded admirably calm considering she was squatting next to a man whose fur was matted with blood.)

Severin groaned again. "What?" he said, or at least that's what Angelique assumed he was trying to say. He sounded garbled—as if he were talking around a mouthful of pebbles.

Thank every star in the sky—he has his mind. Rather than jumping to her feet and squawking with glee, Angelique made herself smile and call out to the soldiers, "Please inform His Highness Prince Lucien that it worked."

Severin tried to rub his eyes, but froze with his hand raised in front of his still-furry face.

Assuming he was on the verge of questioning his sight—understandable after waking up as a large cat—Angelique rested her hand on his shoulder. "Severin, you need to remain calm," she said in the most soothing imitation of Evariste she could muster. "You were attacked."

The prince closed his eyes. "There was a witch." His voice was rough and thick—like a cat's rumble—but he was easier to understand now.

"Yes," Angelique agreed. "She cursed you to live as a beast and for your household to wither away and disappear with you."

Severin sat up a little more and spit, freezing when he saw his saliva was red with blood.

Angelique's heart squeezed in sympathy for the young prince as he turned to the side and retched. She dared to place a hand on his back. *This poor man. I might have saved him, but this is going to be a blight on his life.*

When he stopped gagging, he sat down and stared at the wreckage of the garden. "I injured people."

Angelique gazed at the garden with him, nodding in approval when she saw the medical attendants rushing around the bodies of fallen soldiers, helping those that they could.

She swung her gaze back to Severin. *Should I soften what happened? But he seems like the sort who would prefer a hard truth.* "You did," Angelique said bluntly. "The witch's curse stole your mind. You didn't know what you were doing." She watched his face, trying to decipher any recognizable expressions in his feline features. "She made you a beast in body and mind."

"Why am I alive?"

Angelique rested her hands on the slight puff her skirts created. "Your brother would not give the order for the soldiers to eliminate you. Luckily, I happened to be on hand, as I was intending to request an audience with you."

The prince squinted at her. "Who are you?"

Angelique offered him a slight smile that was hopefully reassuring. "My name is Angelique. I am an Enchantress-in-Training."

"You saved me?"

And here comes the fun part. "In a partial meaning of the word, yes. I can't entirely undo a curse that has been laid; my master hasn't taught me that art yet. But once, I was at a christening, and the child was in a bit of a bind, which is where I learned how to modify and weaken curses," she said, opting to explain it slowly rather than bluntly tell him the boundaries of his curse straight away.

"So, I changed your curse. Instead of living as a complete beast, you are only one in body. Your mind is still yours; it is human, and it will be so for the rest of your life."

As she spoke, Severin seemed to take inventory of his new face. He traced his angular ears, flat nose, and protruding muzzle, then stared at his blood-spattered fur.

Angelique cleared her voice. *Shock is probably setting in, poor boy. But at least all this is temporary. It should be relatively easy for him to break the curse in comparison to his other...options.* "I was also able to stop the curse from spreading further on your servants. They are no longer disappearing, but I'm afraid they cannot speak, and to save their faces, I had to encase them with masks."

"Will they ever speak again?" Severin asked, a slight tremor to his voice.

"Perhaps. It depends on you. I cannot entirely undo the curse, but you can," Angelique said.

"How?"

"By falling in love, by another falling in love with you. Love is a powerful emotion. Working it into the curse was the easiest way out I could forge for you." Angelique's smile waned slightly. *Personally, it seems like a ridiculous way to break a curse when something like brotherly love might have been stronger given the way Prince Lucien was acting, but it works, and it's the only one I know, so there is no sense complaining about it. Really, I ought to be grateful I could use romantic love in this instance, or there would have been nothing I could have done to save him.*

Severin grasped his feline face with a hand.

Angelique inched a little closer to the prince. "You don't look very happy. It might sound impossible"—*or just plain stupid*—"but allow me to assure you that love will not evade you."

He did not respond.

"Severin?" Angelique frowned slightly, wondering if he was listening at all.

"Brother!" Lucien plowed through a line of protesting soldiers, fell to his knees—ruining his fancy pants—and threw his arms around Severin.

"You...big...why?" Lucien struggled to speak as he squeezed his brother—who was now *much* larger than he—in a tight hug.

Angelique stood to mask her eye rolling. *Yes, using brotherly love would have been* much *more logical. Oh well.*

"You should stay back, Lucien." Severin's voice was still deep and growly—a new feature, probably, of his new body. "We don't know for certain that I'm safe to be around yet."

"Don't be an idiot," Lucien snapped. "You're no more dangerous to me than a pony!"

"The curse has been altered, Your Highness; your mind is yours again," Angelique said gently. "You will not regress."

Severin's ears flattened on his skull, and he looked away.

Lucien abruptly stood. "Thank you, Lady Enchantress, for your aid."

"Enchantress-in-Training," Angelique said.

Lucien ignored the correction. "I don't know what we would have done…" He glanced back at Severin, then shook himself as though casting off a dark dream.

The Crown Prince gave Angelique a rakish smile and grabbed her hand. "What can I give you that will properly express my thanks?" He kissed her hand. "Money? Jewels? Land?" With each word, he kissed her hand again.

Angelique yanked her palm out of his grasp and attempted to discreetly wipe her hand off on her skirts. "Actually, I have a request."

CHAPTER 2

"You saved my brother—my commanding general and dearest companion—and this is all you wish for? To view his magic mirror?" Lucien complained.

Severin ignored his brother and was instead gazing at himself in a small hand mirror.

"Yes, Your Highness," Angelique said. "As a user of magic, it is my duty to help those in need. I am only glad my desire to use the enchanted mirror brought me here at such a time." She stood in front of the enchanted mirror and tried not to feel awkward.

Apparently because Severin was the commanding general of Loire's armed forces, the royal family had given him the mirror to use at his discretion.

This meant the thing was kept in his personal quarters. So, in facing the mirror, Angelique was standing next to two wardrobes of Severin's clothes, and somewhere behind her, Lucien was lounging on his brother's bed.

This isn't awkward at all. Angelique forced her spine straight and clasped her hands in what she hoped resembled a thoughtfully elegant pose. *And how am I going to get them out of this room so I can ask the mirror to search for Evariste? I can't risk the Conclave hearing I'm making my own investigation.*

Angelique eyed the mirror. It was the same one she had verified with Evariste years ago—when Severin and Lucien were mere children.

The thought made her grimace.

She studied the mirror's surface, gazing particularly at Severin's reflection as he stared at his hand mirror. *Why did the witch curse him, anyway? The curse laid upon him used a different sort of magic than what was used on Evariste...does that mean there are two groups of black mages running around? But black mages aren't typically...collaborative.*

But why would a rogue magic user choose to attack Prince Severin of all people? He couldn't have been an easy target, and nothing would have been gained by seeing him die—he isn't even the crown prince.

Severin suddenly whirled around, as if coming out of a reverie. "Back in the gardens. Did you say my *servants* were affected by the curse?"

Angelique turned around to address him. "Your entire household, yes."

Severin swiveled and made for the door.

Lucien scrambled off the bed. "Severin—wait! You can't just run willy-nilly through the castle without an escort!" he yowled as he followed after his brother, leaving Angelique alone in Severin's quarters.

Angelique listened for a moment, but Lucien's complaints continued down the hall, growing quieter and quieter.

Now was her chance.

Angelique licked her lips as she faced the enchanted mirror once again. "Mirror, show me Lord Enchanter Evariste."

She held her breath...but nothing happened.

Angelique's heart fell. "Mirror, show me Lord Enchanter Evariste's home, Wistful Thicket," she said.

Instantly, the glass surface swirled before showing a front

image of Evariste's house. The thicket was dark, but the windows were cheerfully lit, and the magic balled at the apex of the roof cast a silver light across the house.

"Mirror, show me Lord Enchanter Evariste of the Fire Gates," Angelique tried once more.

The mirror's surface returned to her reflection, leaving no doubt in her mind that the mirror couldn't find her master.

Angelique's legs trembled, and she sat down heavily in front of the mirror.

I knew there was a chance this wouldn't work—the Conclave must have similarly searched for him when I first got news to them that Evariste was captured. But...I had hoped...

The mirror's inaction was possibly the worst news possible, for it meant one of two things: wherever Evariste was, the black mages were magically shielding him so he could not be found...or he was dead.

He can't be dead. Angelique took a deep breath as she tried to combat the despair that threatened to engulf her. *He's too powerful. If black mages went through the effort of capturing him, it must mean they intend to use him for some terrible purpose. They wouldn't toss aside a magic user of his caliber so easily.*

Angelique stretched so she could brush the edge of the mirror with a fingertip. She paused, then cleared her throat. "Mirror, show me Roland Archibald Whisperpaws the Fifth."

When the mirror swirled, Angelique scrambled to her feet.

He's alive! Roland is alive! If I can find him—

She blinked rapidly as the image sharpened into something recognizable.

Roland peevishly peered off into the distance, his bronze eyes glowing in the moonlight. Though it was dark, Angelique could still see the way he twitched his black tail as he walked down what looked like a city street. The wretched and bespelled black leather collar with the aqua jewel Angelique had made for practice and put on him was still fastened around his neck.

I was such an idiot to ever put that on him! But where is he?

Angelique frowned as she tried to make out more of his surroundings.

The magic cat paused under a flickering torch before he jumped onto a hitching post outside what appeared to be an inn or tavern.

She squinted and leaned forward, trying to make out the furled flag that hung from a flagpole by the window. A gold, double-headed phoenix on a field of deep reddish purple marked the cloth. That was the *Baris* flag!

Angelique grabbed the edges of the mirror and peered at the image. "What is Roland doing in Baris?"

She opened her mouth, intending to tell the mirror to show her the city Roland was in, before she realized it was night, and she'd only get a view of darkness.

Angelique backed away from the mirror, and the image of the black and white cat faded as the reflective surface returned. She barely noticed as she pursed her lips and turned to the door, her eyes settling on the floor as she thought. "I'll have to track him myself...but how did he get all the way over to *Baris*?"

"Who is in Baris?" Lucien asked as he strolled back into the room. Severin stalked in behind him, walking with a man wearing an eye-catching peacock blue jacket and waistcoat and a black mask over his face.

Angelique felt the spark of her own magic as she studied the masked man. *He must be one of Severin's servants.* "Have you spoken to your servants, Your Highness?" Angelique asked, choosing to ignore Lucien, who was smirking at her with the confidence of one who is used to having his appearance much admired.

"I have." Severin's cat ears swiveled as he glanced back at his servant. "It seems I did not understand how terribly the curse affected them. Thank you, Lady Enchantress, for saving my household." He bowed deeply to her, and it struck Angelique that he was more grateful to her for his servants' sake than his own.

Even so, Angelique had to smile to keep herself from screaming, *Enchantress-in-Training! GET IT RIGHT! If the Conclave thinks I'm presenting myself as a full enchantress, I'm going to get in trouble!* "As an Enchantress-in-Training, I am glad it was within my abilities to aid you," Angelique said.

"Who is in Baris?" Lucien repeated.

"A particular friend of mine," Angelique said, choosing to keep things vague. (She did not want to involve the smarmy prince in her life more than necessary.) She brushed her skirts as she thought of the black and white cat. "I believe he means to travel north to the Veneno Conclave in Mullberg."

It was a logical thought. It had taken Angelique some days to get back home after Evariste had pushed her through a magic portal that spat her out in a northern country just as he was captured. Roland might have taken it upon himself to seek out help from the magical community.

"But I don't understand why he went east to Baris instead of going north through Erlauf and winding through Loire," she murmured.

Unfortunately, Lucien had sharper hearing than she expected, for as he picked at a loose thread in his jacket, he snorted. "Probably to avoid the war."

Angelique blinked. "War?"

Lucien scratched his neck and frowned slightly. "The war between Erlauf and Trieux? Though I suppose it was so brief, it may not even qualify as a war." He shrugged. "Regardless, Trieux was invaded and successfully overtaken by Erlauf. It was officially dissolved several weeks ago."

"I see," Angelique said.

Internally, she was not quite so calm.

Trieux—a sovereign nation—had just been taken over? How had she missed such a thing? It sounded like it took place shortly after Evariste was captured, which would explain her preoccupation. But something like a *war* should have stirred the magical community!

She cleared her throat so she didn't sound strangled when she asked, "And you are not upset by this?"

Lucien adjusted his jacket. "We're not happy—with Trieux under their control, Erlauf gained quite a bit of land and money—but I don't think anyone was surprised. Trieux had all but publicly announced their plan to wage war on Erlauf, which was rather cheeky of them."

"A lesson you would be wise to learn," Severin growled.

Lucien waved his brother off and continued. "Erlauf just beat Trieux to battle and took them unprepared."

Although she nodded politely, Angelique was still rather dazed. *A war. There has been a war on our continent, and we mages did nothing about it? What is our world coming to?*

"Though the takeover was quick, I don't think merging the two countries has been all that peaceful," Lucien said.

"That is hardly surprising," Severin said. His lips curled back, revealing his jagged teeth. This seemed to startle him more than anyone else as he took a staggering step back and slightly shook his head.

Angelique brushed her skirts off. *He has some adjusting to go through. And I don't want to be stuck here when King Rèmy and Queen Nicole find out what happened. I need to leave. Now.* "Thank you, Your Highness, for the use of your mirror."

Severin slightly inclined his head. "I hope it was of use to you."

Angelique smiled, but she couldn't help the sad tinge that leaked through. "Yes. Now I'm afraid I must say my farewells. You have the limits of your curse; you may proceed as you see fit."

The cursed prince bowed. "Thank you, Lady Enchantress."

Enchantress-in-Training! A muscle jumped in her cheek, but she kept her expression strong. "It was my honor," she said.

Lucien grabbed her hands and squeezed. "Ought you not stay,

Lady Enchantress? It is late. You must allow us to extend an invitation to remain in the palace." He started to raise her hands to his lips, but Angelique yanked them from his grasp before he could proceed.

"It is very kind of you but unnecessary. Good evening, Prince Lucien, Prince Severin." Angelique bolted from the room, but she froze when she entered the hallway.

It was crowded with people wearing masks. *They must be more of Severin's servants?* She tried to smile at them but awkwardly cleared her throat when they either bowed or curtsied to her.

"Good evening," she murmured. "If you'll excuse me, I was just looking to leave the palace..."

A young boy trotted forward, his smile big despite the mask that covered half his face. He gave her a wobbly bow, then motioned for her to follow him.

Angelique glided after him in her best elf-imitation, but she glanced back over her shoulder at the cursed servants.

I wish I could have done more. But...

Despite Evariste's belief, she was a mere student—with frightfully dangerous magic to boot.

As much as it pained her, such work was far beyond her abilities. She'd more than likely kill them by accident than fix the situation.

Which is why I need to find Evariste. I owe him. She nearly cringed as she remembered her last real conversation with her teacher, which had been a shouted argument.

They had always disagreed about Angelique's magic. She knew it was dangerous; Evariste insisted it was not.

But while Angelique still believed she was correct, she would give anything to wipe the argument away. *I have miserably failed him.*

When Evariste woke, he knew they had moved locations again.

The black mages that had captured him kept him unconscious most of the time. In fact, he was awake only when they were using his magic to bestow a foul curse.

They used me to call out Emerys. Evariste barely held in a groan at the torturous memory.

They had used his close relationship with the Elf King to place a curse on all elves—with *his* magic. And he had been powerless to stop it.

Evariste reached for his magic, but as it had been ever since the black mages captured him, he felt nothing. There was a bone-deep numbness in his chest and nothing where his magic should be.

Even so, I might be able to get free if I can startle them and throw off whatever spell they put on me.

With that hope ever in his mind, he kept his eyes closed and listened.

Murmuring voices created a soft backdrop, disrupted by the occasional crackle of a fire. The icy cold stone floor was hard and unforgiving beneath his cheek, and the air was chilly in its pureness and a little wet, but it lacked any real scent, which meant it was likely they were indoors—a new experience, as the mages had been dragging him through the wilds of the continent.

Feet shifted near him—a guard, most likely. And faintly, in the distance, Evariste thought he heard the cackle of a goblin.

What is a goblin doing indoors? The sound echoed faintly through the room.

The murmuring voices grew louder, and Evariste could hear the faint tap of footsteps. More black mages were approaching. If he was going to attempt an escape, now was the time.

He cracked his eyes open.

There was only one mage standing guard—a male with a

white, puckered scar that slashed diagonally across his face. He was one of the two mages to place the sealing spell on him.

The black mage wasn't even watching Evariste. He was staring at the back of the room and rubbed his hands together, his eyes squinted in longing.

Evariste couldn't look that direction without craning his neck, but he didn't hear any other shuffles or exhales, so it seemed likely this mage was the only guard.

Perfect.

Evariste kicked his feet out, nailing the robed mage in the back of the knee.

The man shouted in surprise and staggered to right himself, but Evariste caught the loose cuff of his robe and yanked, pulling him over.

"He's awake!" the black mage yelled.

Evariste lunged to his feet and kicked the man in the gut, silencing him.

The mage made a gasping noise as he tried to recover from the blow, and Evariste jumped over him.

Every muscle in his body protested—he was stiff and sore, and the lighting was dim. There was just a single fire to light the cavernous room.

Weapon. Find a weapon.

Evariste turned around and almost walked into a razor-sharp dagger forged out of black metal.

"Well, well, well, even the goody-two-shoes mages have some savagery in them after all." A young man sauntered across the room—which Evariste could now see was not a room but a chamber in a *cave*.

As the man drew closer, he held his hand out. Shadows streaked from his fingertips, solidifying into the shape of a broadsword. When the man grabbed the shadow by the hilt, the darkness condensed into a sword of a similar make to the dagger pressing against Evariste's throat, held there by the man's magic.

A war mage. A powerful one. His looks are too exotic for him to be marginally talented in magic.

The war mage appeared to be approximately Evariste's age—perhaps a few years younger. Though if he was strong in magic, his appearance could be deceiving.

His black hair was carefully tousled and smoothed away from his forehead, and he was dressed like an enchanter, in trousers and a shirt of black with gold trim and embroidery. His goldenrod cloak fell over one shoulder, and if it weren't for his startling red eyes, he could have been mistaken for a prince or high-ranked nobleman.

The war mage stopped a few strides short of Evariste and glanced at the still-gasping mage that writhed on the ground. "Get *up*, Funus," he sighed with impatience. "He's without magic. Whatever he did, you ruddy well deserved it for failing to keep him down."

The mage with the jagged scar gagged.

The war mage rolled his eyes, then lowered his sword and dragged it across the cave floor so sparks jumped from it.

Evariste kept still, but he carefully studied the war mage, looking for anything his appearance might tell him.

Although the mage was willowy and muscled leanly, his grip on the sword was familiar—he was well trained. His skin was porcelain white—almost ashen—which meant either the cave system was enormous, or the mage was a recluse.

The war mage tilted his head and rested the flat of his blade on his shoulder as he studied Evariste, a mean smirk twitching on his lips. "You seem hardly worth the fuss that's been kicked up over you."

Evariste ignored him and tried to discreetly get a better measure of the room. The cave—evident by the rocky walls and sloping stone ceiling—lacked any discernable opening besides the one door. It seemed that it didn't even have a ventilation system, for the fire—Evariste could now see—hissed and crackled, but it must have been magic-fed, for it consumed no wood or fuel.

The room was ringed with chests, items, and artifacts of all sizes and kinds. Evariste suspected if he could sense more than the infernal numbness, his senses would be lighting up from magical artifacts.

When he finished his inspection of the room, his gaze returned to the war mage.

The war mage flicked his dark eyebrows up. "Satisfied?" He didn't wait for Evariste to respond before he continued. "Try running again, and I won't trouble myself with the bother of keeping you unblemished."

The edge of the dagger pressed into Evariste's neck, cutting a thin slice in his skin. Evariste kept his expression placid despite the bite of the dagger.

The war mage turned his back to Evariste so he faced the entrance of the cave chamber. "It seems your new toy has finally woken up, Mother."

Two women stepped out of the shadows. One, Evariste recognized—a black-haired sorceress named Suzu who had the personality of a harpy. She had aided the other mages in using Evariste to curse Emerys and the elves.

The second, however, was radically different. While everyone in the room was dressed in dark clothes—even Evariste—she wore a gauzy, pinkish-white gown with intricate, gold beadwork. Her pale blond hair spilled down her back and shoulders in ringlets, but they were covered by a white veil held in place with a crown of flowers. She appeared to be in her late thirties or perhaps early forties but was youthful and beautiful with her pink lips budding in a smile, an unwrinkled and warm complexion, and her eyes that sparkled invitingly.

She was a bright spot in the darkness of the shadows, and everything about her presence felt wrong.

Evariste kept his gaze level, even though instinct had him reaching for his walled off magic as she drew closer.

"Thank you, Acri." The woman smiled fondly at the war mage and briefly cupped his cheek with what appeared to be maternal affection. "You have done well—as always."

The war mage bowed slightly in response.

"Funus, Suzu, you may leave." The woman's voice was musical.

Suzu bowed her head, then glared at the scarred mage as he peeled himself off the ground. "Can't do anything right, can you?" the sorceress growled.

Funus gave a coughing retch and hobbled after Suzu as she swept from the room.

The woman waited with a tilted head and a slight smile until their footsteps retreated past hearing, then she turned her bright gaze onto Evariste. "Welcome, Lord Enchanter Evariste of the Fire Gates. We are so glad to have you here." She grasped the edges of her skirts and curtsied slightly.

"Who are you?" Evariste asked. It was hard to speak around the edge of the dagger, but this was the first time his captors were directly communicating with him. *I need to gather as much information as possible.*

"I am Liliane," she said.

"You're the leader of the black mages?" Evariste asked.

Her smile turned rueful. "I suppose you could say that, yes. Though it is a rather inelegant and small-minded way of looking at it."

Evariste clenched his jaw and glanced from the mother to the son.

The young man, Acri, turned a chair around and sat backwards on it so he could rest his chin on the backrest, his sword balanced on his lap.

"What do you want?" Evariste asked. "What are you trying to accomplish?"

Liliane blinked in surprise. "*Trying?*" She asked. "My dear Lord

Enchanter, you might wish we are merely *trying*, but rather it is that we have already succeeded. Now, we only need to harvest our hard work." She smiled as she glided closer to him. "You will be given the chance to aid us—though I can tell by that mulish look of yours, it will not be your pleasure to do so."

Evariste narrowed his eyes. "What is it you think you've accomplished?"

Liliane shook her head and tapped her nose. "No, I shall not entertain your curiosity today—it would make me such a bad hostess. And one must keep up their manners. Acri, be a darling and fetch the mirror."

Acri left his chair. He placed his shadow-forged broadsword in the air then strode away. The weapon bobbed after him like an animal on a tether.

Evariste tried shifting, but the spelled dagger bit deeper into his neck, to the point where it was painful to swallow.

"Now, Evariste—may I call you that?" Liliane smiled at him, then adjusted her crown of flowers. "Let's talk about *you*. As you've probably realized, your magic is sealed."

She looked expectantly at him, shaking her head in amusement when he stubbornly failed to respond. She strolled around Evariste, tapping his shoulder to gesture that he should swivel to follow.

Her hands were warm, and her touch was soft, but Evariste couldn't help the disgusted curl of his upper lip that made him sneer.

She didn't notice; she was watching Acri approach the far wall of the cluttered chamber. "I am a generous woman, which is why I'm going to explain the boundaries of your seal." Liliane clapped her hands together. "You have a particularly terrible curse placed on you, I'm sorry to say. Or rather, you will think it's terrible. It was the strongest spell we could find that could contain someone of your power—even if you were not the intended target."

Angelique. It was supposed to be for Angelique. Evariste had managed to thwart them in shielding her—something he couldn't regret, even if it meant he was blocked from his magic.

"The smaller mirror, Acri," Liliane called to her spawn.

The young man had paused in front of a giant mirror taller than the average male. It had an ornate, gold frame shaped with tiny flowers and elaborate swirls. A giant, blood-red ruby was sculpted into the top of the frame. It was beautiful, but even without his magic to warn him, something felt *off* about the mirror. Whatever it was, it had seen action—for there was a shard missing from the mirror's surface near the lower right corner.

Acri lingered in front of the large mirror.

"*Acri.*" Liliane's voice was still melodic, but a note it in jolted the young man, so he grabbed the plain, full-length mirror leaning against its more ornate brother instead.

Liliane nodded in satisfaction, then glanced at Evariste. "Admiring the crown jewel of our collection, are you?" She smiled affectionately at the ornate mirror. "That one is due to leave us in a few weeks—a gift to a grieving queen for her birthday, though we will have to spell it before it goes to cover up the crack. But I'm afraid such a beautiful prison is beyond you—for now."

Acri carried the mirror back to Evariste and Liliane, setting it up so it leaned against a hip-high chest.

"Thank you, Acri. Now...where were we?" Liliane tapped her full lips with a finger.

"You were about to drop the terms of his curse on him." Acri smirked maliciously as he dropped back down into his chair, plucking his sword from the air. He eagerly leaned forward and watched Evariste.

Whatever this curse is, it's not going to be fun if he's that excited by it.

"Ahh, yes." Liliane clasped her hands together. "The curse blocks you from your magic. You have no way to access it, use it, twist it, or even feel it. There's no one alive strong enough to break it. It's impossible—because this particular curse is really supposed to be more of a motivator, and while no mage can use magic to crack it, *you* can break it off yourself."

Evariste stared at Liliane as she picked a stray flower petal from her hair. *Is she nuts? Is everyone here absolutely mad?*

"The term to ending your curse is this: you must perform the deepest, darkest desire of your heart." Liliane smiled as she watched Evariste. "Simple enough, is it not?"

Evariste furrowed his brow, but he didn't respond. *The deepest, darkest desire of my heart—what is that supposed to mean?*

"For someone like myself or Acri, such a thing would be providing an excuse to do as we wish! But for someone like you—Enchanter Evariste—who so highly prizes his duty as an enchanter and is known throughout the continent for his valiance and honor..." Liliane drew closer to him and peered up into his face. "What is *your* darkest desire? Not the hidden ambitions of your heart, but the vilest whispers of your very being. Would you kill someone who has been an irritant to you? Use your power to bring those who are less to their knees? Twist your magic to make a fortune, or perhaps set yourself up as a ruler so it is your name on the lips of every man?"

Liliane leaned forward so she could whisper into his ear. "Follow the feeling of the spell, and it will tell you what you must do to appease that dark savage that is within you."

Evariste opened his mouth, intending to say no, but the dagger kept the word in his throat. *Should I test her?* Reluctantly, Evariste felt for the numb feeling that radiated out of his chest.

The closer he drew to it, the more it spread through his body, until he couldn't feel his legs or fingertips.

He found the curse—dark and shadowy, oozing like gooey tar. Uneasily, he listened, and tried to access his magic so he could *see* the spell, though the attempt failed.

He was about to shake it off and scoff at the obviously mad woman when he felt it.

"*Angelique*," whispered a voice that sounded like his own.

Evariste froze.

"*You must give Angelique a kiss of true love.*" Evariste broke away from the spell, his chest heaving as he tried to contain his emotions.

It can't be true. She's lying about the terms of the curse. Angelique has nothing to do with it.

"What is your wish, Lord Enchanter?" Liliane asked. "Murder? Mayhem? Power?"

It's love. Evariste closed his eyes and was unable to keep his shoulders from drooping. *Which might not be so bad...if I didn't know that Angelique will disdain me forever for it.*

She had told him plainly in an argument that she didn't need him. And he'd seen it again and again in her eyes. If she noticed any hint of his feelings for her, she'd leave him in a second.

Moreover, the Veneno Conclave would *make* her leave him.

A relationship between a master and a student? It was inappropriate to say the least. And Evariste had the sinking suspicion that most wouldn't blame him, but that it would be Angelique who would pay the price for his traitorous heart. That it was the *darkest* desire of his true self was telling.

Kissing Angelique might seem like an easy price to pay...but I wish it was something—anything—else.

"Why tell me this?" Evariste asked. His voice cracked, and the dagger made another cut in his throat, but he didn't care.

Liliane patted his shoulder and backed up. "I believe in the fairness of letting you know just what a bad spot you are in. You can't escape, Evariste. Given that you will be our companion until I decide you are no longer useful, I thought it best to lay a foundation of honesty."

I don't believe her for a minute. Why would she tell me the truth? If I give up trying to escape, it will only make it easier for her.

For a moment, his hopes soared. *Yes, that's it. This whole spell is a lie. She's just trying to cow me into apathy.*

"Now then, although *you* cannot use your magic, I intend to make certain that my people can make use of it," Liliane said. "Your powers are so vast and potent, it is simply marvelous. I can see why many called you a prodigy and a legend. Acri?"

The war mage stood and strode behind Evariste.

A moment later, Evariste felt a sharp prick between his shoulder blades. "Walk towards the mirror, *Lord Enchanter*," Acri said mockingly.

Liliane tapped the frame of the full-size mirror with a smile. "This shall be your prison. Without magic, you cannot escape it, and it will make it easier—and less dangerous—for us to drain you of your magic for our use. I wish we could do something that might be more comfortable for you, but you are too strong and too full of your own self-righteousness. Perhaps later."

"You're going to put me *in* a mirror?" Evariste managed to ask.

"Yes. With the right spells, it's rather easy to do so."

Mint-green magic flickered around Liliane's wrists, and she spoke in the language of magic—not the black words of dark magic, but phrases Evariste recognized from his own studies.

How can she—only enchanters or enchantresses could use their magic like this.

Mint-green magic twisted around Evariste—who was still shocked by Liliane's skills.

"Now, Acri," Liliane instructed.

Acri kicked Evariste in the lower back, throwing him against the solid surface of the mirror.

"Prepare yourself, Evariste. This will hurt quite a bit," Liliane said.

White bolts of magic sizzled, traveling up and down the mirror and making the jump to Evariste.

It felt like his blood was boiling, and his innards were being ripped apart. Pain consumed him. He couldn't think, couldn't do anything except try to *breathe* as it knifed through his body.

Angelique. Her name was on his lips as he felt his world fracture around him. *Angelique.*

CHAPTER 3

Spring turned into summer, and the weeks ticked by. And yet any kind of progress on finding Evariste—or those who had taken him—eluded Angelique.

She had tried tracking spells, location charms, had even returned to Evariste's home and—upon finding a young unicorn and a water dragon that were frequent visitors—asked them for aid in finding Evariste. But even they were unable to locate him.

Since *spells* to find Evariste seemed inadequate, Angelique had shifted her focus to sniffing out the dark pockets of the continent where the black mages may be hiding.

For that reason, she had—using one of Evariste's many pairs of horses and carriages kept in stables around the continent—ventured to Arcainia, nonchalantly circling the perhaps single most dark and plagued area on the continent: the lands of Carabas, which had been taken over by an ogre years ago.

Though the lands showed sign of the abuse they suffered under the ogre—crops were failing, the woods were infested with goblins, and almost no wild animals could be found in that stretch of land—Angelique had been unable to find any hint of black mages in the area.

She considered checking the rest of the country. Magic had been outlawed for several decades in Arcainia due to its king, King Henrik, marrying an enchantress (because of course an acting enchantress couldn't marry royalty—that would be *far* too political). But tragically, Queen Ingrid had died unexpectedly and recently, and without the enchantress-queen alive to intimidate any black mages, it was possible they had moved into the country.

But it seemed unlikely given what bits of the country Angelique had seen.

She angrily shoved her chestnut-colored bangs out of her face. *I've been searching for weeks, and I haven't found anything!* She wanted to scream, and her eyes welled with angry tears.

It was frustrating. She was putting everything she could into the search, and she hadn't found a thing. It felt like failure. It felt like *defeat*.

She sighed and pinched the bridge of her nose. "But I can't give up. Maybe it's time I focus on finding Roland."

The black and white cat was nowhere to be found. When she saw in the mirror that he was in Baris, Angelique had assumed he was making his way north to Mullberg and to the Veneno Conclave.

But the magical cat had never arrived.

Angelique groaned and thumped her head against the wall of the carriage. *I'm an Enchantress-in-Training, one of the highest practitioners of magic on the continent. I should be better than this!*

And yet she was not.

Apparently harboring dangerous magic was not her only shortcoming. A general inadequacy seemed to plague her.

She sighed and tugged on the hem of her dress. She was wearing one of Evariste's gauzy creations of cream and purple, with gold coins draping from the bottom of her skirts that made her perpetually jingle whenever she moved.

"Is there an apothecary or a healer?" The shout came from just outside Angelique's carriage, making her jump in surprise.

She miserably lifted her head just enough so she could peer out the window of her carriage. Just outside, a beautiful young lady with lovely blonde hair and puffy eyes crashed off the side of her horse, twisting so she landed on her back, clutching something furry to her chest.

This sounds like one of those aid-those-in-need moments. Angelique sighed and tried to dispel the cloud of poor humor that plagued her.

"Lady Gabrielle?" A villager took the reins of the young lady's horse, stroking his neck and trying to calm the creature.

"What happened?" A woman crouched next to the fallen young lady. "Are you hurt?"

Angelique nudged open the door of her coach and swung the carriage stairs down so she could descend without tripping and breaking her neck. (Which, with this string of luck she was stuck with, was a real possibility.)

"I'm fine; it's Puss." The young lady peeled herself off the ground and unbuckled a saddlebag from her waist.

"The Master Cat is injured?" the man holding the horse cried. "It cannot be!"

Angelique paused. *A cat?*

"Not Puss in Boots!" a child yelled.

Villagers crowded around the young lady so Angelique could barely see her. Angelique squinted a little and started to tug at her magic—before she remembered she was in Arcainia, and all magic was outlawed. *I still should be able to help in some way...*

"What happened?" a woman asked, her hand planted on her intimidating bosom.

"Never mind that—someone call Edna with her herbs," another woman ordered.

Angelique cleared her throat. "Excuse me, did you say a cat is injured?" she asked.

The villagers parted, allowing Angelique a better look at the young woman.

Though her face was tear-streaked and dirt-spattered, the young lady was clearly beautiful. Her hair was golden and shiny, and her face was so beautiful it made Angelique wonder for a moment if she was a fellow magic user.

But, no. She must have been a warrior of some sort, as she wore a leather doublet, boots, and trousers. "Please," she hiccuped as she held out a limp bundle of black and white fur. "Save my magic cat."

Angelique started to reach for the bundle, then felt her heart stop when she recognized the cat's face. "*Roland?*"

"You know him?" the beautiful girl sniffed.

"Yes." Angelique scooped Roland up and started running her hands across his still body, checking for injuries. "What happened?"

"He was flung into a wall by an ogre."

What was Roland *doing near an ogre? He barely ever left Evariste's house and complained endlessly about the toils of traveling!* Angelique grimaced as her magic told her what she had already guessed. "He has internal injuries—and some broken bones, I think."

Roland's lovely companion rubbed her eyes. "Will he make it?" she asked in a shaky voice.

Her heart in her throat, Angelique stared down at her old friend. "Not if I don't use healing magic on him."

"Then use it!" the young lady begged. "Please, I'll pay any price."

"I'm afraid I can't." *At least not in sight of anyone. I'm not going to let him die, but how do I play this so the Council doesn't use it as an excuse to throw me out?*

She tried to puzzle out a proper plan, but her thoughts couldn't settle down. She needed to heal Roland, but how? And *how* did it come to pass that the entire village seemed to know him? And what was he doing this far east in *Arcainia*, the country where magic had been outlawed!

"But you must! Please, Lady Enchantress," the female villager said. "We will offer you whatever price you desire. Master Puss has done so much!"

"Not just for us but for all the northern villages of Arcainia," the man holding the exhausted horse rumbled.

"He's routed bandits and killed man-eating snakes," another villager said.

"And fought goblins and vanquished witches," a young lad shouted.

"He and Lady Gabrielle got rid of the Lech river pirates."

"And they single-handedly stopped a fire from spreading to a hay barn in Muarg!"

Drat. I guess I should have chosen my words with more care, but I can't let them think I'm going to break the law.

"Dear people," Angelique started, "you misunderstood me. I am not unwilling, but as most kinds of magic are outlawed in Arcainia, healing magic among them, I am unable."

"The border—it isn't far from here," Roland's companion said.

"Ride straight north, and you'll find yourself at the foot of Mullberg's mountain range," the man holding the horse directed. "You'll have to go through Carabas lands, though."

"Carabas is long from east to west. North to south, it's quite stubby; the lady can reach the border in under an hour on a swift horse," a villager said.

Really? We're that close to the border? Angelique glanced north, where a mountain range divided Arcainia from Mullberg. Craggy peaks loomed on the horizon, but she had assumed they were farther away than they appeared to be. *Maybe I won't have to break the law to save Roland. He'll last that short of a ride, and then I can really hit him hard with my magic instead of trying to be secretive about it.*

"Please," the beautiful young lady begged.

Her mind made up long before (as soon as she saw the cat), Angelique nodded. "Of course," she said. She glanced at Roland—who lay in her arms—then slightly tilted her head as she briefly studied the young lady. *I do look forward to hearing Roland's explana-*

tion for how he came to be here, traveling with a non-magical young lady for that matter."

"You can use my horse, Lady Enchantress," a villager offered. "Gaffer is one of the fastest in the village."

Angelique shook her head. "My coach will be faster." Evariste owned only the fastest of horses and spelled all his coaches and wagons for durability and speed. The horses would have no problem pulling the coach through the wilds of Arcainia. They would be swift. "...But not faster than *his* steed." Angelique paused next to her carriage and gazed at the sky.

Do I dare try it? If he gets it in his mind, he could kill me and ruin the village. But Pegasus is a constellation. Not even an elven steed can outpace him.

"Please, Lady Enchantress," Roland's friend whispered.

Angelique briefly shut her eyes. *I failed Evariste in my cowardice, and I haven't been able to find him. I cannot fail Roland as well. If I can get him to the border and heal him faster, I owe it to him.*

"For Roland, I will dare to attempt it," she said.

Angelique shifted Roland to one arm, blanching when he dangled limply from her grasp. She grimly tilted her chin up and thrust her hand into the sky. "Pegasus! It is I—Enchantress-in-Training Angelique, student of Lord Enchanter Evariste of Fire Gates. I summon you from the skies to carry me across the lands. Come!"

There was a roll of thunder, and if Angelique hadn't been paralyzed by fear she would have sucked her neck into her shoulders. *That doesn't sound like a good start.*

"There—what's that?" a villager shouted.

A black equine plummeted from the sky. His mane and tail—comprised of blue flames—glowed and sparked. His insubstantial body was a black smear in the sky, though even from this distance she could see the glitter of stars in his coat, and his glorious black wings shone in the morning light.

His front hooves touched the ground with a mighty crash of

thunder, which shook the ground. Soon after, his wings burst into hundreds of feathers that spiraled up to the sky, disappearing soon after.

The equine—for Pegasus was too magical, too *dangerous* to be called a horse—reared and screamed an ear-piercing challenge.

A cold sweat crawled up Angelique's spine when she saw the small crater and singed earth his entrance had made. (Thankfully, it seemed the villagers were too much in awe of the constellation to notice the damage he had caused.)

Angelique licked her dry lips. "Where's the saddlebag?"

"Here," Roland's friend scrambled to give it to her. She was the only one who ventured closer, for the villagers—despite their admiration of the wild magic that was Pegasus—backed away in fright.

"Thank you," Angelique said. Gently, she slipped Roland into the pack, then turned her attention to Pegasus.

The steed struck the ground with its front right leg—eliciting another thunder-crack.

I am going to die, she thought with absolute certainty. *Not black mages nor my own magic could take me out. Nope, instead a flaming magic horse is my end. This will be one for the bards.*

Despite her dour inner monologue, Angelique took a step closer to the mount. "I know I'm not Lord Enchanter Evariste," the enchantress said, her voice grim. "But I'm desperate enough that I'll try to make you yield as you do for him. Now will you test me, or shall we fly?"

Pegasus lunged at her.

Panicking, Angelique thrust up an arm and made a back-handing motion—shouting in the language of magic. (Though she didn't realize until the words were out of her mouth that her spell was one that would make squirrels attack the target. Because Pegasus was absolutely going to submit to her when a bunch of fluffy tailed vermin jumped on his back.)

Perhaps I won't blame him quite so much if he does decide to kill me...

In her defense she had learned it for the sake of inflicting Roland whenever he was being insufferable.

Pegasus danced backwards. He flicked his tail, shedding blue sparks, and stretched his neck so his head was pointed in her direction.

Angelique showed him the pack. "It's for Roland." She hoped the beast knew who she was referring to. (Roland had disliked Pegasus even more than Angelique. He claimed he "wasn't natural." Which, really, was ironic coming from a talking cat.)

The celestial equine snorted—its nostrils flaring red—and looked away. After a moment, it hefted the front of its large body down.

Angelique tried not to gape. She wouldn't put it past Pegasus to get up just to spite her if he realized how shocked she was that he was actually going to let her ride him. So she straightened her shoulders and turned to Roland's friend. "I will find you again when this is over."

"Thank you," the beautiful young lady whispered, her eyes glassy with tears.

Gingerly, Angelique hefted herself onto Pegasus' back, trying not to shiver when the constellation rose to his feet.

She tried to give the villagers an assuring nod as she motioned north; the equine made a tight circle and aimed her towards the Mullberg mountains. When she felt his muscles stiffen beneath her, however, she clung to his back and to Roland.

Pegasus took off like a shooting star.

His hooves pounded, and his long strides ate up the ground, taking Angelique out of the village and into the wild.

They traveled north and slightly west, looping away from the coastal area and heading for the mountains.

Pegasus plunged them into a forest, and Angelique could feel his displeasure—or was it distaste for her—in the way branches smacked her shoulders and yanked on her clothes. She crouched low against his neck.

Bear with it, she told herself. *For Roland. Besides, I'd rather take a branch to the face than a stomp from a constellation.*

Trees flashed by faster than Angelique's eyes could take them in. The wind whipped at her hair, and tears from the heart-stopping pace Pegasus had adopted blurred her vision.

She had no idea how the constellation was able to gallop so fast and avoid trees. Her heart pounded, and every moment, she expected to crash into the rough and unforgiving trunk of a tree.

Still, as terrified as she was, Angelique felt it the moment they passed into Carabas lands.

The air was stagnant but heavy, and the trees and vegetation switched from smears of greens to dry and brittle browns.

Even as Pegasus extended his stride, galloping faster still when they left the woods for rolling hills of dying crops, Angelique could feel the earth itself cry out for relief, violated by the darkness coming from the east.

This is the ogre's doing. It's a miracle it didn't snuff out Roland with its magic.

Pegasus shot across a field. Angelique cringed, knowing he trampled planted crops beneath his hooves, but judging by the unhealthy colors, the crops had failed weeks ago.

Perhaps Evariste really was in Carabas lands. If the lands themselves had been this inflicted, hiding a Lord Enchanter of Evariste's power would be easy.

The Mullberg mountains drew closer on the horizon, stretching towards the sky like the jagged teeth of a dragon.

Almost there.

Pegasus galloped up the first of the foothills clustered at the base of the mountains. From what little Angelique could make out through her tears and the light the equine shed, it looked like they had at least one more hill to cross before they were at the mountains and safely in Mullburg.

Angelique's legs burned with the exertion of clamping herself to the constellation's back, and her fingers were numb from clinging to him.

She glanced at the saddlebag that was smashed in her lap, which is why Pegasus' shriek and abrupt buck came as a surprise.

Angelique flew through the air and landed on her side with an inelegant splat, knocking all air from her lungs and rattling even her teeth. She had curled around the saddlebag, hopefully cushioning Roland's fall, but as a result, her entire side was going to be a massive bruise.

Angelique gasped as she tried to breathe again. Her ears rang, and everything hurt. But when Pegasus shrieked, Angelique was incredibly motivated to peel herself off the ground and stand, as there was more than a slight chance the constellation would run her down if he was feeling nasty.

It took a moment for Angelique's vision to clear before she could make out her surroundings.

They were on or near the border. Angelique could feel the taint of Carabas, but no one lived on this stretch of land. The hills were overgrown with scrubby bushes and weeds—the only thing that could grow in this rocky soil—and they were at the base of one of the impassable mountains. (Any Mullberg village would be located closer to one of the passes or at least the more gem- and ore-rich mines of their mountains.)

Pegasus was positioned slightly in front of her, tossing his head and screaming a challenge.

Angelique, clutching Roland and his saddlebag to her chest, squinted in the light, trying to make out what had upset the starry equine.

Seemingly out of nowhere, an arrow shot through the air, passing by Angelique close enough to ruffle her dress.

Properly incentivized, Angelique finally made out the goblin pack that stood between her and the Mullberg mountains.

She had missed them previously because they crouched low to the ground, and their dappled-gray skin blended well with the bland color of the hills. But with their cover gone, the goblins stood, taller than her and rail thin.

Mountain goblins. Just to complete this terrible experience, of course.

Mountain goblins were sly creatures—they had to be in order to survive in the rocky mountains where game was more scarce than in lush valleys and forests. But mountain goblins rarely descended from their treacherous homes. It was rare that they came even halfway down their mountain, much less into the foothills at the base. Moreover, this seemed like an unusually *large* pack.

Angelique impatiently pushed her curiosity away as she started gathering up her magic, twisting it into a usable spell—one that wouldn't involve her core magic.

The goblins stood, no longer bothering to hide. Even from this distance, Angelique could smell the scent of rot they oozed. Several in the front grinned, displaying serrated teeth, and they licked their lips as those with crude bows took aim at Angelique.

We're close to the border, if not on it. As long as I use regular magic here, I don't think I'll be noticed by the Conclave. Besides, I could probably claim ignorance if they did pick up on this and hauled me in.

And if they weren't satisfied...

Angelique clutched Roland closer. *I'll take the risk. I can't fail Roland again. I only hope I can win this.*

Her mind made up, Angelique struck.

She didn't bother trying to barter with or warn the goblins. She hit them with a water spell that burst above them, creating a torrential downpour.

The goblins emitted garbled screams—more bothered than hurt—but most importantly, the ones with bows were too busy wiping their faces to get another shot off.

Angelique crept closer to Pegasus as she released another spell.

The scrubby bushes closest to the goblins swayed. Their roots

—growing unnaturally fast under Angelique's direction—shot out of the ground and wrapped around the goblins' ankles.

The goblins squawked, but most of them cut through the roots with crude knives or rusty battle axes.

One of the lead goblins snarled and chucked a crude wooden spear at her.

She ducked, and it whistled past, just barely missing her head.

Muttering a few words she never would have let loose in Evariste's presence, Angelique channeled more of her magic as she prepped her next spell. Her actions grew frantic as the goblins started to step away from the ring of still-wet ground, and she released the spell as she finished twisting the final piece.

The ground beneath the goblins—softened by the water and shrub roots—snapped open, closely resembling the gaping jaws of a troll.

Goblins fell in the pitch-black hole, screaming as they tumbled down. Some scrambled at the mouth of the hole, but the rocky soil gave way beneath their claw-like hands, and they plummeted to their doom.

The lead goblin—who had jumped to freedom before Angelique managed to loosen her spell—sprinted towards her.

Angelique stiffened and started to form another spell, but Pegasus charged ahead of her, loosening another few curse words of surprise from her.

It looked like he would collide with the goblin, but at the last second, he spun around and kicked out with his hind legs, hitting the goblin with an earth-shaking crack.

The goblin screamed as he was tossed backwards, hitting the earth with such force, he rolled and skidded straight into the gaping hole.

Just as his shrieks started to fade, Angelique's earth spell finished running its course, and it snapped shut. Brown grass smoothed over the barren patch, making it indistinguishable from the rest of the ground.

Angelique readjusted her grasp on Roland's saddlebag as she eyed the remaining goblins.

Most of the pack was swallowed up by the earth, but six of them had survived. They spread out, making it impossible for Angelique to hit them all with a single spell.

Grimacing, Angelique twisted her powers into weather magic.

Pegasus pawed at the ground—shedding blue-hued sparks that made Angelique nervous given the dry state of the vegetation surrounding them—and tossed his head.

With my luck, we'll defeat the goblins and start a massive fire. Because it's not good enough to be fleeing the country so I can break the law and have a run in with goblins. No, we have to toast my buns while we're at it.

"Pegasus," Angelique called in her friendliest voice. "Could you perhaps be persuaded to return to my side?"

The equine's ears went flat, and he bared his teeth at the closest goblin.

Angelique made a face at the constellation's backside, but her voice stayed pleasant as she continued to channel her magic into a new spell. *"Please?"*

The equine screamed a challenge at the goblins again, then turned around and pranced back to Angelique, circling around her.

The six goblins crept closer, hefting their weapons and cackling to one another.

Angelique mentally marked the two standing closest together —who unfortunately were also the farthest from her—and loosened her spell.

Black clouds swelled in the sky, and two white-hot lightning bolts struck the two goblins, frying them to a crisp.

The lightning strikes shook the ground and crackled with such a loud, thundering boom, Angelique's ears rang, and she only saw white for a few moments.

When she could finally see again, one of the four surviving goblins was running for the mountains.

Pegasus took off after it with a snort, catching it in the span of a breath. The constellation clamped on the goblin's neck with its teeth and flung it, snapping its neck.

Angelique would have given the constellation the bug-eye treatment, but her lightning strikes had started a smoldering fire.

Angelique flung a water spell, putting out the patches of blackened grass that had caught fire.

Based on the squeals of the goblin and the thundering of hooves, Pegasus was descending on another goblin. (And Evariste thought it was a good idea to *ride* such a creature? If she hadn't been so desperate on Roland's behalf, she would have planned to walk the remaining distance to Mullberg!)

That means there are two goblins left...

A shrub rustled, and Angelique started slapping another lightning spell together. When she looked up to narrow in on the last two goblins, her heart flung itself into her throat.

One of the goblins stood in front of her, an arrow knocked in its crude bow.

She tried to discard her lightning spell and instead cast a defense shield, but the sluggish change was too slow.

The goblin peeled its lips back in an unholy smile and loosened its arrow.

Angelique steeled herself for pain and clamped her eyes shut... but felt nothing.

She slowly opened her eyes, her pulse throbbing in her ears when she saw the arrow hovering a hand's width from her right eye. It floated there, the end of the arrow quivering slightly as if the arrow had been jammed into a rock wall.

What the...?

A spark of silver floated past her nose, followed by a silvery flourish of magic. It took Angelique a moment to realize her core powers—her *war magic*—had reacted, stopping the arrow midair.

Her arms prickled in fear, but Angelique took a gulp of air and loosened her lightning spell, frying the archer where he stood.

Everything went bright, the earth shook, and the goblin was taken out.

Numbly, she cast another water spell when she could see again—putting out any tiny flames the lightning might have caused—and tried not to think about what her magic had just done.

It wasn't entirely shocking that her magic reacted on its own. Elemental mages commonly had such connections with their powers.

But Elemental mages don't control bladed weapons. If my magic reacts on its own not to defend me, but to attack...

Pegasus screamed, jerking Angelique from her thoughts.

She looked up to find the horse galloping towards her, and stiffened. "What—"

Pain exploded in the back of her head, and she toppled like a chopped tree.

The ache made it hard to think, but she curled around Roland's saddlebag, shielding him as best as she could. Her stomach rolled with the pain, and it was hard to see straight.

A goblin screeched over her, and Angelique peered up, squinting through the pain.

The mountain goblin clutched what looked like a club. Its eyes seemed to glow as it wound up for another hit, once again aiming for her head.

Angelique grabbed her magic and twisted it as quickly as possible before jabbing a finger at the goblin.

Her spell hit him mid-swing, throwing him back head over heels.

As Angelique pushed herself up onto her forearms, her stomach protested, and the world tilted. But she grabbed for her magic, yanking a rock as big as Pegasus' head from the earth. A push of a spell, and the rock sailed through the air, smashing the goblin in the head, downing it with a single blow.

CHAPTER 4

Angelique groaned and let herself collapse back on the ground.

She was vaguely aware she should use a healing spell on herself, but her skull throbbed with pain.

Her eyes started to flutter shut, until pain knifed through her foot.

"Ouch!" Angelique snapped upright, teetering for a moment, until she realized Pegasus had bitten her foot.

She blinked, her thoughts slow to come as the constellation got down on his knees and stared expectantly at her.

Angelique shifted, making Roland's saddlebag crinkle.

That's right! Roland—I have to save him!

Gingerly, Angelique clutched the bag to her chest and crawled to Pegasus, easing herself on to his back. Once she was on and Roland was secured, Pegasus rocked to his feet.

Every bone in her body ached as Pegasus trotted across the barren hills, forging his way to the mountains. His trot was jarring, but Angelique was thankful—it kept her awake.

A few minutes later, Pegasus splashed his way through a

shallow stream, soaking Angelique's dress, then stopping when he reached the other side of the water.

Angelique groaned. "Are we in Mullberg?"

Pegasus snorted.

Angelique squinted up at the mountains, which cast periwinkle shadows across the land, chilling her despite the warm summer breeze. She slipped off the constellation's back, staggering a few steps before she caught her balance.

She plopped down on a patch of dirt and carefully eased Roland out of the saddlebag. He was still unconscious and limp in her arms, but now his breathing seemed labored.

Angelique's head ached as she stared down at her friend. Her eyes clouded with tears, and her teeth started to chatter.

He looks so fragile. Can he really make it?

In that moment, Angelique felt horribly alone.

She thought she was used to taking care of herself. She believed that even as an apprentice, she had been self-reliant, and though Evariste provided a home and education, she didn't need any kind of support.

Now she knew better.

Evariste's absence was a hole in her chest. If she was with him, he would embrace her in one of his wretchedly warm hugs, and he would coach her through healing Roland.

But now...she was alone.

Her shoulders started to shiver before Angelique impatiently shook her head. *No, I can't let myself panic. Roland needs my help. I must* do this.

She scrubbed at her eyes with her free hand, rearranged Roland on her lap, and took a deep breath.

Next, she reached for her magic. It hit her—a cold and sharp sensation—with enough strength to make her hiss. But she took only what she needed, then started twisting her terrible magic.

It lost its heartless, metallic feel, and instead grew warm and inviting as she transformed it into healing magic.

Angelique held her breath as she carefully rested her glowing hand on the talking cat, using her magic to fix internal injuries, stop internal bleeding, and slowly restore Roland's health.

Time ticked by, and moments turned into minutes as the healing magic pulsed through Roland's small body. Fatigue started to gnaw at her—not for lack of magic but because of the intricate spells she was working. Never before had she been required to heal such a broken little body.

Angelique swallowed as she waited for a response of any sort from Roland, any sign that he would pull through. Finally, his chest stopped heaving, and his breath evened out. Then, he opened his bronze eyes.

He blinked and slightly shook his head. "Gabrielle?" he croaked. "Mistress?"

Angelique finally released the breath she had been holding. "It's all right, Roland. You're safe." The tight band squeezing her heart eased, and she smiled shakily as she shoved another tendril of healing magic into the cat's chest.

"*Angelique?*" Roland peered up at her, his whiskers twitching.

Angelique smiled lazily as exhaustion finally caught up to her. *He's okay, and I've finally found him.*

Roland, however, was not quite so assured. He twisted his head, wildly looking around. "But the ogre—where's Gabrielle?"

"I assume you're talking about your traveling companion? A beautiful girl—"

"Yes, where is she?" Roland tried to claw his way into a standing position, but Angelique firmly held him down.

"I left her in the village of Jagst. She's fine—she was more concerned about you. You were horribly injured. I had to ride north to Mullberg to get out of the no-magic zone of Arcainia so I could heal you." Angelique tickled Roland under his chin, making him relax.

"Gabrielle was uninjured?" he asked, his voice soft and so very un-Roland-like in its worry.

What has happened to him since he left our home? Angelique smiled. "She looked a little rough but was uninjured as far as I could tell."

Roland nodded once, then looked up at her again. "...Angelique?" he repeated.

She smiled. "Hello, old friend. How are you feeling?" She nudged her magic, doing a final check for any injuries or bruising she might have missed.

Roland purred as he leaned into her hand. "Stiff, but otherwise acceptable. I'm glad to see you."

"And I, you. I tried looking for you. I used a magic mirror and saw you made it to Baris, but I couldn't find you after that." Finished with her healing magic, Angelique let her hand fall to her lap.

Roland stood so he could stretch, then turned around once and settled down again, nestling against her stomach. "You're alone."

"Yes," Angelique said quietly.

"So the blackguards really took Evariste, did they?" he asked.

Angelique cleared her throat and tried to ignore the stinging sensation of tears in her eyes. "I was hoping you might be able to tell me."

Roland sighed. "I'm afraid I don't know much. I saw Enchanter Evariste push you through the gateway to Verglas. After he shut it, they jumped him. The magic that hit him after he got you through—whatever it was, it was bad. It pained him so much he wasn't able to fight back." He hesitated. "I tried to help him. I clawed the face of one of the black mages, but he threw me into a wall, and I fell unconscious. I'm sorry."

Angelique shut her eyes in disappointment. *So, I still have no new leads, no new clues to track down.* She pressed her lips together. *But Roland is alive. He's my friend, and he made it through the encounter. I am so very thankful for that.*

She glanced down at the cat, who was studiously peering at his white paws. The angle of his black ears spoke of misery—he wasn't even sinking his dratted claws into her dress.

It was obvious that he felt he had failed her—and Evariste.

I might be disappointed, but none of this is Roland's fault.

Angelique carefully slipped her hands under Roland's belly and picked him up. She held him against her chest and waited for him to look up at her with his bright eyes. "Thank you, Roland, for trying to help him. Thank you for risking yourself on our behalf. But I am so happy to find you well and alive. When I came home and couldn't find you…"

"When I woke up, I waited in the house for several days," Roland said. "I hid in your bedroom before I finally decided I should leave and try to find help—see if I could encounter a mage or something."

Angelique adjusted her hold on him. "How did you end up in Arcainia?"

"I meant to gradually travel north, to the Veneno Conclave," Puss said. "I hoped and thought it was likely that I would encounter a mage along the way." He flicked his tail in irritation. "Unfortunately, I found not a single magic user. By the time I reached Loire, though, it felt as though I was being *followed*."

Angelique frowned. "By who—or what?"

Roland licked a paw and violently scrubbed at his face. "I'm not sure. It was just a feeling. But it was why I stayed in the border town where Gabrielle is from for some weeks instead of continuing north to Mullberg. I was trying to see if my hunch was correct." He sighed. "I never did confirm it. As much as I am loathe to admit it, it is possible I was overly paranoid after experiencing the attack upon you and Evariste."

"Perhaps." Angelique was not so quick to brush off his suspicions. *If the mages were initially unaware of what he truly was, they might have sent someone after him with the intension of cleaning up loose ends.*

Puss growled low in his throat. "I should have gone to Sole to track down that fire mage and war mage you and Evariste sent to guard Princess Rosalinda. They would have at least recognized me and freed me from that *wretched* collar."

Angelique winced. "I apologize for putting it on you."

"You should," Roland sniffed. "Do you have any idea how *terrible* it is to be mistaken for a normal cat? Why, when Gabrielle first met me, she *manhandled* me and inspected my backside! Inexcusable!"

Angelique couldn't help the snort that broke through the cloud of her misery.

Roland glared up at her with narrowed eyes. "Did you just *laugh?*"

Angelique kept her expression benign. "I wouldn't find amusement in something that embarrassed you so."

"You *would!*" Roland's voice was almost a hiss. "You absolutely would! You are the hoodlum who uses chickens and fashion as weapons! Of course *you* would find amusement in my desolation!"

Angelique laughed but tried to cover it by pressing her palm to her mouth.

This only seemed to egg the irate cat on. "How can you laugh when the world was denied the wonder of my voice and knowledgeable opinions for so long? Ingrate! I have lived with peasants—*peasants!* Children stuff me in boots and doll clothes, and Gabrielle insists on calling me *Puss*! As if I were a common cat! The horror!"

Angelique curled over, she was laughing so hard.

"Why, when I traveled through Baris, an innkeeper tried to give me a *dead mouse* his cat had caught because he felt pity for me and thought I was too stupid to catch anything!" Puss complained.

Angelique, finally having caught onto the cat's attempt to put her in a better humor, paused. She lifted Roland higher so she could press her face into his black fur. "Thank you, Roland."

Roland responded with a deep, rumbling purr that made his chest vibrate.

Angelique took a deep breath and finally set him down. "So...Gabrielle?"

Roland sat down and curled his tail around his feet, then studiously looked away from her. "She's a peasant," he said in a voice that was...*warm*. "Or rather, she was. She's brave and filled with more courage than a person has any right to have, and she was rotting in her home village, slowly smothered to death by her desire for more in a place where everyone expected her to be a cog in a wheel."

Angelique brushed a black hair off her skirt. *Why does it seem like he's talking about more than just Gabrielle?*

"She eventually pulled off my collar. I decided she would make a fine pack mule, so I goaded her into a promise of adventure if she traveled with me as I continued to search for a mage," Roland said.

Angelique heard the clear lie in his voice. "What you mean to say is...you couldn't leave her there."

Roland was silent for several long moments before he finally said, "No. I couldn't. She reminded me too much of myself."

Angelique pressed her lips together as she played with the hem of her dress. "Were you unhappy living with Evariste and me?"

"No," Roland said. "But I had regrets. I wished for the courage to travel with you. I wanted to see more than the familiar corners of the workshop and Evariste's home. But I never regretted the times I spent with you—though that became less and less frequent as Evariste took you trotting across the continent for your studies and practice."

Angelique stared at Roland, feeling as if the world had taken an unpleasant twist.

I never knew. I considered Roland my closest friend—after...whatever it is I have with Evariste—but I never knew he was unhappy. "I'm sorry," she said, her voice soft.

"None of it was your doing, Angelique." Roland finally met her gaze. "It was my own actions I regret."

Angelique studied him, her heart sinking. "You're going to stay with her, aren't you?"

The cat hesitated for a moment. "Yes. Though you will be forever my friend, Gabrielle..."

Angelique nodded and leaned back so she could peer up at the afternoon sky. "A lot has happened. A lot has changed. I understand."

And she did, though she was still sad about it. *But Roland is my friend, which means I need to be happy for him instead of thrusting my sadness upon him.*

She cleared her throat, strengthening it, then found herself strong enough to look at Roland again. "I'm happy you found your place, Roland."

Roland purred and rubbed his head against her knee. "You'll find your place too, Angelique," he promised.

"I already have—I'm an Enchantress-in-Training."

"No." Roland twitched his whiskers. "That is your role, but not your place. The Veneno Conclave has done its best to box you in. But really, with Evariste gone, you are under no one's thumb. *This* is your chance to reach."

Angelique quirked a smile. "Are you becoming poetic in your old age?"

"Old age?" Roland hissed.

Angelique laughed as she stood and brushed her skirts off. "I'm sorry to say it, but I think we'll have to camp here for the night." She glanced at the sky, which was starting to show deeper shades of blue. "I'm not particularly skilled at healing magic, so taking care of you took quite a bit out of me. And Pegasus and I ran into goblins on our way here. I hit my head pretty hard.

Honestly, I don't know that I could hold onto him for the ride back."

"You just need practice to build up your magical stamina." Roland, scoffed, then abruptly twisted to face her. "You rode *Pegasus* here? Without Evariste?"

Angelique grimaced. "I was desperate to save you."

Roland purred deeply and leaned into her skirts.

Angelique picked him up, then took a reluctant step towards Pegasus, who was sniffing a moss-covered rock with suspicion as he twitched his flaming tail. "Pegasus, I thank you for the ride—because of you, I was able to save Roland. But we will be camping here tonight. I can put up some defensive spells that will keep goblins at bay. But you may go."

Pegasus flicked his ear but stayed still.

"Thank you," Angelique added awkwardly when the equine did nothing more.

The constellation snorted and went back to sniffing the rock.

"What is he doing?" Angelique whispered Roland.

"How am *I* supposed to know? What do I look like—a speaker of stars?" Roland scoffed.

Angelique cleared her throat. "Does this mean, Pegasus, you intend to spend the night with us?" She held her breath, hoping she was correct.

Pegasus was, above all, a creature of the night. If he stayed with them—something Angelique hadn't dared to dream he would deign to do—she would be as safe as if she were traveling with Evariste himself.

The thought made some of her enthusiasm dim, but she snapped to attention when Pegasus snorted again and tossed his head.

"I assume that means he's staying?" Angelique whispered to Roland.

"Assuming when it comes to a *constellation* can be dangerous," Roland said sourly.

Angelique licked her lips and wished she could summon a bit more of the courage she had when Roland's life was on the line. "Haven't you told me before that I should fake confidence until I have it?"

"Perhaps, but at the time, I was not referring to your dealings with magical equines!" Roland clambered up onto her shoulder.

Pegasus finally abandoned the rock and sauntered past Angelique and Roland, meandering back down the slight incline that funneled down to the stream they had splashed through. When he reached a piece of flat ground, he stopped and pawed a hoof.

"I suppose that's as much confirmation as we're going to get," Angelique grumbled.

"Perhaps," Puss said. "On a happier note, if you have the courage to ride a formation of wild stars, I won't feel nearly as bad asking you to help Gabrielle and me defeat the ogre in Carabas."

"Gabrielle mentioned something about that—are you jesting? Trying to defeat an ogre?" Angelique hesitated before she joined Pegasus on the flat piece of earth.

Roland jumped from her shoulder, but she noticed he winced when he hit the ground and moved a little stiffly. "I have decided to get Gabrielle a title," Roland began. "Clearing out the ogre is the easiest way—not to mention the March of Carabas is ripe for the picking."

Angelique groaned as she started to gather up some of the magic that floated freely around her, preparing to weave it into a defensive spell. "Your adventuring days have made you *insane*."

"Quite the contrary, they have been the making of me." Roland ducked his head when Angelique lifted up her skirts to step over him.

"Fine, fine, we can do something. I was hoping I might run into black mages in Carabas—hiding in the shadow of the lands— but I've found nothing," Angelique grumbled as she made the finishing touches on her spell and began spooling it out. "I might as well make my efforts worth it."

"The ogre is too powerful for black mages to squat on his lands." Roland joined her in watching her silvery magic trace out a large chunk of the land, briefly filling the area with the sound of many spears striking the earth and creating a pearlescent shield that briefly bubbled around them before fading.

Roland glanced up at her when the spell finished. "He would have killed them if they tried."

Angelique sighed. "It was worth a try, I suppose." She reached into the small leather bag attached to her waist—a gift from Stil that was spelled to hold more than it should—and yanked out a fluffy blanket that she spread on the ground.

Roland hopped on the blanket with a pleased hum but paused and looked up at her as she yanked a few dried provisions from the bag. He cleared his throat. "Angelique...there is one thing I might be able to share about Evariste."

Angelique froze, her heart brimming painfully with hope. "Yes?"

Roland looked away for a moment before he sighed. "As I was attacking one mage, the pair that attacked Evariste with the vermillion magic loosened another spell." He paused. "I don't know for certain because I was doing my best to claw a man's eyes out, but I think they might have sealed his magic."

CHAPTER 5

To Angelique's surprise—and puzzlement—Pegasus did choose to spend the night with Roland and her, and the following day, he took them back to the village of Jagst at a brisk trot.

The pair blew into the inn The Turtle & Doves, run by a kind, elderly couple, who informed them that Gabrielle had left early in the morning and headed north. (The couple had also added that a little, orange cat had left with her, though Angelique didn't understand the significance of this.)

"Perhaps she meant to meet up with us?" Angelique asked as they left the inn. (She was surprised to see Pegasus was still there, arching his neck and looking dark and intimidating in the bright and cheerful village.)

"No, she didn't, that little idiot!" Roland growled, and his back seemed to arch against his will. "That impulsive little brat went to Carabas!"

"To face the ogre?" Angelique frowned. "By *herself?*"

"I said I love and admire Gabrielle; I never said she was smart," Roland growled. "We have to go after her."

"Obviously." Angelique said. "We can use my coach."

"Will it be fast enough? How long has she been gone?" Roland twitched his tail back and forth and worriedly looked north.

This Gabrielle girl really is special to him, Angelique realized as she watched the cat fret. She sucked in a breath of air and eyed Pegasus.

He was the fastest option, but Angelique frankly didn't know how much longer his good—or perhaps apathetic was a better description—mood would last.

Her palms were a little sweaty as she approached the equine. "Pegasus, er, I'm aware I'm imposing on you, but, could you—um —possibly give Roland and me a ride to Carabas?"

Pegasus snorted, making his nostrils glow red, and pawed at the ground with a hoof, eliciting a deafening thunderclap.

Roland flattened himself against the ground. "That didn't make him happy."

"Oh, didn't it?" Sarcasm dripped from Angelique's voice as she rubbed her ears.

Roland stood and started stalking in a circle. "We need to leave now to catch up with her. Don't you have any speed-boosting spells?"

"I don't have that kind of war magic," Angelique said.

Roland growled. "Stay here, I'm going to see if I can get a more precise estimate of when she left." He bounded back into the inn, forgoing his usual saunter in his anxiety.

Angelique sighed and scratched her head—until she noticed a little girl watching her, then she pushed her arms to her side and did her best to look serene. She watched the girl run off, then allowed herself to droop.

She scrunched her eyes shut and leaned against the hitching post just outside the inn.

I don't know what to feel anymore. I'm sad Roland is leaving me but happy for him that he found Gabrielle. But now Gabrielle is in danger, and I need to keep up my search for Evariste, but Gabrielle means so much to Roland, I can't just leave him.

Her shoulders shook briefly, until she took in a big gulp of air and shook her head. She didn't open her eyes, however, until she felt something press into her shoulders.

Swiveling to see the source of the weight, Angelique almost jerked backwards when she found Pegasus's muzzle migrating from her shoulder to her hair.

"Um, hello. Er, greetings." Angelique stiffened automatically, but she didn't dare shy away.

Pegasus shook his head, tossing his flaming mane into the air.

"Um, you may leave whenever you wish," Angelique said. "I'm just waiting on Roland, or rather for more information." She frowned slightly as she let the hitching post take more of her weight. "It seems that his friend—or his mistress, really, since he has chosen to follow her—has gone to Carabas to fight the ogre. She and Roland tried attacking it earlier—that's how he got hurt. She must have gone back to avenge him..."

Angelique trailed off.

Though Roland was obviously angry with Gabrielle, in a way, Angelique could understand her actions. *I feel similarly, I guess, though I'll admit guilt is part of my motivation. Not only did Evariste take the spell aimed at me, but I never apologized for our disagreement.*

Pegasus shifted next to her, and it took Angelique several long moments before she realized he was lowering himself to the ground.

Angelique's eyes bulged slightly as she stared at the equine, but before she could ask him anything, Roland came tearing out of the inn.

"Michi says she left early, so it's certain she's already in Carabas—what is going on?" Roland skidded to a stop just before he crashed into Pegasus.

"I think Pegasus has changed his mind and is willing to take us?" Angelique studied the constellation with narrowed eyes, searching for a clue to his intentions.

Pegasus blinked his liquid black eyes and remained still.

Roland's tail formed the shape of a question mark before he nodded. "I'll chance it." He leaped onto the constellation's back, his puffed tail betraying his nerves.

Angelique sucked in a deep breath. *Evariste might be beyond my reach right now, but we can still help Roland's Gabrielle if we hurry.* She studied Pegasus' face, blinking when she thought she saw a comet streak across his forehead. *I can risk getting tossed off if it's for Roland.*

Angelique slid onto Pegasus' back. Roland climbed into her lap just before the equine rocked to his feet. "So," she started. "Where do we go?"

"North," Roland said as Pegasus started to trot, rapidly exiting the village. "And then east. To Carabas."

Pegasus bore them steadily and hastily to Carabas. Even when they tore through the abandoned city, his pace—fast enough to cloud Angelique's gaze with tears—didn't falter.

Carabas—from its empty streets and battered gates to its quiet-as-death castle—made Angelique shiver. The sky was thick with clouds when Pegasus dropped them off in a courtyard. The castle felt disconcerting.

Angelique had shivered upon seeing that the gray stone of the castle was covered by black moss which only added to the gloom of the place, but her fear shifted to irritation when she got stuck in a window.

"You have adapted entirely too easily to the lifestyle of an adventurer," she grumbled as she tried to wriggle through a busted window frame.

"Do you have the location spell going?" Roland demanded as he waited inside the castle, nervously twitching his tail.

On the way to Carabas—which Pegasus had blasted through fast enough to make both of them windswept and rumpled—Roland had proposed the idea of Angelique creating a tracking spell (as she had gained *great* proficiency with them since beginning her quest to find Evariste) to locate the ogre, making it easier to creep through the castle.

Angelique scowled as the spell curled around her like a cat. "*Yes*, I have it running. It can't find the ogre."

"I thought you said you were good at tracking spells," Roland hissed.

"I *am*!" Angelique finally made it through the window and had to adjust her dress once inside the castle. She scowled at the dust-covered room. "It can't find the beast at all. Maybe he has magical protection."

"Unlikely. He's bloody strong, but intellectual brilliance is not his strong suit." Roland hustled across the room and reached up to bat the door handle with a paw.

"It was able to defeat you," Angelique reminded him as she pulled the door open.

"I *know that*," Roland hissed. "Which means Gabrielle is in grave danger!" Roland slipped into the hallway, his paws silent on the stone flooring.

Angelique grimly reached for her magic. *I'd better prepare for a fight—something to stun the ogre maybe. If I pack enough power in it, I should be able to make him pass out.*

Angelique caught up with Roland when he reached a door that appeared to lead into a hall.

"She's through here," the cat said.

"How do you know?"

"I can smell her—because I taught her everything she knows," Roland said.

Angelique furrowed her brow. "What?"

"Just blow the doors down!"

A bead of sweat dripped down Angelique's back as she struggled to juggle the location spell and the stunning spell for the ogre. "Fine, fine, keep your claws on."

Just when she was about to begin a third spell—to open the

door—Roland hissed at the doors. "Never mind, you're too slow! I'll take care of this."

Angelique blinked. "Really?"

Roland batted at one of the doors, then skittered backwards. A moment passed, then the door was ripped from its hinges and thrown twenty feet into the hall before hitting the floor.

Steam and smoke—byproducts of the more-powerful-than-necessary-spell—filled the air.

Well. I hope the ogre isn't nearby, or Roland just alerted him to our presence.

Angelique expected the magic cat to use more caution, but he was already charging into the hall.

"Gabrielle, you ungracious—ugh—*foul-smelling* child!" he yowled.

Angelique edged her way after him, squinting in the haze. *And if the explosion didn't alert the ogre, Roland's caterwauling will. Yes, he has definitely changed—for the better, I think.*

"I am gone for one day, and you *replace* me with that orange-haired interloper who has not a lick of sense." Roland made it through the clouds of smoke, and Angelique staggered after him, adjusting her hold on her spells as she peered around the hall, looking for the monster.

It was empty, except for Roland's beautiful, blonde-haired friend.

"*Puss!*" Gabrielle shouted. The young lady scrambled across the room and scooped the persnickety cat up, snuggling him to her shoulder. "You're alive. You're *here!*"

Angelique was distracted from ogre-searching long enough to openly gape at the way Roland—ever-correct *Roland*—let her refer to him by such a name.

He didn't seem to mind it, for he rubbed his cheek against Gabrielle's chin. "Of course. You doubted I would survive such trivial wounds?"

"They weren't trivial," Gabrielle said.

Angelique grunted in quiet agreement.

Gabrielle continued, "You almost died! I didn't know if you would make it or if you would be the same afterwards."

Roland twitched his whiskers. "You feared I would be dim-witted?"

"Well, blowing up doors in a castle occupied by an ogre is not the most intelligent thing to do," Gabrielle said.

"Well stated," Angelique muttered under her breath as she continued to survey the room. It really was as empty as it appeared—with the exception of a small orange cat that lingered near Gabrielle. (Perhaps she had a particular affinity for cats?)

She made a slow circle as Roland continued to lecture his traveling companion. "You are scoffing at *my* intelligence?" he demanded. "Good heavens—what little cleverness *you* had has been beaten out of you. Coming here alone? What were you thinking? Now hush. We must flee and regroup. We'll take the ogre out when I grace us with a fresh plan. Angelique, have you successfully pin-pointed that vile creature's location?"

Angelique's eyes watered—she wasn't sure if it was from the smoke or the pungent, musky smell that filled the hall. "No. I must have performed the spell wrong."

Roland hopped out of Gabrielle's arms and stalked his way over to Angelique. "What has you drawing that conclusion?" he asked.

"I can't find a sign of him anywhere." Angelique frowned as Roland twined his tail around her skirts.

"You won't be able to." Gabrielle said nonchalantly. "He's dead."

CHAPTER 6

Gabrielle grinned when Roland whipped around to address her.

"What?" Roland thundered. "How?"

"I tricked him into becoming a mouse, and your *feline* lady friend ate him." Gabrielle approached a chair and picked up the orange-colored cat sitting next to it.

Angelique tried not to gape at the adventurous girl. "You're certain the ogre perished?"

"Oh, yes." Gabrielle looked a little green as she sat down, hard, still holding the orange cat. "I heard her crunch on his bones."

Angelique held in a grimace at the description. *Roland was wrong; she must be brilliant to defeat an ogre by herself. No wonder she can keep pace with him.*

Roland must have still been upset with his friend for venturing to Carabas alone, for instead of approaching her—as Angelique was certain he wanted to—he sat down next to Angelique. "Are you well?" he asked.

Gabrielle's smile looked tight—and perhaps a little forced—

and she cleared her throat. "Of course. I just...I haven't gotten much sleep for the past two nights."

She's upset...but why?

Puss must have sensed the emotion as well, for he left Angelique's side and meandered up to Gabrielle's chair. "Beat it," he hissed at the orange cat before jumping onto his mistress's lap. "Ugh—you smell like you've been cavorting with fox cubs."

Gabrielle scooped him up into a tight hug.

Angelique wondered if the young lady would start crying, so she purposely looked away, casting her eyes across the dusty and dilapidated hall.

Roland's voice was gentle when he spoke. "It's all right, Gabrielle. Angelique fixed me up quite nicely, even if her bedside manners are poor."

Hearing the obvious cue Roland had made to insert some humor into the tense moment, Angelique drawled, "Now I remember why Master Evariste and I always left you behind."

"How do you two know each other?" Gabrielle released Roland and slowly stood as if it made her bones ache.

Roland hopped onto the ground. "She was my original mistress."

Angelique thought she caught a flicker of dismay in the beautiful girl's face. *Does she think Roland means to part from her?* Aloud, Angelique said, "Master Evariste—the Lord Enchanter to whom I serve as apprentice—gave him to me for my birthday many years ago."

"You were her pet?" Gabrielle asked.

"Assistant!" Roland snapped. "I was given to her because Angelique has the focus of a child being lured with a sweet."

"Magic cats of any age are hard to come by," Angelique said, "but Master Evariste somehow found Roland...er...Puss when he was still a kitten. He was supposed to be a companion and a reference, as he is quite knowledgeable in casting magic—even charms that are beyond his abilities."

Gabrielle looked down at the magic feline. "You must have been expensive."

"Yes, but that man squanders money on Angelique all the time." Roland swatted at the orange cat when it ventured too close.

"I see," Gabrielle said.

Angelique tilted her head slightly as she studied the young hero. *Did she sound...sad?*

Roland didn't seem to notice. Instead, he peered around the room. "Where have all the humans gone? I haven't seen any scurrying about—mind you, Angelique and I blew through the city, so I shouldn't be surprised."

"They're hiding," Gabrielle said.

Roland twitched his whiskers, and Angelique could almost *see* the schemes of his brain coming to fruition.

She grinned. "Perhaps we should find them and inform them of their new master,"

"Their what?" Gabrielle asked, sounding confused.

"Their new master. They have a right to know the despot-ogre was ousted and to be given a chance to follow you willingly," Roland said. "Though, mark my words, if they refuse to acknowledge your leadership, they deserve to be chopped up into mincemeat!" He padded from the room, his glee apparent in the sway of his black tail.

Gabrielle took a staggering step towards the wrecked doors. "Why would they follow me?"

Angelique started after Roland but paused in the broken doorway long enough to offer the obviously confused Gabrielle what she hoped was a reassuring smile. "Because you're the new Marquise of Carabas."

"No, I'm not." Gabrielle followed Angelique and Roland down the empty hallway.

"Save your breath, Angelique. Gabrielle can be as stubborn as a mule," Roland advised.

Angelique snorted, then tried to alter it into a more appropriate peal of laughter. "So you've met your match then? I can see how you enjoy yourself." She opened a set of doors, and together they slipped outside.

Roland's voice was thick with satisfaction. "It has been a refreshing change."

Gabrielle hung back, holding the door so the orange cat could follow after them. "What made you two decide to part ways?" she asked.

"We didn't decide," Roland led the way across the courtyard. "It is more that our lives were torn asunder."

"Oh?" Gabrielle asked, her voice polite.

I can't get a read on this girl. Does Roland—or do I now call him Puss?—need to assure her he's staying at her side, or does she know that already?

Angelique grimaced. *Regardless, we do owe her an explanation.* "There was an attack," Angelique began, unable to keep all the sorrow out of her voice. "Late this past winter. Master Evariste and I were home—"

"Which was something of a rarity," Roland inserted—though he didn't sound as know-it-all as he usually did.

"And we were attacked," Angelique said.

Gabrielle's eyes widened. "Two enchanters were *attacked?*"

"In Master Evariste's home—perhaps one of the best guarded places on the continent," Roland's voice was soft as they reached the outer circle of the castle.

"The attackers tried to...to capture me." Angelique paused as a flicker of guilt gnawed at her. "They would have gotten me if Master Evariste hadn't thrown me halfway across the continent with a transportation spell. I wasn't able to return home until spring and..." She stopped before the rush of emotion could overwhelm her.

I am so sick of feeling sad!

Roland jumped on a windowsill and peered inside before he

nodded at the door. "They ransacked the place and carried Evariste off. I don't know where to—I was thrown unconscious before they left. It was no matter; I couldn't have done anything. Angelique had placed a silencing collar on me earlier in the day, cutting off my means to cast magic."

Gabrielle slunk into the empty building, leading the way as Roland and Angelique dawdled behind.

"I'm sorry," Angelique said, guilt gnawing at her again.

"You couldn't have known." Roland must have finally forgiven her, for his voice was kind. "I left, hoping to track down a mage. I never found one—although I narrowly missed the craftmage Rumpelstiltskin when I met Gabrielle and resolved to embark on an adventure with her." He gave Gabrielle his version of a cat smile.

"Really? Stil was around here?" Angelique asked.

Her comment went ignored, for Puss and Gabrielle were staring at each other. "You thought we would eventually run into a mage, and then you planned to return to Lady Enchantress Angelique?" Gabrielle asked.

"I hoped to find a magic user, yes, but that wasn't why I chose to travel with you," Roland acknowledged.

Gabrielle was silent as they started down the hallway, their footsteps echoing.

Angelique flicked her eyes between the hero and the cat. *Gabrielle is definitely making some assumptions, and I'm not entirely certain Roland has picked up on all of them.* Angelique smiled and made an effort to keep her voice bright. "As I have already alerted the Veneno Conclave to Master Evariste's capture, and located Puss, I am free to follow my leads. Or rather, *find* leads."

"So…you will travel with the Lady Enchantress now, Puss?" Gabrielle's heart was in her eyes as she studied the magic cat.

"What? No!" Roland glared at the orange cat, who rubbed her head against him.

Angelique was filled with the desire to kick her old friend. *Does he really not see how upset Gabrielle is?*

"I would understand, if—" Gabrielle started.

Roland, sounding quarrelsome, interrupted her. "I have my own free will, Gabrielle. I choose with whom I stay."

That had all the sweetness of a skunk. The little idiot—he's not making her feel any better!

"Yes, but if you were a gift to the Lady Enchantress—"

Angelique hastily intervened. "Please, Lady Gabrielle, you don't understand." Angelique rested a hand on Gabrielle's shoulder, stopping their progress forward. She used what she hoped was an understanding smile as she met Gabrielle's unusual, amber-colored eyes. "Roland—Puss, that is—has been, and will continue to be, my dear friend. But it is clear you are his true mistress."

Gabrielle shook her head.

I was right—the poor thing thought Roland was going to leave her. It took everything in Angelique to keep from giving the black and white cat a murderous look. Instead, she settled for lightly squeezing Gabrielle's shoulder.

"No, you must listen to me, ogre-defeater," Angelique said. "Seeing Roland with you, hearing him talk about your adventures? He is happier with you than he ever was with me. And he has chosen you."

Gabrielle's eyes glazed with tears, and although she blinked rapidly, a few of them still fell, leaving wet tracks down her cheeks. She blushed a little, then bent over to pick Roland up, cuddling him close.

"Ugh, you really do reek," Roland grumbled, eliciting a choked laugh from Gabrielle. He continued, "Angelique is my friend, Gabrielle. But I will follow you until the day one of us takes our last breath."

Angelique smiled as she watched the pair, but she felt like a bit of an intruder. She glanced away and considered forging ahead without them. *They probably need to talk...*

"Thank you, Puss," Gabrielle said. "And thank you for saving him, Lady Enchantress. I was so worried."

"It was my pleasure." Angelique peered up the hallway, trying to decide if she should make an escape or not. "I mean to leave soon to renew my search, but first I will help both of you settle into Carabas. Our tour has made it apparent that it is quite neglected."

"It is, but I think Gabrielle will have the funds to renovate it," Roland said. "Phew, after she bathes, that is."

"What? How?" Gabrielle asked.

"By crawling in a tub filled with hot, soapy water," Roland said.

"That's not what I meant."

"The funds? The answer is easy—the ogre has been hoarding wealth and treasure since he first thundered his way into Carabas. He must have quite the treasury by now," Roland said.

Angelique narrowed her eyes. "How do you know that?"

"I read it in one of Evariste's correspondences," Puss said, his black tail twitching.

"You read his *mail?*" Angelique's first instinct was to snatch Roland from the protective cradle of Gabrielle's arms and shake some sense into him, but that would absolutely tarnish her enchantress image, so she planted a hand over her heart instead and privately promised herself retribution later.

"Yes."

"You sneaky—"

"I already said I'm not going to be the new marquise," Gabrielle said.

"Of course you are. You're the lost heir of Carabas—or at least King Henrik promised to let us pretend you are." Roland's voice was smug and pleased.

Gabrielle stared at her cat. "When did he agree to that?"

"That time Prince Steffen accidentally peeped at you," Roland said. "I had an excellent conversation with King Henrik in his carriage."

Angelique studied Gabrielle with new interest. *A prince spied on her? Well, she is gorgeous. I would still bet my best dress Roland had a paw in it.*

Gabrielle groaned. "I can't keep up with you."

Angelique smiled but fixed her attention back on the castle. If she wanted to return to her search for Evariste in a timely manner, she needed to begin working right away—especially since her stamina wasn't the greatest these days.

I can help them here in Carabas and safely use my magic, I think. While it's technically in Arcainia, these lands are below poverty level and have been under siege by the ogre's foul presence. She wouldn't have to hesitate if she had anything besides war magic—the Council would approve of her aiding them, then.

But she was what she was. And she knew Evariste would never leave Carabas in the dire mess it was in, so neither could she.

If I could help and avoid getting in trouble, I would much prefer that, but it's not like I can cast spells to help Carabas from the border of Mullberg.

Angelique nodded, her mind made up. "I believe I will start with some repairing spells—though it will take me twice as long to cast as it would a full enchantress." Angelique tapped her lip as she stared down the hallway, her eyes fixated on a smashed pillar.

"I will begin designing Gabrielle's letterhead. Your crest will, of course, include a cat," Roland said.

"I give up," Gabrielle muttered.

"It's always the wisest course to bow to my superior intelligence," Roland said. "By which I mean to say, you could begin by taking a bath."

"Oh, go roll in some *Essence de Fox*," Gabrielle muttered, stomping off.

Angelique whirled around. "*What?*" she asked in horror.

"Essence de Fox," Gabrielle repeated.

Angelique grimaced. She recognized the name as one of Stil's early creations meant to inhibit all olfactory abilities. (It was a rousing success, but Angelique would never want to actually *use* the stuff.) "Do you know what's *in* that?"

"She doesn't want to know," Roland was quick to say. "Come, Mistress. While Angelique gets started with her magic, we should continue searching for your new subjects."

"But what—"

"Hush. We've already wasted hours, and the residents of Carabas deserve to learn that they've been set free!"

BY THE TIME NIGHT FELL, Angelique felt like a frayed dish towel.

She had spent the afternoon walking through the ruined castle and city, doing her best to mend the direst of the wreckage. (She had never used so many building- and construction-based spells in her life!)

At least I'll have a solid case if the Council lectures me for this. It's a wonder the castle didn't fall down on top of the residents years ago!

Angelique sagged against a stone support pillar as she stared up at the wooden ceiling beam she was repairing. Her magic came at a slow trickle—not because it was running low, but rather because she was so tired she couldn't muster any greater amount.

She stood in the shadows, apart from *Lady* Gabrielle's subjects, who scurried through the great hall, cleaning and setting furniture and ornaments right. Though they had only been at it for an afternoon, already the castle seemed lighter—and *smelled* better. The air was fresh and scented with ocean brine rather than the rotten smell of ogre or the pungent scent of *Essence de Fox*.

"This is pathetic," Angelique grumbled as her eyes drooped with exhaustion. "I took rests throughout the day—why can't I do more?"

"Because you're doing bigger spells than you're used to."

If she had been any less tired, Angelique would have jumped in place. Instead, she looked down at Roland, who was fastidiously licking a paw and using it to clean his face.

"What do you mean?" Angelique asked.

"Evariste taught you a great deal, and you used many spells," he conceded. "However, you normally didn't fire off so many spells in a row. It's the same reason you were tired yesterday—you defeated goblins and then worked a major healing spell. Besides, Evariste taught you spells to strengthen wood timbers and reform broken stone in *Noyers*, not a crusty city that is little better than ruins."

Angelique sighed and watched a rather determined-looking woman roll up her sleeves and attack a fireplace with enviable exuberance. "Normally I'd argue with you and say it's just proof of my deficiencies, but I suspect you are right. It's still disappointing." She pushed a little more of her magic into the spell she was using to strengthen the ceiling beam. "Otherwise, do you think I'm finally reaching my price?"

"Hardly," he scoffed. "You've used a bucketful compared to the ocean of magic you possess. No, you just need practice. Evariste taught you well and gave you a great framework, but what you are experiencing now is the messy-ness of the world that those without magic must face."

Safely hidden in the shadows, Angelique pursed her lips.

"You will find that you'll improve—rapidly, if you keep this pace up." Roland purred as he briefly rubbed against her skirts, making the coins on her hem jingle. "A year from now, you'll be as stalwart as any scruffy mage."

"We'll see," Angelique said, unconvinced. "But Roland—do you want me to call you that, or Puss, now?"

Roland flicked his tail. "Both names are special to me," he said. "Either will do."

Angelique smiled. "Then I shall call you Puss."

He twitched his whiskers. "You hope to irritate me?"

"No. Because I think it's proper—to acknowledge this new life that you've embraced," Angelique said. "Though I might mess up sometimes."

"I'm still your Roland." He again pushed against her skirts.

His words made her throat ache a little with emotion, but she swallowed it. "I know, and I'm thankful. But I won't hold you back." The last part almost came out as a whisper, but she managed to say it. And that was the important thing.

She tested the wooden beam with her magic but wasn't yet satisfied, so she twisted some more of her powers, further reinforcing the timber. Once she had it going, she let her attention wander and spotted Gabrielle.

She was at the far side of the room, helping a footman roll up a moth-eaten, hole-riddled rug. When they finished, she shouldered the rug with ease and walked over to the open window, flinging it into the courtyard where they were temporarily throwing all unusable items.

The footman winced as he scurried at her side, obviously pleading to take her burden from her, but Gabrielle laughed him off.

"She's going to be a wonderful Marquise," Angelique said.

Roland—no—Puss grumbled. "She'll be an oddball of a Marquise is what she'll be with her insistence on helping her people and getting dirty."

"I disagree," Angelique said. "Those outside Carabas might not understand, but everyone here…they lived through the ogre. Once they adjust to your adventuring mistress, I suspect they will be almost as loyal to her as you are."

"I imagine so. But the rest of the continent might not view her actions with such favor," Puss said.

Angelique glanced back up at the beam again, checking on her silver magic that encased it. "Perhaps. But she'll be the kind of Marquise nobles *should* be." She frowned, remembering her encounter with the greedy Loire duke whose illusionary clothes she had "accidentally" dropped during an important speech. He had bled his lands dry to pay for his exorbitant spending on clothes. "In fact, I think nobles everywhere could stand to learn a thing or two from her."

"They could," Roland, er, Puss said. "And they might, if that peeping prince of hers persists."

"You don't like him?" Angelique asked.

"As a general rule I don't like *anybody*," Puss snidely replied.

Angelique chuckled as she tested the beam one last time, then released her magic, finally satisfied. She tipped her head back and tried to roll her stiff shoulders. "I was hoping we would finish soon for the night, but based on the torches they're bringing in, the people of Carabas mean to soldier on."

"Go outside and rest," Puss advised her. "They're making food in the kitchens. I'll find you when the preparations are complete."

Angelique nodded. "I'm not too proud to admit I can't do much more. Thanks...Puss." She half expected him to say something snarky about her testing the waters, but he didn't.

He didn't even acknowledge it, for he was already padding off after Gabrielle, his white paws gleaming in the torchlight.

Angelique smiled at his preoccupancy, but there was a small pang in her heart, too. *Even though I know Roland is still my friend, somehow...seeing him with Gabrielle makes me lonelier than ever. I have no one.*

Angelique shook the thought from her head and inhaled deeply. She drew herself up, gathering up her practiced enchantress bearings.

She smiled at the servant or two who noticed her when she made her way to the door, and quietly slipped from the hall.

A footman carrying wood bowed so low, Angelique worried he might stumble, but he was the only being outside the hall, and after she passed, he hurried in to join his countrymen.

The castle was quiet as Angelique made her way from the

inner part of the castle to the courtyard nestled between the inner and outer ring.

Summer kept the air warm even after the sun was down—though Angelique could feel a nippy breeze roll in from the ocean and hear the gush of the waves.

She spotted a stone bench nestled next to a dead bush and started for it.

The sound of her steps echoed in the courtyard, and flames of blue flickered in the darkness.

Angelique tripped and almost screamed, but she managed to keep it in when she realized the blue fire was only Pegasus. When her heart resumed beating at a normal pace, she managed a strangled, "Good evening, Pegasus."

It was hard to see the constellation in the dark of night—besides his glowing mane and tail, of course. But when she spoke, he snorted, and his nostrils briefly flashed red.

Angelique shook her head and made herself smile. "I apologize. I didn't know you were still here in Carabas. I assumed you had returned to the skies." She inched closer to the bench and waited for Pegasus to move or...something.

He didn't.

She slowly sat down on the seat, her shoulders drooping, and tipped her head up at the sky.

Though a few rooms were bright inside Carabas castle, outside, it was so dark that the stars in the sky could shine at full power.

It was beautiful and quiet, but it made her feel rather small and reminded her that she had no one, now.

Concluding that she'd much rather fill the silence with her own voice than allow herself to wallow in self-pity, Angelique addressed the magical equine. "The ogre has been defeated—as I'm sure you concluded. He was already dead by the time we arrived, actually. Gabrielle—she's Roland's, sorry, no, Puss' friend. Anyway, Gabrielle said she talked the ogre into turning into a mouse. I've been told she planned to crush him with a shovel, but the little orange cat that followed her to Carabas ate him instead."

Angelique shivered at the thought. "I don't know if I should be impressed with Gabrielle or marvel that a cat achieved what dozens of heroes, mages, and even armies could not. Regardless, Roland has now set Gabrielle up as the Marquise of Carabas."

She stretched her arms above her head as the tension in her shoulders and heart started to loosen. "I'll spend the night here, but I hope to leave tomorrow and continue my search for Evariste. That is, Lord Enchanter Evariste. I think I might return to our home in Torrens to do a bit of research." She dropped her hands into her lap and smiled at Pegasus.

Now that her eyes had adjusted to the dimness, he was easier to see, for his coat faintly glowed with flickers of stardust.

"Thank you," she said, "for taking me to Mulberg so I could heal Roland, and for bringing us here. I don't know if I could have saved Roland without your speed."

Pegasus flicked his tail and twitched his lower lip.

"Are you going to return to the sky tonight?" Angelique asked.

Pegasus moved closer to Angelique and dropped his head to sniff her feet.

Angelique offered her palm for him to sniff, but he ignored it and instead briefly lipped at her hair. A moment passed, and he turned his attention to the dry bush by the bench, but he didn't leave.

Angelique wasn't sure what to make of it, but she was grateful for his company.

He stayed with her until Puss, true to his word, came for Angelique to summon her to dinner. And when Angelique arose the next morning, ready for the return trip to Torrens, he was waiting outside—his coat pitch black in the early morning light—then laid down in his wordless invitation for her to climb on his back.

CHAPTER 7

Angelique plucked a promising book from a shelf and only glanced at the title before adding it to the stack she held precariously balanced in her other arm. The next one she pulled out appeared to be written in an entirely foreign language, so she slid it back into place with a quiet "tsk."

The arm that held all the books ached something fierce, so with only one additional glance at the shelf, Angelique hopped off the stool and made her way over to the desk, carefully setting the books on its wooden surface.

She massaged the back of her neck and looked from her stacked books to the library—which was now looking markedly vacant given all the tomes she had piled around the desk. "Somewhere in here, there has got to be something that can help me find Evariste."

She rearranged a few stacks, choosing what books to prioritize, then plopped down in a chair and opened the nearest book to its table of contents.

Her eyes traced over the list of topics—mostly advanced techniques for craftmages, but she was hoping to find a charm or spell that might help her find her teacher. "Heat charms, invisibility spells, warding off mice, spinning gold—nothing on locating lost people or items." She sighed and pushed the book aside, already reaching for the next one.

She had already used all well-known spells and charms to search for Evariste, but she was hoping she might be able to stumble on something less known, or something that used archaic and long-forgotten methods.

The old methods weren't often used or dabbled in because they were considered potentially dangerous or nearly impossible to harness. (There was a reason why they were part of the old ways.)

Conversely, the older methods were more prone to being negatively or positively affected by emotions—which technically meant if she found the right spell, she might be able to use love to power it. But as she hadn't found anything helpful, Angelique wasn't ready to go scour the Conclave in search of one of Evariste's many female admirers. Yet.

She was hoping, however, that she might be able to use the bracelet Evariste had given her when she first became his apprentice. It was supposed to serve as a tracking spell so he could find her, but Angelique was rather hoping she could reverse the spell and use it to find him.

Angelique skimmed through the table of contents of another book. This one had a spell to find lost items. *Perhaps it could be modified?* she wondered as she set it aside.

She grabbed the next book, and tried not to grimace at the piles she had to sift through, but she had no shortcuts for her research. If the Conclave knew she was looking into old magical methods, the officials wouldn't be pleased.

The Elves of Alabaster Forest likely would be able to help —it was said they used old magic to cross the ocean and arrive on the continent years ago. But Angelique had used the portal in the salon to trod their borders when she first arrived back from helping Gabrielle and Puss in Carabas nearly a month ago. And though she shouted, they had not come.

Something suspicious is going on with the elves as well, Angelique vaguely noted.

Something tapped on the window pane.

Angelique pulled her attention from the book, putting it aside when she saw a butterfly hovering outside.

It had wings edged in black with swirls of forest and olive green. Its wings were long—so much so that the ends of its lower wings trailed slightly behind it, making it look like a cloak swept behind the butterfly.

She hurried from the library, running to the front door. When she threw it open, she saw the butterfly making its way around the corner of the house, its delicate wings fluttering in the nippy fall breeze that was starting to tug on the half-green/half-orange and -yellow tree leaves.

Angelique jogged up to the butterfly and held out her hands, cupping them together.

The butterfly landed on her palms and glowed before its wings unfolded into a paper letter. The magic-made butterfly faded away, leaving only the message behind.

Angelique grimaced when she saw the stylized V and C that made up the Veneno Conclave seal. Reluctantly, she broke the seal and opened the message.

Apprentice Angelique, Enchantress-in-Training:
You are to report in to the Veneno Conclave Council at your earliest convenience to discuss your recent actions.

Angelique groaned and trudged back to the house. "It's been almost a month. I thought maybe they hadn't noticed my work in Carabas. But it's been too long for them to be upset about my modification to Prince Severin's curse. Unless they're disturbed that I'm running around without supervision?"

Angelique locked the door when she entered the house, gulping at the thought. *I haven't done anything wrong, really. But given how little they like me, it's possible they might punish me for any of the above.*

Angelique rubbed her brow as she climbed the stairs, making her way to Evariste's quarters—where he had a portal that connected to his office in the Veneno Conclave fortress.

Dread filled Angelique, turning her fingers cold as she opened the door to his bedroom.

The portal to the Conclave was still active. It glowed a crimson red and was framed by goldwork and foreign scripts. She could see the massive wooden desk and the plain white walls of his Conclave office through the gate.

She took a breath and stepped through. The strange-ness of portal magic surrounded her—oddly enough, it actually seemed to spool tighter around her than usual. But she stepped through, and the feeling of Evariste's rare portal magic evaporated.

She straightened her dress and double checked that the illusion spell she used to change the unusual hue of her silver-colored eyes was active, then decided to make her hair an ashy blonde color for the occasion—for she might as well try to appear as bright and innocent as possible for this trial—before leaving Evariste's office.

She wandered through the Veneno Conclave fortress, leaving behind the workshops and offices of the mages and magic users who lived and worked in the Conclave, and instead entered the wing of the fortress that held the rooms for the conclave's governing body—meeting rooms, offices for the various heads of the different departments within the Conclave and, of course, Hallowed Hall: the large hall where the Council met.

Two men were posted outside the doorway to Hallowed Hall—a war mage and his apprentice, it appeared. The war mage was taller, broad shouldered, and held two sabers, while his apprentice—a youthful and wide-eyed teenage boy—gripped a staff.

"Good afternoon—I have a summons from the Council." Angelique held her letter up for inspection.

The war mage waved it off. "I am aware of who you are, Lady Enchantress Angelique." He bowed, giving her far more respect than she deserved.

His apprentice bowed even deeper, but he craned his neck so he could still watch, gawking at her with a mixture of awe and delight.

While I am thankful for my fellow war mages' support, it is a bit awkward to have them look at me with stars in their eyes when a day of using construction-based spells is enough to mentally fatigue me. Angelique awkwardly cleared her throat. "I'm afraid I'm only an Enchantress-in-Training."

The war mage quirked a brow and smiled handsomely at her. "Soon, Lady Enchantress," he said as he motioned for his apprentice to help him open the door. "Soon."

Angelique pressed her lips together but stepped into the darkened Hallowed Hall.

She had no fondness for the hall. The only good memory involving the place was the day Evariste stepped in to take her on as his apprentice, blocking the Council from sealing her magic.

It was still as dark as ever. The only light sources fell on the high desks that belonged to the Council Members.

Angelique squinted in the dimness, but she couldn't make out anyone sitting in the poorly lit seating section available for mages to sit and observe the Council's rulings and judgements.

"Ahh, Apprentice Angelique," a cheery voice called. "You are quite prompt!"

"Approach us," ordered a much deeper, male voice.

Angelique followed the orders and stopped on the threshold of the intense light. She had to look up to see the Council Members—three enchanters and three enchantresses—but made her curtsey low out of respect. "I used one of Lord Enchanter Evariste's permanent portals to get here."

"We see," Enchantress Felicienne said icily. (As the enchantress was Angelique's most outspoken critic, Angelique was not surprised at the cold reception. None of the Council Members liked her very much—except perhaps cheerful Primrose and fun-loving Crest who tolerated her.)

"Where does the portal drop you off?" Enchanter Crest asked, leaning forward. He gave her a slight smile that made him look even more handsome than usual. (As he appeared to be in his late thirties, he was the youngest member of the Council, but given the slow aging process of powerful magic users, he was likely old enough to be Angelique's father or grandfather.)

Angelique, already on guard, slightly bowed her head. "The Conclave side of the portal is located in Lord Enchanter Evariste's office."

Enchantress Galendra—a quiet, mousy-looking woman—frowned. "Is it appropriate for her to use what is obviously supposed to be Evariste's personal method of transportation?"

She and Felicienne frowned in Angelique's direction.

Angelique fought to swallow as the familiar—and bitter—taste of defeat filled her mouth. "Enchanter Evariste frequently took me through that particular portal before he was...taken."

The enchantresses didn't look satisfied with the answer.

The persecution begins with my travel arrangements, of course. How could I have expected any less?

"You are worrying needlessly, Galendra, Felicienne," Enchanter Tristisim said unexpectedly.

Was he defending her? Usually Tristisim disliked her almost as much as Felicienne!

"Traveling through Evariste's portal without him is the least of her most recent sins," he continued.

Ahhh, yes. There we go—that's the jolly Tristisim I know.

"Tristisim is right." Crest flipped through his papers. "We've received a few troubling reports about you, Angelique."

Angelique kept her expression bland and said nothing.

"It seems you used magic in Arcainia on two separate occasions." Crest read off the report. "Lazare, would you list the charges?"

Charges? Angelique's stomach began to curdle.

A moment passed, followed by another.

A loud, growling noise that rather reminded Angelique of a screeching raccoon was the only uttered reply to Crest's request.

Enchanter Crest leaned forward so he could peer down the lineup. "Lazare?"

"He's fallen asleep again," Felicienne said dryly.

"Oh dear." Primrose clasped a hand to her plump cheek before she tapped the old enchanter on the hand. "Lazare? *Lazare*."

Enchanter Lazare only snored louder.

Enchanter Tristisim slammed his hand on his desk. "Lazare!"

The elderly enchanter finally sat up. "Eh? What do you want?" he demanded. He fumbled with his monocle before getting it into place, his gaze falling on Angelique. "Oh. You. *Again*." His mouth screwed up with obvious distaste. "Guilty!" he declared.

Felicienne sighed and rubbed her eyes, but Enchanter Crest chuckled. "Sorry, old boy, we're not making a judgement quite yet. Could you read off the instances of magical misuse we have received on Apprentice Angelique?"

Enchanter Lazare scowled and scratched his cheek. "If we say she's guilty, we can break for lunch."

"*Lazare*," Tristisim said in exasperation.

"Fine, fine, fine. Have it your way," Enchanter Lazare grumbled. "When we're forced to skip lunch again, and you embarrass us all with that growling bear you have in your stomach, don't complain to me!"

Tristisim frowned and folded his hands over his belly as Lazare cleared his throat.

"Apprentice Angelique, we've received reports of you using magic on two separate days in Arcainia—where magic is strictly forbidden," Lazare read. "Additionally, you have performed magic on a member of the Loire royal family—of your own volition—and have been recorded as traveling the continent and performing magic without the supervision of your master." Lazare dropped his paper and peered at her. "What do you have to say about that?"

Now is when my acting really matters. Angelique thought of the beautiful elven Lady Alastryn and did her best to mimic the lady's serene but slight smile. *I must appear to be as innocent as a lamb, even if I am really a fox.* "It is true that I used magic *near* the border of Arcainia, but I was in Mullberg at the time. The only spells I used were against goblins—which were attacking me—and a healing spell."

Enchanter Tristisim frowned but Enchantress Primrose smiled encouragingly. "Self-defense near the border, was it?" she asked.

Angelique nodded.

Enchantress Felicienne tapped her fingers on her desk. "And the second occasion?"

I don't like that no one gave any indication of what they think—that doesn't bode well. Still, Angelique kept the mask of her smile in place. "The second time I used magic was in Carabas—which, as it has been under the rule of an ogre, is all but a city-state and wasn't a part of Arcainia at all."

Enchanter Lazare adjusted his monocle. "Why do you say that?"

Angelique made her smile just a smidgeon larger and hoped she looked charming instead of angry. "It's not as if the King of Arcainia was collecting taxes from the ogre or providing support of any kind. The Carabas March was cut off from all outside contact. If the King's will cannot be decreed in a city, is it truly part of the country?"

Enchanter Lazare grunted and leaned back in his chair.

"What kind of magic did you use?" Enchantress Galendra asked.

"Repair and construction spells." Angelique tapped her lower lip and tried to appear deep in thought. "I repaired support beams and timbers—mostly important structural repairs that the people of Carabas would have a difficult time fixing."

"That's right. You were there when the new Marquise of Carabas defeated the ogre, were you not?" Enchantress Felicienne asked.

"I was near, but I was not present, Lady Enchantress," Angelique said. "By the time I arrived, Lady Gabrielle had already outsmarted the brute."

"And what have you to say about meddling with Prince Severin of Loire?" Enchantress Felicienne asked.

Here's the challenging part. If I'm careful enough, I can twist this to drag them into the matter as well. But I have to make them believe I'm asking this out of wonder, not spite. And I also need to make sure they don't ask me why I was sashaying up to the palace right then! Angelique let her smile droop slightly. "I was in Noyers when Prince Severin was attacked. He had a curse placed on him, which gave him the mind and body of a beast and doomed his household—"

"To fade away with him," Enchanter Tristisim said. "Yes, we're perfectly aware of the terms of the curse."

Thank you, sour grapes, you are as charming as ever. Angelique made herself nod. "Then you are likely also aware that Prince Severin was out of control, and it was only a matter of time before the soldiers would be forced to kill him for the safety of his family?"

Enchanter Crest nodded. "In our report, Prince Lucien said as much, yes."

Angelique waited a few spans, but no one spoke. *Excellent, then here's the trap.* "But it seems my actions displease you?"

"You—an apprentice—used magic without your master on a royal," Enchantress Primrose furrowed her brow with sympathy. "It could easily be construed as a political move."

The other Council Members nodded in agreement.

And I've got them! Provided I don't mess up my delivery, that is.

Angelique slightly tilted her head and allowed her forehead to wrinkle with concern. "I see. I was unaware it would be considered less political if I were to let Prince Severin *die*."

Enchantress Felicienne sat up. "I beg your pardon?"

"I assumed that the Veneno Conclave would act to save a prince in danger because *not* extending help would show a lack of concern not only for the royal family, but it would also fail to meet our duty to protect the continent from dark magic—for it was an evil witch who *cursed* the prince," Angelique said, verbally twisting the dagger.

"Apprentice Angelique," Enchanter Crest began gently. "That is not to say we did not wish for you to help him at all."

"Then what would you have had me do?" Angelique asked, false earnestness bleeding through her voice. "I am a mere apprentice, so the only thing I could think of at the time was to alter his curse, as Lord Enchanter Evariste taught me to do when Princess Rosalinda of Sole faced a similar crisis."

The Council Members exchanged glances, and Angelique barely kept a satisfied smile off her face.

They might be able to punish me for my other instances of not toeing the line, but I'm not going to let them bully me over Prince Severin—not when Evariste had me do the same thing for Rosalinda!

"It seems we can dismiss any charges for modifying Prince Severin's curse," Enchanter Tristisim rumbled with clear reluctance.

Angelique exhaled in relief—she didn't know if they'd buy her "serene enchantress" act. She wanted to stick her tongue out at the Council for even bringing the bogus charge against her, but if she was to clear her name on the rest of the charges, she needed to act pleasing.

"I second the motion," Enchantress Felicienne said finally. "Under the provision that it was an emergency situation involving black magic."

"Yes, of course!" Primrose chimed in.

"And the other charges?" Enchantress Galendra timidly asked.

Tristisim frowned. "I think her line about Carabas not being a part of Arcainia is untrue."

"I don't know." Enchantress Primrose looked thoughtfully down at her papers. "She spoke the truth that as long as the ogre was there, Carabas really was not acting as an Arcainian city."

Yes! Angelique smiled politely and didn't allow her inner glee to show. *Thank you!*

"And the time she was performing her magic, Lady Gabrielle was the new Marquise, oh, dear," Enchantress Primrose looked dismayed, "which brought Carabas back into Arcainia, I suppose."

No, no, no! Angelique wanted to groan. Enchantress Primrose's good will seemed to be a double-edged sword—if she'd just stop *speaking* her thoughts aloud!

"I used my magic the day Gabrielle defeated the ogre," Angelique said, unable to keep silent. "As the Royal Family was not yet aware of Gabrielle's new position, the future of Carabas was still uncertain, so to speak."

Enchanter Lazare scratched his chest. "And you did all of this unsupervised?"

"Yes," Angelique said. "Because Lord Enchanter Evariste is still missing."

"Why did you leave your home to begin with?" Enchanter Crest asked.

It was only through great self-control that Angelique managed to hold in a grimace. *Darn. I hoped they wouldn't ask me that—because they aren't going to be pleased with my answer, even if they cannot fault me for it.*

"I was searching for Enchanter Evariste," she said.

Enchanter Crest smiled sadly. "While it's valiant of you to look, Angelique, the Conclave already has an official investigation *and* a committee searching for your dear master."

Yes, and how many months have passed with the committee lacking anything to show for it?

Angelique bowed her head. "I am aware of this, Enchanter Crest."

"We have yet to resolve if she willfully performed magic in Arcainia by using it in Carabas," Tristisim said coldly.

"I suppose that is the greater issue," Enchantress Primrose agreed. "We can interpret her tracking around the country and using magic at will despite her being a student as loyalty to her master."

Angelique winced. *Primrose. Please. Stop. TALKING!*

Enchanter Tristisim looked thoughtful at Enchantress' Primrose's words. Enchanter Lazare, however, yawned widely and smacked his lips.

"Why are we fretting about semantics?" he complained. "Tell the girl's master to punish her, and be done with it."

"Lord Enchanter Evariste is missing, Lazare," Enchantress Felicienne reminded the older enchanter.

"Eh?" He said, leaning forward, which underlined the stooped shape of his aged back.

"Lord Enchanter Evariste cannot punish her, as he is missing," Enchantress Felicienne spoke loudly.

"Then what are we sitting here for?" Enchanter Lazare complained. "Until he gets back, we can't discipline the girl—unless she does something worthy of being sealed. Has she?" He eagerly planted his elbows on his desk and looked up and down the line of Council Members.

"Not yet," Enchantress Felicienne slowly said.

"Agreed. The charges are serious, not endangering," Enchantress Galendra said.

Serious? Which of my actions are at all serious? They are dubious at worst!

Unfortunately, Galendra's words stirred up Enchanter Tristisim again. "Consider this your warning, Apprentice Angelique. Continue with self-studies at your home, and cease using magic without the supervision of your master."

And how am I supposed to practice magic without casting any? The sarcastic comment was on the tip of Angelique's tongue, but she forced herself to swallow it.

"If you continue to willfully ignore the regulations placed upon you, the Council will have no choice but to act," Enchanter Tristisim continued, "which could lead to sealing your magic if you prove yourself not trustworthy."

Angelique didn't have to falsify her dismay. "W-what?" she stammered.

"You heard correctly," Enchanter Tristisim said.

"Surely we could let an exception or two pass," Enchanter Crest intervened. "Although we are supposed to treat all mages equally, it is a special circumstance. Lord Enchanter Evariste is missing, after all."

This made Enchantress Felicienne frown. "We are the ruling body of the Veneno Conclave. We *cannot* make exceptions or special pardons. It would mean unequal treatment." She fixed her gaze on Angelique and narrowed her eyes. "Which means, Apprentice, you had best trod carefully." She looked back at her fellow Council Members. "We are finished, are we not?"

Enchantress Primrose sighed. "I suppose so."

Crest smiled kindly. "Apprentice Angelique, you are dismissed."

Angelique demurely bowed her head and glided for the door, pressing her palms against her thighs so she wouldn't clench them into angry fists.

I was lectured—and threatened—*for helping people. Helping!* Angelique made herself smile at the war mage and his apprentice as she passed through the doorway, but she stormed down the hallway without stopping.

She clenched her teeth as she rounded a corner and almost smacked into a man.

"I apologize." She backed up a step or two.

"Chewed you out, did they?" he asked.

Angelique blinked as she realized she had almost collided with none other than Enchanter Clovicus—Evariste's old teacher.

Enchanter Clovicus was a handsome man with a sly smile and an eyebrow that was fast to quirk and betray his good humor. His copper hair was striking, but the slight dusting of silver at his temples gave him a more refined air than his smile would normally afford him.

His grin was very slight at the moment, and the slant of his eyebrows spoke more of sympathy than humor.

Angelique cleared her throat and forced her posture to straighten. "You knew I was to meet with the Council?"

Clovicus pushed off the wall and motioned for her to follow him with the twitch of two fingers. "With Evariste missing, I've taken it upon myself to make you my business. What did they want?" He strolled up the hallway, leading the way back to the section of the Conclave where both his and Evariste's offices were located.

Better keep it simple, or the bitterness will leak out of me...though I suspect Clovicus has me figured out. Angelique re-fixed the small smile on her face as she followed behind him. "They wished to speak to me about some of my actions as of late."

"They didn't lecture you for altering the Loire Prince's curse, did they?" Clovicus asked. "They're lucky you were there to act and modify the curse, or Loire would be raising seven different kinds of hell right now."

"That was one of the things they mentioned," Angelique said. "Though they seem more concerned that I'm traveling by myself and using magic without supervision."

Clovicus glanced back at her long enough to roll his eyes, but he didn't speak again until they entered his office, and he shut the door behind him. "They're being fools. You were months away from being made enchantress before Evariste was captured. You're perfectly capable of casting magic by yourself, and I've never heard of another experienced apprentice—enchantress or otherwise—being disciplined for it. It's well recognized that you're *supposed* to be able to cast magic by yourself by the time you make your proper rank."

Angelique shrugged and dropped into a chair when the enchanter motioned for her to sit. "They might be worried that I will use my core magic. When Evariste took me on, I agreed to use it only in his presence."

"And then you had a fourteen-year apprenticeship," Clovicus snorted. "Unless they expect you to stay with Evariste for the rest of your life, eventually you'll have to use your core magic at your own discretion." He grumbled under his breath. "Bunch of dimwitted, lily-spined twits."

Angelique shrugged slightly, which made Clovicus' eyebrow pop.

"You disagree?" he asked.

"While I do not appreciate my every action being evaluated with suspicion, I cannot say I disagree with their fear and reluctance to let me use my core magic," Angelique said.

Up went Clovicus' other eyebrow. "Angelique," he said. "You've been able to run free for several months now—without Evariste around to act as your conscience—and all you've done is help people."

Angelique shifted slightly in her chair. "Yes. Well. That is our duty."

Clovicus smirked slightly. "I see. I rather think you *should* use your core magic, but I also believe you need to exercise caution."

Angelique nodded. "It is dangerous."

"No, bother that," Clovicus grunted. "It's your price. You haven't figured it out yet, have you?"

All mages—no matter their rank—had either a limit to their power, or a price. A limit limited the ways a power could be used. Evariste was a perfect example, for although he had the rare and powerful magic of creating portals that could move a person thousands of leagues in a single step, there were checks to his power.

He could not, for example, set up a portal in a place recently tainted by black magic.

Prices were more common. They were—simply put—the cost of using magic. The most famous case of a price was the Verglas Snow Queen herself—who was also considered the first enchantress ever, even though she lived centuries ago. The Snow Queen fell unconscious for days when she used great amounts of her ice and snow magic while fighting a band of twisted magic users called the Chosen.

"No," Angelique finally replied. "I haven't discovered if I have a price or a limit yet as I haven't used enough of my magic—though most people seem to think I'll have a price."

Clovicus nodded. "And that is why I'd like you to be careful when you use your core magic."

When? Angelique wanted to scoff, but considering Clovicus was one of her few allies in the Conclave, she thought it better to remain quiet.

"When you finally do use enough of your magic and discover your price, chances are it's not going to be pretty," he warned her. "It would be better if I were there—or if you could hold off until we get Evariste back, but that's not very likely. How goes your search?"

Clovicus is insane if he thinks I'm going to plan to use my war magic. But I think any more protests are just going to fall on deaf ears. Angelique let a slight sigh leak out of her. "I haven't been able to find any leads on Enchanter Evariste's location. I've been researching spells in hopes of finding something those on the committee haven't used yet."

Clovicus nodded. "If I hear anything I'll let you know, but I checked with Enchantress Lovelana this morning, and she had no words of encouragement," he said, referring to the beautiful enchantress who was in charge of the committee.

"Thank you, Lord Enchanter Clovicus. I appreciate your aid," Angelique said.

Clovicus shrugged. "Seeing as Evariste was my student, I feel a bit responsible for you. And I know it would grieve him to see how you've struggled since his capture."

Angelique wasn't entirely certain on that count, due to her rather loud clash with Evariste about her magic before he was captured. *But even though he was angry with me, he still threw me to safety and was hit by a spell aimed at me. With a nature that good, perhaps Clovicus is right.*

"If you need anything, Angelique, whether it is aid with magic, general advice, or someone to stand with you when the Council calls you in again, call me," Clovicus said.

His certainty that Angelique would get called in again by the Council made her cringe, but there was truth in his words.

"Thank you," Angelique said. "I greatly appreciate your support."

He offered her a smile. "What will you do next?"

"More research," Angelique said. "I have some books to go through. Hopefully one of them will have something I can use."

Clovicus nodded and stood. "Very well. I'll walk you back to Evariste's office—unless you wanted to spend the day here?"

"No," Angelique dryly said. "I would prefer to return home."

Clovicus opened the door. "Very well, then. This way, Apprentice."

Angelique once again fell in step behind Clovicus, although this time she carefully studied his back.

I think he truly means his offer of assistance, she thought as she puzzled over his actions. The sick feeling in the pit of her stomach—brought on by the accusations of the Council—subsided, and Angelique relaxed slightly. *Evariste might be missing, and Roland—Puss, that is— has moved on, but at least I am not utterly without allies.*

THE INSIDE of the mirror was a watery gray. Everywhere.

There was no horizon line, no line distinguishing the floor from the ceiling, just nothingness.

The only thing besides the gray nothingness was the rectangular shape of the mirror's surface, which served as a window into the world.

The first few days Evariste had been in the mirror, he tried to walk away from that window, but no matter how long he walked, when he turned around, the spot was still there.

He could see directly out of the mirror and hear things. But even if he kicked the glass with his heel or rammed against it with his shoulder, the glassy surface held, keeping him captive inside.

Evariste was flat on his back, staring up at the gray that filled the skyline. *I wonder what Angelique is doing. How much time has passed since I was taken?*

Time was hazy inside the mirror. Days bled into one another, and nights were a smudge. Eating was unnecessary given the magic that held and sustained him, and he slept, but it was impossible to separate his waking hours from his sleeping hours, for the gray invaded there, too.

The one thing that was safe were memories.

Emerys' scoffs during the hours they spent riding through Alabaster Woods...Enchanter Clovicus' growls and booming laughter during Evariste's lessons as an apprentice. The grayness hadn't yet started to invade those memories, but as months slipped past Evariste's control, he feared it was only a matter of time.

Evariste stared at the grayness. *I think I just might go mad if nothing changes.*

He inhaled deeply, then shut his eyes and thought of Angelique. He recalled the pinched expression she put on her face if he suggested buying her a new wardrobe and the incredulous look she gave him whenever he referred to Stil as their child.

He could almost hear her garbled squawks of outrage, and cracked a smile.

Of all his memories, those of Angelique were the only ones strong enough to make him smile in even these grim circumstances.

Unfortunately, they're also the only ones that make getting this curse off me less palatable. What will happen if Liliane is telling the truth, and the only way for me to get rid of it is to kiss Angelique? What do I tell her?

In his mind's eye, Angelique's expression switched from a smirk—for he had been recalling the way she affectionately pushed Stil around like an older sister—to an expression of rage, her eyes hot with an unforgiving fire.

She'd never believe him. She'd never forgive him. She'd view him with suspicion again, the same way she looked at all other mages, because in acting on his feelings, she would carry the burden. She'd be the one the Council punished. And he'd lose what relationship he'd managed to forge with her, and he'd be alone. Again.

Didn't that get dark fast?

His smile transformed into a frown, but he'd use the moment as a motivator.

With his eyes shut, Evariste again mentally plunged into the internal well from which his magic flowed.

The numb, sinking feeling of the curse greeted him instead. Despite the numb feeling, Evariste tried to pull on his power.

Though he had tried for hours and days before, he tested it again and again, never giving up.

If even a drop of my magic could seep through a crack in the spell, I could escape. He had hopes that if he just kept pulling, maybe the spell would weaken.

So he kept pulling until the numb feeling sank through his entire body, and he almost choked as he finally let go and took in several heaving gulps of air.

Nothing. Again.

He groaned and threw his arms wide. *Why hasn't the Veneno Conclave been able to find me? It's been so long...*

Evariste heard footsteps echo outside the mirror surface.

He cracked his eyes open and, staying on the ground—or rather what he thought of as the ground—slithered his way over to the mirror, keeping himself as flat as possible.

Liliane—in a dress of pale purple—smiled adoringly at her son as he carried a white canvas and an easel. "Thank you, Acri. If you'd set it up right here."

Acri did as he was told, his expression lacking the warmth of his mother's, though he didn't seem irritated. "Will this chamber be large enough?"

"Yes, unfortunately. The Marquise of Carabas killed most of the goblins before I even knew what happened. I won't be summoning many, for there weren't many who escaped. But it cannot be helped." Liliane sighed and waited for Acri to pull a stool from the wall for her and set it in front of the canvas. "After so many years of being left alone, we assumed Carabas was permanently taken, even if the ogre was not strictly one of ours. But it matters not. Our plan for Arcainia is already in motion."

Evariste frowned and squinted into the room.

It was plain, empty, and dark. (They'd taken him out of what he suspected was a treasure room several weeks ago when he'd startled Suzu one evening by abruptly roaring so she dropped a glass artifact, which shattered. The satisfaction over that had been rather short-lived, given that now besides the grayness of the mirror, the only thing he could look at was the blackness of the empty cave chamber.)

Acri adjusted the two torches posted on either side of the cavern entrance. "I'll go prepare," he said.

"Yes, do, please. Thank you, dear!" Liliane called after her son.

Acri nodded, then disappeared through the darkened doorway.

Evariste watched as Liliane set up what looked like dabs of paint and began painting the canvas.

What is she painting in this empty room? Evariste narrowed his eyes and saw the mint-green flicker of her magic as she started to make the black outline of what resembled a goblin.

As it had become his policy to be as annoying as possible to his captors, Evariste silently swiveled so his feet were closest to the mirror. He lined himself up, then waited just until Liliane started to make another mark on the canvas and kicked.

Though the glass held, the frame rattled and made a loud thud.

Liliane jumped mid-stroke, her paintbrush making an unsightly streak. She sighed at her canvas. "I see you are still as lively as ever, Enchanter Evariste."

Evariste stood and brushed off his clothes, then leaned against the glassy surface. "What are you doing?"

"I'm so glad you asked," Liliane brightly said. "I'm using my core magic."

Core magic...that implies she's stronger than a regular mage and is on the level of an enchantress.

"You've been captured for almost a year now, you know." Liliane spoke conversationally, as if they were holding a discussion over tea.

Evariste rubbed his face. "I thought you said it was your policy to be honest."

"It is; that's why I'm telling you." Liliane finally turned to face him, her mouth circular with her surprise. "I don't know why you don't believe me when I tell you these things—it's silly. What could I possibly gain by lying?"

"The Veneno Conclave wouldn't take a year to find me."

"They are searching—there's an entire committee dedicated to the cause." Liliane pursed her lips as she studied her canvas—she had painted what looked like the outlines of a small goblin pack. She nodded, then dabbed her paintbrush in an ashen-green paint. "But I might be so bold as to say they won't find you. I do not have green mages under me but rather seasoned professionals. The same cannot be said of the Conclave."

Evariste only half listened to her. The other piece of his attention was on her painting as he watched her minty green magic fall from her fingertips and latch on to the wet paint of the canvas. "Hmm."

"Of course, your apprentice is searching for you on her own. But I expect she's even less likely to find any hint of you than the Conclave." Liliane filled in several of the goblin bodies with her green paint. "She may be powerful, but that hardly means she's competent."

Evariste stood up straight, every muscle in his body tensing. "What do you know about my apprentice?"

Liliane smiled bemusedly. "To begin with, it was she we were aiming to capture. But this turned out much better. She's young and green—so easy to crush in both mind and spirit even if she is not with us. It is a loss we cannot drain magic from her—our reports say she has a great deal of it. But then again, even I never dared to think we'd ever manage to capture you. And given that you'd likely be a nuisance to us over time, this really is the better arrangement." She nodded as she filled in the last goblin shape, then dipped her brush in an earthy brown paint.

Evariste rested his palms on the surface of the mirror and fixated on the one important thing out of Liliane's chattering: Angelique was looking for him.

I don't know whether to be happy or terrified. If they capture her... He frowned as he mentally replayed Liliane's explanation. *And what did she mean that it would be easy to crush Angelique?*

Evariste shifted as he thought about the best way to ask Liliane without making it obvious just how concerned he was for his student.

"There, finished!" Liliane set her paintbrush aside and held her hand out invitingly to the image.

Her magic flowed from her palm to the canvas until the painted image of the goblin pack was nearly obscured by the green of her powers.

Several feet away, in the empty expanse of the chamber, Liliane's green magic churned in a large circle—almost like a whirlpool.

Liliane cut off her magic and stepped around her canvas, watching her swirling powers with clear expectation.

Her magic frothed and boiled, creating a cloud of green.

Goblin cackles pierced the air.

Evariste flattened his face against the mirror surface as he watched, shocked, when the magic settled, leaving behind nine goblins.

The goblins staggered a few steps—two of them fell flat on their faces, and several more plopped down on the stone floor.

"Yes, yes, it's very upsetting I know, but it was necessary." Liliane spoke in a soothing voice. "Go, now, into the main chamber. Suzu is waiting with new orders."

Evariste watched, shocked, as the goblins trooped through the chamber, passing into the hallway. *She has teleportation magic? No—it's more like summoning magic. And there must be limits to it, or she'd have just painted Angelique or myself here.*

Evariste knew summoning magic existed, but it wasn't as common as weather magic, illusion magic, or even craft magic. There were several mages in the Veneno Conclave who had differing variations of it.

But he hadn't expected a *black* mage to have summoning magic.

Liliane chuckled as she strolled closer to his mirror. "You look surprised. Did you imagine my magic was something dark and terrifying?"

Evariste looked past her to her canvas that still looked wet and glittered with fading sparks of her magic. "You're Conclave trained," he realized.

Liliane clapped politely. "I suppose I should say one should expect such observations from an enchanter, but frankly I'm surprised you didn't realize it sooner."

Evariste stared at her, unsettled by this new dimension of her powers. She didn't have the mark that made her an exile, which meant the Veneno Conclave was unaware of what she really was.

She mentioned core magic—which implies she's on the level of an enchantress. But there are no living enchantresses with summoning magic, nor have there been any in almost a century.

"My husband thought it was a silly idea to attend Luxi-Domus, but I wanted to see how the Veneno Conclave taught magic. I expected too much of them, of course, but I was given all the painting lessons I wanted while I was a student." She laughed and blushed prettily as she held up her hand to her cheek.

"You're a registered mage," Evariste said.

Liliane brushed her bangs. "I'm afraid my honesty must end there—for it would be terribly *boring* of me to speak so much of myself. It is now your turn." She clasped her hands together, intertwining her fingers. "Your apprentice is ever so *earnest*. Did you know that?"

Evariste stilled.

"She seems rather duty-bound as well. She's searching for you, you know."

Don't let her see. Evariste nonchalantly leaned against the solid pane. "You've already said that."

"I know, and you feigned apathy then, as well—which is rather more revealing than you'd like, given that you don't often bother to censure yourself."

Evariste set his jaw but purposely kept his stance relaxed. "Oh?"

"She's going to be crushed," Liliane said. "Without you there to shield her, all it will take is a few whispers and some quietly voiced suspicions. Given her magic, she'll be hauled in for so much as a sneeze." She was quiet for a few moments. "We don't have to physically attack her to ruin her, Evariste. In some ways, perhaps a physical attack would be a kindness to her."

She was right. Angelique was already so suspicious of other mages and faced so much prejudice, it wouldn't take much to push her over the edge or to convince the Council that she was a danger.

But they cannot exile her or place any significant punishment on her without me there...unless they decide to handle her differently because of my capture.

"And when the moment comes, I can imagine her despair," Liliane said.

Evariste's fingers twitched against his will. *Steady*, he told himself. *She's testing me for weaknesses.*

"The master she has so sought to find is still gone, and the other mages are uncaring of her situation. There will be no one with her, no one for her as she struggles to fill the duties you so faithfully taught her."

Don't move. Don't give her any more power over me!

Liliane sighed. "All of that power, snuffed out, strangled by the weight of expectations and the cruelty of this world."

Evariste roared as he threw himself against the mirror, making it shake and rattle. "Leave her *alone*!"

Liliane daintily held a hand to her mouth. "Oh, my. I thought she was just your student, but it seems you haven't been entirely honest with me, hmm?" She winked and glided to the cavern entrance.

Evariste kept shouting long after she was gone, yelling until he was hoarse. He tried yanking on his magic, but only the numbness enveloped him.

Hours later, he slumped to his knees, his entire body shaking from fatigue and barely-held-in-check emotion.

Angelique...please...Angelique.

CHAPTER 8

Unfortunately for Angelique, combing through Evariste's library yielded nothing helpful. (At least, nothing that was within reach of her abilities.) A year passed.

Angelique was invited to Lady Gabrielle's wedding to Kronprinz Steffen of Arcainia, making her Prinzessin Gabrielle according to traditional Arcainian titles. (The handwritten note included with the invitation mentioned that Steffen was the peeping prince Puss had grumbled over.)

She continued her research but also spent her time going out on covert missions, furthering her search for Evariste under the guise of searching for more magic books.

Her unusual lifestyle of travel was how, roughly two-and-a-half years after Evariste was captured, Angelique learned of the massive storms that were springing up off the coast of Ringsted, making travel to the country difficult.

What was worse, Angelique received word from Firra and Donaigh—the war mage and fire mage Evariste and Angelique had asked to watch Princess Rosalinda—that there were signs Carabosso was beginning to look for the hidden princess.

"Perfect, just perfect," Angelique groused as she fit a telescope to her eye and peered at the angry swell of clouds crouched over the ocean. "Because there's not already enough bizarre things happening, now we have to have a potential threat to an entire country."

As she watched, lightning streaked through the clouds, followed by a peal of thunder. Standing on Erflauf soil, she was safe from the storms. But the weather made passage from Erlauf —or any other country on the continent for that matter—to Ringsted, rather ugly.

Angelique collapsed her telescope and scrunched up her face as the wind relentlessly yanked and pulled at her cloak.

Winter had just arrived, but it seemed determined to sweep across the continent with a vengeance as it kicked icy, stinging snow into Angelique's face while she watched the storm.

She coughed and brushed the snow off and continued to scowl at the storms.

Ringsted was the southernmost country of the continent and boasted a great deal of shoreline. It was cut off from the rest of the continent, however, by the giant mountain range that spanned the northern length of the country.

Ringsted—famous for its fleets of ships and merchants—could still get through storms of this size. Even so, Angelique didn't like it.

The storms aren't moving on or running out of power. They're just... there. It has to be unnatural.

Angelique tapped her collapsed telescope against her thigh and considered the implications. *Could it be the work of the black mages who kidnapped Evariste? But what do they gain from making storms?*

A piercing shriek echoed behind Angelique.

She spun around, peering up at the mountain range that loomed to the east, separating Erlauf from Baris. *That sounded like a goblin...*

She held her breath as she listened, straining to hear above the howling wind.

Silence...and then another scream.

"It's always goblins," Angelique muttered as she scrabbled up the rocky shore. "Pegasus!"

The ground shook as the constellation jumped a boulder and landed not far ahead, white sparks fizzing from his hooves.

Since aiding Puss in Carabas, the magical equine had become her primary method of transportation—and her greatest confidant in truth.

Pegasus pranced next to Angelique, slowing down long enough for her to fling herself at his back and pull herself on by the leather strap he had allowed her to place around his neck. (The winds on the coast were so strong, she needed it to hold on.)

Once she had her cloak wrapped around her, Angelique leaned forward and grasped the strap. "I'm ready—let's fly!"

Pegasus bugled a challenging cry as he tossed his head, then plunged into the snow-covered hills.

Thankfully, there was only a thin layer of powdery snow that crunched under Pegasus' black hooves—it wasn't deep yet—but the salty smelling air was icy, and Angelique crouched low on Pegasus' back to keep warm.

"It sounded like the goblin cry was at the base of the mountain," Angelique shouted above the whistling wind. "More mountain goblins, I think."

Pegasus altered his course, and Angelique started to spool her magic into a spell, preparing to attack.

Her teeth rattled as Pegasus charged up the side of a hill. *Irritating goblins*, she thought mutinously. Over the last few years, they had become a more common sight—particularly in Erlauf.

Though Angelique was now experienced enough at spellslinging that they were little more than an irritant, she always did her best to take out any that had the bad misfortune of crossing her path. Because although she could handle them, the townspeople and farmers in the area were not nearly as strong of opponents.

Pegasus reached the crest and began speeding down the other side, galloping closer to the pace of a falling star than Angelique wanted.

When he reached the bottom of the hill, the goblins screamed again, and Pegasus abruptly turned.

Angelique roared, hoping to intimidate the creatures before even catching sight of them. *"Your doom has come for you, gob*—and that's not a goblin."

A young boy—at least Angelique *thought* it was a boy; it was hard to tell under all his clothes—came skidding down a small foothill. He was swaddled in at least two cloaks, a scarf, mittens that were too big for his hands, and a hat that made him resemble a sheep. He kept looking back over his shoulder, and as a result fell over his own feet and smacked the hardened ground.

"N-no!" he shouted. He struggled to get up, still focused on the hill behind him.

Angelique followed his gaze and saw a stooped figure appear on the peak of the hill.

The shape resembled an old woman, except she wore thin ratty clothes that reminded Angelique of rat pelts. Her rust-colored lips were malformed into a permanent grimace that was spotted with black, rotten teeth, but it was her watery white eyes that gave her away.

"Mountain hag," Angelique growled. *But what is one doing all the way down here?*

Mountain hags were magical entities of warped and dark magic. Though they only lived far north, in the icy country of Kozlovka, they were known to wander during winter, searching for young women they could kill so they could devour their hearts.

However, in all her reading and classes, Angelique had never heard of one coming this far south, *ever*.

So what is one doing here in Erlauf?

The mountain hag started to totter down the hill, heading straight for the fallen boy—whose cries echoed off the mountains.

"Pegasus," Angelique started as she tightened her legs around the horse. "We have to—"

Pegasus shot off without further instructions, pounding across the turf.

Angelique hurriedly changed her spell, spinning it into something that could kill the mountain hag.

The mountain hag had picked up speed and was now only two horse lengths from the boy.

The boy struggled to rise, but he must have hurt himself in the fall, for he collapsed before he could fully stand.

Angelique blinked, and Pegasus shot forward faster than ever, coming between the mountain hag and her prey. He had to lock his legs to skid to a stop, then reared and screamed in anger—a sound that made the trees shake.

Angelique wove her spell around her fingers and clung to Pegasus, waiting for him to stop so she could get a clear shot.

The mountain hag's cloudy eyes went from the injured boy to Angelique, and she cackled. "A *maiden*! How fortunate! You will become my—wait—not you!" the mountain hag shrieked.

"Yes, me. Farewell." Angelique pushed her hand forward, and a giant icicle as sharp as a blade shot out of the ground, piercing the hag through the heart.

The mountain hag screamed like an animal. Her body turned into ashen snow and swirled away in the relentless wind.

Angelique frowned as she watched the mountain hag's remains fade. *What did she mean by "not you"? I'm not famous in the magical community—or rather, I'm infamous. But I don't think my dubious reputation would proceed me among twisted magical beings.*

Resolving to ponder it later—and perhaps even ask Enchanter Clovicus or Sybilla, a fairy godmother—Angelique turned her attention to the mountain hag's intended victim.

She smiled at him—or was it a her? She still couldn't tell—and gripped the hood of her cloak to keep the wind from ripping it off her head. "Did the mountain hag hurt you?"

"It's you!" the child shouted in a distinctly boyish voice.

Angelique blinked in surprise. "I beg your pardon?"

"You're the Lady Enchantress who altered His Highness's curse!"

"Enchantress-in-Training," Angelique automatically corrected.

The boy tried to stand again, but when he put weight on his left leg, it collapsed under him.

"Allow me to help you." Angelique slipped off Pegasus' back and crouched next to the boy. She gave Pegasus a smile when he moved so he stood between them and the wind, acting as a partial block. With a deep breath, she grabbed a glob of her magic, twisting it into a healing spell.

"I finally found you! I've been searching for you for *days*! Though that mountain hag almost did me in. Could you not tell His Highness about the mountain hag? He'll sigh at me, and if Elle finds out, she'll box my ears for sure," the boy chattered away, words tumbling endlessly from his mouth.

Angelique did her best to listen as she used her magic to probe his leg. Finding bruising in his ankle, she set about fixing it.

"We haven't any time to waste, either, because Elle said she was going on a long trip, and His Highness needs to know that she really loves him! He doesn't believe her, but if you tell 'im, he'll understand!"

I haven't the faintest clue what this boy is talking about. Who is His Highness? She needed more healing magic, so she tried to tug on a small flicker of her magic. Unfortunately, her tug seemed to loosen a gushing river of her powers that smacked her with enough force it almost pushed her over.

Angelique clenched her teeth and breathed out whispered curses about irrational magic while half-listening to the boy continue his story.

"She broke his curse, but everyone's real upset because she's not a villager like she said she was—I don't understand why that matters, though. And even though Elle saved His Highness, Emele tells me I can't talk to her. *Rot that*. I'm still talking to Elle no matter what bossy Emele says," he complained. "But I think Elle is in danger, and His Highness needs to help her, but he *won't* because he doesn't believe her!"

Angelique squinted at the boy's leg and nodded in satisfaction. "Your ankle should be better, now. It's not all healed—so you need to be careful with it—but I placed a slow healing spell on you, so it will be better by this evening. You may now stand."

"Thank you, Lady Enchantress!" The boy hopped to his feet with the spryness of a rabbit, testing his foot.

Angelique stood and smoothed the skirts of her gown. "Now, who is His Highness?"

"Prince Severin of Loire, of course!" The boy pushed his scarves down long enough to give Angelique a look that clearly communicated he thought she was dense for not knowing that.

Angelique frowned. "Prince Severin? Is something wrong?" *But if there were, I would have thought it would be Prince Lucien chasing after me given his loyalty to his brother.* "Was there a change in his curse?"

The boy threw up his hands in exasperation. "That's what I've been trying to tell you: his curse is broken!"

She relaxed and patted Pegasus' neck when he bumped her shoulder with his velvet muzzle. "Oh, that is wonderful news."

"Except it's *not*, because he doesn't believe Elle loves him!" the boy said.

"And this Elle is the lady who broke the curse?"

When the boy nodded, Angelique's frown returned. "That doesn't make any sense. The curse could only have been broken if she loved him."

"I *know*," the boy said. "But His Highness and none of the other servants believe her because she misled everyone about who she is! You need to come tell His Highness! That's what I've been trying to tell you!" The boy's voice quivered between frustration and sadness, and he inhaled a deep and shaky breath.

Angelique glanced at Pegasus, but the mount was already getting down in response to her unasked question. Satisfied, she turned back to the boy. "I apologize, for although you know who I am, I'm afraid I don't know your name."

"I'm Oliver." The boy sniffed loudly. "His Highness' stable boy."

Angelique slid onto Pegasus' back. "I see this is a far more complex matter than I thought. Come, Oliver. We can return to the inn where I'm staying, and you can explain the whole ordeal." She held out a hand, guiding the boy so he sat in front of her.

When Pegasus rose, the boy whooped with obvious delight, bringing a faint smile to Angelique's lips.

I only hope I'll be able to help as Oliver seems to think I can. It sounds like a disagreement between the prince and the lady, and magic can do many things, but it can't help matters of the heart.

AFTER GETTING the full tale from Oliver, Angelique took Oliver and began traveling back to Loire, taking the occasional side trip to warn local mages about the mountain hag. Between that and being unwilling to let Pegasus ride at full speed while carrying the small boy, it took them over a week to make the return trip.

She wasn't entirely certain she understood the full tale of Prince Severin's woes—mostly because Oliver, as a child, didn't understand or care for romantic love very much. (He described the prince and his lady love's meetings with rolled eyes and the occasional faked gag.)

But what she interpreted was that after spending over two years as a beast, a young lady named Elle fell through the roof of the prince's chateau. Due to a broken leg, it was decided by

Severin's servants that she couldn't leave until the bone mended, stranding her—an eligible young lady—with Prince Severin—who needed the love of a woman to break his curse.

Apparently the two did fall in love, and Severin's curse broke... but the lady hadn't been entirely honest with who she was, and as a result, Severin felt she had lied about her feelings for him as well.

Frankly, either the prince is so emotional he cannot see straight, or he is an idiot. Both are disturbing possibilities considering he is the commanding general of Loire's armies, Angelique thought as she followed Oliver through the halls of the Loire royal palace.

"—And then I ran into a *mountain hag!*" Oliver said, chattering away to another one of Severin's servants—a male valet. "She had black teeth and looked like a bunch of mice bit her in the face. She would have *killed* me, but that's when the Lady Enchantress found me!"

Enchantress-in-Training, Angelique mentally sighed. *If everyone insists on ignoring my actual rank, I am certain I'm going to hear about it from the Council.*

The valet held up his hand as he stopped outside a door. (The stable boy instantly silenced himself.) "You did quite well, Oliver. Quite well indeed." He smiled affectionately at the boy, then raised his eyebrows. "Are you ready to face His Highness?"

Oliver was almost jumping in place. "Yes! Yes, Lady Enchantress Angelique will handle all of it!"

"I am a mage, not a match-maker," Angelique pointed out (and was ignored) as the valet and stable boy exchanged sage nods.

The valet straightened and knocked on the door. He then cracked the door open and poked his head inside. "Someone is here to see you, Your Highness."

"Show them in," said a deep, growling voice.

The valet swung the door open and stepped aside, moving just in time to avoid Oliver as he leaped through the doorway.

"I found her, Your Highness! I found her! I couldn't hardly

believe it—she was real hard to track down, but now she's here, and she'll fix *everything*," Oliver said.

Angelique followed the stable boy into the room, but she paused just inside.

She was relieved to see they had been shown to a private study instead of Severin's bedroom as she had been during her previous visit to the palace, but that wasn't what made her pause.

The last time she had seen Prince Severin, he was a combination of cat and wolf. Now he had returned to his human form.

He was a soldier in build and posture—straight back, broad shoulders, and a tidy appearance with his charcoal-black hair pulled back in a ponytail at the base of his neck. His eyes were the same golden amber they had been as a beast—though now the pupils were round and not slitted.

His appearance made Angelique pause. Not because he looked different than expected, but rather because for the first time ever, she was truly aware of what her ageless future meant.

When she had first come to the palace to inspect the magic mirror with Evariste, Severin had been a *child* newly adopted into the royal family despite his illegitimate beginnings. Now, he looked older than she did and was in charge of a country's military.

So this is what it is like, to watch those around you age while you remain the same. Very little has changed for me; I'm still a student, and I still struggle with my magic.

It was haunting, in a way.

Angelique briefly closed her eyes to collect herself, then strode into the conversation.

Severin hadn't yet noticed her presence and was scowling down at the sheepish boy. "Oliver, calm down. Where have you been? I've been sending soldiers and search parties all over Loire looking for you. What possessed you to leave without warning?" he rumbled.

Angelique put on her well-practiced "ethereal enchantress" smile. "He was looking for me."

Severin glanced her way, then immediately bent over in a bow. "My lady."

I guess I know where his servants get their insistence on inflating my station from. "There's no need to bow. I am an Enchantress-in-Training, not nobility," she said.

Though Severin's lips did not form a smile, Angelique saw the warmth in Severin's eyes. For a moment, the warmth there was snuffed out, but he slightly shook his head, and it was back again.

"I disagree," he said. "One with your standing deserves every display of respect."

Angelique tilted her head as she studied him carefully. There was some truth to Oliver's appeal for help. For although Severin was human, Angelique could see tiny cracks in the stoic expression he wore—it was in the twitch of his fingers and the light of his eyes.

Since he doesn't appear overly emotional, I guess idiot it is. Lucky me that I get to walk him through the obvious conclusions one can draw as a result of his broken curse. Angelique stifled the desire to roll her eyes. *Funny, during his lectures of duty, Evariste never said anything about tutoring slow-thinking princes.*

Angelique inhaled and began what could quite possibly become a long and lengthy process. "Severin, what is wrong? You are human again. Every joy in life should be yours. Why is your heart heavy?"

Severin looked away, choosing to stare at a wall. "Oliver, find Bernadine and report in."

"Yes, Your Highness." Oliver gave Angelique a bright grin and glanced back at Prince Severin before he slipped from the study.

Angelique tucked her loose hair—using her illusion magic, she had made it a honey brunette today—behind her ear. "You have a loyal servant in that one. It takes a lot of courage to track an enchantress across two countries."

"He has more courage than I would wish for him to possess," Severin said dryly.

Angelique's smile grew less elegant and more affectionate as she thought of the boy—for she could see bits of herself in his actions. "Perhaps, but it speaks loudly of his love for you...and for this Elle he has told me so much about."

Severin briefly shut his eyes.

Ahhh, yes. There's the idiot. Angelique made her voice soothing and as inviting as possible, hoping to pry an answer out of the taciturn prince. "Severin, what happened? Something must have gone terribly wrong to make you so miserable. Please, explain."

Severin clenched his hands into fists. "Elle, the girl Oliver told you about, won over my servants before attempting to befriend me."

When Severin briefly turned his back to her, Angelique rolled her eyes. *How dare she be a kind person, hm?* Keeping her inner sarcasm from her tone, she asked, "And that is a bad thing?"

"She is a liar. Everything she told me was a lie."

Angelique narrowed her eyes. "Everything?"

Severin hesitated. "No, not everything. But she did not tell me she was employed by my brother."

Angelique furrowed her brow. *Is he afraid she will fall in love with Lucien? Why? Lucien is handsome, but he is so smarmy it makes me shiver just thinking about it.* Aloud, she asked, "And what does her livelihood have to do with your curse?"

Severin was silent for a long time. "She didn't love me." The words sounded like they were torn from his chest, and sorrow lined his face when he glanced in Angelique's direction. "She was just like every other woman who loved my wealth or family."

Angelique held in a sigh. *Perhaps its unkind to call him an idiot. He has been through much due to the curse, and they say love makes you a fool. Maybe he just has an excess amount of love.* Gently, Angelique said, "That cannot be."

"But it is!" Severin said. "Her love was nothing but a *lie*."

Stars above, give me patience, Angelique grumbled. "But your curse—"

"The curse broke because *I* fell in love with her! My servants know it; I know it. Our curse was removed not because Elle loved me, but because I loved her, and she does not return my love," Severin said, clenching his hands. "I didn't fall in love with any of those other women, although Heaven knows I tried. But Elle...I knew I loved her the moment before I realized she was a liar."

Angelique pinched her eyes shut as she prepared to make Severin carefully repeat his tirade, when she finally realized what he said and froze.

Wait...he said the curse broke not because she loved him, but because he loves her. Did he not understand—did I not explain it properly to him?

Guilt circled Angelique as she tried to remember exactly how she had explained the boundaries of his curse to him. *"By falling in love, by another falling in love with you." That's what I should have said. Is that what I said? Perhaps I could have been a bit clearer. He must have interpreted it as one or the other, not both, as I meant for it to be.*

Angelique eyed Severin with great remorse. *This will teach me. I'm just a bit careless with my words, and apparently it has made two people—and an entire household—miserable. I only hope I can right it—and remember this for the rest of my life!*

"Oh, Severin." She rested her hand on his shoulder, her regret coloring her voice. "I am so sorry."

"Yes. Now you know." Severin squared his shoulders, putting his emotion behind him.

Goodness, he is unknowingly twisting the knife of my incompetence—but I only have myself to blame. "No." Angelique shook her head. "I am sorry. I must not have explained your curse well enough. In order to break the spell that doomed you to live as a beast, you had to fall in love with a girl, *and* she had to fall in love with you. It was not one or the other."

Severin hesitated. "You mean...?"

Angelique almost stooped in relief. *Thank goodness; he's going to take this news well.* "Because your curse broke, I know Elle must love you deeply as well."

The shock that flooded his handsome face and the dismay in his voice made another dagger of guilt stab Angelique. "What have I done?" he murmured.

Time for me to clean this mess up. Angelique rubbed her hands together as she sifted through possible plans. "Oliver tells me she has gone on a journey?"

The shocked prince stared at his feet. "A mission. She's a Ranger, an intelligencer."

"You don't know where she is?" Angelique asked.

He shook his head. "I know what she was sent to do, but I'll never be able to find her."

That's easy enough to solve! Relieved she could perhaps make amends for her verbal flub, Angelique nodded when she espied the prince's magic looking glass leaning against the wall of the study. "Ridiculous. Of course you will. You have a magic mirror."

Severin stirred behind her. "I'm not certain it works anymore. I tried having it display Oliver, but it wouldn't."

Angelique thoughtfully scanned the mirror from top to bottom. "That's because he was with me, and I shield my presence from all kinds of magical tools."

Ever since Evariste was captured, anyway.

Angelique pushed the thought aside and continued, "But Elle will not have that same protection. Mirror, show me this Elle girl that Prince Severin is in love with."

The moment the glass surface started to swirl, Severin was at Angelique's side, almost bumping her out of the way.

Angelique hid a grin at such an obvious sight of his devotion, until she noticed the disheartening image the mirror displayed.

A pretty young lady with black hair and bright and intelligent eyes leaned against a skeletal tree, panting as she clutched one of her legs. She peered around the tree—seemingly watching for something—then darted to a bush, quickly crawling beneath it.

Flattened against the ground, she pulled cloth bandages out of a pouch tied to her belt and started wrapping a nasty gash on her arm.

Angelique studied the image for a moment. "Is that her?"

"Yes," Severin tightly said. "But how can I find her? She could be anywhere."

What does he mean? We are looking at a magic mirror, a tool built for this sort of purpose. A tiny frown spread on Angelique's lips. "You mean you don't know how to use this?" She gestured at the mirror.

Severin hadn't peeled his eyes from the image of his lady love. "I apologize; I don't understand."

Ah, well. He's not a magic user, and it's not like books titled "How to Use Your Magic Mirror: The Beginner's Guide" are floating around. Angelique turned back to the mirror. "Mirror, show me the area this Elle girl Prince Severin loves is in."

The image zoomed out, as if they were watching through the eyes of a bird who suddenly took flight. It showed craggy mountains smoothing into white plains before hitting a thick forest.

"Aha," Angelique said, fighting to keep her voice pleasant. "I recognize that area. It's in Verglas, a dozen or so miles from your border. That mountain on the horizon is called Gelus. She's heading for Frigus Forest."

The only reason she so easily recognized the area is because she had passed through it when fighting her way back to Torrens after Evariste had flung her to Verglas with his portal spell.

Evariste. He's going to laugh until he cries when I tell him how I bungled this. Her smile faded as she realized there was no telling how long she'd have to wait to share the story with him.

Angelique shook her head, then blinked when she realized Severin was no longer behind her but was shoving folded clothes in a pack. He strode swiftly and efficiently through the room, grabbing things he might need.

"You are going after her?" Angelique guessed.

Severin grabbed two waterproof maps, then unearthed a crossbow, three hand axes, and a rolled cloth case of daggers from a chest. "Yes."

He is a good boy, she thought fondly. (Angelique figured it might be strange to call him a boy given his age and station, but she couldn't help but feel that he was still her junior.) "Bring clothes for her as well," she suggested.

Severin nodded and opened the door to bark into the hallway, "Send for Emele, and have Fidele and a spare mount of similar build and temperament saddled. Also ask Bernadine to make up a saddle pack with provisions to last two people a week." Severin shut the door and swung his attention back to Angelique. "Will you remain here long?"

"I will be here when you return," Angelique said. "I am interested in meeting this Elle girl."

"I will inform a steward; he will have a room cleaned out for you."

No, no, no, no! The last thing I want is to be stuck in this palace with Lucien scurrying around! Angelique thought frantically for a moment, before she recalled her latest communication with Stil—the craftmage she and Evariste had found in Baris all those years ago.

"No need," she said brightly. "I have friends in the area with whom I wish to stay. I would appreciate it if you did not alert your family to my arrival."

Severin paused for a moment. "Lucien recited poetry about you for some time after you left."

Angelique couldn't help the scowl that twitched across her lips. "Lucien is a toad. Or he will be if you tell him I am here."

Darn it—I shouldn't have let that slip!

She glanced at Severin but was surprised to see him crack a half-smile at her comment. He said nothing in response and instead slung his pack over his shoulder and picked up his weapons. "Then I apologize for my abrupt exit. I cannot thank you enough for your help. Is there any way to repay you?"

It was partially my fault you had this misunderstanding to begin with, but if you don't remember that, I'm not going to bring it up. Angelique smiled. "Seeing you with Elle will be enough."

Severin bowed. "If you need anything, seek out Burke. He is discreet and will grant you whatever you desire."

"Thank you, and take care, Your Highness. I look forward to your return."

"Thank you for everything, my lady," Severin said before leaving his room.

Angelique smiled fondly at his exit, before she realized it was rather awkward to be left alone in the prince's private study with the prince gone. *Well. I guess I had better go find Stil. It's perfect timing, really. I can see if he found any spells for me!*

CHAPTER 9

Angelique found Stil's home just outside Noyers. It appeared to be nothing more than a tattered tent that was in grave danger of collapsing under the slightest breeze.

An ornery donkey that was the size of a small horse was picketed next to it, his giant ears hanging out to the side, though he didn't seem to mind the snow that covered his fur.

"Hello, Pricker Patch," Angelique greeted the donkey with familiarity, for he was Enchanter Evariste's graduation gift to Stil.

Looking at the donkey, she snorted as she recalled Evariste's explanation for the gift. ("He's a craftmage, which basically means he will become a hoarder. It's inevitable given all the tools and materials he will use in his career. Since I care deeply for our child"—*He is not our child!*—"I will provide him with the best method possible to transport his goods.")

She cracked a smile at the memory. She had given Evariste a lecture about continuing to refer to Rumpelstiltskin as their child. The lecture ended only when the Lord Enchanter had unrepentantly and nonchalantly asked her if she thought a male or female donkey would suit their son better, and Angelique had given up out of sheer disgust.

Pricker Patch snorted, drawing Angelique back to the present.

"Sorry," she apologized. "I don't have any treats with me. But why are you standing in the snow? It looks like Stil set up a little shelter for you." She pointed to a canopy nestled between two trees that blocked the wind.

Pricker Patch stared at Angelique and didn't even look back at his provided shelter.

"I see," Angelique finally said. "Good talk." She left the donkey and made her way to the dilapidated tent. She paused, giving Stil's magic imbedded in the tent a moment to recognize her, before she peeled back the fabric flap of the structure.

Instead of revealing the threadbare innards of a tent, the flap opened up into a large, tasteful parlor. Luxuriously padded armchairs and settees were carefully arranged in front of a marble fireplace, where a fire crackled and popped as it burned through a new log.

Stil crouched in front of the fireplace, a stack of books on his left and a pile of precious gems arranged in a haphazard pile on his right.

He hadn't noticed her presence yet; his attention was on the ruby he was muttering over as his magic rolled across his fingers.

Angelique smiled fondly at him. Long gone was the brat in the ill-fitting clothes, leaving a handsome young man in his place.

His blue-black hair was cut short at the moment—but like Evariste, he enjoyed changing his hair length with the use of his craft magic, so there was no telling how long that would last—and his hair, combined with his high cheekbones and long and slender chin, gave him a rather princely air. However, it was his eyes that were the most remarkable—as most mages' eyes, his were special —for they were beautiful swirls of sky blue spiraled with royal blue.

Though they now looked the same age—perhaps Stil looked even a bit older than Angelique—she still watched him with the fondness of an older sister.

"My, my, you've grown up into such a fine adult." Angelique continued inside, gratefully escaping the cold and the snow.

Stil blinked as he peered in her direction, and his face transformed into a bright grin. "Angelique! Welcome to my comfortable home."

Angelique sighed. "I should have tried harder to instill a sense of humility in you; although with your skill level, I suspect your pride was inevitable."

Stil—or Rumpelstiltskin, as his mage name was—had finished his apprenticeship years ago, but his most remarkable feat was to be granted the title of Master Craftmage at such a young age.

Then again, it had been a long time since a craftmage as skilled as Still had passed through the Veneno Conclave.

"I *am* a genius," Stil modestly said. He stood up and offered her a sweeping bow.

Angelique snorted. "Come here, you." She hugged the craftmage, ignoring his squirm. "It's good to see you, Stil."

At her words, he stopped moving and finally hugged her back. "It's good to see you, too, Angel."

Angelique jabbed him in the side as she stepped back. "I told you, it's Angelique!"

Stil rubbed his side and frowned. "But you let Evariste call you Angel."

"How many years have I told you, it's *Lord Enchanter* Evariste!" Angelique said—though after years of correcting Stil's informality, it was more an old joke than any attempt to fix it.

"What brought you to Noyers? Any word of Evariste?" Stil motioned for Angelique to sit down as he rolled a tea cart over to her—the drink still piping hot.

"I'm afraid not." Angelique settled into one of the armchairs, relaxing in the warm comfort of the cushions. (Stil's home benefited greatly from his craft magic, particularly all seats and beds, as they were all spelled for comfort.)

Moreover, it was a relief to let her façade down—for Stil already knew just how sarcastic her personality was.

"A stable boy who serves Prince Severin found me," she continued. "I apparently was unclear with my explanation of what would break the prince's curse, which allowed for unnecessary drama. I returned here to clear the matter up."

Stil poured her a cup of steaming tea. "Wasn't the modification of his curse based on romantic love?"

"Yes," Angelique said dryly.

Stil laughed outright. "They called *you* in to mend a lovers' spat? Hah!"

"Not entirely, thank goodness—for I probably would have made things worse," she acknowledged.

Angelique had very little patience for romance and love—particularly people who went all gooey and useless over such things. She had a missing master to find and goblins to kill. What use was love in all of that?

"All I had to do was explain—more clearly—the rules of the modification. Prince Severin is off to take care of the rest. Thank you." Angelique inhaled the fruity scent of the tea and sipped it—blueberry—before she added a little cream. "I thought I'd drop by to see if you found any useful spells for me."

Stil snapped his fingers. "Actually, I have! I'll be just a moment." He disappeared through a door on the far side of the parlor, striding off through the rest of his roomy house. (Though the doorway was in a tent, Stil's home had multiple bedrooms, a kitchen bigger than Evariste's, a dining room, and more. He managed it through the same clever spellwork he used to make the inside of pouches, satchels, and the like, far bigger than they should be.)

Angelique waited impatiently for his return, hoping that whatever he had unearthed was useful.

He ambled back a few minutes later, carrying a book with a

blue leather binding that was so faded, it was more of a watery gray. The pages were tattered, and a few were torn, and the ink words on the page had faded with age.

"Here we are." Stil set the book on the table and flipped it open, making a small cloud of dust. "It's an old spell, and it requires a lot of power, but since it's you, I think you might be able to make it work."

Angelique sipped her tea—which tasted, now with the cream, like blueberry cobbler—then set it aside so she could join Stil on a settee. "What kind of spell is it?"

"It's another location spell, but it's rather advanced and uses a different method—one I believe would be harder for the black mages to block out." Stil sat back as he rubbed his chin. "Most location spells are set loose on the continent and seek out a person. Since they're very general, they're also very easy to deflect."

"And this spell isn't quite so general?" Angelique asked.

Stil shook his head. "It uses the bond between two people to locate the other one. The spell follows the tie of the relationship, and there you find the missing companion. It's rather complex—I think even Evariste might find it challenging—but I'm sure with a bit of practice, you can complete it."

Angelique frowned slightly. She wasn't too concerned about the complexity—she could keep trying the spell for as long as it took to master it, but... "It sounds like a better option, but how close of a relationship does it require?"

Stil frowned at her. "Does it matter?"

Angelique rubbed at her temple as she carefully chose her words. "My claim on Evariste might not be strong enough. I would take it to King Themerysaldi of the elves, but I still can't reach him or his people."

"Angelique, you were Evariste's student for fourteen years. He jokingly referred to me as *your joint* child. If your bond isn't strong enough for the spell to work, *no* relationship would be able to weather it." Stil used the scoffing tone he occasionally trotted out whenever he thought she was acting dense, but Angelique was not quite so certain.

She didn't doubt that Evariste cared for her—he showered her with endless affection and gifts—or even that she had a bond with Evariste.

Her voiced worries were a cover, really, for Stil wouldn't understand the true problem—which wasn't so much the emotional tie, but the magic of it. How would she affect the spell? She had seen her powers *devour* the magic of others. Could it actually work on such an old and advanced spell without self-imploding before finding Evariste?

I guess I will just keep trying until I reach him, then. It's a lead, and I'm desperate enough to try anything right now.

"Thank you, Stil, for finding the book—and the spell." Angelique smiled at him, carefully taking the tattered book when he offered it to her.

"I'll keep looking," Stil promised. He rested his hand on top of hers and squeezed. "We'll find him, Angelique. We won't stop until we bring him home."

ANGELIQUE FROWNED as she carefully re-read the spell from the book Stil had brought her, peering from it to the circuit of magic she had twisted her powers into.

It's shaped oddly. I must have done something wrong...but where?

Her silvery magic twined through a complex weaving pattern that was shaped like a flower with defined petals. Glowing glyphs and scripts—words of magic—glittered around the edges of the petals, completing the spell.

But it couldn't be right, for her spell had turned out rather domed, whereas the book insisted it was meant to remain flat.

A door opened, and Angelique froze. She strained her ears for footsteps or conversation, but there was nothing.

Suspicious, she narrowed her eyes and peered around one of the large bookshelves, but it appeared she was alone.

Prince Severin had returned from Verglas with his lovely lady, Elle. Given that she had apparently injured herself while in Verglas, he had taken her to his Chateau until her health improved, and they had only recently returned to Noyers.

Severin had invited Angelique to the palace to meet this Elle, but when she arrived, the prince and his lady were still meeting with the royal family.

Having no wish to intrude on what was clearly an important time, Angelique had opted to wait for the happy couple in the library...because she thought it was the room Lucien would be least likely to enter if he "happened" to wander away from the family visit.

Even so, Angelique was suspicious that the handsome prince might have accounted for her actions and would outmaneuver her and corner her in the library with his smarmy attitude and ridiculous compliments.

Angelique shook her head slightly as she returned to her work, comparing her spell with the book's example.

I got the words of magic correct—for my glyphs and symbols are right. But why, then, does it have this funny shape?

Angelique frowned as she drummed her fingers on the table. "I," she announced, "am not the student I once was."

She sighed and considered her magic some more. *I really can't see where I went wrong. Maybe I should release it and see what happens?*

Another moment of table drumming, and she nodded. *Yes. Let's try it. The library is spelled against damage anyway. It should be fine.*

Angelique studied her magic, took a breath, and spoke the release word.

Her magic glowed fiercely, the symbols in it starting to move. *It's working!*

The spell slowly crawled forward, then abruptly shot in her direction.

It collided with her, zapping her with a surge of power that sent her tumbling to the floor. She hit her elbow on a chair on the way down and smacked the floor with a thump.

"*Ow!*" She scowled as she stood up, glaring at the wisps of her magic that floated around her. "That hurt." She got back on her feet and brushed her dress off, then studied the book again. *Though at least now I have a hunch where I went wrong—ah-hah!*

Angelique exhaled a wheezing breath and hunched over the table. "Of course! I reversed the sender and searcher positions. I should have put myself on this end and Evariste here, but instead, I tried to fill the spell out as if Evariste was searching for me. That was the *first part* of the whole spell!"

She groaned but straightened and suspiciously swiveled when she heard a door open. There were footsteps, so Angelique darted behind a bookshelf—abandoning the book on the table—and watched through narrowed eyes.

"Lady Enchantress?" Severin called in his easily recognizable voice—for it was rather deep and still a bit growly.

Angelique fitted her mask of elegance on her face as she minced out from behind the shelf. "Prince Severin, it is good to see you again." She smiled at the tall prince, though her gaze drifted to the young lady walking arm-in-arm with him. "And you must be Elle."

Elle was a beautiful girl—not in the classical sense or the breathtaking way Puss's Gabrielle was, but rather the way fire was beautiful.

Her ink-black hair was soft and shiny, her eyes bright, but her smile was big and had more than a hint of mischief. With her expressive face and eyes that seemed like they didn't miss much, Angelique could see how the girl was a good match for the taciturn prince. She'd force color and humor into his life.

"And you are Lady Enchantress Angelique," Elle said. "I have heard much about you from Oliver."

Angelique chuckled. "Evidently, however, he failed to tell you I am only an Enchantress-in-Training. Regardless, I am glad I finally have this opportunity to meet you, Elle, and I am happy to see you are in good health."

"Thank you for bringing Oliver back here, to Noyers," Elle said, "and for explaining the curse to Severin again."

Angelique winced as guilt pricked her conscious. "Yes, I fear it was my incompetence that started the misunderstanding. I apologize—I did not mean to cause so much pain."

Elle snorted. "Nonsense. Severin is the commanding general—he should have asked for a clearer description. Besides, you saved his life—something no one else could have done."

Severin nodded gravely. "I rather agree with Elle. You should not blame yourself, Enchantress Angelique. Without you, I fear I wouldn't be here today."

Angelique's smile returned. "I am glad I happened to be on-hand to help."

"Yes, I imagine it was particularly good fortune, as it likely took a lot of power to modify such a spell," Elle said

"It would require a mage to possess either a certain type of rare magic or an enchanter or enchantress with the power to weave his or her powers into different magic, yes," Angelique said. *Elle is a sharp girl. I can see why she worked as a Ranger—but for Severin to love her, I suppose she'd have to be incredibly clever.*

Elle disengaged her arm from Severin's so she could clasp her hands together. "I wanted to ask you: are *all* traces of Severin's curse truly gone?"

"There is nothing to fear, Elle. His curse has been completely destroyed," Angelique assured her.

She expected Elle to brighten or perhaps smile, but strangely, she sighed, and her shoulders drooped a little. "Oh, I see..." Her grin was back and just as mischievous as ever when she winked at

Angelique. "I was rather hoping it wasn't *completely* gone because I really miss his cat ears, you know?"

Severin groaned and pinched the bridge of his nose. "Elle…"

"I don't suppose you could give those back to him?" Elle rushed to say.

"*ELLE!*" Severin roared.

Elle was not at all intimidated; instead, she chortled and unapologetically clapped her hands in glee. She wriggled her eyebrows at the prince, then fake-whispered to Angelique, "I was *gravely* disappointed that when he was cursed, he didn't have a tail."

Angelique stared at Elle for a moment, until laughter finally bubbled past her lips.

Yes, Severin and Elle will be just perfect for each other.

Severin glared at his lady, but even Angelique could see the gleam of humor that sparked in his eyes. He shook his head, then turned his attention to Angelique. "I wanted to talk to you again, Lady Enchantress. I've finally gotten the entire story out of Oliver, and he told me of the mountain hag."

"I find it hard to believe one had shuffled all the way to southern Erlauf," Elle frowned. Gone was her humor. Instead, she narrowed her eyes, and Angelique could almost see the wheels turning in her mind.

"Erlauf has also seen an increase in goblins," Angelique said. "A few mages have theorized that since Carabas has been purged, the goblins that used to be there moved on."

Severin narrowed his eyes. "You don't agree with the theory?"

Angelique shrugged. "I am acquainted with Prinzessin Gabrielle, who is also the Marquise of Carabas. She *hunted* all the goblins in her lands and eradicated them. If any escaped, I'm certain they were few in number and not nearly enough to account for this sudden increase."

"It's said the princesses of Farset have been cursed," Elle

added. "All *twelve* of them, though no one knows exactly what the curse is, only that they wear through their shoes each night."

"The witch who cursed me was never caught?" Severin asked.

"Not to my knowledge," Angelique said. She paused, then added, "It's been a strange past few years."

"Yes," Severin acknowledged. "We can only hope that it's merely *strange* and not the start of something worse."

CHAPTER 10

Angelique crouched behind her desk in Evariste's workshop and suspiciously eyed her latest attempt at the complex search spell Stil had found.

All winter she had worked on it—between continuing her research and sending messages to Clovicus asking if there were any updates on Evariste from the committee. (There weren't.)

And despite the long winter months that had passed into spring, Angelique hadn't gotten the spell to work correctly. Or rather, in the beginning, she had made tiny errors that always made the spell deflate or fizzle; but the last few times, she had done everything perfectly...but after the spell whizzed off to search for Evariste, it crumbled.

"But this time, this time I think I finally have it," Angelique muttered to herself as she eyed the flower-shaped, silvery spell. "Or at least I have the start of something that might work." She glanced worriedly at her bracelet—a silver thing with a blue glass bead encased by a silver cage—that sat on her desk directly below the spell.

It seemed to Angelique that the spell crumbled when it hit

whatever defensive magic the black mages were using to hide Evariste because it lacked the power to push through.

Angelique theorized that she could supplement the spell by adding her bracelet—a gift from Evariste to her which *also* contained the added benefit of a locating charm. She hoped it would give the spell the extra oomph needed to make the distance. So, she added a bit of her own spellwork that brought the bracelet into the magical circuit the spell created.

I hope I'm right, or I'll have to give up on this spell, too, and go back to combing the countryside for sparks of black magic.

The thought made Angelique sag, but she shook her head in determination. "This will work," she stubbornly said.

She shuffled her feet to adjust her crouch so her thighs didn't burn quite so much, but she didn't dare stand. (This spell had knocked her over on more than one occasion, and once she had set her dress on fire when she took a candle down with her.)

"Okay...here we go." Angelique took a deep breath, then cautiously spoke the release word in the language of magic.

The silvery spell glowed brighter and brighter as the script twining around her magic turned white-hot.

A silver mist encased the bracelet, and for a moment everything was still.

Abruptly, the spell veered off, shooting through the wall of the house and disappearing.

"Thank goodness," Angelique breathed a sigh of relief. "I was half-worried it was going to blow the house up with the bracelet added in. Now I just have to wait."

Search spells were not instantaneous—it took time for the spells to cover land. Based on how previous iterations of the spell had gone, she had approximately an hour to spare.

She stood up and walked around her desk so she could sit down in a chair. She busied herself with reading more books in search of other helpful spells, but after half an hour, she gave up pretending to get anything useful done. The spell was a faint tingling sensation in her mind as it chugged along, following the bond.

She stiffened as she closed her eyes, immersing herself in her magic. Her heart thudded in her chest as she waited and hoped.

Angelique wasn't entirely sure where her spell was, but she felt it when it thumped into something—this was always the moment when it faltered and was then snuffed out.

Her magic sang like a blade slicing through the air, and Angelique cracked an eye open to peer at the bracelet. The mist surrounding it had become more of a cloud, and some of the magic of the spell now flowed around the bracelet, circling it endlessly.

Her magic powering the spell sputtered for a moment, then roared back to life, pushing through.

Angelique again shut her eyes, concentrating on her spell.

It was *supposed* to give her a mental image of where Evariste was, but there was only gray.

Angelique scowled—she *felt* the spell still running its course... so what was the problem? Had it not yet reached Evariste?

"What a hack of a spell," Angelique grumbled to herself. "I've wasted how many hours on this blasted thing? That's it: I'm setting this book on *fire* if this doesn't work!"

She pursed her lips but still felt only emptiness.

Until...

EVARISTE TROD BACK AND FORTH, pacing in front of the glass of the mirror as he tried not to go mad. He stretched his arms above his head, then paused when he heard a shout.

"*What is that?*"

"*Stop it! Don't let it get through!*"

Curious, Evariste peered down the hallway. A silvery spell charged into the chamber. The script used to construct it churned for a second before it veered in Evariste's direction and struck the mirror.

Even with his powers walled off, Evariste would have recognized the cool and unfathomable depth of this magic.

His ears rang, and his heart nearly burst out of his chest.

It's her. But how? This isn't a spell I know. Is it a trap?

For a moment, Evariste's color-starved mind staggered. He had been double-guessing every bit of information Liliane and her cronies deigned to feed him; he could hardly believe this was *real*.

He took a shuddering breath and cautiously pressed his palm at the spot where the spell was attempting to push through the mirror.

"Angelique?"

ANGELIQUE CAUTIOUSLY OPENED HER EYES, but the workshop was still. The bracelet was growing even brighter, but that wouldn't have made a voice in her head. *But that was Evariste's voice. I heard it as clearly as if he were standing next to me.*

She felt for the spell and tugged on it. It whirled, but it didn't feel like it was *moving* any more, even though it was still consuming power, gnawing at what she had drawn on for the spell.

"What's happening?" she murmured.

HOPE BEAT PAINFULLY in Evariste's heart as he stared at the spell. She had reached him—Angelique had found him!

She'd make sure the Conclave came for him, and he'd leave this terrible grayness!

Acri sprinted into the room, black daggers in hand. "It's here for Evariste!" he shouted. "It's still active—can we trace it?"

Evariste ignored the dark-haired spawn and pressed harder

against the glass, as if he could forcibly push his hand through the mirror so he could touch the spell and tell Angelique his location.

Suzu swirled into the room, Funus on her heels. "Do it!" Suzu snapped. "Whatever mage is strong enough to get through needs to be taken out!"

Evariste's world froze for a moment. *No.*

They didn't know the depth of Angelique's power—no one did, really. They suspected, of course, but if they learned its *true* extent...

They'd hunt her like an animal. She'd never be safe, and she wouldn't even know they were coming for her! He turned his back to the spell and stared, anguished, into the horrifying gray of the mirror. It made his heart shudder to think of staying there, in the smothering gray. *It doesn't matter. I can't let them find out it's her. Even if it means she doesn't locate me.*

Evariste took a deep breath and let his hope of escape die. "Angel, you have to stop this! It's too dangerous," he hissed, trying to keep his voice low so Acri and the others wouldn't hear him over their shouts and the sizzle of magic.

He could mentally feel Angelique's shock, and he had the faint impression she bolted into a sitting position. *"Evariste? Where are you?"*

Evariste shut his eyes. He'd rather see darkness than the gray that only served as a reminder of his future. "You have to stop the spell."

"Are you crazy? No! Not after I finally found you!"

Her familiar squawk was a dagger to his heart, and Evariste smiled and grimaced at the same time. Stars, he missed her.

"Cut the spell off!" he ordered.

He peered over his shoulder and saw Suzu pressing a black flame into Angelique's spell. *If she succeeds in burning through Angelique's spellwork, they'll be able to trace her location.*

His heart rate ratcheted up, and he stopped breathing. "Cut it off *now*!"

Angelique clenched her jaw as she ignored the order. She could feel the spell straining, but she wasn't certain what the problem was. *I'm feeding it plenty of power, so why does it feel like something is holding it back?*

"Where are you?" she repeated, louder. "Can you describe what you hear or have seen?" The spell isn't—"

A quiet crack filled the workshop.

Angelique opened her eyes to see the glass bead on her bracelet disintegrate, and the magic surrounding it snuff out. "NO!"

Without the bracelet, the spell began to falter.

"Thank you for trying, and tell Clovicus everything. Keep alert; stay safe. If you are safe, I can survive this."

Angelique barely heard him. She was struggling to keep the spell going, but she couldn't stabilize it. In her panic, she tried shoving a glob of her raw magic into it, but that only made the spell shatter into a million tiny fragments.

But before the spell faded into nothing, Angelique got one clear picture: a mirror—one that was full length and simple but had mint-green magic circling around its frame.

"A mirror," Angelique whispered as she collapsed in her chair. "They're keeping him in a mirror."

Evariste sagged in relief when he felt the connection sever. *She's safe. They can't track her now.*

Behind him, Funus roared in anger when the last flickers of Angelique's magic faded.

Suzu sighed in aggravation. "It must have been Clovicus—he likely figured out we were on to him."

Funus raised an eyebrow. "That spell looked poorly constructed for someone of Clovicus' experience."

"Then *you* tell us who it was," Suzu said.

"He doesn't have to," Acri drawled. "Lord Enchanter Evariste knows who it was. Don't you?"

Evariste took several steps into the murky gray of the mirror before he turned around to face the glass pane.

Acri stood just outside it, smirking as he pressed the flat of one of his daggers to his lips.

I don't know that there is a word foul enough to describe what he is. Evariste narrowed his eyes as he studied the war mage.

"He recognized that magic," Acri continued. "It was all over his face when I came in the room. He thought this was his escape."

Funus scowled. "He's not going to just blab that information."

"Obviously," Acri snorted. "But can't you think of the right incentive?"

Suzu snapped her fingers, and black fire bloomed in her palms.

Evariste took another cautious step backwards, but he laughed —a jaded and cynical sound. "You've already taken so much from me. Do you really think I'll give this one up?" Mockingly, he leaned forward. "Do. Your. Worst."

Acri laughed. "I was so hoping you would put up a fight! Suzu, do it."

Evariste stiffened himself for pain, but he wasn't concerned.

Pain was temporary, and while it was consuming, it didn't threaten to steal away his very self like the grayness of the mirror did.

No, whatever torture they tried wouldn't loosen his lips. *At least it will break up the monotony*, he cynically thought before the burning started.

CHAPTER 11

With the bracelet broken and useless, no matter how Angelique tried to recreate the spell, it didn't work. She tried supplementing it with some of the gifts Evariste had given her: dresses, pearl hair pins, books; nothing worked.

In the end, she concluded that the mages holding Evariste might have realized she got through their defenses and doubled down on them.

It makes sense, Angelique thought gloomily when, two weeks later, she busied herself with sorting through the various correspondences—magical and otherwise—she had received. *The mages are crafty enough to capture Evariste. There is no possibility that the spell went unnoticed—particularly given Evariste's concern. It's likely they would increase their defense to make certain I couldn't get back again.*

For a moment, she stared unseeingly across the library. *But at least I got something out of it. They've imprisoned him in a mirror. I need to stop by Enchanter Clovicus' office and tell him.*

Angelique paused when she found a letter stamped with the wax seal of the royal Arcainian family.

It must be from Gabrielle—but it came through the Veneno Conclave? Why wouldn't she send it to me directly?

She tugged on a scrap of paper stuck to the seal and saw it had a message scrawled across it.

Angelique—thought you might want to look into this given your friendship with the Prinzessin. It was a general message sent to several enchanters and enchantresses, but to my knowledge, no one has the time or ability to investigate the matter at the moment.

-Clovicus

Curious, Angelique broke the seal and unfolded the letter, scanning the contents.

It was a request from Prince Erick of Arcainia.

King Henrik of Arcainia had married a new bride shortly after Severin and Elle had been married in early spring.

Unfortunately, it seemed the circumstances surrounding King Henrik's new marriage were rather suspicious. (He had met the woman in the woods and kept her a secret until they announced their engagement, and the woman—reading between the polite garbage Prince Erick had written—had the personality of a shrew. Moreover, King Henrik seemed almost *addled* by his love for this woman, and he had made several questionable decisions over the past few weeks.)

Prince Erick's request was for a high-level mage to come to Arcainia and meet the queen to see if it could be discerned whether she was using magic or any sort of enchantment on the king.

Angelique scratched her collarbone as she looked around the library.

Outside, the lawn was green, and the mid-spring flowers were blooming with a vengeance, creating a colorful picture. Even through the walls of the house, Angelique could hear the birds chirping and singing.

It's been three years since Queen Ingrid of Arcainia died. It's not a bad thing for King Henrik to marry again, but given the famous passion of his romance with Ingrid, I would have thought he would not enter into something with such secrecy—for the sake of his children and his country.

Angelique chewed on her lip. "I suppose I could drop by. It would be nice to visit with Gabrielle, and I'd like to talk to Puss about Evariste being sealed in a mirror. Though we'll have to do that in secret—if I recall correctly, he's posing as a regular, non-magical and non-talking cat at the moment."

Angelique tapped the letter on her hand before she nodded, her mind made up. "Yes. I'll do it. I don't think I'm going to have any more success with this spell, so I had best start pursuing the lead I *do* have."

Angelique tossed the rest of the correspondences on the desk and left the library, making the trek to her room.

I'll visit Clovicus before I head to Arcainia and tell him about the mirror. If I am lucky, Sybilla won't be out on an assignment, and I can speak to her as well.

The fairy godmother was a firecracker with an extensive knowledge of spells—she was trained to recognize *all* types of magic, as her main role was to search out children with it and invite them to Luxi-Domus.

Angelique was feeling better about the plan as she climbed the stairs and barged into her room, grabbing an enchanted satchel Stil had made for her long ago that could hold approximately a closet's worth of items inside but remain light enough to carry.

She approached her wardrobe, intending to grab one of her fancier dresses for meeting with the Arcainian princes (more out of respect for their deceased mother, as she had been an enchantress, than out of any social propriety) but paused when she saw the gown hanging from the door.

It was the one Evariste had been saving for her, the one the investigative team found when combing through the house once he was gone.

The gown itself was beautiful, with fitted sleeves, an off-the-shoulder neckline, and a thick skirt, but what was most eye-catching about it was the way it changed colors.

As Angelique stared at it, the dress changed from a pale pink to a deep red. Another minute, and the red mellowed out to a pumpkin orange that shifted into gold.

It was a dress worthy of a Lady Enchantress...something Angelique was most emphatically not. (Yet, anyway.)

Angelique hesitated, then brushed the skirts with her fingers, reveling in the soft cloth.

I don't deserve the kind of distinction Evariste tried to give me, she thought sadly. Softly, the memory of Evariste calling for her through the spell that broke her bracelet tugged at her.

She pressed her lips into a thin line, then nodded. *So, I guess I had better become someone worthy of it.*

On an impulse, she tossed the satchel onto her bed and changed into the new gown. Her image in the mirror was lovely—clearly whoever had made the gown had worked with Evariste to create a style that perfectly suited her.

Dressed like this, Angelique really did look like a Lady Enchantress.

She stared at the mirror, eventually raising her eyes so she gazed upon her face. "I'm not an enchantress yet, but I'll need the power of one to find Evariste. And I'll make whatever sacrifice is necessary to see him home."

ANGELIQUE FURROWED her brow as she clung to Pegasus. The constellation was cantering—a less neck-breaking speed than he usually adopted—along the road that led to Castle Brandis, home of the Arcainian royal family.

Despite a (painful) week sojourn to the Veneno Conclave where she consulted both Clovicus and Sybilla, she had nothing to show for it.

Both the enchanter and the fairy godmother were overjoyed with the shred of information she had uncovered, but neither were knowledgeable about the kind of magic that would be required to seal a person inside a mirror.

She had left Clovicus scouring the library, and Sybilla had promised to keep her ears open during her travels, but she had hoped for a greater step forward with this finding.

I should talk to Enchantress Lovelana and see if she has found anything—or if knowing he's in a mirror changes anything.

Pegasus abruptly stopped, breaking into a rear of anger.

Angelique clung to his back like a particularly determined squirrel, even as he took a few dancing steps sideways and snorted. "Pegasus, what's wrong?" She patted his shoulder when he stilled, and that was when she felt it.

Dark magic.

Evil magic.

Angelique clenched her teeth as she started channeling her powers. "Think we can take it?"

Pegasus snorted and pawed at the road with a hoof, making the ground shake.

"I think so, too," Angelique agreed. "Let's go!"

Pegasus shot forward, galloping at full tilt. The wild magic that pulsed through his body rose to the surface, turning the world white and making his hooves sound like rumbles of thunder.

Up ahead, Angelique could see the black magic spell that soured the air. It was a dark fog that crept through the forest like the fingers of a living creature. It was searching out something and smothering everything in its path.

As Pegasus bore down upon it, Angelique braced herself. "Here we go!" she shouted as they plunged into the smoggy mist.

She released her powers—which she had twisted into sunshine magic—lighting the area up with the brightness of a star.

The fog started to retreat, but *nothing* could outrun Pegasus. They reached the center of the black spell—a tar-like core.

Angelique hurriedly gathered her magic up—trying to ready another spell—but it was unnecessary.

Pegasus screamed as he collided with the core. The stars in his coat shone, and a cosmic boom shook the forest.

The black core shattered, spattering the ground with a thick, jelly-like substance before it burned away, disappearing.

"Ewww." Angelique scrunched up her nose as she peered over the side of Pegasus' shoulder, watching the last traces of the gel fade.

Pegasus snorted and looked to the side of the road. Angelique joined him and spotted a young lady, surrounded by seven swans.

The girl had unruly brown hair that was pulled back in a ponytail with a red ribbon, and appeared to be wearing a uniform of sort—a black gown with white sleeves, gold trim, and a red sash, but it was the gem-studded circlet nestled on her forehead that caught Angelique's attention.

Only Arcainian royalty wore such a thing.

That meant this girl had to be King Henrik's foster daughter. *What was her name again? Ah, that's right!*

Angelique smiled at the princess. "You certainly aren't Gabi, so Princess Elise, I may presume?"

Princess Elise—or, rather, Fürstin Elise if one was to call her by her Arcainian title—gazed wide-eyed up at Angelique, her face pale as she shifted closer to the swans. "W-who are you?"

"I am Angelique."

"You're an enchantress."

Angelique considered correcting her, but based on the swans flocking the area, proper titles were of no concern at the moment. "Correct. Your brother, Prince Erick, invited me to Arcainia. He asked me to observe your step-mother. It seems that I am too late."

Angelique looked over the swans again. *Seven of them, and they are clearly touched by magic.* On a hunch, she crooned, "It is all right, princes. Please, come out of hiding."

The seven swans glided out of the forest, joining her on the road as she slipped off Pegasus.

Angelique slid her hands under the head of one of the swans, making it look up at her. She gently stroked its face as she studied it, trying to make out what pieces of the spellwork she could. She murmured under her breath, hoping the swan stayed calm.

The princess waded out of the trees, dragging a large horse with her. The horse snorted at Pegasus and watched it with bugged eyes but thankfully did not try to flee from the unnatural equine.

Pegasus ignored it and watched the swan princes.

Angelique slowly turned the head of the swan, holding in a growl.

The princes of Arcainia had been cursed—assumedly by the King's new bride, the one the princes had been concerned over.

But why? Why would she risk such a blatant and harmful spell? This isn't like the witch attacking Severin; all of the continent will know where to find the new queen.

Angelique cringed as she continued to consider the curse. It was powerful—far stronger than what Severin had been struck with. Like Severin's curse, there were several different parts to it. Unfortunately, it was arranged in layers rather than sections.

It *looked* like the spell that forced the princes into the shape of a swan was relatively harmless—if not a little devious. Unfortunately, it was the very bottom layer upon which everything else was piled—a spell to take their minds, the curse in general, and more.

It was so entangled that Angelique couldn't outright modify it —at least not with her limited knowledge of curse modification.

She sighed and let a frown tug on her lips. "This is a serious curse," she said. "I assume Gabi escaped it because of Puss?"

"Puss?"

Angelique glanced at the princess. "Her cat."

Elise scrubbed her face with a dirty hand, her eyes glassy with unshed tears. "I don't know. She wasn't cursed; I don't know why, though."

Yes, it was definitely Puss' doing, then. But that doesn't explain Elise's state.

Angelique tried to offer the princess a sympathetic look. "And how did you remain unhindered?"

"I'm not sure." Princess Elise looked half dazed as she played with the red sash of her dress. "Clotilde tried to curse me, but it bounced off me and went back to her."

Bounced off? Is she wearing some kind of charm? Angelique scanned the girl but didn't notice anything that leaked magic on her. "How very odd."

Elise, if possible, looked even more miserable as her chin dropped in defeat. "Maybe it's because I'm not a real member of the royal family. I am a foster child."

"Unlikely. This curse was not crafted specifically for the royal family, and it was made with black magic. Anyone who took the time to create such a vile curse would not make a beginner's mistake." Angelique released the swan.

Elise crouched on the ground, covering her head with an arm. "Can it be broken?"

Angelique, who had been trying to recall the names of the seven princes with little luck, jolted out of her contemplations. "Pardon?"

"Is there any way to end this curse? Could we make Clotilde take it off them? Or... if she dies?" Elise's lost look was starting to be replaced with an expression of determination, visible in the slant of the princess' eyebrows and the strong line of her lips.

Angelique lowered her gaze to the swan princes and stared at them for several moments. *I can't modify this the way it is. But if I attack the source of the curse, this Clotilde, I should be able to do something. If Puss and Gabrielle remained behind, I can recruit their help.*

Out loud, Angelique said, "The safest place for you and your brothers is to be far away from Clotilde. As for breaking the curse...I will see what can be done."

"How?"

"I will approach Clotilde."

"What if she attacks you?"

Angelique was silent for several moments. *And that's the fly in the pudding in all of this. If I want to harass her to get the princes' curse loosened up, I'll have to do magic in Arcainia again, and the magic ban here hasn't been lifted. The Veneno Conclave is not going to be happy. But I can't abandon the princes just to waltz off to seek permission. Saving them would be worth the lecture—just hopefully the Council won't follow through on their threat to seal me.*

She finally sighed. "There will be no 'if,' for I plan to attack her first."

Elise peered in her direction. "Will you be punished for it?"

"Perhaps," Angelique said with false cheer.

"I'm sorry. I would pardon you, the royal family would pardon you if we could." One of the swans waddled up to the morose princess and started tugging on her hair with its orange beak.

"I thank you. But it is not the Arcainian government that outlawed magic in Arcainia, but the Veneno Conclave itself." Angelique leaned slightly into Pegasus' shoulder, encouraged by his nearness. "There is a good chance I will not be punished, as the attacks originate from a twister of magic. However, no matter who made the law, I would not stand for this. My master taught me that as a magic user, it is my responsibility to right whatever wrongs might have been made with magic. What Clotilde has done is not only wrong, but evil."

As Angelique explained the situation, her resolve grew. *Yes, this is the right thing to do, even if it makes the Council upset. It's what Evariste would do.*

"Thank you," Elise whispered. The swan pecking at her hair whistled, drawing a weak smile from the princess.

"Of course." Angelique turned to Pegasus, but he was already lowering his front end in a bow, extending his leg to make it easier for Angelique to climb on in her fancy dress. As she twitched her skirts across the constellation's back, her skirt color changed to match him, fading from a dusky orange to a dark blue. "You must leave the country. Keep going west to Loire, and from there, go north to Verglas. Your stepmother could never touch you there, for the magic of the Snow Queen still runs strong in Verglas in spite of the centuries that have passed. I mean to find Gabi and Puss to form a plan for attacking the queen. It may be some days before I find you."

The princess brushed her palms off on her dress as she stood. "Lady Enchantress, please...can my brothers understand me at all?"

How do I phrase this to keep from entirely discouraging her?

Angelique nodded when she finally settled on an explanation. "They understand more than you would think, but not much of their humanity remains. I would guess that they recognize you as someone important to them, although they certainly do not understand the conversation we just had."

The princess pushed her shoulders back and raised her chin, rallying her spirit. "I see. Thank you."

"They will stay close to you." Angelique discreetly tugged on her skirt when it started to ride up Pegasus' withers. "Do not worry that they will fly off. It will be easier for you to reach Verglas if you lead them rather than attempt to drive them, I think."

"Thank you," Elise repeated. Though her expression was stoic, her warm eyes betrayed the pain of her situation.

Pegasus snorted, and Angelique patted his shoulder. "I will find you after my encounter with your stepmother. Until then, stay safe."

"Thank you, Lady Enchantress. My family owes you a great debt," Elise said.

"Hardly." Angelique wryly replied. "It is the fault of magic users for allowing this to happen in the first place, but I thank you all the same. Until Verglas, Princess Elise." Angelique clicked encouragingly at Pegasus, and he set off at a trot.

"We're heading to Castle Brandis, Pegasus." Angelique ducked a tree branch that jutted out to the road. "To consort with Gabrielle and Puss, it would seem."

Pegasus huffed but tucked his head and picked up the pace when they left the woods, galloping for the country's capital.

CHAPTER 12

Rather than announce her presence to the witch-queen, Angelique chose the option of subterfuge. She left Pegasus outside (after arguing with him for a good ten minutes, he *finally* agreed to return to the sky) and walked into the capital, an invisibility charm hiding her from sight.

She chose a charm that used very little of her magic—she didn't want to be throwing any around without knowing how skilled Clotilde was at black magic, as the witch-queen might be able to sense it being used.

It meant making her way through the city and to the royal castle a harrowing experience, however, as the charm was really just a thin illusion that would falter if someone ran into her.

I need to send word to Enchanter Clovicus, Angelique thought as she wove her way through the busy city streets. *While I'd like to believe I will be forgiven for using magic here when the situation is this dire, it's very likely someone in the Veneno Conclave is going to throw a fit, and the Council will to have me dragged in again.*

She sighed. The knowledge was disheartening, but she was surprised to realize she was more bothered by the time she'd waste arguing her case than knowing no one trusted her even when she was risking her life to do what was right.

I guess all my years of being treated with suspicion have finally helped me reach enlightenment. She cracked a smile at her own dark joke as she circled a city fountain, taking a moment to get her bearings before continuing on. *I now expect to be treated like a villain. In fact, I welcome it. If I march into their den expecting to be doubted, it means their hard words and blatant disbelief hurt less.*

In her heart of hearts, though, it still made Angelique doubt. Was she doing the right thing? The Veneno Conclave was supposed to be the moral guidance for magic users. And if they were so suspicious of her every action…

Angelique shook her head and instead turned her thoughts to her examination of the curse stamped on the princes. *There was something* familiar *about some of that spell work.* She side-stepped a man carrying buckets of water and increased her pace. *Or perhaps not even the spell itself, but the power in it. But that's impossible. I'm not familiar with black magic.*

She peered ahead and spotted the gate that divided Castle Brandis from the rest of the city. A few quick strides and she was through.

She tried to go around by the stables, but they were buzzing with frantic activity, making it too risky for her to pass through with her delicate spell. So she continued around to the back of the castle, passing through a small garden.

"Angelique?"

She paused at the voice and poked her head past a hedge. Gabrielle wove her way around a bird bath, with Puss on her shoulder and her hand grabbing fistfuls of her fine, silken gown, lifting up the hem so she could walk faster.

Angelique dusted off her invisibility charm. "Over here—and slightly disheartened you found me so easily. It does not bode well for my attempt to arrive undetected."

"Don't be stupid," Puss crossly said. "You were my owner for years. Of *course* I'd recognize your magic—even if you *have* improved its subtleties," he grudgingly said.

"I doubt anyone else felt your arrival," Gabrielle added. She stopped just short of Angelique and offered her a bow.

"Please, we are past formalities," Angelique said.

Gabrielle grinned, adding to her beauty, and laughed. "I'd like to think so, too, but I didn't want to assume."

To Angelique's surprise, the younger girl stretched out her arms and embraced Angelique with a tight squeeze. Puss added to the embrace by rubbing his head against Angelique's cheek.

The affection startled Angelique—besides Evariste and occasionally Stil, she hadn't often been hugged by others. But the hug let Angelique feel the slight shake to Gabrielle's shoulders, and though Puss purred for a moment, when he placed a paw on her shoulder, his claws dug in despite his usual control.

They are afraid. Not that it's unexpected—one curse, and almost the entire Arcainian royal family is out of the picture.

"What are you doing here?" Gabrielle squeezed Angelique once more then released her.

Puss tottered on Gabrielle's shoulder before he regained his balance. "Indeed, there's no way for you to have so swiftly heard of the tragedy that has happened here." He twitched his whiskers, and jumped into Angelique's arms.

"Actually, I have," Angelique said. "I was on my way here to discreetly study Clotilde at Prince Erick's request, to see if she was using magic." She smiled wryly. "I met Fürstin Elise on my way to Brandis, so I've already had a look at the princes' curse, and I sent her north to Verglas."

Gabrielle sighed. "I'd normally laugh at the horrible irony, but I'm glad, at least, that you are here with us."

Puss let Angelique shift her hold on him but flicked his tail. "What did you make of the curse?"

Angelique glanced down at her feline friend then across at Gabrielle. The hero-turned-princess watched her with an even gaze. *They need the truth because they're going to fight this.* "It's bad," Angelique admitted. "It's a powerful, multi-layered curse. I don't know how to modify it, or I would have tried at the time. A more experienced enchanter or enchantress would be able to do something, but I'm not well versed with curses. The only option I could see is to attack Clotilde. If she dies, the curse will end."

"And if we fail?" Gabrielle asked.

Angelique pressed her lips into a thin line. "If we can rattle her enough, I think we can weaken the curse, but that is all. I am in contact with a powerful enchanter. I can get word to him to help us—he will be more than a match for Clotilde."

"Who?" Puss asked. "Unless, have you found...?"

"No," Angelique said, the word falling heavily from her lips. "I meant Enchanter Clovicus."

"Evariste's old mentor? I see." Puss twisted so he looked back at Gabrielle.

Correctly interpreting the motion, Angelique passed the black and white cat back to his mistress.

"While it's true he would be more than a match for Clotilde, you forgot one thing," Puss said.

"What's that?" Gabrielle asked.

Puss reclaimed his perch on Gabrielle's shoulder. "That to get permission to come here and use his magic, he'll have to struggle through the painfully *slow* machinations of the Conclave. He won't be cleared to fight Clotilde for several weeks, if not more than a month."

"I'm aware of the time it would take," Angelique said. "But I thought I would make the offer. Based on the strength of that curse, I'm not up to Clotilde's strength."

Gabrielle nodded, but Puss stared at her, his bronze eyes glowing.

Angelique could see the same truth in his eyes that she knew herself.

She was more than a match for Clotilde—if she used her war magic.

But I can't. I'm willing to break Conclave law and use magic in a no-magic zone and interfere in country politics if it means saving a life...but I can't use my war magic. I can't.

The metallic taste of panic briefly filled her mouth as she recalled the times she had used her core powers. She had injured Evariste, and in a pre-test for her Enchantress examination, the raw form of her war magic had nearly flattened a village.

Then again, if she had used her war magic, she could have stopped the black mages who took Evariste.

But she *couldn't*. She couldn't shake the feeling that if she did start to freely use her war magic, it would lead her down the path of carnage and blood, and it would turn her into the monster the Conclave seemed to think she was. *I'll do everything in my power to help people, but I can't let this last piece of me go. I can't throw away the last proof I have of my innocence.*

"As it stands," Gabrielle started, "I don't think we can wait for this Enchanter Clovicus." The prinzessin's gaze turned hard. "If we let her sink her claws into Arcainia without fighting back, Clotilde will bring the ruin Carabas saw on the entire country."

"I am inclined to agree," Puss said. "Even if all we do is waylay her plans, it will help. If we let her carry out her plots without stopping her, it will make it that much more difficult to end her later, and Arcainia might not recover from her actions for decades. Additionally, I don't believe she is as strong as you seem to think she is, Angelique."

Angelique frowned. "Why do you say that?"

"Because the curse she cast on the princes was not her power," Puss explained. "She has a magical artifact that oozes black magic. She used it to cast the curse."

"So if we can separate her from the artifact, we can win." Angelique thoughtfully tapped her lips with a finger as she thought. "That does change things."

Gabrielle grinned, looking more like the reckless hero she was than the gorgeous princess she appeared to be. "What do you have in mind?"

Angelique narrowed her eyes. "I'm thinking...a trap."

ANGELIQUE CROUCHED with Gabrielle in a narrow hallway, stretching her invisibility illusion to cover the prinzessin as well—a slightly more difficult task given the naked blade the blonde brandished. They waited at a cracked doorway, which opened up into the throne room.

Clotilde apparently possessed an enormous ego, and as such, spent a great deal of time preening on the throne.

While it made Angelique roll her eyes, it also made it quite easy to spring their trap. After several days of planning and plotting, all they had to do was wait for the witch-queen to retire for the evening, then they could enact their plans easily and without the fear of being discovered.

Regardless, Angelique's nerves still prickled as they sat in the servants' hallway, waiting for the wretched woman in silence.

"Puss," Gabrielle called in a whisper. "Are you there?"

"Of course I am," the cat hissed back. "Now shut your yipping mouth before you reveal us!" Though he was invisible to the eye, his voice came from the throne King Henrik usually occupied.

Angelique scrunched her eyes shut and rubbed her forehead. *Naturally, Puss would choose to sit on the King's throne.*

The main door to the throne room entrance creaked as it swung open.

Queen Clotilde marched across the chamber, climbing the dais and smiling triumphantly when she reached her throne. She was tall and broad shouldered for a woman. She likely could have been considered a beauty with her fair hair and pleasing figure, but her dress—bedecked in lace and sporting a train several yards long—and the crown perched on her head that was so decorated with gems it was gaudy—spoiled the picture and made her look more like a little girl playing dress-up.

King Henrik ambled in behind her, swaying like an elderly man. Gabrielle said Clotilde had a magical hold on him, but Angelique hadn't expected it to be this bad. His eyes were open but vacant. Angelique doubted he heard or saw anything around him.

It's a good thing he's so slow—we can attack Clotilde while he's still near the door.

She tapped the floor in the pre-agreed upon signal.

It was time.

Gabrielle slipped through the cracked door, Angelique's spell falling from her and making her visible once more.

"Clotilde," Gabrielle called in a strong voice that sounded of steel and iron.

"You!" Clotilde stood, her face twisting with rage when she saw Gabrielle. "Guards, arrest the princess!"

Gabrielle, wearing the leather doublet and men's breeches she used to wear during her adventuring days, laughed as she rested the flat of her blade on her shoulder. "They're not going to come, Clotilde. You might call yourself a queen, but you're not." She stalked toward the witch-queen, moving dangerously close to her.

Clotilde's face turned red. "You might have gotten away before, but you won't today!" She thrust her arm in front of her, holding what looked like a black diamond that was approximately the size of a crab apple.

The sheer evil encased in the gem made Angelique cringe, for it radiated malevolence like a stench. But she forced herself to stand and burst out of the door, shedding her invisibility and shouting a spell for a shield that enveloped Gabrielle.

Clotilde's forehead wrinkled, and her eyes turned small and beady as she stared at Angelique with obvious confusion.

Come on, Puss. Hurry!

Finally, Puss' invisibility spell fell off him, revealing him just as he reached the apex of his jump and knocked into Clotilde's hand.

The black gem fell from her grasp, clattering to the floor.

"*Don't* touch it," Puss growled at Gabrielle.

"Then hurry up!" The prinzessin growled right back.

Puss snarled but closed his teeth around the gem. Gabrielle then grabbed him and the two sprinted back to Angelique, who released another spell.

"Come back here!" Clotilde shrieked. "You awful—ACK!" she screamed when Angelique's spell knocked into her, tossing her head over heels so she hit the dais with a painful smack.

Angelique flicked some of her magic at one of the curtains drawn back behind the thrones to create a backdrop, and the golden cords used to tie them in place slithered free and scurried to Clotilde, wrapping around her arms.

(Angelique had come a long way since she and Evariste had encountered the black mages in Baris; *that much* was for certain!)

It was too early to celebrate a win, but everything was falling into place better than Angelique had hoped.

Gabrielle—still carrying Puss—*almost* reached Angelique's side...when the gem was yanked from Puss' mouth and went flying back to Clotilde.

The golden binds around Clotilde shredded to pieces as the witch-queen stood.

Angelique's spirits fell when she saw the second black diamond clutched in Clotilde's other hand.

Oh no...we hadn't accounted for two *artifacts of such power—but where did she get them?*

Clotilde caught her original gem, her lips pulled back in a snarl. "You think you can attack *me*? With these I have great power; I am limitless!" She laughed as she jabbed a finger at them.

Black lightning exploded from her fingertip and raced in their direction.

"Get down!" Angelique shoved a spell out, forming a clear shell of protection around them.

The lightning crackled, then exploded when it hit Angelique's defenses, rocking the throne room. Angelique clenched her teeth and added more power to the spell, but it crumbled like dust.

"We need to retreat," Puss shouted.

"Come on, Angelique!" Gabrielle shouted.

Angelique stubbornly shook her head. *This is the one chance we have—she's going to be better guarded after this. I have to do something, or she'll only get stronger.*

"Just let me get one hit in." Angelique hurriedly threw up another barrier when she saw Clotilde chuck another spell. "If I can pitch it right, I might be able to change the princes' curse!"

She clenched her teeth as she braced herself for impact, heaving more power into her barrier when the black lightning struck.

Clotilde using artifacts changed the basis of the princes' curse. It wasn't a circuit—self-contained—but rather it was tied to the artifacts themselves. Angelique could physically see flickers of the curse drifting from the dark gems like thread.

If I can hit them, I might be able to do something.

Sweat beaded on Angelique's forehead, and her arms *ached* under the strain as she tried to hold her barrier together long enough to fend off the crackling black lightning. When she saw the black, scorched marks the lightning left in a red carpet, she cringed.

"You better hurry up," Puss said. "She's going to overpower you if you don't do *something*."

The black lightning faded, and Angelique let her barrier fall. She threw together a spell she could have woven in her sleep, and a massive fireball roared to life.

Clotilde screamed in pain as Angelique's fireball sprang on her hands. She dropped the black gems—which sat at the center of Angelique's flames.

Come on, Angelique thought as she threw more power into her magic, making the flames turn blue. *Break it!*

Her fire hissed, and she saw it. A tiny crack appeared in the princes' curse.

Yes!

"Gabrielle, don't you dare, you brash thug!" Puss howled as Gabrielle crept towards the still-burning artifacts with obvious intent.

Clotilde screamed in rage and dove, plucking up one of the gems, having wrapped the fabric of her train around her hands. She brandished the gem in Gabrielle's direction with a howl.

"Angelique—help her!" Roland shouted.

Angelique snapped off her fire spell and then flicked her fingers at the flooring in front of Gabrielle.

The rock that made up the dais stairs peeled up, mortar crumbling as they hastily stacked in front of Gabrielle just in time to shield her from watery mist that crept towards the princess.

Clotilde retrieved her second gem, and her eyes—such a light blue they were nearly colorless—fell on Angelique. "You will pay!" she screamed.

Angelique struggled to raise a defensive spell in front of her when pain exploded in her back.

She fell forward, her breath knocked from her as a sharp, stabbing sensation dug deeper and deeper into her shoulder. She struggled to twist her neck at a painful angle and saw what looked like a decorative flourish of metal snapped off a candelabra jutting from her shoulder.

Hm. That's a new one, she thought dimly.

The metal dug deeper and deeper, and with every push, air left Angelique's lungs. She couldn't scream; she couldn't get up.

Her magic pounded in her ears, pumping ruthlessly through her body as it demanded release. It sparked at her fingertips and snapped at her calves, hurting almost as much as the pain in her shoulder.

No. Angelique held it back, even as she felt like the power of her magic might eat her alive. *If I lose it here, I'll kill everyone—including Puss and Gabrielle. NO!*

Puss' muted voice flickered through her senses. "Gabi!"

"I'm coming!"

Clotilde screamed, and cooled hands tough with calluses briefly brushed Angelique's arms.

"Get rid of that before you drag her off."

"You think?" Gabrielle's voice was warped, as though she were underwater.

But the digging pain in Angelique's shoulder focused into one painful, jarring stab...and then there was merely waves of dulled pain.

Someone wrapped their arms around Angelique's waist and began to haul her away, dragging her across the floor.

She knew it had to be Gabrielle, but for a fleeing moment, she thought it was Evariste, and she relaxed in his grasp...until she remembered that was impossible.

Her magic flooded her, overwhelming her senses and threatening to loosen itself on the world, as pain ate away at her shoulder.

But as Angelique drifted off into the soothing darkness, she clamped down on her magic. *No. Not here.*

CHAPTER 13

Several days later, Angelique tried to discreetly roll her shoulder, attempting to ease some of the pain that still festered in her muscles.

Gabrielle noticed the gesture and narrowed her eyes. "Are you sure you're good enough to do this?" She glanced up at Puss, who was perched on her shoulders. "Puss' healing spell isn't that strong, and you were out of it for a day."

"I beg your pardon; my healing abilities are *quite* potent," Puss squawked. "If they weren't, you would have been dead the first time a bandit thumped you upside the head!"

Angelique offered what she hoped was a reassuring smile. "I was unconscious only because Puss placed a sleeping spell on me with his healing magic. I am much better now." *And since I lost a few days, I have to get moving, fast.*

Between Puss' meddling and the shoulder wound, Angelique had lost valuable time. Now that she was healed—or at least healed enough—she needed to see just how she had damaged the princes' curse, observe Clotilde, and plan for the next step.

Clotilde couldn't be left in power. The consequences would be disastrous. She'd have to take the matter back to the Veneno Conclave for help.

Gabrielle sauntered down the hallway, waving to a guard in thanks when he—unprompted—opened the door for her. She held a finger to her lips, and the guard nodded. Satisfied, the Prinzessin trotted through the door, beckoning Angelique to follow.

Angelique joined her, holding her breath when they crept onto the narrow, stone balcony that edged the throne room.

Officially, it was for soldiers only—even now, six soldiers were stationed at different corners of the balcony, each wielding crossbows. The soldiers glanced in their direction, and for a second, Angelique's heart stopped.

Will they sound the alarm? Gabrielle is safe from Clotilde because of Puss, but the rest of the castle workers are not.

The soldiers' expressions didn't even flicker as they went back to observing the queen with stony expressions.

Angelique exhaled. *Bless their loyalty. And bless Gabrielle for being worthy of it.*

Gabrielle crouched down and inched up to the stone balcony, peering over the side into the throne room.

Roland re-arranged himself so he half-stood on her sloped back, making sure he didn't poke too high above the balcony wall.

Angelique joined them, awkwardly crouching in her beautiful dress. She leaned her side against the wall until the muscles in her still-healing shoulder prickled in pain, pulling her skin tight. Grimacing, Angelique gave up the pretense of elegance and instead lowered herself to her knees, pressing her chest against the cold stone of the balcony so she could also peek down into the throne room.

Clotilde sat on her throne, wearing another one of her so-fancy-it-was-gaudy dresses. A crooked scowl was etched into her lips as she listened to the castle steward's morning report.

(The poor steward kept trying to address the King, but Henrik didn't move—or even blink—during his entire talk.)

Even this cursory glance made Angelique sigh.

Clotilde was fine. She showed no ill effects of their fight. And now that Angelique knew what she was looking for, she could sense the presence of the queen's black artifacts, which radiated malice and contempt.

It confirmed Angelique's suspicions: Clotilde herself was nearly powerless. The artifacts were the bigger threat. It was also worrying, however, because if Clotilde was such a poor magic user…where had she gotten the artifacts?

"Can you tell what your attack did?" Gabrielle whispered.

"Sorry, I was thinking," Angelique admitted. "Just a moment." She blinked as she let her sight expand and began picking up on more shimmers of magic from herself, Puss, and Clotilde.

It took Angelique a couple of moments before she saw the occasional glitter that represented the curse which held the princes in Clotilde's power.

As she had hoped, her fire spell had damaged it—but in a rather strange way.

"Well?" Roland prompted.

Angelique squinted at the curse then leaned closer to the magic cat and Prinzessin to whisper. "I simultaneously damaged it less and more than I thought."

"How?" Gabrielle asked.

Angelique paused as she tried to think of an accurate explanation.

Seeing her expression, Gabrielle started to edge away from the balcony and motioned for Angelique to follow her. They crept from the balcony and slipped back into the hallway from which they had come.

As Gabrielle waved to the guard and they retreated farther away from the throne room, Angelique sifted through her thoughts.

When she used the fire spell, she'd been *attempting* to do what she had done to Severin's curse: destroy the part that cursed the princes to forget their true selves and have the mind of swans.

She hadn't succeeded to that end, probably because the spell was built more in layers than in separate chains like Severin's curse had been.

Instead of destroying just that part of the curse, she had sliced through and damaged the bottom layer—the part that kept the princes in swan bodies.

"Think of this curse like layers on a cake," Angelique finally settled on. "I was hoping to scrape off the top layer of the spell, but instead my fire cracked all the way to the base, and it removed a slice of it."

"How will it affect the curse?" Gabrielle leaned against another door, pushing it open.

The room inside was undecorated and held several cots and a few chairs—the break room for soldiers guarding the floor, likely.

"It hasn't gone into effect yet because I'll need to yank on it, but once I do, the curse *should* loosen up enough so that after sundown, for one hour every night, the princes will transform and become their true selves."

"Only for an hour?" Puss asked.

"I'm afraid so, yes." Angelique frowned as she sat down in one of the sturdy, plain chairs and rested her hands on the table.

Gabrielle nodded thoughtfully. "What does that mean for the curse? Can you modify it, as you modified Prince Severin's curse?"

Angelique tapped her fingers on the table. "I *could*, but I'm not sure it's the best option."

Puss hopped off Gabrielle's shoulder and sat on a chair, his head just clearing the table top. "Explain," he ordered in that instructive-but-bossy tone he used to use on her when Evariste sent her out to practice spells on the dummy in the yard.

Something hot clogged her throat for a moment, and she had to blink before she could continue. "I can see there is a thin slice where I could use the same modification I used on Severin: the curse will break if one of the princes fell in love, and the girl he loved returned the feelings. The prince *and* his lady would have to be mutually in love." She carefully enunciated the rules, given the disaster that had occurred the last time she hadn't been so careful.

Gabrielle hopefully bit her lip. "Will it work if we're already in love."

"I'm sorry to say it won't. The spell requires the power that comes from the kindling of a relationship, not the ongoing blaze."

Gabrielle exchanged a look with Puss, furrowing her forehead. "Ahh, yes. That might be a problem. Two of the princes are in love already, but the lady…"

"The Bumpkin Head would kill them first," Puss said. Catching Gabrielle's arching eyebrow he added, "That is, Prince Steffen would kill them."

"Even when he's a swan?" Angelique asked.

"Some things transcend magic," Gabrielle carefully said.

"Like the bossiness of an older sibling," Puss added.

"I see." Angelique shrugged. "I didn't think it was a very viable option anyway. Falling in love when your country is on the line seems impractical and silly."

Puss twitched his whiskers. "I'm not surprised to hear *you* say so. You have the romantic sense of an angry badger."

"Normally, I might agree that being in such peril might not be an ideal time to fall in love," Gabrielle poked the top of Puss' head and gave him a warning look before she smiled at Angelique. "But it has been my experience that people can learn to love in all kinds of situations. However, given the…obstacles the princes face—for even if we ignore the two who *might* succeed if not for Steffen, that still leaves only an hour a day for the lads to remedy that—you might be correct that it is not a practical modification. But you said this wasn't the best option; does that mean there is another possibility?"

Puss smugly licked his chops. "You can be impressive with your intellect when properly focused, mistress."

Gabrielle shot the cat a glare but folded her arms across her chest and leaned back against the wall as she turned her gaze to Angelique.

"The second option won't directly be a part of the spell at all but rather will act as a counter-weight to Clotilde's magical artifacts," Angelique started. "The curse doesn't come from Clotilde herself, but from the artifacts, and it is linked to them. If an act of great sacrifice born out of love is committed on behalf of the princes, it should shatter the curse entirely."

Gabrielle tilted her head. "But if it's not tied directly to the curse, how is that possible?"

Puss raised a paw and placed it on the table edge, digging his claws into the worn wood. "I think I see it. Clotilde's artifacts are filled with a dark and evil power. Love and sacrifice are the exact opposite. Since the curse is still tied to the artifacts, an act of sacrifice would undermine that connection and destroy it."

Angelique nodded. "Exactly."

Puss's tail twitched behind him. "It's nothing to fret over, Gabrielle. Such a thing has long been proven and accepted in the magical community for centuries. There're multiple acts of love and sacrifice that can be completed that have proven and recorded results—you could say they are almost natural modifications set into any curse caused by a magical artifact. They are practically considered a tradition or part of magical lore. It's merely the matter of picking the right one."

Gabrielle warily brushed the hilt of her sword that hung from her belt. "What kind of sacrifices?"

Angelique stared at the ceiling as she tried to remember some of the acceptable methods she had been taught as a student at Luxi-Domus. "There's a long one where you have to travel to the east wind, west wind, then south wind, and north wind. It's rather time consuming and blustery."

"Collecting gold apples—they grow on the Isles of Mythos," Puss added.

"The one that will likely be the swiftest and least deadly—though it's rather taxing—would be to sew or knit shirts of stinging nettles," Angelique said. "Though the person sewing them cannot speak from when she first starts until she finishes the last shirt."

Gabrielle frowned. "I know a little of sewing. Hopefully it will be enough."

Angelique glanced at Puss, and the two nodded.

"You won't be breaking the curse, Gabrielle," Puss announced.

Gabrielle pushed off the wall and stalked over to her cat. "What do you mean?"

"You're more useful here," Puss said.

Angelique rolled her eyes. "You're *needed* here," she said. "Whoever undertakes breaking the curse will have to remain with the princes. And Verglas is the safest place for them as long as Clotilde is alive."

Gabrielle hesitated. "I promised Steffen when we married that I would guard Arcainia with him, that the country had to come before us."

"Which is why you can't go." Puss gently nosed her hand until she stroked his head, eliciting a deep rumbling purr from his white chest.

"You have Puss with you," Angelique said. "He's uniquely gifted to withstand Clotilde. And even if you asked him to remain behind—which would be rather cruel—no one has gone through the life and death situations you two have. No one will do as well with him as you will."

"Worry not, mistress." Puss's voice was soft and gentle with affection. "Together we can guard your country...and wait for the Bumpkin Head to return."

Gabrielle picked Puss up and cradled him in her arms. She

sniffed, and Angelique wondered if she would cry, until she saw the princess' shoulders settle.

Clotilde doesn't know what she's in for, Angelique realized as she watched Gabrielle lift her chin.

"We'll stay," Gabrielle said. "It means we'll be dumping the sacrifice on Elise, though," she said, referring to the princess/foster-sister of the seven Arcainian princes.

"I don't think she'll mind," Puss said. "I am of the opinion that she is even more stubborn than you are and will go at the curse just as doggedly as you would."

"At the very least, we can send her help—perhaps a soldier to help her stay safe." A brief frown twitched across Gabrielle's lips. "I feel bad, though, that we aren't giving her a choice."

"There is a possibility it might not be necessary," Angelique said. "Though I am not powerful enough to take care of Clotilde by myself, surely the magical community will see the need to act and will take care of her—which would shatter the curse as well."

Puss narrowed his eyes, and Angelique could sense he still longed to remind her that if she used her core magic, that wouldn't be so.

And yet, she couldn't. Something in Angelique couldn't let that happen. The few times she had used her core magic since leaving Luxi-Domus, Evariste had been with her. And now…

Technically, given the vast amount of power I have, it shouldn't even be necessary to use my core magic.

The thought made her frown—and if she had been alone, she would have been tempted to hiss.

It was almost ironic. The Council, instructors at Luxi-Domus, and Evariste were forever telling her how powerful she was. And yet she hadn't really succeeded at *anything*.

I couldn't erase Severin's curse, only modify it. I couldn't hold off against Clotilde and her wretched artifacts—I'm not nearly as strong as everyone believes, or perhaps I'm just very bad at magic. But I thought I had learned well. Evariste always told me I learned faster than expected.

Angelique cut the thought off—lest it linger and made her think even more of her master.

A gentle tap rattled the door.

Gabrielle stood, her hand on her sword, and Angelique readied her magic.

"Yes?" Gabrielle cautiously asked.

The door cracked open, and a rather harried-looking guard peered inside. "Prinzessin," he began, when something small and white scurried past his feet. "Stop that!"

He made a dive for the white object, which wove around him with a surprising amount of agility. It *appeared* to be a human shape—about hand-length—fashioned out of paper.

With a spry leap, the paper human jumped onto the soldier's head, then the table. It came to a quivering stop just in front of Angelique.

Angelique could feel the faint magical signature that radiated off the paper man. "Enchanter Clovicus?" she muttered.

"I apologize, Prinzessin." The guard peeled himself off the ground and bowed. "That *thing* arrived at the gate not ten minutes ago. We've been trying to grab it, but it kept evading us and coming in this direction."

Puss tilted his head. "It's safe," he declared. "If not a bit crudely made."

Gabrielle smiled at the soldier. "Thank you for letting us know, but it's fine."

He bowed again and backed out of the door, closing it behind him.

Once they were alone again, Angelique held a finger out, which the paperman held as if in recognition.

He abruptly stiffened, then fell, unfolding into a crinkled letter.

Angelique,
Leave Arcainia, now.

Couriers have been sent out by Veneno Conclave officials with express orders to bring you back.
They are aware there has been an upset in Arcainia, and I don't believe anyone thinks you are to blame for it, but reports have also outlined your use of magic.
Unless you mean to stand your ground, you need to leave before the couriers arrive. I'll inform the Council what is going on.
Enchanter Clovicus

Gabrielle went back to leaning against the wall, politely looking away. Puss had no such compulsions.

"What does it say?" he demanded.

Angelique stood. "The Veneno Conclave has sent out couriers with orders to bring me back," she said, her chest tight.

"Is that bad?" Gabrielle asked.

Puss twitched his tail back and forth. "For Angelique? Yes, *very* bad." His bronze eyes glowed as he stared unblinkingly at her. "I apologize, Angelique. It seems we have caused a great deal of trouble for you."

Angelique snorted. "A witch has cursed the seven princes and brainwashed King Henrik. You have done no such thing—it is merely because the Conclave hasn't yet learned all the details of the situation." *I hope.*

"Evariste is still absent," Puss said.

Angelique glanced at her old friend, puzzled by the statement. *What does Evariste have to do with me being punished?*

"We can sneak you out of Castle Brandis," Gabrielle said. "This place has a million passages, and once you get out to that... horse...of yours, no one can catch up with you."

Angelique glanced down at the crumpled letter. "First, I need to get word back to Clovicus."

"What, did he ask for your opinion on his stationary?" Puss drawled.

"No, but I need to make arrangements to *meet* with him so I can explain what's happened," Angelique snapped.

"Oh." Puss blinked. "I suppose that's acceptable."

"No, it's not," Gabrielle unsheathed her sword—though Angelique suspected it was more for personal comfort than any plans to hack something to pieces. "You need to leave, now!"

"You said yourself: nothing can outrun Pegasus," Angelique said. "And Clovicus is our best bet for help, as it stands."

Gabrielle groaned and slid her sword back in its scabbard. "*Fine*! I'll get you paper and ink." She stomped across the room and kicked open a few supply crates before she found what she was looking for.

It only took Angelique a few moments to scrawl out her reply—a request for Lord Enchanter Clovicus to meet her in Erlauf—and they were out the door, Puss leading the way with his tail extended straight up like a flag pole.

"I'll ride north to Verglas and explain the situation to Fürstin Elise," Angelique said.

"Thank you," Gabrielle said, the relief evident in her voice. "For everything."

"I am glad I was on hand to offer aid," Angelique said. *Even if it means I'll be dodging messages for the next few months.*

Gabrielle motioned for Angelique to follow her down a spiral staircase. "I don't know what we would have done if you weren't here."

"Do you want me to tell Steffen anything?" Angelique asked.

Gabrielle hesitated at the base of the stairs. It took Puss rubbing against her legs to prod her into motion so she strode down the hallway. "No, I spoke to him before they left. And he's not going to take this situation very well." She smiled wryly. "He hates it when things spiral out of his control."

"A common worry of the unprepared," Puss muttered.

Gabrielle rolled her eyes as they ducked outside. "If he wasn't worried, you would accuse him of being stupid and unaware of the danger we're in."

"Naturally," Puss said. "I retain the right to criticize your husband no matter what circumstance, or there will be a terrible imbalance to his ego." He almost skidded when the hallway opened up into the stable courtyard, making all three of them squint in the sunlight.

Angelique's shoulder twinged again as she swept down the three stairs that separated the hallway from the courtyard. She pushed off the sensation and turned around to offer one last smile to the Prinzessin. "Thank you..." she started, then trailed off at the worry that stole over Gabrielle's face. "What is it?"

Gabrielle slowly tipped her head. "Are those two mages?"

CHAPTER 14

Angelique turned around and saw two males. One was short and stout, the other tall and blank faced.

It took Angelique a second to place where she had seen the taller one—he was a mage who had been present at Princess Rosalinda's christening in Sole, and his name was Finnr, if she remembered correctly.

"Falling stars," she muttered. "I bet he's not here to admire the castle."

"This way, Angelique." Puss leaped outside and started around the castle, moving in the opposite direction. "Can you dampen your presence?"

"I've been wearing charms that ward off location spells ever since Evariste and I were attacked," Angelique said. "But I'm fairly certain the Conclave has a deep tracking spell on me, given their surety that I'm going to turn on them like a rabid dog."

Gabrielle fell in line behind Angelique, seemingly doing her best to block her—though it was a lost cause with Angelique's eye-catching gown.

Angelique relaxed slightly when they rounded the corner.

Though she and Puss continued at a brisk walk, Gabrielle lingered behind them, looking back at the mages.

"There is a small gap in the wall—it's meant for drainage, but you'll be able to fit through it," Puss said.

"Fantastic," Angelique muttered.

Behind them, Gabrielle swore. "Pick up the pace, Puss; they're following us!" She ran after them, jumping a stone step with ease.

Angelique also ran, but not with as much ease. Though her dress was breezy and comfortable and spelled against wear and tear, the poofy skirts still snagged on the branches of hedges and bushes.

She risked glancing over her shoulder and saw Finnr round the corner, his brows lowering as he saw her run.

"Don't you think they could be reasoned with?" Gabrielle asked as they peeled away from the castle and skirted around a shelter that covered bales of hay. "You attacked a witch; you didn't go dancing through a city stirring dust-clouds and striking unlikable people with lightning."

"Sometimes you are entirely too innocent," Puss groused.

"Maybe they'd be more lenient, but I'm not well liked." Angelique gathered up an armful of her skirts so she could run easier. "Or rather, I'm not liked *at all*."

"Here we go." Puss skidded to a stop, digging his paws in so he left tiny trenches in the gravel-strewn path. "Between these bushes."

Gabrielle pushed a bush aside and yanked on the lever. "This will pull a grate up—the gardeners have to clear it out of greenery every year, so it can only be toggled on this side."

Angelique stared at the gap in the wall—which was about as large as a stool—as the rusty grate that crossed was slowly raised parallel to the wall. "I'm honored you think I'm slender enough to fit through there, but you may overestimate me," she said doubtfully. "Though on the positive side, if I *can* squeeze through, Finnr certainly won't be able to."

"Now is not the time for your inappropriate sense of humor," Puss snarled. "Just get through the wall and go summon your snooty constellation!"

"Stop!" a deep, rumbling voice shouted.

"He's here." Gabrielle swiveled so she faced Finnr, her hand edging towards her sword.

Angelique dropped to her knees. *"Don't* fight him!" She poked her head through the hole, scooting into an awkward angle to push her shoulders through.

"What am I supposed to do? We can't just let him chase you," Gabrielle said.

Puss growled deep in his throat and hissed. "He's getting closer, Angelique. Hurry!"

Angelique heard footfalls as she wiggled her hips through. She clawed at the ground, dragging herself free. *Why is it that enchantresses have to wear beautiful dresses and float around like flowers on the wind? What's wrong with trousers and a good belt?*

The second she pulled free, Gabrielle toggled the grate, so it crashed back into place.

Angelique pressed herself against the wall and crouched down in the dry gutter so she could partially peer through the grate, watching Finnr jog into view with a stormy expression.

"I said *stop*," he rumbled. "And you aided in her escape?"

"You wanted to speak to Angelique?" Gabrielle asked, her voice warm and innocent. "Whatever for?"

Angelique grinned and heaved herself to her feet before she started running through the backstreets of the city.

She followed the wall that separated the palace from the city, starting the trek to the city gate.

"You—Apprentice Angelique!"

Angelique twisted to look behind her, groaning when she saw Finnr's short and squat companion. *They must have split up for this very reason.*

Angelique again grabbed at her skirts and ran, twisting through back alleys.

"Stop—by the law of the Veneno Conclave!" the man shouted.

He slowly closed in on her—drawing Angelique's irritation.

After all of the physical training Evariste shoved at me, I would have thought I'd be able to outpace him! Sheer determination drove her up a quiet street, even as her lungs burned. *Instead, I meet the human equivalent of a horse!*

Finally, she started to hear the hustle and bustle of the main street that divided the city in half and went from the central gate to the palace entrance.

Angelique zipped in that direction, narrowly dodging when he lunged forward in an attempt to grab at her.

She shot into the main road, frightening a few caged ducks and barely avoiding an oncoming ox cart.

"Angelique—stop!" the mage ordered.

Angelique cast about for an appropriate spell. *I can't do anything harmful—for both him and the city's sake, but what would—oh.*

She'd done the spell enough times that her powers sprang readily into the necessary form. She whispered a few words in the language of magic, then turned around and stabbed a finger at the oncoming mage.

Abruptly, the main road was an eruption of chickens. White ones, gold ones, dark red ones, black ones—chickens of all size, shape, and color filled the street, making it impossible to hear with their clucking. Their heads wobbled on skinny necks while they studied the world with bugged eyes.

A bunch of them gathered around the feet of Angelique's chaser—pecking at his shins and tripping him as they continuously jostled to be underfoot.

Angelique would have laughed if the situation were any different, but she settled for a quick grin before she hurried on, running down the street. *Puss will be horrified when he finds out that move was actually useful.*

She threaded her way through the busy street, panting in a very unseemly manner by the time she burst out of the city. She had paused for a moment to suck in more air when she thought she heard a faint, "*Stop—Apprentice Angelique!*"

The cry threw her into action again, so she shouted, "Pegasus! It is I..." When she turned around and saw the short, squat mage about a block down, the rest of the reverent speech fled from her memory. "It's me, Angelique, I need a ride—*now*!"

Before she could finish babbling, Pegasus answered.

In the blink of an eye, he crashed to the ground—not in his usual grand and fancy way, but in a ball of blue flames and a crash that made a *crater* in the ground.

Ooohh, Puss is going to complain about that, too.

Pegasus' black wings were still attached to his shoulders, and the blue flames that danced at his hooves hadn't gone out yet, but Angelique awkwardly threw herself onto his back, struggling through the material of her skirts to sling her leg over his back.

"*Angelique!*"

Pegasus snorted and turned tightly as his black wings started to disintegrate. He swiveled to face the oncoming mage, snorting and pawing at the ground.

"No, no, no, no." Angelique recognized the signs of his rage, even as she got a face full of his black feathers. "We're not attacking; we're fleeing. *We're* the villains here—wait." She paused at the rather ungraceful framing of her explanation, but Pegasus brought her back with a slight crowhop that threw her onto his neck but also slid her into place on his back.

He took off at a gallop, the last few feathers of his wings spiraling away as they fled Castle Brandis.

AFTER A SHORT STOP on the Loire/Arcainia border to send off her response to Enchanter Clovicus (it only took a few moments to fold the letter into the butterfly spell that would make it mobile and self-delivering) Angelique headed northwest, to Verglas.

Verglas was a land of cold. Its people risked hard winters with abundant snow and ice but were repaid with beautiful summers, plentiful rivers fed from mountain glaciers, and safety. For Verglas had been the home of the Snow Queen—the first enchantress ever who had imbedded her magic into her country, forever safeguarding it from any dark and malicious magic and from the enemies she had fought: The Chosen.

Unfortunately, the magic couldn't guard the people from their ruler. King Torgen was known to be mad, but the land was gentle and the water was sweet, making the country idyllic despite its crazed monarch.

Angelique spent more time in Verglas than she wanted to, mostly *looking* for Elise and her seven swan brothers. After she finally found them in the early evening hours—witnessing the brothers' temporary return to normalcy due to the crack in the curse—she explained to them the failure that was the attack on Clotilde and the intricacies of their altered curse.

I think I'm beginning to understand why Gabrielle and Puss were also against using romantic love to break this curse, Angelique mused as she watched the seven princes of Arcainia argue.

All of them were fair haired, handsome, and *excessively* opinionated on whether their foster-sister should or should not attempt to break the curse by knitting shirts of stinging nettles. It was fairly hard to tell them apart in the glittering moonlight—though their varying heights and builds helped some.

Angelique sighed and pushed her locks of hair—which had tumbled free of her pinned hairstyle during her run from Castle Brandis—over her shoulder. She was positive she had at least a brush or two of dirt on her cheeks—though her dress was spotless.

Evariste must have really spelled this gown straight to its seams. Her faint smile fell from her lips at the thought of him, and she took a breath, forcing her attention back to the conversation.

Elise's eyes were furrowed, and she looked thoughtful as her brothers chattered around her.

Yep, she will attempt to break the curse—regardless of what they decide for her.

Angelique gently placed her hand on Elise's shoulder, drawing the princess' attention so she could speak in a quieter tone. "There is one small consolation I can give you," Angelique said. "For the hour your brothers are human, you may speak. But *only* when they are human. If you utter a single word—even if it is while they make the switch from swan to prince—your work will be ruined." She tried to put a warm smile on her lips, but in the privacy of her thoughts she knew Elise faced a monumental task.

Elise's cloudy expression cleared. "Thank you."

Angelique shifted a step closer to Elise, making it easier to hear over the quarreling princes. "You will do it, then?"

"Yes."

Angelique tried to give the princess the kind of warning a benevolent fairy godmother might give. "Be careful. One of the princes mentioned the dangers of being voiceless and without human aid. He spoke the truth. Verglas is free of evil magic, but it has its share of bandits and brutes."

"Wouldn't it be safer in another country?" Elise asked.

Angelique shook her head. "No. Verglas is still safest. It offers you protection from Clotilde and any vile magic she may have up her sleeve. No evil or tainted magic can breech the borders of Verglas. It has been so for centuries."

Elise set her shoulders. "Then we will remain here," she said in a soft but determined tone.

Angelique's smile returned as she observed the stubborn set of the princess' chin. *I suspect—no—I believe she's going to succeed. She seems determined, and I suppose any princess who can survive these seven patience-trying-brothers must have her fair share of guts.* "I suggest you travel east, and a little farther north. There is a bigger pond there that is more hospitable for humans. It also has a large number of stinging nettles in the forest that borders it," Angelique said, trying to keep the wryness out of her voice.

"I thank you for your wise council," Elise said.

Whether it was her exhaustion or general moroseness that the Conclave had sent mages after her, a snort—the sort she'd never use in public—slipped from her. "It is hardly wise. I circled it about five times when I couldn't find you. I had to release the weakened curse and watch which way it went," she admitted.

"I don't understand what you mean. The curse wasn't instantly weakened when you fought Clotilde?" Elise asked.

"It was, but magic—just like everything else—takes time to cover distance. There's only one kind of magic that allows for instantaneous travel, and those able to wield such a power are rare." A pang that was becoming increasingly familiar stabbed Angelique's chest, but she ignored it and continued. "As such, the broken curse ambled along with me as I sought you out," Angelique explained.

Rather, I ran into its magical trail while attempting to tail Elise, but then we get into magical theory I don't believe she truly cares about.

"I'm afraid I don't understand, but I shall take your word for it," Elise said. "Thank you, Lady Enchantress. You do not owe us your help, and I don't know if we will ever be able to repay you."

The thanks almost made Angelique cringe—for if she had been better, if she was more skilled, she could have stopped Clotilde. But there was no judgement in Elise's eyes, only gratitude.

Unbidden, another smile rose to Angelique's lips—though this one was perhaps too true in its sadness. "I know what it is like to lose someone dear to you as the result of an enchantment. I am glad I can help you reclaim your father and foster brothers," she said.

Elise bobbed in a curtsey. "Thank you."

Angelique tucked her hand under Elise's chin, making the princess meet Angelique's gaze and stopping her from showing any additional-and-not-strictly-required signs of respect. "This is a burden they are placing on you, Princess. But I think you underestimate how important you are to them."

Angelique meant to say more, but there was a numb feeling at her fingertips; the sharp sensation of her magic that constantly slithered across her body since she let it be free was muted. *What is that?* She slipped her hand out from under Elise's chin and stared at her fingers.

"Lady Enchantress?" Elise ventured.

Does Elise have magic? But that's impossible—a fairy godmother or godfather would have found her well before now—they search Arcainia carefully due to the magic ban on it. And it should be impossible for the princess to hide it. But...she did avoid Clotilde's curse for unknown reasons. Angelique shook herself. "Something to think about." She headed back to Pegasus, digging into the saddlebag she had purchased when she stopped to send off her letter. "You cannot wear your uniform. Arcainian work uniforms are impossible to miss, and it will mark you out in a country of cut-throats. Here are some clothes that will suit you better." She plucked a burlap bag from the saddlebag and passed it over to the princess.

"Thank you." Elise peered down at her dress, which—even in the dimness of dusk—was clearly ripped and tattered.

The eldest prince—Steffen, whom Angelique only vaguely knew because of his marriage to Gabrielle—disengaged from the brothers' argument and stood with Elise. "We thank you for your aid, Lady Enchantress. When this is all over, if there is anything we can do for you, please do not hesitate to call on us," he said.

Angelique climbed onto Pegasus' broad back. "Thank you," she said. "I wish you all luck."

She paused—because this seemed to be the ideal time in the conversation to spout typical vague and useless warnings higher-level mages seemed prone to say upon departure. "Be on your guard, but do not fear Clotilde. Evil can never win for long. Farewell."

Steffen and Elise, the only two noticing her departure, bowed and curtsied.

"Goodbye."

"Thank you, Lady Enchantress."

Angelique acknowledged their farewells with the flick of her hand as Pegasus trotted into the dark and shadowy forest. *Next, to Erlauf. Hopefully Enchanter Clovicus will know what to do about Clotilde...and the Veneno Conclave.*

CHAPTER 15

With Pegasus as her mount, Angelique reached Erlauf well before she could expect Enchanter Clovicus to arrive. But it gave her time to pick an inn at which to stay where she likely would *not* be recognized, and to ensure the pub where she had asked Clovicus to meet her wasn't frequented by mages. (It was not.)

As such, when Clovicus finally arrived, Angelique was seated at a table, comfortably sipping her pint.

Clovicus entered with a bemused sort of smile, his eyebrow arching when he saw her. "The Dragon's Roar?" he said, naming the pub. "You have interesting taste."

Angelique blinked, then frowned a little. "I tried to choose a location I thought mages would not visit."

The enchanter snorted. "There are *a lot* of pubs mages wouldn't set foot in. I just find it interesting that the one you chose is a known military favorite."

The Dragon's Roar—whether in respect or an attempt to curry favor with its clientele—was swathed with Erlauf colors—gray and a deep shade of burgundy. The furniture was plain but clean and comfortable. Everything was vaguely square in shape, but there were cushions aplenty, and on top of every table was a tiny metal dragon.

Erlauf flags hung from nearly every wall. The country's crest—a burgundy dragon—was fashioned out of glass and hung by every window, and perhaps what was most telling was the large, padded space cleared at the far end of the room...just in case a physical demonstration was necessary.

(Erlauf was renowned for its army. Its officers were, socially speaking, more powerful than the country's nobles, although most sons of nobility ended up enrolling.)

Slightly confused by Clovicus' words, Angelique scanned the pub again. *I don't understand. It's clean and quiet at this hour, and the food and drink are decent considering the prices.*

A few soldiers were seated in one corner—easily recognizable by the gray and burgundy of their uniforms and their swallow-tail jackets.

Another group was on the opposite side of the pub, for although they lacked the uniform, Angelique could tell they were soldiers from the way they stood, spoke, and crowded around a table comparing three different types of swords like old ladies swapping recipes.

Clovicus seated himself across from her and arched his eyebrow even higher—if that was possible. "I have good news to share. The Veneno Conclave no longer has a warrant out for you."

Angelique frowned in her surprise. "Why not?"

Clovicus leaned back in his seat and motioned for the barmaid to bring him a pint, then rested his hands on the table. "It was an automatic measure put on you by workers as soon as your magic was reported in Arcainia. I couldn't stop the initial warrant going out, but I spent two days talking them out of it before resorting to the Council," he snorted.

"...I beg your pardon?"

"It wasn't too terribly hard. Once I made it clear to the Council you used your magic to fight a witch who had cursed the princes, that gave the Conclave something else to be upset about. Tristisim and Felicienne in particular aren't happy with you, but they were more angry with that Clotilde woman you wrote about and understood the situation once it was explained to them—and their ruddy officials," Clovicus grunted.

"So the Conclave is going to do something about her?" Angelique asked.

"Eventually, some day." Clovicus sighed—though he broke it off to give the barmaid a charming smile when she delivered his pint. "Before they act, they plan to send couriers out to other countries, so they are aware the Conclave is acting on behalf of Arcainia and that it is not a show of favoritism but for the benefit of all. Of course, they'll have to wait back for responses, and already it is suspected King Giuseppe of Sole is going to complain given that the Conclave hasn't done much for his cursed granddaughter, Princess Rosalinda."

"In other words, this could take some weeks," Angelique said.

"Months, probably," Clovicus predicted.

"And Arcainia will suffer in the meanwhile." Angelique traced the rim of her mug.

"The Veneno Conclave's strength lies in its size. It gives them the ability to do large things and achieve peace with the greater power backing it," Clovicus said. "Unfortunately, its size is also its greatest weakness as it takes a great deal to get the Conclave moving."

"Am I still in trouble, then?" Angelique asked.

Clovicus scratched his strong jaw as he considered her words. "Not if you keep a low profile. I'd recommend you stay away from the Veneno Conclave and avoid seeing other mages. The less you can remind them of what they view as your transgressions, the better. Even if the warrant was redacted, it doesn't mean another mage won't feel duty bound to drag you back to the Veneno Conclave fortress for a forceful lecture."

Angelique held in a frown. "I was hoping to recruit other

mages—or even enchanters and enchantresses—to attack Clotilde."

Clovicus snorted after taking a swig of his Erlauf beer. "You probably could have...if you had *contacted me* to say you were intending to attack Clotilde. As it is, I have been in damage control, painting you as a worried lady enchantress rather than willfully disobeying Conclave law. With the Council as angry as it is, most highly ranked mages are going to be reluctant to jump into these political matters."

Angelique nodded slightly. "I apologize."

Clovicus waved her off. "Just know that next time—because you seem unusually prone towards walking into these kinds of situations—if you send me a letter, I can smooth things out for you *before* they start taking unnecessary offense at your actions. It's given me a taste of what Evariste endured with your unusual... shall we call it...luck?"

Properly scolded, Angelique peered into her half-empty mug. "It is my fault and my short-coming. Next time I will do better."

His head half-tilted, Clovicus studied her for a few long moments before his expression shifted into a relaxed and barely-there grin. "It wasn't too much trouble. You're an excellent apprentice—the Council's blindness is not your doing. Besides, Evariste was *far worse* than you've ever been."

Angelique straightened in her chair. "But Evariste was a prodigy."

"And the nosiest brat I had ever come across." Clovicus set his pint down with an emphatic thump. "Being a prodigy made him greatly admired at Luxi-Domus. By the time he came to me, his head was so big his skinny neck could barely keep it upright."

Angelique felt her eyes pop from her head. "I don't believe...*really?*"

Clovicus' smile deepened into a smirk. "On the first day of his lessons, we covered weather magic. He informed me he knew all about twisting his core magic into other types of magic. I pointed out he had never done it."

Angelique leaned closer as she tried to picture a young Evariste. "What happened?"

Clovicus shrugged. "He was insistent he knew what he was doing, so I told him if he was so confident, he should make an attempt. He struck himself with lightning and then passed out when he couldn't figure out how to stop channeling his magic into the spell."

A bark of laughter escaped Angelique before she guiltily slapped a hand over her mouth.

Clovicus chuckled. "You *should* laugh—me laughing is the only way the little monster made it through his first month of training instead of getting strangled in the middle of the night." He shook his head. "After that incident, he was a little better about listening to me—though in recent years he *still* willfully ignores me. I don't understand why, for it always comes back to bite him." He rolled his eyes, but Angelique could tell the second he remembered Evariste was gone, for some of the light went out of his eyes.

A moment or two passed before Angelique awkwardly cleared her throat. *I guess it's my turn to say something.* "He was lucky to have you as a teacher."

"Maybe," Clovicus said. "During his first year with me, he didn't know his boundaries, and his previous instructors and fellow students had talked him up so much, he thought he could do anything." Clovicus narrowed his eyes as he studied Angelique. "He was the opposite of you. Your previous instructors urged you to use restraint or to lock up your magic altogether, even though you are just as powerful as he is. Perhaps more so."

Angelique shook her head. "Given how miserably I've been failing at magic lately—failing to defeat Clotilde, taking months to get that advanced location spell to work—I am beginning to doubt I am as powerful as believed."

"You're confusing power with experience," Clovicus said.

"Even after their apprenticeship, nearly every Enchanter or Enchantress is practically useless for a decade or two until they have more experience. Living with Evariste has perhaps misled you there. The truth is, Angelique, you were tossed into an ocean after Evariste left. It's impressive that you've been able to think on your feet fast enough to react, much less keep yourself from getting killed in your encounters."

"Perhaps," Angelique reluctantly said.

"You said in your message Clotilde had two artifacts—you had no way of predicting that given their rarity. It was a mistake even I likely would have made," Clovicus added.

Angelique watched a pair of soldiers demonstrate a grappling hold. "Perhaps," she repeated.

"Speaking of Arcainia, is there no way for its people to take care of Clotilde on their own?" Clovicus asked.

Angelique slowly shook her head. "I don't believe so. As you said, magical artifacts are rare and powerful, and the black diamonds Clotilde used...." She mashed her lips together and stared at her mug. "There is one possibility, though it's a long shot."

"Oh? Do share," Clovicus prompted.

"It's Elise—the foster-daughter of King Henrik. I think she *might* have magic, and it might possibly be a kind that either reflects or deadens another mage's powers."

Clovicus whistled. "Rare stuff. And powerful."

"I can't say for certain that she has it. I'm not quite sensitive enough to gauge another mage's magic," Angelique said. "But it seems rather unlikely given her age and her home country."

Clovicus shook his head. "Not necessarily. Rumor has it Ingrid sought her out and made her the royal foster-child. Though the Veneno Conclave required that Ingrid set her title of Enchantress aside and refrain from using her magic in Arcainia when she married Henrik, she had some natural foresight magic. I imagine she didn't pick Elise out on a whim."

The soldiers who were still demonstrating wrestling skills staggered away from the cleared area.

Angelique, seeing that they were stumbling in their general direction, lifted her mug off the table. "What do you recommend I do, then?" she asked.

"Track down Sybilla," Clovicus advised. "If you describe what you felt, she'll have a better idea—it's her specialty, after all." Both of his eyebrows arched when the wrestlers jostled into their table, spilling some of Clovicus' drink.

"Sorry," one of the soldiers watching from the other side of the room called.

Angelique waved her hand at them and set her mug back down. "I'll do that, thank you. Do you know where she is?"

"She'll be coming through Erlauf this summer." Clovicus bemusedly stared at the puddle of his drink until Angelique swiped a rag off a nearby table and tossed it to him. "Thank you."

"No, it is I who must thank you," Angelique said. "I shall follow your advice and track down Sybilla."

He nodded. "Wise of you. I think that covers everything. Except for the regular platitudes—be careful, watch yourself, and all of that." He waved his hand to express the general nebula of farewells, then furrowed his brow. "How much does a drink cost here? I only have gold coins on me."

"I'll pay," Angelique said dryly. "They aren't going to have change for that." She tossed the necessary coins on the table as she stood, nodding to the soldiers who leaped to their feet and bowed slightly to her.

Clovicus prowled after her, chuckling. "It's interesting what you can tell about a person by the places that make them comfortable." He lazily stretched his arms above his head as they left the pub.

It was raining, so Angelique scooted to the side so they could stay under the overhang of the pub's roof. "What do you mean by that?" She mentally reviewed the contents of the pub, before freezing. "If you think I chose this place because it had bladed weapons—"

"I think no such thing," Clovicus snorted. "You chose that place because you are rather like a soldier yourself."

"My father was a soldier," Angelique corrected.

"Mmhmm, and you are certainly your father's daughter." He winked and smiled roguishly.

Angelique expressionlessly stared at him. *I guess Clovicus not only taught Evariste magic but also the charm he uses on ladies of all ages. How enlightening. I wonder if he is the reason Evariste is so keen on embraces?*

"Why do I get the feeling you are judging me?" Clovicus asked.

"I would never presume, Lord Enchanter," Angelique said.

"Mmhmm." The enchanter peered up at the cloudy sky.

Angelique studied him as she carefully selected her words. Strictly speaking, there was nothing more they needed to discuss, and she was almost afraid to ask what she really wanted to know... "Have you been able to find anything that might help the search for Evariste? I'm aware you might not have had much time given the situation I caused."

Clovicus sighed. "It doesn't look good," he said.

Angelique's heart fell. "In what way?"

"According to what little information I've been able to scare up, sealing someone inside a mirror takes a great deal of power. Getting Evariste out is going to be difficult. Even worse, as long as he is stranded, whoever put him there can use him as they will—most commonly the victim is milked for their magic, but it can also be a method of...torture."

Angelique's heart plummeted to her feet. "No."

Clovicus shifted his weight and stared out into the street. "There is one thing that might help us."

Angelique could barely lift her head. "And that is?"

"No normal mirror can be used for this purpose," Clovicus said. "It has to be a mirror capable of holding or using magic."

"So...a magic mirror, like the one Prince Severin of Loire owns," Angelique said.

Clovicus nodded. "Or something similar. Magic mirrors that can be used to find or watch a person are not the only kind of enchanted looking glass there is."

"I see. That does narrow the target quite a bit," Angelique agreed. "Thank you for researching it."

Clovicus nodded. "Since you'll be in Erlauf searching for Sybilla, you might want to investigate a rumor I heard about magic glass."

Angelique blinked. "Magic glass?"

"Yes—I'm not sure if it means there is a magic looking-glass or just glass capable of holding enchantments, but I've heard a few rumors of such an item coming out of Trieux—or what used to be Trieux, I guess, but is now Erlauf territory." Clovicus gave her a sharp look. "It's just a rumor. I wouldn't put much stock in it, but even if it's only a store that produces glass capable of holding magic, they may be able to tell you other craftsmen who can build similar things."

"I agree; it is a helpful start," Angelique said. *Far better than wandering about like a lost bard, asking after magical mirrors. That practically shouts to the world my intensions and makes it easy to set a trap for me.* She tried to think practically about it, but a smile threatened to bloom on her cheeks.

Finally, she had a lead!

"I'll let you know if I find anything more," Clovicus said. "Take care, Angelique. And don't take too many risks."

Angelique nodded automatically and was surprised when Clovicus flicked her on the forehead.

"I mean it," he said. "If you hurt yourself, Evariste will be devastated." Though his words sounded like a private joke, his voice was steady and his expression serious. He nodded once at her before he strode off into the street, effortlessly throwing up a spell that blocked the rain so it trickled around him and didn't so much as dampen the hem of his robes.

Angelique frowned slightly. *I never know quite what to make of him*, she thought. *But at least I have a clear idea of what my next move is. I need to find Sybilla and check into that rumor of magic glass.*

THE HOOD of Angelique's cloak threatened to slide off her head. Angelique tugged it down as she strolled through the marketplace of Werra—or Arroux, as it used to be called under Trieux rule. There was the typical market fare for a city as large as Werra: produce, livestock, ceramics, carpentry, and more. Unfortunately, there were no stalls for glass workers.

I've already talked to the two glassmakers in the city, and they assured me they knew nothing of magic glass. But all the rumors I heard insisted an object of magic glass was in Werra.

A slight breeze stirred Angelique's cloak—which would have been stifling if not for the charms worked into her gown. She wore the cloak not for warmth or shelter—for it was sunny and not a single cloud lingered in the sky—but to at least partially hide her face.

She had run into two mages during her search for Sybilla and the fabled magic glass. Neither of the meetings were particularly pleasant—though only one of the mages threatened to tell the Veneno Conclave where she was so she could be properly "schooled." The other merely fled, though Angelique was fairly certain he had tattled her location, for she narrowly missed running into Mage Finnr and his stout companion not a few days later.

I don't know that Clovicus cleared my name as well as he thought— for could it really be a coincidence that brought Finnr through Erlauf at the same time?

Angelique stopped in front of a stall selling bright yellow flowers. She turned a circle—trying to see any sign of glasswork, and sighed. *Nothing.*

"May I help you, Mademoiselle?"

Angelique rotated to face the flower stall, blinking a little when she saw the woman who was addressing her.

Her voice sounded more sophisticated than the haggling folk around her, and she held herself with accustomed grace.

"I apologize—I'm blocking your stall," Angelique said.

"Not at all, Mademoiselle. But can I help you? You seem as though you are looking for something," the woman said.

Angelique mashed her lips together and nodded. "Yes, I heard rumors of magic glass here in Werra. I'm trying to find it."

"Magic glass," the woman repeated slowly. "Yes, I might know what you speak of."

Angelique brightened. "Truly?"

The woman nodded. "There is a cobbler's shop past the market, up two streets. It has a pair of magic glass shoes—the likes of which none have seen. The glass itself is enchanted, for the shoes are able to support human weight and are said to be comfortable. They caused quite an uproar when the cobbler displayed them, but of course no one of Trieux can afford them, and such a thing would never interest someone from Erlauf."

CHAPTER 16

Angelique's heart fell. *Ahhh, yes. That makes sense why I could never confirm if the glass was a mirror.* She should have known better than to hope by now, but the disappointment still left a bitter taste in her mouth. She rolled her shoulders back and tried to bolster her sagging spirits. *But the shoes must be forged out of special glass to hold an enchantment, so I had better follow through. The cobbler might be willing to reveal his supplier.*

"I see," Angelique said. "Thank you for your help. By chance, do you happen to know if a fairy godmother has been through Werra?"

The woman shook her head. "I apologize, Mademoiselle, but I have heard of no such rumor."

"No, there is nothing to apologize for. Rather, I must express my thanks for your aid." Angelique smiled—though it felt a little forced in her disappointment. "Good day to you."

"Good day, Mademoiselle."

Angelique made her way through the market, heading in the direction the woman had indicated. *I'll follow this lead, and then perhaps make a discreet appeal to the palace. I've been receiving invitations to this victory ball Queen Freja is soon throwing at the former*

Trieux palace since the day I arrived. If palace officials are aware I'm present, then perhaps they will know if Sybilla is as well.

Angelique reached the edge of the market where she narrowly missed colliding with a person who swept around the side of a stall. (She would have smacked straight into the woman if her years of combat practice hadn't made her jerk backwards at the last moment.)

"I beg your pardon." Angelique busied her hands with brushing off her cloak so as to hide the faint flicker of magic that had leaped to her fingertips at the possibility of a threat. She shoved her magic down. *I'm fine. There's no need to be so jumpy.*

"No, not at all, the fault was all mine...Angelique?"

Angelique looked up and felt the blood drain from her face. *Perhaps I'm not so fine after all.* "Hello, Lady Enchantress Lovelana."

"Apprentice Angelique, greetings." The beautiful enchantress nodded politely. "I didn't expect to see you here."

Angelique furrowed her brow quizzically.

"I heard about your experience in Arcainia," she supplied.

"Ah, yes. Well, Clovicus took the matter to the Council and explained everything," Angelique said.

"I see." Lovelana nodded.

Angelique bit the inside of her cheek as she tried to gauge the enchantress' reaction. Lovelana was infatuated with Evariste, which meant she inherently was not warm to Angelique. (Oddly, it seemed all women who fancied Evariste shared the feeling. Angelique could never grasp why. She was Evariste's student, not his partner. And Angelique would have gladly used her insider knowledge of Evariste's life to forge connections with the other females if she hadn't thought they'd hiss at her for suggesting such a thing.)

Lovelana, however, had softened some after Evariste was kidnapped. She was the enchantress in charge of the committee that searched for Evariste, so it was important to stay on polite terms with her.

But is she feeling polite enough that I can inquire after the committee's activities? Angelique nudged her hood off and straightened. "Do you have a lead you're following in locating Lord Enchanter Evariste?"

Lovelana slightly pursed her lips. "Not just yet. In reviewing all cases of reported black mages, the committee uncovered four abandoned shops and workrooms. One of my agents did capture a black mage in Loire, but he has barely any skill and received his orders by paper. Though he's been questioned extensively, he knew nothing besides the locations of a shop—which was already closed by the time we uncovered it."

"You're still going through old reports?" Angelique asked.

Lovelana smiled. "Yes."

"Have you spoken to Prince Severin and Prince Lucien about the night Prince Severin was cursed?" Angelique asked.

Lovelana shook her head. "No. Given that the prince was cursed after Evariste was captured, it was determined the two events were unrelated."

"Then what about Arcainia?" Angelique asked. "Clotilde—the woman King Henrik married—is clearly a witch of some variation. She cursed the Arcainian princes with two artifacts."

"I left the Conclave before details of your excursion were fully reported." Lovelana's voice was perhaps a little stiffer now. "I'm heading north to Farset next so I won't be able to look into Arcainia just yet. But if it is as you say, I imagine the Council will dispatch someone else to take care of it."

Angelique wasn't so convinced, but she could see what little rapport she had with Lovelana was fading fast. "Yes, I suppose you're right," she agreed—even though she was hardly convinced. "Where are you coming from?"

I bet she was investigating the Ringsted storms—though it would make more sense to send a weather mage there.

"Torrens," Lovelana supplied.

Angelique blinked. Torrens was where she and Evariste lived. (Or *had* lived, as a twitch in her chest reminded her.) "Oh?"

"Yes. According to our reports, many years ago, there used to be several black mages who lived in Torrens but have since gone missing. I went to investigate the facts."

Angelique smiled mildly when she really wanted to groan. *Of course they went missing. King Channing married warrior queen Lisheva from Baris! The year they were married, she went and hunted all those mages down for the fun of it! How does no one know this?* Angelique held in a sigh. *The committee is never going to find Evariste if they are investigating incidents that old.*

"Did you find anything of note?" Angelique was proud she kept her tone inquisitive rather than snappy.

"Alas, no. It seems the Royal Family took care of the mages long ago, so there was nothing to uncover." Lovelana slightly tilted her head back as she studied Angelique. "And what brings you here to Erlauf? I would have assumed you would be prepping for your evaluations."

"I cannot take my enchantress examinations until Evariste is found," Angelique reminded her.

"Oh, I suppose I forgot that. Why, then, are you here?" Lovelana asked.

Angelique weighed her options. *Given the rather narrowed look she's giving me, now is likely not the best time to inform her that I'm searching for Evariste myself.* Angelique straightened slightly. "I'm searching for Fairy Godmother Sybilla, actually. Do you know if she's in the area?"

Lovelana tapped her lips. "No, I don't believe so. But we only arrived this morning."

"We?" Angelique asked.

"Yes, Mage Finnr, Mage Walf, and myself. Mage Finnr and Mage Walf were sent to accompany me on my travels out of fear that black mages might be targeting all enchantresses," Lovelana said.

Angelique blinked very slowly. *Finnr? Out of all people, Finnr is here? And how much money could I make if I bet Walf is his stout companion who came after me at Castle Brandis?* "Is that so?" she finally managed to say. "Well, I shouldn't waste any more of your time. Thank you for all your work." She started edging away.

"Oh, and there's Finnr!" Lovelana smiled beautifully as she looked beyond Angelique—who was now scooting at double the pace.

That's just my luck—grump-face himself is here. Lovely, just lovely. Angelique positioned herself so she could easily flee up the street and angled herself so she could keep an eye on Finnr as he approached.

The daunting man bowed slightly and muttered, "Lady Enchantress." He rocked to a stop when he saw Angelique. "Apprentice," he said in a deep and icy voice.

Angelique sucked a breath in and made her smile even bigger. "Why *hello*, Mage Finnr! Fancy meeting you here!"

Finnr narrowed his eyes slightly and spread his fingers wide.

Yep, it is necessary to get out of here quickly if I don't want Finnr to ponder whether or not the Council would like to talk to me regardless of the warrant being canceled.

"It was such a lovely time to see both of you, but if you excuse me, I *must* be leaving," Angelique said. "Lady Enchantress, Mage Finnr." She was in the process of scurrying away when Mage Finnr called after her.

"If you wish to avoid such unpleasantries in the future, Apprentice, you'd be wise to more carefully choose your actions."

Angelique stopped mid-step and swung around. "I beg your pardon?"

"Arcainia," he said. "You need not fear other mages if you acted according to the law."

Perhaps, but the law didn't account for a power-hungry witch who enchanted a king and attempted to kill his children! And even if I hadn't done it, I'd still fear other mages because other mages fear me! Though the sarcasm burned in her throat, Angelique didn't let it claw free. "Mmm," she said.

Lovelana frowned delicately. "What were you doing in Arcainia at that time anyway? And why are you now here in Erlauf?"

That line of questions does not *bode well for me. Escape!*

Angelique threw on a smile, acting as if she hadn't heard the question. "I wish you both luck in your endeavors!" She waved wildly and skipped off, hurrying up the street at a fast pace she knew Lovelana would not attempt to match.

She only looked over her shoulder twice to confirm Finnr wasn't following her before she found the cobbler's shop that the flower vender had mentioned.

It was a tiny shop with walls lined in varying styles, colors, and sizes of shoes. Though they had everything from beaded ladies' slippers to leather riding boots, there was barely enough room for the cobbler—a short, scrawny elderly man who had a mustache so long it nearly touched his chest. He peered through tinted glasses as he tapped away on the sole of a beautiful boot.

As there was no room for customers, the store instead had three large, open-air windows through which customers could inspect goods and haggle with the cobbler's apprentice—a young lady with lovely, russet brown hair and a spattering of freckles that made her appear innocent even though her eyes sparkled with intelligence.

"Good day, Mademoiselle," the apprentice greeted as she eyed Angelique's dress—probably trying to gauge her position. "How may I help you?"

"I heard rumors throughout Erlauf of magic glass and was told by a flower vendor you have shoes made of such a thing?"

The apprentice tilted her head. "Ahhh yes, you must have spoken to Vitore—she minds the market stall that belongs to Duchess Cinderella of Aveyron. I know just what she meant."

"Duchess Cinderella? I thought all Trieux nobles were deposed in the Erlauf take over," Angelique said.

The apprentice shook her head as she retrieved a wooden chest from under a counter. "No—a few families were allowed to keep their titles and powers. Our Duchess Cinderella Lacreux is one of them."

Lacreux—I don't believe I met any Trieux nobles by that name, but it sounds familiar.

The apprentice dug a necklace from the shirt of her dress, revealing a key that she stuck into the locked chest. "Mademoiselle Cinderella is a marvel, for she cast off her riches and now works her lands with her servants." The lock clicked.

Ahhh, yes, that is how I have heard the name. I heard rumors in Erlauf of the scarlet-haired duchess who works as a servant, yet owns more land than anyone in Erlauf.

"Here, this is what Vitore spoke of when she mentioned shoes of glass." The apprentice reached into the small chest and pulled out a pair of glass slippers, which she set down in front of Angelique.

They were multifaceted to make them sparkle more like diamonds than true glass. Even as she stared at them, a rainbow hue seemed to glide up and down the shoe. Tiny roses were etched into the toe and heel of the slippers, and if Angelique stared long enough, she could have sworn the petals actually *moved.*

They were breathtaking.

The detail and craftsmanship—Angelique had never seen anything like them! *Perhaps they will be able to help me, if they're able to create something like this!*

"They're stunning." Angelique tapped the toe of one with her finger. "Your master must be very skilled to make them."

The apprentice shifted slightly. "Y-yes..."

"I never thought mankind was capable of making such a thing—it clearly does have magic encased in it, though I'm not sure how." Angelique lifted up one of the shoes to further inspect it.

The apprentice bit her lip. "Are you a mage, Mademoiselle?" When Angelique glanced at the girl, she gestured to Angelique's dress—which was changing from a light green to a bright aqua. "It is merely your gown..."

Angelique smiled and set the shoe down. "Yes, I am an Enchantress-in-Training."

The girl's eyes widened. "*Enchantress?*"

"Indeed. I am in search of magic glass—or perhaps someone capable of producing magic glass—so I hope you are able to help me."

The apprentice scratched the back of her neck. "Ah, my master will not be willing to part with any trade secrets, I am sorry to say."

"Could you tell me your supplier of the glass?" Angelique asked. "I'm not seeking to make goods of my own; rather, I'm trying to track down a particular mirror."

The apprentice bit her lip, then glanced over her shoulder at the old cobbler. Keeping her voice lowered, she leaned across the counter so she could murmur, "Then you should know, Lady Enchantress, my master did not make these shoes."

"Oh," Angelique said. "Then could you tell me who did?"

The apprentice shook her head. "I'm afraid not—because we don't know."

Angelique blinked. "What."

"One evening, we closed up shop and went to bed, and when we woke up the next day, these slippers were in the shop," the apprentice said. "There were no signs of forced entry, and nothing was taken."

Angelique frowned so deeply her forehead wrinkled. "Nothing?"

"Not even a crumb of food." The apprentice shook her head. "It's the strangest thing."

"Yes," Angelique agreed. *It can't be a black mage's work*, Angelique pondered as she set the slipper down. *But who—besides a mage—has the magic to go around making shoes like these? I'd say it resembles elf work, but they haven't left Alabaster Forest since Evariste was captured. Regardless, it doesn't seem like whoever did it had any malicious intent. It seems this is a dead end—albeit a rather strange one. But just in case...*

"How much for the slippers?" Angelique asked.

A SMALL FORTUNE LATER, Angelique was the owner of a pair of magic glass slippers. She spent two days in her inn room trying to uncover the magic used in the shoes, but it seemed that the slippers were not forged with real glass but were made entirely out of magic that was tempered to make the shoes strong and comfortable.

"So, yet another dead end." Angelique sighed as she trudged along a dirt road, trying to make it a safe distance from Werra before she called Pegasus from the sky.

The sun was sinking on the horizon, already starting to turn the blue sky a swirl of gold. Soon, the first stars would be visible.

At least Pegasus will be glad to travel at dusk.

"I say, is that you, Angelique?"

Squinting, Angelique turned around, then straightened so quickly her spine cracked. "Sybilla?"

The older woman pushed her glasses up her nose as she marched up to Angelique, a sweet smile brightening her grandmotherly face. "Hello, dear. How are you holding up?"

CHAPTER 17

The question almost made Angelique cry, but she cleared her throat and settled a smile on her lips. "As well as could be expected. I was actually hoping to find you. I have a few matters I need to discuss with you."

"Of course, I'm off to seek out a young lady I need to speak to—she lives a bit farther out in the country. Would you walk with me?"

Angelique nodded and fell in step with the fairy godmother.

"Now, dearie, what is it that needs right?"

As they walked, Angelique explained her tale of the cursed princes, Elise, and attacking Clotilde.

The fairy godmother was a soothing audience to have—she made sounds of encouragement at the right spots and patted Angelique's shoulder during the difficult bits.

"So you're wondering if Princess Elise has the power to defeat Clotilde?" Sybilla guessed once the story was over.

"Yes." Angelique gazed around, blinking as they approached a magnificent and austere chateau perched on a hill.

"Hmm, I'm afraid I can't say for certain without testing her," Sybilla said.

"Is there a test I can carry out? A spell of some sort?" Angelique asked.

Sybilla shook her head. "Not one that will test her strength—which will be necessary to defeat this Clotilde. If she has only a trickle of magic, it's not going to do much damage."

"She has to have a good amount given that she reflected a curse," Angelique pointed out.

"Yes, but reflecting a single curse is entirely different than facing off against two evil artifacts," Sybilla said. "I can tell on sight—it's part of my magic. I'd offer to come take a look, but I'm afraid I have a few important assignments I can't set aside quite yet." Sybilla said. "If it's not resolved by winter, I'll be free by then."

Angelique wanted to groan at the delay—for she'd heard the news coming out of Arcainia, and none of it was good. (She could only imagine how terrible it would be if Gabrielle and Puss were not working to counter the witch.)

"I'm not entirely certain the situation can wait that long," Angelique said. "If we wait much longer, I don't know that Arcainia will be able to recover, and I'm afraid Clotilde will only grow more powerful."

"You should have dropped your ethics and attacked her with your regular magic—regulations or not," Sybilla cheerfully said. She gestured for Angelique to follow her in making a circuit around the chateau's exterior.

"I'm already in trouble for using magic in Arcainia. The last thing I need is another broken rule for the Conclave to wave in my face," Angelique ruefully said.

"Yes, but that wretched queen would be safely dead, and the princes wouldn't be flapping about as barnyard fowl." Sybilla brandished her finger in the air for emphasis.

"But I didn't, so our hope rests in Princess Elise." Angelique glanced at her. "You are sure there is no easy test I can use to sense the strength of her magic?"

"Not with that magic type, dearie. It would take a powerful enchanter to probe her limitations. Your master could do it."

Angelique blinked hard. "Sybilla."

"I know, I know." She paused in the middle of the gravel lane and turned to face Angelique, her hands on her hips. "Well, here is how I see it: send Elise to face this Queen Clotilde and stand in reserve. If it looks like she will lose, step in, and use your real magic. Sooner or later, you will have to face it anyway."

Sybilla's suggestion tasted like ash in Angelique's mouth. "As you say," she managed to reply. *I guess I can go back to Verglas—so much time has passed, it's possible Elise has freed the princes by now.* Rather than voice her thoughts, Angelique looked around the lovely land, her eyes lingering on the immense and lovely home—that strangely had its windows boarded up. "What are we doing here?"

Properly distracted, Sybilla continued to march down the path that wove around the house, likely looking for the kitchen entrance. "We're here to see a girl. My sources tell me the lady of the house had a nasty run in with a mage."

Wrinkles spread across Angelique's forehead, and a faint headache started to brew at her temples. "A black mage?"

"You betcha. I would like to question her to see what more we can learn." Sybilla led the way around the corner of a hedge.

A young lady with short hair a stunning shade of bright red stood in the middle of the path, gawking at them with widened gray eyes. Though she wore faded clothes in the style of servants, she held herself with grace, her posture perfect, even as she gaped at Sybilla and Angelique.

It took Angelique a moment to match the young lady's scarlet red hair, with her obvious elegance and servants' clothes, with the rumors she had heard while searching for the glass shoes.

She could only be Cinderella Lacreux—the destitute duchess the cobbler's apprentice had referred to.

"Hello there, dearie," Sybilla greeted her with the flap of a hand.

Angelique followed Sybilla as she marched up to the young lady. "You did not tell me you were here to see Duchess Lacreux."

Sybilla looked quizzically at her. "I am. How did you know?"

"The duchess is famous for her scarlet-colored hair."

The fairy godmother stared at her. "You've been tramping across the continent for how long on your doomed quest, and you *still* can remember that the Trieux duchess has red hair?"

Past Sybilla, the Duchess stirred a little and appeared to self-consciously swallow.

"It's a fact I recently learned while I was looking for these," Angelique held out her newly acquired pair of sparkling glass slippers to her companion.

Sybilla studied them, her golden glasses sliding down her nose. "Seems impractical."

Angelique refrained from sighing. "I was looking for a mirror. I was told of a 'magic glass' in Werra and thought to give it a try. The rumor never added the last word: slippers."

Sybilla sighed deeply and rubbed Angelique's back like a concerned grandmother. "I'm sorry, dearie."

Angelique shrugged. "What can one do? But I am being rude. Duchess Lacreux, please forgive our discourtesy and allow us to introduce ourselves."

Sybilla turned back to Cinderella and smiled warmly. "I am Sybilla, a First Appraised Isolator Rank Yellow, charged with childcare and development: a fairy godmother."

"And I am Angelique, an Enchantress-in-Training."

Cinderella curtsied beautifully enough to make Angelique envious. "Welcome, madams," she said. "How can I help you?"

Sybilla adjusted her spectacles and pulled a length of parchment and a full-sized quill out of a small pouch. "I was told this afternoon you had an encounter with a black mage. Could you describe him for me—"

Abruptly, Cinderella sat down on the ground, hard.

"Oh, dear," Sybilla said.

"I-I'm sorry." Cinderella struggled to stand. "Please forgive my —" She bewilderedly stared at the ground, and a few tears trickled from her eyes and down her cheeks.

The poor duchess—if the market rumors are only half true, she's had a difficult go of it, and to be attacked by a black mage on top of it all? Angelique knelt in front of the obviously overwhelmed young lady. "Do not be alarmed; it is sometimes difficult for a person to be in the presence of magic as powerful as Sybilla's, even if she is not using it."

Sybilla chortled, "Speak for yourself, dearie."

Angelique ignored her in the interest of projecting her "elegant enchantress" image and spoke in the most soothing tone she could muster. "I can tell your heart is pained. What troubles you, Duchess Lacreux?"

Cinderella burst into tears. Not the gentle, dainty, and falsified tears nobles shed in games of cunning and manipulation, but sobs of heartbreak and exhaustion.

Angelique draped an arm across the young lady's shoulders and shot Sybilla a look of alarm. Sybilla plopped down on the ground with them, murmuring soothingly until the storm partially subsided.

When Cinderella's tears decreased, Sybilla patted her much the same way she had Angelique. "There, there, dearie. A good cry is just what a girl needs sometimes."

Angelique offered the duchess a white lace handkerchief, listening as Sybilla continued.

"Now, what has you so upset?" the fairy godmother asked.

Cinderella clutched Angelique's handkerchief and stared at it. "It is as you said. Today I was attacked by a black mage."

Sybilla nodded. "A run in with one of those brutes is enough to make any lady cry."

Cinderella impatiently wiped tears from her face. "But that's not it. I-I didn't know—or maybe I didn't *see*—how Trieux's hatred for Erlauf and Erlauf's hatred for Trieux is ruining us."

Of all the things the duchess could have said, that was most certainly among the last Angelique would have expected.

As one of the last nobles of Trieux, Cinderella would have suffered under Queen Freja's rule. The fact that she stood before Angelique with short hair and dressed in servants' clothes was a testament to Cinderella's trials. And yet, could she really be reaching past all of that?

"The black mage said we would destroy ourselves, and darkness would rule here," Cinderella blithely continued. "I talked to someone, and he said if we want to survive, our attitudes must change, and our people must change. But I don't know *how*."

Angelique exchanged looks with Sybilla—who was equally surprised, if her wide eyes and the slight O shape to her mouth were anything to go by.

Feeling emboldened, Angelique asked, "Are you not the only Trieux duchess, the highest ranked of all remaining nobles?"

Cinderella sniffed. "Yes, but what can I do?"

Sybilla adjusted her eye glasses, switching over to her instructor mode. "My dear lady, forgive me for being blunt, but what *can't* you do?" she kindly asked. "Every person in your beloved country is born with potential to change the world. But you, who desire to spark the change, have been dealt an incredible hand to play. You are a *duchess*. I have been in Erlauf for just a few days, and even I have heard how you string the Erlauf First Regiment along like a girl leading a lamb."

"I suspect you are thinking of firepower, Duchess Lacreux," Angelique added. "You believe you don't have the power to fight back because you haven't an army to your name or magic to shield those you love?"

Cinderella nodded eagerly. "There are things I can do—things that will affect Aveyron and perhaps Werra. But how can I extend my reach? *All* of Trieux festers with hate."

A warm smile—a *true* smile—crept across Angelique's lips. *Cinderella is a very rare kind of lady. But what in the blazes am I supposed to say to that?* Angelique cast desperately around her mind for a moment before recalling something Evariste had once told her on a day when she had been particularly bitter about her magic. "I believe, Your Grace," Angelique started, "you underestimate the power of kindness. A gentle word, a smile, an act of compassion, these are the things that can turn hate to love."

A mercenary gleam twinkled in Sybilla's eyes. "Or, if that is your worry, ally yourself with someone who *can* reach all corners of the country."

"Who?" Cinderella asked.

Sybilla adjusted her eyeglasses. "Queen Freja, of course."

A shadow of a frown flashed across Cinderella's face. "And how will I win Queen Freja to my side?"

Sybilla patted her hand, as if she could soften the blow she was about to deliver the lady. "Dear, it might not be a matter of 'winning' her. Have any of you nobles from Trieux tried to talk with her?"

Cinderella was silent.

"Speak to her. She is a brilliant queen, not a tyrant," Sybilla recommended.

"But how?"

Sybilla clapped her hands. "There is no time like the present. Isn't there a ball coming up? I nearly drowned in the invitations when the queen learned I was here."

"It is tonight," Angelique confirmed.

"Perfect! There you have it—a ball is a public party. You will be able to approach the queen," Sybilla said. "Or at least a member of the royal family."

"Yes," Cinderella thoughtfully said.

Sybilla watched her for a moment, almost waiting for her to scurry off. When the duchess didn't move, she helpfully added, "If the ball is being held now, you ought to go change so you may leave as soon as possible."

Cinderella blinked. "I haven't any dresses suitable for the occasion. My stepsister said I could borrow something of hers—though she is taller than I am." She frowned in thought. "I know—I can walk to Werra and borrow something from Marie."

"Borrow? *Borrow?* Goodness, *no*. There will be *no* borrowing of ball gowns tonight," Sybilla shivered as if the word was forbidden.

"Then what am I to wear?"

Sybilla looked expectantly to Angelique.

That would be my cue. And for once this is a task easily completed. Angelique stood, her skirts easing back into proper place as they faded from a periwinkle blue to a blue-green color. "I can help you. I am a little skilled in alteration magic. If you do not mind the wait, I should have something suitable in a minute or two."

"In that case, please excuse me, so I may wash." Cinderella rose and hurried off to the well to wash up.

Angelique began spinning her core powers into alteration magic, some of the weight lifting from her shoulders as she began to picture what kind of dress would look fetching on the duchess.

"I thought you were going to talk to her about the black mage?" Angelique asked.

"After seeing her beauty? No. It's not necessary," Sybilla said. "She's known for having a close relationship with the Colonel of the First Regiment, and surely you must know who *he* is."

Angelique wracked her brain to think of what was important and noteworthy in the Erlauf army. "Oh," she said when she properly recalled. "Yes, that would make sense."

"Particularly given that the royal family has been attacked by several black mages since their invasion of Trieux," Sybilla said. "I suspect our dear duchess has been added to the mages' list of powerful people to eradicate."

Angelique froze, and for a moment her powers that had

twisted into alteration magic threatened to revert to her core magic. "*What?*" She asked, her voice sharp, before she remembered herself. "That is to say, there have been attacks on the Erlauf royal family?"

"Indeed." Sybilla sniffed and pushed her glasses up her nose. "They haven't officially asked the Veneno Conclave for their help in the matter, yet. I suspect it's because they're still rather aware that they're on thin ice with mages given their sudden invasion of Trieux."

Angelique was baffled by this revelation, but when she heard the echo of Cinderella's footsteps, she refocused on her magic and hurried to finish the dress.

"Ahh, there she is," Sybilla said, clapping her hands.

Angelique doublechecked her work and carefully studied Cinderella. *Yes, the style and colors I've chosen should look magnificent on her.* Angelique slightly curled her fingers as her silvery magic began to play around them. "Please hold still for a moment, Duchess Lacreux." She walked a circle around Cinderella, first brushing the duchess' chin-length hair.

A twirl of her magic, and long scarlet locks tumbled down Cinderella's shoulders, draping all the way to her elbow before the hair started moving on its own volition, braiding small tendrils that pinned themselves to the crown of her head.

Angelique, recalling some of the hair ornaments Evariste had given her, made the pins in Cinderella's hair topped with pearls and tiny white roses.

Next, Angelique touched the sleeve of Cinderella's dress. The fabric transformed into snow-white silk and crawled across Cinderella's body, changing into a full-skirted gown that brushed the ground.

Trim in a lovely shade of storm-gray crawled across her neckline and fastened in the back, and a bow the same shade gathered at her waist, held in place by a string of pearls.

I don't usually wear gloves or anything that could get in the way of casting magic, but I should give her the whole set.

A flick of Angelique's magic, and storm-gray gloves encased Cinderella's fingertips to her elbows. She added in pearl bracelets and a pearl necklace with a heart-shaped diamond pendant as finishing touches.

Angelique almost tied off her magic before recalling one key detail. "It is a masquerade ball, yes?" she asked.

Cinderella kept her eyes on Angelique, though it was clear she longed to further inspect her temporary gown. "Yes."

"Then you will need this." Angelique slapped her palms together, then slid them apart, using her magic to form a mask covered with white silk and storm-gray lace.

It was a little on the small side—it only covered the bridge of her nose and circled around her eyes—but Angelique suspected it was better if Cinderella was actually recognized, though she wasn't going to tell the young lady that.

She handed the mask off to Cinderella, before inspiration struck. *This would be the perfect opportunity to part with the slippers—there is no sense in carrying them across the continent, after all.* "And for the final touch..." She set the glass slippers she had bought off the shoemaker's apprentice on the ground, positioning them so Cinderella could step into them.

Cinderella shook her head. "I couldn't."

"Please." Angelique smiled. "They are not what I was searching for, and I have no use for them." *In other words, let me pawn my unnecessary belongings off on you, please.*

"I cannot thank you enough." Cinderella slid her feet into the shoes, then smiled so brightly, Angelique felt physically warmer. "You have helped me beyond what I could have dreamed of. Is there nothing I can do for you?"

For a moment, Angelique could almost *feel* Evariste at her side, telling her once again it was a job well done. She even went so far as to glance over her shoulder.

But, of course, he wasn't there.

Angelique took a breath, then shook her head in response to Cinderella's question. "It is the duty of those of us gifted with magic to use it for whatever good purposes we can find. I am pleased I could help you."

Cinderella's cheeks were dusted with pink as she shyly brushed the silken fabric of her skirts. "Thank you."

Once again, Sybilla eagerly clapped her hands. "Now, shall we call for your footmen and carriage?"

Cinderella's smile turned uneasy. "I will walk."

Sybilla blinked. "*Walk?*"

The duchess nodded. "Aveyron does not have a carriage, and I cannot use the horses. They have worked all day and are likely to be eating their evening hay."

Angelique cleared her throat and glanced away. *Yes, Cinderella is someone worthy of helping. Perhaps I should grant her a boon? Or might the dress be considered a help already?*

Sybilla's jaw hung loose, and her glasses slid down her nose again. "No carriage?" she repeated.

"No."

"Hmph. We shall fix that—temporarily at least." Sybilla decisively nodded, making Angelique sit up and take notice.

As a fairy godmother, Sybilla had more magic than the average mage, and though she could only use her core magic and was unable to twist it into anything, most fairy godparents had several strains of magic. Angelique hadn't heard Sybilla was one of those godparents, but knowing the depth of her intellect, Angelique wouldn't put it past her to limit the use of her magic in order to lull others' sense of her.

Is Sybilla about to show off a magic I didn't know she possessed?

Sybilla studied the goats loose on the lawn. "No, but I will be back for you later." She murmured to the unconcerned livestock. "Cows—oh, goodness, no. You can hardly have *spotted* horses. Sheep? Too stupid. Hmm, I know. Attention, creatures. This young lady is in need of some assistance to reach a ball. Are there any volunteers?"

The Duchy of Aveyron was silent.

A few moments passed before Angelique heard the patter-paws of tiny feet, and four clean, well-fed mice scurried up to Sybilla.

Three of the mice went about cleaning their whiskers and patting their fur with the fastidiousness of a court lady. But one mouse leaned back on his hind legs and twitched his nose at Sybilla.

Sybilla nodded as if she could understand the mice, which—knowing her—was entirely possible. "Of course, I see. I'm sure she will not object to that," she said. "In that case, I thank you for your kindness. Now, if you wouldn't mind, be horses."

There was a bang, and a cloud of smoke encased Sybilla.

"Drat! I forgot about that," Sybilla coughed from inside the cloud. "Where are you, mice? Oof!"

Angelique eagerly leaned forward, and, sure enough, when the smoke faded, four horses with coats the same velvet brown color as the mice stood in their place. Perhaps they twitched their noses a little too often, but they didn't seem to mind their new bodies or their matching black harnesses.

"Magic," Cinderella gulped.

"Sybilla's magic," Angelique was quick to add. *Sybilla's* impressive *magic!*

Sybilla ignored the exchange and was wading through the grass, stomping towards the goats. "Yoo-hoo! Yes, you two! I need a footman and a driver. What say you?"

The two nearest goats chewed mouthfuls of grass and looked generally uninspired.

Sybilla put her fists on her hips. "How is that for gratitude? Is anyone else more prone to honor than these two pigs?"

A buck goat—who must have been ancient judging by the

white hair intermixed in his black coat—slowly but regally approached Sybilla. A baby doeling hurried behind him, jumping and leaping in glee.

The buck baaed at Sybilla but stopped when the doeling jumped on his back. When the younger goat hopped off, the buck smacked her in the head with his horns, making her stagger a few steps.

Sybilla beamed at the pair. "Thank you very much. I assure you the mice won't be much trouble. I've already given them directions," she said. "Now, be men!"

Nothing happened.

"Herm. That was embarrassing," Sybilla said as the buck baaed at her again. "I beg your pardon. Be a man and a girl!"

Angelique waved smoke from her face, and thought her eyes might pop from her head when she saw the fruit of Sybilla's magic.

An elderly carriage driver dressed in a fancy suit of white and gray stood proudly with a young girl clothed in gray breeches and a white shirt. She tried to bolt away, but the driver caught her by the collar of her shirt, yanked her backwards, and smashed a white tricorner hat on her head.

Transforming animals into a human appearance was *advanced* and *rare* magic. *Fairy godmothers are powerful and respected, but this... this...* Angelique couldn't even think of a proper description.

Sybilla took no notice of Angelique's awe. Instead, she inspected the goats-turned-people with a satisfied nod. "Very good; you both look grand. If you would stand with the horses, please. Now, a carriage. Duchess Lacreux, have you any pots or apple baskets?"

Cinderella peeled her gaze from the mice-horses. "Pardon?"

"I see a basket over there." Angelique pointed to a lopsided basket that held a few bruised tomatoes.

Sybilla frowned and shook her head sharply. "*That* will *never* work—she'd spill from the carriage before they made it down the lane! What else is there...Ah-hah! I see a pumpkin patch yonder. It is the wrong season, but with luck, that will make the pumpkin more cooperative." Sybilla sailed off to the field, bearing down on the greenery with narrowed eyes and pursed lips.

She returned some minutes later, a suspiciously *round* carriage plated in gold rolling after her. The mice-horses arranged themselves in front of the carriage—their harnesses curling into place by Sybilla's magic—while the goat driver climbed into place.

The goat footgirl opened the door of the round carriage, revealing an inside of orange satin.

Sybilla sniffed angrily when she peered inside. "I could not get it to entirely agree with me, but no one will see the interior anyway." After another displeased look at the pumpkin coach—making Sybilla resemble an aggravated magic instructor—Sybilla turned her attention back to Cinderella, her expression lightening. "Now, dearie, I am sorry to say it, but this magic will only work until midnight. The mice need to be home by then, and I must confess I need to leave the Werra city limit as well. And once I do, my magic will cease functioning."

Slightly alarmed, Angelique stood straighter. "I hadn't thought of that. I, too, must be leaving."

Sybilla fixed her glasses. "Off to see that Arcainian princess?"

Angelique nodded. "Yes. If she can overtake Clotilde, it would be wisest to make our move as swiftly as possible."

"Smart."

"Perhaps." Angelique gave Cinderella an apologetic smile. "I will stay in the area with Sybilla until midnight, but on a night as suitable as this for my mount, I really should ride. When I fall out of range, my magic will fade as well. I apologize, but I cannot stay longer."

Cinderella gestured to her clothes and the carriage. "There is nothing to apologize for. I cannot repay you for this."

"It was our delight," Angelique said. "I wish you all the luck I can spare."

Cinderella smiled shakily. "Thank you."

Sybilla narrowed her eyes at Cinderella. "Do not be afraid, dearie. Your good cheer has more power than you know. Even your animals know you labor for them. Now, run along. You are fashionably late, but you haven't much time to spare."

"Thank you." Cinderella accepted the goat-footgirl's help into the round carriage. The door closed after her, and as the duchess pushed aside an orange, velvet curtain to wave at them, the mice-horses jolted forward, pulling the carriage away from the duchy.

"What a lovely girl." Sybilla waved back to the duchess until the golden carriage was a smear of gold. "Well, then, dearie. What will *you* do next?" She turned her back to the faint speck that was the carriage and fixed her sharp gaze on Angelique.

Angelique scratched the back of her neck, then made herself hold her arms loosely at waist height. "I think I'll ask Pegasus to take me back to Verglas and check on Princess Elise. She should be close to freeing her brothers from their curse. With that matter out of the way, we can discuss what to do about Clotilde."

"And as for Evariste?"

"I'd appreciate it if you kept your ears open for any rumors of magical mirrors or looking glasses, but I think I'm back to combing different countries to search for any evidence of him," Angelique said.

"You've searched Erlauf and Trieux. Once you take care of the witch-queen of Arcainia, where will you go next?"

"Sole, perhaps. Or Ringsted."

"Excellent. You'll stay in touch, dearie, I know it." Sybilla winked and took one of Angelique's hands so she could pat it. "Now, what do you say about getting us some dinner?"

"As long as we stay away from the palace," Angelique said.

"They were that insistent in their invitations, hmm?"

Angelique laughed. "Indeed. It's rather strange to be so popular among royalty even though I am infamous among mages."

"Sometimes it is the non-magical folk who use their eyes." Sybilla ruined the effect of her wise words by rolling her eyes. "Though heaven help us, it's rarely the royals who do. Come, now. I'm feeling a bit peckish."

CHAPTER 18

Angelique started for Verglas at a relaxed pace. She didn't have a solid plan for taking on Clotilde, but Pegasus' trot covered more ground than an average horse could achieve in a day, so they made good time.

She traveled north through Farset, stopping at Alabaster Forest in the vain hope that the elves would leave their forest home to greet her. (They didn't.)

It was there that she felt the Arcainian Princes' curse shatter.

She hadn't expected to be able to feel it or sense it, so it came as something of a surprise to her and nearly knocked her clear off Pegasus' back before she was able to right herself.

She altered her course, intending to follow the river that formed part of the border between Kozlovka and Loire and head east to Verglas.

With Pegasus galloping freely once more, the miles flew by. In fact, just north of the border Verglas shared with Loire, Angelique and Pegasus almost collided with one of the Arcainian princes.

Once she had calmed Pegasus and gotten him settled enough that he wouldn't paw the ground, she smiled at the bunch. The princes looked hale—no worse for the wear due to their curse, which was a blessing—and they must have acquired mounts somehow, for all of them were riding. She noticed there was an addition to their number, a woman who held herself like a guard. *An Arcainian soldier, perhaps? When we were plotting against Clotilde, Gabrielle mentioned sending Elise help.*

"Lady Enchantress," Steffen called. He rode near Elise, in the middle of the pack of princes and was easy to pick out as Angelique knew him as Gabrielle's husband.

"Greetings, princes and princess of Arcainia." Angelique turned Pegasus in a circle so he stopped prancing. "Allow me to extend my happiest of congratulations in breaking the curse. It was fortuitous timing, might I add. I was almost to Loire when I felt your curse shatter; it made finding you an easy task. Elise, your dedication and sacrifice are to be commended." She slid from Pegasus' back—mostly because it was easier to keep up her pleasant mask when she wasn't trying to contain the wild constellation.

"Have you been cleared before the Veneno Conclave?" one of the princes asked.

"Not quite. But I do not think it will matter. I spoke to a close friend of mine, a fairy godmother from Erlauf." *Here comes the pitch—hopefully they don't throw a fit.* Angelique clasped her hands together and put on a winning smile. "We concluded that outside aid would be unnecessary."

"You can defeat Clotilde on your own?" the youngest-looking prince asked.

Angelique almost laughed but successfully covered it with a cough. "No. Not even close. However, there is one closer to you who can do such a thing," She swiveled, turning in the princess' direction. "Elise can—*good heavens*! What happened to you, princess?" She covered her mouth with a hand to keep from revealing her dropped jaw.

Princess Elise, frankly, looked terrible. Her tattered dress was an ashy black color and had numerous burn marks. Her face had smears of soot, her hair was wild, and her hands looked puffy and sported angry welts. The eye-stinging scent of smoke wafted from her like a cloud.

The princess dipped her head in respect. "I was almost burned at the stake. You were saying?" She looked attentively to Angelique, as if being burned at the stake were a common and trivial trial.

Angelique glared at the princes. *What a bunch of lugs. How could they drag her through Verglas when she's just recently broken their curse—and survived almost being burned alive!* She had to physically pry her mouth open and forcibly brighten her voice so she didn't sound as disgruntled as she felt. "No, no. This is unacceptable. We must get you properly cleaned up and fed. I would have thought your brothers would see to that." She *wanted* to take the princes by their ears and shake them, but she settled for waggling a finger at them.

"It isn't their fault," Elise said.

Steffen shook his head. "It is."

"We were, perhaps, overzealous in our desire to leave Verglas," another one of the brothers rumbled.

"You noticed that just *now*?" Angelique snapped. *The princess needs rest, or she'll never be able to face Clotilde. And didn't Stil recently send a message that he was in southern Verglas?* She paused to take in a breath and settle another warm smile on her lips. "However, you are in good luck. It just so happens that a companion of mine has set up camp nearby. We may seek refuge in his house and draw up plans for your stepmother." Angelique clambered onto Pegasus' back. "This way, if you would."

Within an hour, Angelique had the princess and princes settled inside Stil's large tent home.

He wasn't around, and based on the latent magic present, it seemed like he had been gone for a day or so, but he wouldn't mind Angelique inviting the royals in. (Particularly if she fed and cared for Pricker Patch while they intruded.)

Angelique abandoned the princes in the sitting room and delivered Elise to Stil's frankly over-the-top washroom. Although she really wanted to take the tea tray to the princes' heads for unnecessarily pushing their sister, she made herself serve them drinks and food from Stil's ample pantry.

It was then the princes explained what had been the catalyst for their rapid exit from Verglas. Apparently Prince Toril of Verglas had stumbled upon Elise as she silently knitted and invited her north to the capital city. Once there, the prince's mad father—King Torgen—heard about Elise and proceeded to make life miserable for her through escalating meetings that ended with the princess almost being burned at the stake.

I guess it's more understandable that they were in a rush to leave the country, Angelique mused as she poured more tea for herself.

She heard light footsteps down the hallway and smiled when Princess Elise peered into the sitting room. Already she looked more rested. Her hair was tidy again, and the clothes Angelique had set out for her were a perfect fit. (And as an added bonus, she no longer smelled like a chimney.)

"Perfect timing, princess. Your brothers were just asking after you," Angelique greeted her. "Please, come have some tea and scones."

"You look much better. You were quite bedraggled and scruffy before." The prince with goldenrod hair inspected her from head to foot. "Not that you didn't have reason to be," he added.

The brother Pegasus had almost run down smiled fondly and slid a hand beneath Elise's chin. "You look beautiful."

Steffen crowded that brother, forcibly parting him from Elise. "Doesn't she though?"

Angelique offered the princess a steaming cup of peppermint tea, sweetened with honey and a little milk, as she sat next to Angelique on the settee.

Elise's stomach growled, and one of her foster-brothers passed her a plate laden with scones and tea sandwiches.

Elise selected a sandwich and smiled. "Thank you."

"I do not mean to rush you, Lady Enchantress, but you said you knew of someone who could break the curse?" Steffen asked.

Angelique topped off Elise's tea and watched her devour her food. "I do: Fürstin Elise."

Elise choked on her sandwich.

"Pardon?" Steffen blinked.

"No, I see where this is going. We cannot ask Elise to do more for us," said the prince Pegasus had almost run down. (Privately, Angelique was starting to think of him as the touchy-feely one, because whenever he spoke, he reached for Elise, even just to rest a hand on her shoulder as he was now.)

"Her hands will take months to heal, even if I purchase the best creams and plants to make pastes for her. She cannot do a thing more." That came from the goldenrod-haired prince—the one who spoke stiffly but eyed Elise with concern.

"Elise has done more than her fair share," piped in the youngest prince.

"I agree with what you say," said the brother with glasses. (He faintly reminded her of Sybilla, not just because of the spectacles, but because of the sharp mind that gleamed in the shadows of his eyes.) "But perhaps we should hear out the Lady Enchantress first."

The brothers quieted down and expectantly stared at Angelique.

She waited for a moment of silence before continuing. "As I mentioned, after I left you, I called on my friend in Erlauf. She is a fairy godmother and seeks out young boys and girls who are gifted with magical talents."

That's a vast oversimplification, for she does far more than that, but it would do me no good to break out into a lesson on the duties of a fairy godparent at this time.

"I discussed with her the oddity that the curse worked on every Arcainian royal—Gabrielle excluded—except for you," she continued, looking at Elise. "After conversing further, we concluded that the only logical explanation is you have the ability to use magic, as well."

Elise shook her head and shifted so she sat on the edge of the settee. "I'm sorry, but that's impossible. There would have been signs. I wouldn't be the royal family's foster child," she said. "Magic is not something a person can hide. Furthermore, I would know! There's no possible way I could be ignorant of an ability like that."

Angelique shook her head as she picked up her teacup, inhaling the minty scent of the tea. "You are ignorant because of the way your powers manifest. Observe."

She drew her fingers together and tugged on her magic, making a glittering ball of light. A flick of her fingers released the ball, rolling it lazily in Elise's direction. Angelique held her breath—she wasn't entirely certain Elise had this kind of magic. *And if I'm wrong, we have no way to attack Clotilde that won't involve weeks or months of waiting.*

She swallowed and watched the ball roll closer to the princess. When it touched Elise, it bounced off her and faded away like smoke.

Angelique relaxed. *Finally, something has gone right for a change! Clotilde will have no power over Elise, making her far easier to defeat.* She looked expectantly to the princes, but they were all watching her with varying levels of suspicion.

I guess another example is necessary to illustrate the difference.

Once again, Angelique created a ball of light. This one, she flung at the prince with eyeglasses. The blob of light stuck to him like a thorny plant until the prince crushed it with his fingers.

Elise crinkled her brown eyes as she thoughtfully pursed her lips. "What does this mean?"

Angelique cleared her throat and folded her hands to keep from clapping them in glee. "It means your powers, probably as a result of the country you live in, lie in magic cancelation. Magic cannot survive around you. Thus, a curse, even one as powerful as the one Clotilde used against you, will not work," she said. "The curse couldn't hit you, but it was powerful enough to survive contact with you, so it bounced back and hit Clotilde."

"It is my understanding that it is difficult for other magic users to hide their powers from each other. How could no one have discovered Elise before now?" Prince Glasses asked.

Angelique rearranged the tea tray, just to give herself something to do. "Probably because Elise's magic doesn't feel like magic. I didn't notice it myself until I touched her and felt my powers go mute." She glanced at the princess. "Elise does not give off the aura of magic because, to put it simply, her presence devours all traces of magic."

Another prince—one of the twins, based on the nearly identical face he sat next to—rubbed his chin. "And our curse?"

"Yeah, how was Elise able to break our curse if her touch cancels magic?" the other twin asked. (Though they were identical, it was easy to tell them apart given that the one who smiled more and wriggled his eyebrows at inopportune times had a crooked nose that looked like it had been broken. Multiple times.)

Angelique mulled over the prince's question for a few moments. "Breaking a curse is an entirely different matter than human-made magic. It deals with a deeper power that would easily override Elise's magic."

Now it was Elise's turn to frown. "I still don't understand."

Angelique tilted her head. *What's the easiest way to describe something as complex and diverse as magic without launching into confusing details?* "The magic I use—the magic any enchanter or enchantress uses, Elise included—is a sort of surface magic. It is using your personal powers to change things. The magic that went into breaking your curse was a far deeper and older kind of magic that existed long before any enchanter walked these lands. Using love to conquer darkness is a power as old as the oceans. It is not surprising that Elise's powers would have no effect on such potent magic. Once the steps are taken, *no one* can stop the consequences of a sacrifice made from love."

This explanation seemed to satisfy Elise, for a steely expression settled on her face. "So how can I destroy her? Do you mean for me to wake Father from his stupor?" she asked.

Angelique sipped her tea. "I'm afraid the task before you is much greater than that. You must cut her off from her power source. Clotilde's powers are nothing special, but if you cancel the magic of the artifacts she uses to prepare her big curses, she will expire."

"Why?" Prince Glasses asked.

"Clotilde has put her life into those artifacts. If you destroy them, you destroy her," Angelique said.

Steffen pressed his fingertips together. "Can you guarantee Elise's safety?"

Ah yes, this is the tricky part that they aren't going to like. Not that I blame them after what she has been through already.

Angelique took a deep breath before replying. "No. We know nothing about Elise's abilities. There may be limitations, but I do not know how to properly test a magic student—I'm still an apprentice. Additionally, the testing process is a lengthy one. Based on the news I heard in Erlauf, I'm not certain Arcainia can hold out much longer."

"News? What news?" Rune asked.

Angelique rubbed her tea cup with her thumb. "You royal siblings have worked to increase Arcainia's power and wealth under your supervision. You have succeeded, but the country does not flourish without you."

Steffen relaxed. "Of that we are well aware."

Angelique winced. "As such, Arcainia has not prospered under Clotilde's rule. Her presence is evil, and the land is rejecting her. There was a famine this year—almost all crops were lost to blight or fungus. A storm hit Carabas harbor and nearly destroyed it.

Without Prince Rune's frequent patrols, more magical creatures with ill-intensions entered the country. Several villages were destroyed by those creatures. The army is underfunded and will not be able to survive much longer without proper finances, and as Clotilde lacks access to the majority of the country's funds, she has raised taxes to support her spending."

Elise narrowed her eyes. "How high are the taxes?" she asked in a hard voice.

"Too high. After the massive crop failure, many of your subjects are unable to pay the tax. Normally, they would leave and become refugees, but your subjects trust you, and they're waiting for your return," Angelique said. "But Clotilde does not let them go unpunished."

Angelique fell silent and watched Elise stare at her welt-covered hands.

Simply put, Arcainia was suffering. And Angelique didn't know how much longer the country could last before it was dealt irreparable damage. *The only reason it has held out this long is because of Gabrielle and Puss. If they weren't there...I think the whole country would have fallen by the end of the first month.*

"*We* will have to do something," said the twin without the broken nose. "Not Elise."

"It's about time we take some of the burden," Prince Broken Nose said.

The youngest prince took a marmalade tart from the tea tray. "I try to look useless, but I don't relish the idea of Elise being the only one in our family responsible for our country's freedom," he said.

Steffen rubbed his eyes, but Angelique could see his refusal of the idea in the tightness of his shoulders. "We can do nothing more today," he said. "That much is clear."

"Daylight is all but gone. If we set out for Arcainia, we would not get very far," Prince Touchy-Feely said.

"We may spend the evening here," Angelique said.

Elise finally looked up. "Your friend will not mind?"

"Stil? No." Angelique held in a snort. If the sassy craftmage knew he had princes in his home, he'd be pawning his charms and magic to them—royalty were always his best customers.

She cleared her throat and continued. "Even if he comes home, I doubt he will notice our presence. Although I must apologize, for he does not have enough rooms for us all."

"No matter, we men will sleep here. There are plenty of cushions, and we're used to spending our nights in much more uncomfortable places these days." The corners of Steffen's mouth wryly turned with his words, a reminder of the twisted times that had fallen on the continent.

IN THE LATE hours of the night, Angelique left the royals—Elise and the guard, whose name she learned was Brida, in a guest bedroom and the princes splayed out in the sitting room like ungainly puppies—to sleep the darkness away.

She, on the other hand, slipped outside. Fall was creeping through the land, making the air chilly and filling it with the sound of falling leaves.

Angelique released a deep sigh, exhaling all the tension that had been holding her upright, and stared at the sky. Sure enough, she saw Pegasus' constellation brightening the night and smiled fondly.

The celestial equine had traveled with her longer than he had ever escorted her and Evariste. She hadn't even *known* he could spend so much time away from his starry domain. But he wasn't showing any detrimental signs. Rather, he seemed to greet her each morning with increasing enthusiasm—and property damage, given his powers.

Lulled by the beauty of the stars and the serene silence of the night, Angelique rolled her head in a circle and massaged the back of her neck.

I am just an apprentice, and yet I'm running across the continent putting out fires, and it takes more out of me than expected. I guess I thought enchantresses just...floated around granting boons and practicing magic.

She snorted. *What a great joke that is!*

The whisper of cloth behind her betrayed the woman—or rather women—who tried to creep through the tent's entrance.

Still feeling at ease, Angelique turned around and smiled at the pair. "Princess Elise, Captain Meier. How surprising."

Elise looked shocked to see her, but she recovered quickly and smiled politely. "Good evening, Lady Enchantress. What brings you outside at this hour?"

Angelique pointed to the sky. "I was checking on my mount. I rode him longer than usual, and I wasn't sure what condition he would be in."

Elise squinted a little. "Oh?"

Angelique studied the princess and her silent guard. *Elise was awfully angry to hear about the state of Arcainia. I'd bet my most priceless book that they're trying to sneak out so the princess can face Clotilde regardless of whether her foster-brothers agree with her or not.*

Elise fidgeted under the scrutiny, then blurted out, "Do you really believe I can take on Clotilde?"

I'm getting better at reading people! Or perhaps it's just that everyone has less...hidden depth than Evariste. I could never really pin him down. The thought renewed the festering ache inside Angelique, so she pushed it away and forced her attention on the princess. "I do."

"What do I need to do?" Elise asked.

Angelique tapped her lower lip as she thought. "Your bare touch should be enough. It seems that you do not toggle your powers on and off, but you constantly use them. As a result, you do not need to worry about activating anything on your end. Clotilde keeps her tools for her dark magic on her at all times. If your magic is strong enough, your touch will cancel her magic, as well as the artifacts' magic. It will be her end."

Elise narrowed in on Angelique with impressive single-mindedness. "If my magic is strong enough?" she bluntly asked.

Angelique tried to come up with a more polite way of phrasing it, but nothing came to mind. She eventually gave up and nodded. "I have no way of measuring your magic, so I cannot tell you if your powers are enough to smother everything. The way you attack her would make a difference, I suppose. Skin-to-skin contact would provide the best channel for your magic to reach her. The more contact, the better."

Elise fussed with the sleeves of her dress. "I see."

Brida spoke, perhaps for the first time since she was officially introduced. "Your powers were enough to keep you from being cursed, Fürstin. I am certain you are strong enough to defeat that witch." She slid a pack off her shoulders as she approached her tethered mare.

"Thank you, Brida. I wish I had your confidence," Elise said. "We are leaving tonight, before my brothers wake. They will never let me face Clotilde, and I feel that I must try."

Angelique patted the skirts of her iridescent dress, trying to smooth them so they didn't puff quite as much. "I think you underestimate your powers of persuasion over your brothers, Princess. If you tell them you feel strongly on the matter, I suspect they will bow to your wishes."

Elise's gaze went glassy. "Perhaps," she agreed. "But, but...I cannot risk them again. I almost lost them, and I could not live with myself if Clotilde cursed them a second time." Her voice was barely more than a whisper when she finished.

Angelique studied Elise. *Because she is so stoic and quiet, I find it hard to connect with her. But really...she understands the pain of losing someone. Even if she knew where her foster-brothers were, for all practical purposes, they were still lost to her.*

But is it wise to let her go alone? Gabrielle and Puss will be on-hand to help her... Angelique glanced at the sky again. *I would do anything to be given the chance to face those mages again, to stop them from taking Evariste.*

"I understand," Angelique finally said.

Elise perked, her bright eyes and shining face a sharp contrast to the solemn little thing she usually was. "You do?"

Angelique's smile felt painful. "More than I wish I did. You must leave now if you are to have a chance of confronting Clotilde without your brothers. When they wake, I will hold them off as long as possible, but they know you. The instant they realize you have left, they will set out after you."

Brida handed Elise the reins of her mare, having tacked it up during the princess' exchange with Angelique. "Then we'll have to make the best use of our head start," the guard said.

Angelique reached for the bracelet Evariste had given her, frowning slightly when she remembered she had broken it. "You will need to go slowly. It is dangerous to ride in the dark. It is your good fortune that tonight is a full moon."

Brida picked a different horse out of the line—this one Angelique vaguely remembered as the mount Elise had with her when she first encountered her in Arcainia. "We're a stone's throw from Loire. Arcainia isn't far beyond that. What time we gain by leaving tonight should be enough to keep us ahead," Brida said.

"One can hope," Angelique said, unconvinced. *Based on the way they fussed over her, I'm surprised none of them have realized she's out here already.* Reminded of the squabbling princes, Angelique turned towards the tent. "If you excuse me, I will take my leave of you here. If your brothers ask, I can truthfully say I did not see you leave. I wish you a safe journey and great luck in your venture."

"Thank you for everything, Lady Enchantress," Elise said.

Angelique offered the pair one last smile. "I am glad I can be of assistance." She slipped inside the parlor and carefully navigated her way around the sleeping princes, heading to her favorite (and best) of Stil's guest quarters, the Frost Room.

The hues of blue décor and warm honey tones of the room's furniture always struck Angelique as calming. When she slipped inside it, she sagged slightly and leaned against the wall.

"I have a duty," she reminded herself, "to help those in need. Even if I am growing a little weary of it."

CHAPTER 19

Angelique was hiding in the dining room of Stil's rather large home, surrounded by several musty books, when the princes discovered their foster-sister was missing.

Magic mirrors, magic mirrors—nope. Nothing. You'd think a book of craft magic would have information on the steps done to create a magic mirror. She set another book aside with a sigh, having decided to take advantage of Stil's impressive book collection of craft magic to research magic mirrors.

Thus far, her efforts had been in vain.

She was about to start in on the final book when she heard the thud of footsteps running down the hallway.

They've finally gone and looked in the princess' room, I bet.

Angelique flipped the book open and began paging through it, looking up only when the door slammed open and Steffen staggered inside.

"They're gone," he panted.

Angelique made a show of blinking. "Who is gone?"

"Elise and Brida. Did you see them leave?" He sagged against the doorframe as if he didn't have the willpower to stand.

"No," Angelique truthfully said.

"We've wasted an hour trying to find her in this wretched maze of a house tent," Steffen muttered under his breath and pushed his blond hair out of his eyes. (Angelique suspected it was only her rank that kept him from demanding a more detailed answer.)

"You've confirmed they're gone. Isn't that all that matters?" Angelique pushed back from the table and stood. "I would think it's fairly obvious where they intend to go."

"I *know*," Steffen snapped. He paused and corrected himself, putting on a handsome smile. "That is to say, I am well aware of the end location Elise likely has in mind." He bowed politely to her.

Oh, he's good, Angelique thought with a smirk.

"If you are able, Lady Enchantress, we would like to leave in a quarter of an hour." He struggled to keep the civility in his voice, and his smile turned brittle in his worry.

"I will be ready, Your Highness," she said.

Steffen nodded his thanks and started to duck out of the room.

"Steffen," Angelique called after the prince. "She'll be fine."

Steffen slowly shook his head. "She's my baby sister. I don't care if she should be fine; she shouldn't have to do it without me." He ducked into the hallway, his footsteps fading as he pounded back up the hallway.

Angelique stood in silence for the odd moment, her gaze resting on Stil's books. "Family loyalty," she murmured. "It is a wonder to behold."

Would anybody do the same for me? Pegasus keeps me company, but I'm fairly certain that's as far as his good will goes. Stil would help as he could, but I don't know that he would run after me. Evariste, though, he would likely be there with me dropping vague hints every step of the way...

She shook her head and gathered the books up, intending to return them to their proper place before going outside to summon Pegasus.

She had a feeling the princes would hover if she wasn't ready as quickly as possible.

BLAST THESE PRINCES! Angelique thought as she sagged against Pegasus' neck. *I'm starting to understand why Elise is so quiet and purposeful. It's because they're a bunch of broody hens!*

The princes set a merciless pace to get back to Arcainia. That hadn't mattered much to Angelique—Pegasus could outlast any horse, and she had developed a posterior of steel after riding as much as she had during the past few years.

No, what was hardest to handle was the *constant pestering* and quarrels between the brothers.

"Are we there yet?"

"This is your fault, you know."

"My fault? Why should it be my fault?"

"You *told* her she couldn't do it. This is Elise—that means you practically dared her to attack Clotilde on her own!"

"She won't be alone. Gabrielle is there—with her dratted cat."

"I still don't understand how a cat can be of any help at all."

"It's a *magic* cat."

"And you're a loon if you think that's true!"

"Little Gerhie, you're too cute and young to be so jaded."

"Stop *touching* me!"

"I wish I had been born an only child."

"Would someone ask the lady enchantress if she can track Elise?"

"*You* ask her. I asked when you wanted to know an hour ago if she could raise a wall of magic to keep Elise from entering Arcainia. She wasn't very cheery in her response."

"Your face annoyed her, probably."

And on and on it continued with the brothers arguing over

one another endlessly so she couldn't even be certain who was speaking!

Angelique had no doubts the princes were charming and amusing...when one didn't stand between them and the foster-sister they wished to protect.

As it was, she spent most of her riding hours actively reminding herself that she couldn't murder them all because Elise, Gabrielle, and Puss could use their help at Castle Brandis.

We're almost to the border. I should send a message ahead to Gabrielle so she knows Elise is coming. We can't be too far behind her despite the lead she had. The princes are pushing too hard for that.

She sat up and peered around suspiciously, but the brothers were occupied with watering their horses, giving them a short break before they started out again.

Satisfied that they were otherwise occupied, she rooted around in her bag and pulled out the letter she had written the previous evening when they had stopped to rest.

She began folding the letter into the shape of a bird, imbedding it with bits of her magic. Once finished, she held it out, and the paper bird flapped its wings before jumping off her palm and soaring into the sky.

It was a risky method of communication—a rain could ruin the spell and, since the bird was very obviously made of paper, occasionally messages were swiped by enemies or nosy folk. But Angelique was willing to bet the bird would make it to Gabrielle one way or another with the help of other Arcainians.

"Are you ready to continue, Lady Enchantress?" Steffen asked. He led his horse closer to Pegasus—though kept ample space so as to not irritate the constellation.

"Yes," Angelique confirmed. "Though I'd like to remind you and your royal brothers that we are about to enter Arcainia again. It's rather possible Clotilde might feel you entering the country, depending on how her affinity with her artifacts has grown over the summer."

Steffen bowed slightly. "We'll be alert." He swung up onto his horse's back and nodded to the twins, who started the parade of princes and crossed the stream bed.

For once, the princes were blessedly quiet as they rode.

Several of them reached for the various weapons strapped to their horses' backs, reassuring themselves—or perhaps preparing—as they rode into their country.

The border between Loire and Arcainia was rather nebulous. Angelique thought they still had a few minutes of riding as they rode across hills, the wind whipping at their clothes, when a geyser of black liquid shot off.

The horses reared, and even Pegasus shied at the gurgling noise.

The liquid plunged back to the ground and was still, but Angelique saw a glob of it shoot east.

Angelique swallowed several rude phrases. She yanked hard on her magic, twisting it and throwing it in the span of seconds. She formed it into a lightning bolt that she shot at the glob. But whatever dark magic Clotilde had used dodged the strike and continued east.

Angelique shaded her eyes as she watched the magic slip out of range. "I'm afraid Clotilde knows we're here," she grimly said.

Prince Touchy-Feely frowned as he patted his horse's neck, calming it. "You think that was an alarm?"

"Most likely," Angelique said.

"Then we should continue with the expectation that she's waiting for us," Steffen said.

Angelique nodded, when one of the brothers shouted, "Look out!"

A whistling hiss sounded from deep within the earth.

Pegasus swung around just in time to let Angelique watch a creature emerge from the large geyser hole.

The creature had silver belly scales with a gold and coal-gray scale pattern on its back. Sharply ridged black feathers flowed down the creature's sides. They were beautifully deadly—Angelique knew each feather was coated in poison. Feathers also sprouted from its tail, and a black crown shape made of spines and reptilian webbing perched on the basilisk's head. Though its body was snake-like in shape, its muzzle was longer and crowded with teeth, though it still possessed prominent fangs.

It was a basilisk, a beast considered the king of snakes and incredibly dangerous to fight.

"That's a basilisk!" Prince Touchy-Feely shouted.

"Thank you, Manual for Field Identification of Magical Creatures," Steffen drawled. "Have any other useful tidbits to share?"

"It's poisonous, and there's no way we can outrun it," said Straight-Nosed Twin.

Smashed-Nose Twin flung a dagger at it, which bounced off the scales of its back. "Seems like it's impervious to blades." He scratched his broken nose as he peered at the hissing creature.

"The softest scales are on its underbelly," Prince Touchy-Feely said. "Aim there."

"With what?" the youngest prince snarled. "We weren't given a bow or crossbow!"

"I'll take care of it," Angelique shouted. "You princes ride ahead!"

Trying to end the basilisk with them would be a miserable experience if riding with them is any proper measure.

"It's deadly, Lady Enchantress," Steffen said. "Are you certain you can handle it alone?"

Angelique gulped as she eyed the creature, which was slowly rearing its head back—probably so it could see them better. It wasn't full grown—for although it could wrap around a cottage and crush it, its head was about the size of a large dog. (Legends said they could get to be as big as dragons.) But behind her—even with the basilisk staring them down—she could still hear the princes arguing.

"Rune could go in with a spear while the rest of us act as bait?"

"It's poisonous. Rune isn't going anywhere near that thing when all he has to wear is a cotton shirt and trousers!"

Yep. All they'll do is argue. As long as I stay back far enough, I'll be safe from it. "I'm certain," Angelique said.

Steffen looked east and squinted.

Angelique could see the war on his face—chase after his sister, who was untrained and pitting herself against a witch, or help the enchantress who had done so much for them.

I'm fairly certain I can tip the scales to motivate him to leave. Angelique cleared her throat. "Steffen."

The prince swung back around to face her. "Yes?"

Angelique raised an eyebrow. "Gabrielle is waiting."

Steffen's eyes burned, and he swung his horse around. "We're moving on," he shouted to his brothers. "Lady Enchantress Angelique will take care of the basilisk."

The princes started to fall in line behind their eldest brother, except for the twins.

They exchanged looks before they dumped a spear, two broadswords, and several daggers onto the ground.

What are they doing? They can't possibly know my core magic! Angelique eyed the basilisk, which hadn't moved from its coiled position, then slipped from Pegasus' back. "Princes, I am a mage, not a warrior," she lightly reminded them.

"Perhaps, but just in case," Smashed-Nose said.

His more serious twin nodded in agreement.

They clicked to their horses and hurried off after their brothers, who were already cresting a hill, continuing their push to Castle Brandis.

Angelique kept her eyes on the basilisk but patted Pegasus' shoulder. "You might want to leave for this part, friend."

Pegasus tossed his head and snorted, making the flickering flames of his mane and tail spark.

Angelique pressed her hand into his neck, reveling in the warm feeling of his coat, then edged away. She kept her distance from the basilisk—which she was relieved to see ignored Pegasus and kept its eyes on her.

A basilisk's greatest weapons are its poison and size. But since this one isn't fully grown, the poison is my first concern. I just have to stay out of range, and I should be able to attack it.

The monster hissed again—a strange, slithering, whistle noise that made Angelique's ears ache.

It started to uncoil, and Angelique hurriedly plucked at her magic, rapidly twisting it into a stun spell.

CHAPTER 20

When the basilisk began slithering her way—withering any greenery that touched its poisonous feathers—Angelique threw the spell, hitting the creature.

Its eyes grew unfocused, and its head wobbled dazedly.

Angelique twisted her magic into a fire spell. *I'll have to be careful with this—I shouldn't use water magic around the basilisk, or I'll just spread its poison everywhere.*

She smiled proudly when she finished twisting her magic—she was getting faster—and shot two massive fireballs off at the basilisk's unguarded chest.

The fireballs crackled as they sped towards the stunned monster. When they had breached half the distance, the basilisk shook its head, and its gaze cleared.

It dropped its head and coiled over itself, protecting the soft scales on its chest. The fireballs smashed into it but swiftly winked out.

The fire didn't seem to damage the monster's scales, but it did singe its feathers.

Angelique's jaw dropped in dismay, but she was already prepping a lightning spell. *How did it shake that stun off so quickly? It lasted for only a few moments!*

The basilisk slithered closer to her, its golden eyes glowing eerily.

Angelique shouted her spell, shooting lightning at the monster.

It laid flat, so the spell hit its back. Lightning crackled up and down the basilisk's spine—burning more of its feathers—but it didn't appear to do any lasting damage, for before the last spark of lightning was gone, it again bared down in her direction.

The smell of its burnt feathers was a bitter and foul scent that made it hard to breathe. *I hope I'm not poisoning the air.*

Just in case, Angelique held her breath as she formed and released her next spell. A spike of earth shot out of the ground—her attempt at impaling the creature. All it succeeded in doing, however, was making the basilisk whistle in anger and briefly stop its forward progress as it course corrected.

Desperate, Angelique threw up a thin defensive shield. *Fire and lighting are out—the air is definitely tainted with something from its feathers. And I can't use water. Earth doesn't seem especially effective. I could use strength magic, but I don't relish touching the creature.*

The basilisk whipped its tail at Angelique, striking her ice-like shield.

The shield held, but when the basilisk battered it with a second hit, it cracked, and tiny lines like spiderwebs spread across its surface.

Angelique rushed to pour more power into it, but the basilisk was faster. It hit the shield again, and it disintegrated.

Its tail smashed into Angelique, hammering her into the ground.

Her bones rattled from the impact, and it was difficult to breathe from being slammed into the earth, but her mind screamed.

Those feathers—the poison is going to eat through my dress!

The basilisk started to curl around her when Angelique finally managed to sit up.

Before it could encircle her and dig its spiny feathers into her side, she shot another stun spell at it. When it was safely dazed, she followed it up with two spikes of earth that peeled its belly off the ground like a convenient bridge for her to pass underneath.

Angelique scurried away, weaving together a wind spell as she fled, and readying healing magic as well. But when she looked down at her dress, it still gleamed—flawless and iridescent, with not a tear to be seen.

What did Evariste do *to this gown?* she wondered bewilderedly.

The basilisk cracked her with his tail, sending her face-first into the ground with such force, for a moment, Angelique thought she might have broken bones.

Everything hurt and blazed in pain.

That stun was even shorter than the first one. The thought was fuzzy and came to her slowly as she tried to think through the haze of pain. *This fight is going much more poorly than I estimated.*

She felt the cool sensation of her magic twine through her fingers, but she pushed the sensation away.

I won't use my core magic!

She felt the basilisk looming above her, its hot breath making her shiver.

Angelique clenched her teeth and slammed her hands onto the ground, releasing the wind magic she held. The magic exploded across the ground, raising a gritty cloud of dust.

The basilisk hissed its irritation as Angelique pushed herself off the ground and scurried away, wincing as her right knee radiated a hot, searing pain up and down her leg.

With the pain spurring her on, Angelique mentally sifted through some of the more brutal forms of magic Puss had insisted she learn.

She waited until the dust cleared before she threw magic that would temporarily blind the monster.

A milky white membrane spread over the basilisk's eyes. It shook its head back and forth, writhing in vain as it tried to see.

Angelique shifted so she didn't put so much weight on her injured leg, then uprooted a fir tree that sat on the crest of a hill. She smashed it into monster's back, attempting to crush it.

The basilisk flung its head back as it roared in pain. It struck the tree, its strong jaws and jagged teeth ripping through the needled branches and sturdy trunk.

While it was preoccupied, Angelique used her magic to scoop several large rocks that bordered on the edge of being small boulders, and hefted them higher and higher into the air.

When the basilisk threw the tree off its back, Angelique dropped the rocks.

They smashed into the monster's head with a skull-crunching thud.

The basilisk shook its head, throwing the rocks off.

Angelique ducked to avoid one, but her knee gave out, and she flopped to the ground—injured knee first.

She tried to hold in her growl of pain, but the blinded basilisk had already heard her. It swiveled it's head in her direction, rearing back in a strike pose as Angelique stumbled to her feet.

It lunged at her, and Angelique took a few staggering steps backwards, but it was only a feint. The monster pummeled her with its tail, smashing her into the ground again and again until she was sure her body had to have made a crater.

Everything hurt.

Pain sliced through her with such efficiency, she could feel the soft edge of unconsciousness beckoning her closer.

I'm going to die.

The realization struck her like a sword to the gut.

I can't escape. I'm going to die here.

Her eyes fluttered open, and she saw the milky white of her

blinding spell retreat from the basilisk's golden eyes, having run its course.

Everything hurt. She couldn't move, even as the basilisk shifted into another strike pose, its golden eyes piercing her. A yellow-tinted drop of liquid fell from one of its fangs, eliciting a burning hiss when it fell to the ground and killed all the grass around it.

Angelique's eyes stung with unshed tears, and her pain intensified when she moved her fingers, trying to stir her magic into something useful.

Just as the monster leaned in to strike, Pegasus screamed a challenge.

The constellation jumped over Angelique, skidding to a stop as he stood between her and the snake. He tossed his head and reared, shaking the earth and making thunderclaps when his front hooves hit the earth again.

"Pegasus, no," Angelique weakly called. *No matter how magical he is, he can't withstand a direct strike from a basilisk! Its fangs will pierce him through!*

Pegasus ignored her and snorted, red sparks flying from his nostrils.

He's going to get hurt!

Panic spread through Angelique's body, numbing her so she could peel herself off the ground. "Pegasus!"

The basilisk hissed a warning—which Pegasus ignored when he slammed his front legs into the ground, creating bolts of lightning.

The basilisk struck Pegasus with his tail, pushing the horse sideways and opening a cut on the equine's rump with a spiked feather.

Horror filled Angelique. She couldn't breathe; she couldn't move. Only one thought filled her mind: *He's going to be killed. For me. He's sacrificing himself for me.*

Her magic started to stir within her like a caged beast.

Again! It's happening again!

"NO!" Angelique screamed.

She didn't think. She didn't hesitate. She grabbed on her war magic, ripping as much free as she could.

It came to her—cold, sharp, and blazing. Angelique flung it out from her, and the spear, swords, and daggers the twin princes had left behind floated in the air.

But that wasn't all.

Angelique's deadly magic surged across the ground, levitating the sharpest splinters left from the fir tree, raising rusted arrowheads long lost, sharpened shards of rock, and an axe left behind in a nearby forest. Ancient, rusted swords in a style Angelique had never seen before were ripped from deep within the ground, covered by centuries of rust and dirt. They, too, rose into the air, the sharpened edges of the blades visible even through the muck that caked them.

The basilisk bared its fangs at her, but...

Her magic struck with an explosion of power—a release of pressure that had been building up for years—shaking the ground and raising clouds of dust.

The weapons—both true and make-shift—plunged into the basilisk's bared chest with such force, they knocked the creature backwards and nailed it to the ground.

It flopped once, twice, then was still.

Angelique stood, her magic filling her. It was invigorating and intoxicating as it arced around her, and everything glowed silver.

She shifted her gaze to the pinned basilisk, and the weapons dug deeper and deeper into its flesh as they dug into the ground.

It didn't matter; the monster was dead. One of the ancient swords had pierced straight through its heart.

But Angelique didn't care. It had almost hurt Pegasus. She was going to grind it into the dust for the sake of certainty.

Furthermore, there was now a sense of *wholeness* she hadn't felt in a long time. She hadn't used her war magic this freely since her earliest days in Luxi-Domus, when she had loved the way it flowed through her, cool and precise but dangerously reassuring.

She reached for more of her magic, when a warm muzzle pressed against her temple.

Angelique blindly reached up, gingerly touching Pegasus's velvet muzzle as he lowered it so he could lip her shoulder.

She turned slightly so she could gaze upon her equine companion, searching him for injuries. *That's right, Pegasus. He's safe now.* She glanced back over her shoulder at the basilisk's body, and it finally dawned on her what she had done, and what was done.

Oh, stars. Angelique immediately cut her war magic off, shivering at its sudden loss. She leaned into Pegasus, readily immersing herself in his warmth—which calmed her and gave her something to cling to.

I don't regret it. I've already failed to protect Evariste. I couldn't let that happen again. But it's terrifying how right my magic feels.

Her shivering increased as the last bits of her magic faded from the battlefield, and she realized just how much her body hurt.

Angelique summoned flickering bits of healing magic, placing a slow healing spell first on Pegasus for his cut, and then on herself. Just as she finished, nausea hit her. She wasn't sure if it was the leftover stench of the basilisk's feathers or the personal knowledge that she had used her deadly powers, but her stomach twisted with gut-wrenching pain.

She groaned and felt like she wanted to retch, but although her body shuddered, the only thing she did was feel ill.

Pegasus lowered himself next to her. Angelique took several deep breaths, waiting for the worst of the nausea to subside before she crawled onto his back.

By the time Pegasus heaved himself to his feet and set their course east, the twisting pain in her gut was already subsiding.

Angelique clung to the constellation's back, threading her hands through his flickering mane.

Dimly, she wondered, *Did I just reach my price?*

RIDING PEGASUS, it didn't take long for Angelique to catch up to the Arcainian princes—though she still sat a little too loosely, her stomach occasionally twinging.

"You destroyed it? That quickly?" one of the twins asked as they slowed their horses to a walk.

Angelique held in a grimace—it hadn't *felt* like a quick fight—but nodded. "It's dead," she said. *And when the Council finds out about this escapade, I can probably look forward to another summons. Hopefully they'll be as sympathetic about a basilisk as they were about Clotilde.*

Steffen reined in his horse. It pranced in place for a moment so he dropped back to ride with Angelique. "Did it hurt you? You look pale."

Angelique paused, trying to choose her answer.

"Basilisks are poisonous." Prince Glasses watched her with narrowed eyes. "Do you think you have been compromised?"

Angelique couldn't quell her shiver as she shifted on Pegasus' back. Physically, she was already feeling better from her slow-burn healing spell on her bruised muscles. But her stomach hadn't settled, and icy dread was now crawling up her spine. (She could have hurt Pegasus, a million things could have gone wrong, and what would happen now?)

"No," Angelique finally answered. "I'm not much injured, just rattled."

Her stomach unexpectedly rolled again, and Angelique almost tipped over Pegasus' shoulder with the sick feeling.

"Perhaps we should separate into two groups," Prince Touchy-

Feely said. "Some of us can ride ahead, and a few of us can stay behind with the Lady Enchantress."

"Isn't it dangerous to split up?" the youngest prince asked.

Prince Touchy-Feely pressed his lips in a line. "Perhaps, but if we don't pick up our pace, we won't catch up to Elise in time."

Why isn't my slow-burn heal helping this sick feeling? Perhaps it really is my price? But I don't know that I used that much of my power.

Angelique tried to sit tall with dignity, intending to inform the princes she was well enough to push forward, but the sick twist to her stomach traveled up to the back of her mouth. She almost gagged before she gave in and slumped forward again.

Her shivers increased, and her teeth would have chattered if she hadn't kept her jaws clenched.

She closed her eyes and pressed her head to the crest of Pegasus' neck. Instead of smelling of the usual horse scents—hay, straw, and maybe grain—Pegasus gave off a slightly smoky scent. "It seems I require time to recoup. But I don't think it is necessary for you princes to split up—you may all ride ahead." The words tasted just as sick as her stomach—it was wrong to let the princes ride off without any magical aid. But between her shivering and the gurgles in her stomach, it was likely she wouldn't be able to continue much longer.

If I try to push on, I'll only hold them back.

Steffen slowly shook his head. "You are Gabi's friend," he said, surprising Angelique.

When was the last time a human being called me friend?

"She'll have me quartered if we leave you behind in this state, even if Elise needs our support," the prince added.

"We're near a village, aren't we?" Smashed-Nose asked. "Why don't we stop there to see if Elise passed through. We can leave the Lady Enchantress at the Green Ivy Inn."

When Steffen swiveled back to her, Angelique sat up so she was only crouched over Pegasus's neck rather than draped across it like a rag doll. "That would be agreeable," she managed to say.

Steffen nodded. "Then it's settled. Alter our course, Rune."

"Happily."

Angelique collapsed back on Pegasus' neck, squeezing her eyes shut as she greedily clung to his warmth, which—even if it did not make her shivers subside, reminded her of home, the warmth of the workshop, and Evariste's laughter.

CHAPTER 21

Angelique felt it when Clotilde died—mostly because the land itself seemed to gasp in relief once the darkness polluting it disappeared.

The princess was able to do it—bless her, she thought numbly.

She felt better...ish. Every so often, her stomach would roll and she'd gag, so she wouldn't be trotting off after the princes, but she was able to lie on the bed, safe in her inn room, while feeling only mildly uncomfortable.

It was late—if not near the midnight hour—but she couldn't sleep. (Her stomach made certain of that.)

A knock shook the door.

Angelique snapped upright and regretted it immediately. "Yes?" She cautiously eyed the door and pressed a hand to her grumbling stomach.

"I beg your pardon, Lady Enchantress," the innkeeper—a lively woman—said through the door. "But there is a visitor who insists on seeing you despite the late—and *rude* hour—"

"Oh, bother this!" a familiar voice snarked.

The lock toggled before the door blew open, and Roland sauntered in.

"That was entirely unnecessary, Master Puss," the innkeeper said.

"Quite the contrary. Thank you, Lena. You may go now." Roland's tone was imperious as he lifted his black-and-pink nose high.

When the innkeeper raised her gaze to Angelique, Angelique smiled. "Thank you, but we'll be fine."

"Then good night, Lady Enchantress, Master Puss." The woman closed the door again.

Angelique raised an eyebrow. "Master Puss?"

Roland sniffed. "I am not unknown in these parts from Gabrielle's adventuring days."

Angelique chuckled, but she let herself flop back on the straw-stuffed mattress. "Then it worked? Elise won?"

"With help from *me*, yes," Puss confirmed. "She broke the artifacts and defeated Clotilde rather swiftly."

"I am very glad to hear it," Angelique said.

"I assume so. But I am rather worried about whatever it is that has you rolling around like a beached whale," Puss said. Though his tone was haughty, Angelique heard the notes of concern in it.

Angelique briefly closed her eyes, as if she could so easily shut out the knowledge that she had used her war magic. "How did you arrive so swiftly?"

"As Gabrielle and I are no longer in hiding from Clotilde, I used the Carabas carriage." Puss jumped onto the bed and sauntered around the mattress. "There are some advantages to having a titled mistress who is independently wealthy of the royal family." He climbed onto her stomach and curled up in a tight ball.

He purred deep in his chest, which made Angelique's belly tingle and, strangely, soothed her stomach. She rested her hand on his back, relaxing slightly as the cramping in her stomach eased.

Minutes passed before Puss spoke again. "When Steffen told me you were here, he mentioned you faced off with a basilisk."

"Yes."

"What happened?" His voice was soft but unyielding. He wasn't going to let her screen her answer as the princes had.

Angelique sighed. "I used my war magic," she admitted. "It was going to get Pegasus, and I just *couldn't*—I can't see another sacrifice for me..."

"Basilisks are difficult to fight, particularly alone," Puss said. "It was a wise move."

Angelique covered her eyes with her hands. "Was it, though? I didn't just levitate sharp stakes of wood or a dagger, I stabbed the thing through with buried weapons my magic ripped from the ground. My powers came out so strong, there was an explosion."

Puss sniffed. "Hardly surprising given how you've kept it locked up."

"It was so strong and intoxicating," Angelique whispered. Her throat clogged, but she made herself speak. "What if I let it overtake me one day?"

"Your magic is intoxicating because it is powerful, there is a great deal of it, and—like *all* magic—it longs to be used," Puss sourly said. "If you used it regularly, it wouldn't have such an effect on you—not just mentally, but speaking of your price as well."

"Price?"

"The princes said you appeared ill."

"Ahh, yes." Angelique sighed. "I've been feeling sick since I used my magic. It's better now, but it's not encouraging that I still feel ill."

"You haven't used your magic since your days in Luxi-Domus," Roland said.

"Not true," Angelique countered. "I used it when Evariste and I were attacked by a troll."

"*Fine*, you haven't used your powers *on this scale* since your days in Luxi-Domus. I imagine your body is unused to handling it—a rather poor thing considering your war magic is at the very core of you."

"Not helping, *Puss*," Angelique growled.

"I would not be surprised if this sick feeling plaguing you really is your price, and I would expect next time, it won't last nearly as long. If your magic exploded on release, it's likely the lingering is a side effect from its unnecessary imprisonment and sudden mass usage."

"I hope so," Angelique groaned. "This isn't fun."

"It's actually a very mild price," Puss said. "Enchanter Jaxon goes blind for a number of hours after extensive usage of his magic. Enchantress Aubrey has to eat a great deal, or she passes out, which happens frequently. Enchanter Levidon loses control of his body, and it's said the Snow Queen herself used to fall unconscious for days after using her snow magic. You can still function...to a certain extent."

"Yes, I can do so much when I can only sit bent at an angle," Angelique snorted.

"At least you can drag yourself to safety," Puss pointed out. "You should prepare a pack with commoner cures—carry ginger, mint leaves, and the like. It might make you feel better."

Angelique's body twitched at the suggestion. "I don't plan to use my magic often enough to require such a thing," she said.

"Better to be prepared than caught off guard."

"Puss—no—Roland, I'm not going to use my magic."

"And what if another creature attacks Pegasus?" Puss stood and hopped off her stomach. He strolled down the length of her body and sat down next to her head. "What happens when you finally find Evariste, and you are forced to use your war magic to free him?"

Angelique was silent.

"You'll do whatever you need to." Puss placed one of his pink paws on the tip of her nose. "You needn't punish yourself for when that happens. Carry precautions, Angelique."

Angelique finally nodded. The motion didn't dislodge his paw, but she grimaced slightly. "Do I want to know where your paws have been the past few days?"

"Would you rather I present you with my posterior?"

"No, thank you."

"That's what I thought—ungracious child."

"I'm older than you are!"

"You are but a babe in enchantress years." Puss twitched his whiskers. "Gabrielle could likely be considered older than you are—you've aged only two or three years since I met you."

Angelique's eyes drifted shut again. "Time passes strangely," she said. "I don't sense it like I used to. I knew Evariste has been missing, but only recently had I realized it's been *years* that he's been gone."

"You will find him, Angelique." Puss laid down, this time curling around her shoulder. "Have you made any progress?"

"A bit, but not enough to be encouraging," she sighed. "And now the Council is going to send me a summons for using my core magic without supervision."

"You were fighting a basilisk; they can hardly complain."

Angelique was silent because both she and Puss knew they *would* complain regardless of the situation.

Their silence was oppressive, until Angelique decided to break it. "Enchanter Clovicus was able to smooth things over with the Council when I used magic against Clotilde. Perhaps he can do the same thing again," she bleakly said.

Roland's tail pulled loose from the curve of his body, and he violently flicked it. "They're fools."

"They're concerned with the entire Continent," Angelique corrected. "I'd be suspicious of me as well."

"You acted to save the princes of Arcainia who only recently ended their careers as wild fowl." Roland's voice was hot with anger as his tail lashed up and down.

A ghost of a smile settled on Angelique's lips. "Thank you, Roland."

Roland scooted closer to her so he could rub his cheek against hers. "Thank you, Angelique," he said. "You didn't have to help Gabrielle or the Arcainian royal family. It was a sacrifice—one I'm thankful for."

Angelique squirmed when his whiskers tickled her. "I didn't do much."

Puss rested his head against hers. "You did. And you face persecution from your own people for it. But the royal family knows, and Arcainia is grateful. *I'm* grateful."

Angelique had to raise her hand at an awkward angle to be able to pat his back. "Even if I were to ignore my duty as a magic user...you're my friend, Puss. If you—or Gabrielle—ever need help, I will stand with you."

"And we will stand with you," Puss said. "If the Council gives you too much guff, send for us. Gabrielle can be *quite* convincing and commanding when properly incentivized."

Angelique laughed. "Do you need to leave for Brandis right away in the morning?"

"Oh goodness, no. I hope you were joking, or shame on you for wishing such a horror on me. Gabi hasn't seen that Bumpkin Head of hers in months, and I very much wish to escape *all* of their reunion. It's sure to be a sickeningly sweet encounter." Puss shuddered in revulsion.

"So you are saying we should take our time in riding Pegasus back to Castle Brandis tomorrow?"

"Have you not been listening to a word I've said? I mean we shouldn't leave *at all* for at least three days!"

Angelique laughed, and finally the last nauseating twist in her stomach dispelled.

The Council would send for her, but she didn't regret aiding Arcainia, and she would *never* regret protecting Pegasus.

She only wished she could have done the same for Evariste.

EVARISTE STARED at the pile of canvases Liliane had recently painted to summon several different goblin packs. *How has she made an alliance with those creatures? And to what end?* He sat on the ground, his arms resting on his knees as he stared out through the glass pane.

Liliane and her cronies kept him in the empty chamber that Liliane used—it seemed—to summon different creatures.

Goblins, harpies, trolls, and more had traipsed through the cavern. The presence of so many creatures was not a good sign, for it meant Liliane and her people were more than a rag-tag bunch of black mages.

In fact, based on the numbers of dark creatures he had seen, it seemed Liliane was more like a general waging a war.

But why? Who has the power and fortitude to spend so much time readying plans and waging secret battles? The Chosen, the only magical enemy the world has ever faced, were stamped out centuries ago!

Evariste watched them stubbornly, trying to ingrain any and all details in his memory. *It will be useful to know when I get out.*

He tried to keep his hope alive, though he hadn't heard from Angelique nor any other mage since she nearly succeeded in tracking him with a location spell, and he was fairly certain it had been months.

His eyes drifted shut, and the grayness of the mirror invaded him, making his mouth taste like cobwebs as he felt the muted haze of the area threaten to swallow him whole.

No.

Evariste opened his eyes again and took a deep breath. *No,* he repeated. His fingers twitched, and he forcibly dredged up memories of complex spells he had learned as a young apprentice, mulling them over as he tried to match the spell Angelique had used with one he knew.

He didn't particularly care if he figured out what she had done, but the act gave his mind something to fixate on and beat back a bit of the drab grayness of the mirror. Of course, remembering some of Emerys' muttered curses or one of Angelique's funnier expressions did the same, but the mental activity made him feel marginally more useful. So he spent his hours pondering the spell, saving up questions he'd ask Angelique about what she had done to power it, where she had acquired the spell, how long it took her to create something so advanced, and if she missed him as keenly—no—as wholly as he missed her.

Better not ask that last one. She'll freeze like a frightened deer or think I've lost my wits.

Footsteps interrupted his thoughts. Evariste leaned his head against the glass pane of the mirror and watched when Liliane emerged from the darkness.

His muscles tightened when he saw she didn't carry her canvasses, but a black jewel. *Not again.*

"Good day to you, Lord Enchanter Evariste!" Liliane cheerfully called.

Evariste stood and edged his way back as far as the grayness would allow. "Bugger off."

She smiled serenely. "Now, that is hardly a cordial greeting."

"Hardly cordial? Obviously I wasn't trying hard enough. Please allow me to rephrase that: I hope you choke in your sleep and die," Evariste growled.

"I know you're testy because of this." She held the black jewel—which was the size of a small apple—up for inspection. "But I'm afraid I must drain you regardless of your bad humor. One of my underlings is in need of your power to strengthen a spell."

Evariste's fingers twitched again. He was desperate enough that he tried to reach for his magic, but as always, there was only the numb embrace of his sealing spell.

Liliane and her minions frequently used Evariste as a power pack, draining him of his magic and using it to forge potent spells. Getting drained was a pain Evariste had never known before. And he recognized the black gems—Liliane had drained him months prior to charge up two similar jewels.

He clenched his jaw and sat down hard—as far away from the pane as he could get. *I'm not going to give her the satisfaction of my pain. I can't win much in this state, but in this I can.*

He took a deep breath as Liliane dragged a stool in front of the mirror and sat down. She sat primly with her feet tucked under the hem of her dress, her skirts pooling over the sides of the stool.

But sitting this near to her, Evariste saw the tightness around her eyes. *Something happened. Something big—for she's never shown signs of strain before.* "One of your plans failed," he said.

A corner of her mouth briefly twitched down, but it was the only sign Liliane gave that indicated just how right he was. "Your insults are going dull, Lord Enchanter, if that is the best you have."

Evariste chuckled as he leaned back on his hands. "It's not an insult but rather an observation. Everything isn't falling into place as you had planned. You're *losing*."

Liliane chuckled. "Hardly," she said. "I can admit there have been a few hiccups, but nothing worth troubling ourselves over. We have much in store. Centuries of planning won't be disturbed or ruined by a few lucky fights." She made a show of settling in and sniffed a little.

Evariste wasn't fooled. He actually considered getting up and running around of the inside of the mirror, cheering.

Liliane may not be losing, but whatever is happening out there, it's unsettling her. Which means there is great potential to damage her plans. That she called them lucky fights is even more telling.

"Chin up, Enchanter Evariste," Liliane said consolingly as she cradled the black gem in her hands. "It's only one jewel this time—though I'm afraid I'll require quite a lot of power for this one. Lightning, thunder, high winds, all cost much in power when done on such a large scale, even if it's only to get things started."

Evariste frowned. "*What?*"

"This will only take a few minutes," Liliane said sweetly before she flicked her magic at Evariste.

She used a combination of her mint-green powers and foul black magic that oozed like tar.

Evariste shifted uncomfortably as the swirled mixture coated the glass that separated him from the outside.

It oozed in around the edges and crawled towards him like a snake. He tried to kick it away, but it encased his foot and climbed up his leg.

The pain was unimaginable.

Even though Evariste was walled off from his magic, it still was a part of him, and it was getting dug out and sheered from his soul. For the spell forcefully drained his magic from him and used it to power whatever Liliane was crafting.

It made his heart spasm and his lungs ache. His body shook from the pain, his vision blurred, and the unsteady thumps of his heart filled his ears.

He clenched his jaw, unwilling to release the roar of pain that clawed at his throat. The pain consumed him, ripping through his body with the savagery of a sword.

The gray around him dimmed. Desperate, Evariste reached for the darkness and the comfort of unconsciousness. He retreated to his memories, retreated to a happier time and place.

"And that was when—Evariste, are you even listening to me?" Emerys growled. Pookie, his black war unicorn, pawed at the ground and snorted red.

Evariste blinked at the shock of finding himself on horseback. He twisted in the saddle to look back at Angelique, who was riding an elven horse and chatting with Lady Alastryn. It took him a few heartbeats to recall the memory—it was the day of a large summer feast the elves threw annually. They were riding to Brandy Crest, the spot in Alabaster Woods where the elves held their biggest celebrations.

Angelique laughed at something Alastryn said, then turned and met his gaze, her eyes sparkling with joy.

Yes, it was just a memory, and when Evariste came to again, every piece of him was going to ache from the pain of being drained. But here he could escape. Here he could see the green of the world, the beauty of Alabaster Woods, joke with Emerys once more, and watch Angelique—beautiful, brave Angelique...

CHAPTER 22

"You used *war magic*, unsupervised!" Enchanter Tristisim thundered so loudly he dislodged dust from the ceiling beams of Hallowed Hall.

Angelique winced but forced herself to stand tall as she stood under the well-lit dais placed in front of the Council Members' seats. "The basilisk was going to attack Pegasus—a constellation. No one was with me, so I couldn't seek help. I didn't see any other way."

"That matters not!" Enchanter Tristisim shouted. "You made an agreement!"

Enchantress Primrose coughed politely, and Tristisim finally looked away from Angelique and growled into his papers. Primrose set her folded hands on top of her desk and smiled sadly. "What I believe Tristisim meant to say, is that as part of us giving permission for you to be made an apprentice, you agreed not to use your core magic without Enchanter Evariste's supervision."

Angelique mashed her lips together. *I did, but how can I convince them I had no other choice?*

"Might the Council take into account that the *only* reason Apprentice Angelique has not yet made Lady Enchantress is because her master is not here to advocate for her, and without him, she cannot take the evaluations," Enchanter Clovicus said loftily. He leaned against the fence that enclosed Angelique's dais and folded his arms across his chest.

Enchanter Crest rested his chin on his hand. "I will admit I'm slightly baffled regarding your presence, Clovicus, when this is supposed to be a closed-door meeting."

Clovicus smiled—which was more debonair and daring than polite. "I'm here to represent the interests of my previous student, of course," he said. "The skies know Evariste would be here if he could—and perhaps he would be *if* you put more manpower into finding him."

"If the committee charged with seeking out his captors needs more manpower, they will request it themselves, without your meddling," Enchantress Felicienne said in a voice that was taut like a violin string.

"As you say, Council Member," Clovicus said smoothly. "Regardless, henceforth I'll be attending any meetings involving young Angelique—for the sake of my dearly beloved previous student, that is."

Enchanter Lazare squinted. "When we dumped Evariste on you as a lad, you complained you didn't want to babysit a spoiled brat who was too small to ride anything bigger than a pony."

"And yet look how well he turned out," Clovicus said. "Besides, we became quite close. Eventually."

Though the Council did not look amused, Angelique couldn't help the slight smile that ghosted across her lips. *The more I get to know Clovicus, the less Evariste's ability to manipulate surprises me.*

"Fine," Enchantress Felicienne said with an aggravated smile. "Be here if you *must*. But all the worming in the world won't erase the fact that Apprentice Angelique used her war magic without Evariste's supervision."

"To save Pegasus," Angelique said.

"Yes, to save the constellation," Enchantress Galendra murmured. "But why was he in danger?"

Angelique refrained from rolling her eyes. "Because I was facing a basilisk, and if I had not fought it, it would have gone after the seven Arcainian Princes." It was a fight to keep her voice pleasant, but she won.

"That's right, the seven princes have been recently freed from their curse, yes?" Enchanter Crest asked.

"Yes," Angelique said. "I was with them when they rode to Arcainia, but we separated when the basilisk was unleashed."

"But they went on to defeat Clotilde, did they not?" Enchantress Felicienne asked.

"It was a family effort, yes." Angelique phrased her response carefully.

Steffen had made it clear he didn't want the Veneno Conclave to know about Elise's magic. Sybilla would hold her peace, Angelique was sure. The real danger was that she needed to speak the truth when answering the Council's questions.

The Council Members frowned.

Clovicus sighed loudly. "Since none of you seem keen to remember, might I remind you that because he is not from our realm, Pegasus falls under special protection while here."

Enchantress Felicienne's mouth twitched, and Tristisim's expression grew hard.

"Yes, Clovicus, we are aware of the constellation's status," the enchanter growled.

Clovicus winked. "I thought so—you were definitely acting as though you remembered such a thing."

"Be that as it is, we—*again*—cannot charge Apprentice Angelique," Enchantress Felicienne said.

Though normally Angelique would have sagged with relief, instead bitterness swept through her.

They're disappointed. They're aggravated they can't seal me because I followed the rules, because I saved Pegasus. It's been the same way every time. Why do they want *me to be evil? Why do they act disappointed when it's made clear I've acted on behalf of the greater good?*

Enchantress Primrose smiled warmly at Angelique. "You are cleared, Angelique. But while we are here, I would like to discuss the possibility of transferring you to another enchanter or enchantress."

Ice filled Angelique's veins. "I beg your pardon," she croaked.

"We really don't know how long it will be until Evariste is found," Primrose continued. "It seems unfair to leave you in an uncertain position."

"It's *dangerous*," Tristisim said with great certainty, "to let her frolic, unfettered, around the continent."

"New supervision is required," Enchantress Felicienne agreed.

"We will create a list of enchanters and enchantresses who could properly *manage* someone of your...talents," Enchantress Galendra squeaked.

"But I don't want a different master," Angelique said.

"Your loyalty is admirable, Apprentice, but with Evariste's future uncertain, this is the best move for you," Enchanter Crest said. "With a new master, you'll soon be able to take the necessary tests to become an enchantress." Though his voice was warm and his smile inviting, Angelique wasn't fooled.

After what I just witnessed? Not likely. There is no chance that they would ever let me become an enchantress. They're just trying to shift me to someone else so they can seal—and possibly exile—me with a new master's permission.

Clovicus tsked, and all the Council Members shifted wary gazes to him.

"What *now?*" Tristisim demanded.

"I just find it regrettable that the Council—the most esteemed members of the Veneno Conclave—know so little about our organization's laws." Clovicus sighed and slightly shook his head.

Angelique held her breath. *Is he going to get me out of this?*

A look of puzzlement settled over Primrose's face as she patted her plump cheeks. "Oh dear, did I forget a law?"

Enchantress Felicienne rubbed her eyes with the palms of her hands. "What is it, Lord Enchanter?" she asked.

"Unless a master has either died, been sealed, or is in the process of being charged with a serious crime, the master must approve of the change," Clovicus said.

"Evariste died?" Enchanter Lazare leaned over his desk and squinted at Clovicus. "Why didn't anyone tell me?" he demanded.

"Enchanter Evariste is still alive, Lazare," Primrose assured him.

"I am familiar with the rule," Tristisim said. "But there are other exceptions—if a master is taken suddenly ill or if he disappears. Evariste might not have disappeared in the traditional sense, but we've lost all sign of him."

"Yes," Clovicus agreed. "But the rule also states that at least one to two years must pass since the master was recorded as missing before the apprentice can be changed over."

"Agreed," Enchanter Crest said. "Which is not a worry because it's been three and a half years."

"That's for a regular mage student. For an Enchantress-in-Training, the timeline expands due to the longevity of our kind." Clovicus brandished a finger in the air. "For at least ten years."

"Oh," Primrose blinked.

Tristisim screwed up his mouth so it looked like he had swallowed a toad. "He is correct."

Enchantress Felicienne's groan was only slightly muffled by the arm she slung across her face.

Clovicus directed his gaze up to Angelique and smiled—an infectious sort of smile that made Angelique's mouth start to move as well. "I usually am," he said.

"Then I guess we must leave Angelique under Evariste's care?" Enchantress Galendra asked as she sank deeper in her chair.

"Unless!" This time, Clovicus turned to the Council with such energy, Angelique suspected this was the point he had been aiming to drive home the entire time. "You give her apprenticeship to *me*. As Evariste's old teacher, my claim on Angelique is exempt from the waiting period. It would be *natural*, in fact, to take her under my wing."

Enchanter Lazare scratched his beard, making a dry, crackling sound. "That's very true, and law-abiding to boot!" he said, sounding like he was considering the matter.

Every other member of the Council scrunched their face up.

Felicienne scowled at her desk in a mixture of disdain and horror—as if Clovicus had just presented her with a hairy spider.

Tristisim was busy mashing his fingers into his forehead, and even Enchantress Primrose looked a little green at the idea.

"No, no," Primrose laughed uneasily. "I think Angelique will manage quite well on her own."

"But you were so *eager* to let her seek help from another master." Clovicus smiled like a wolf. "And here I am!"

"You would make her into the most crooked magic user to ever grace these halls," Felicienne flatly said.

"Lady Enchantress, how you wound me! Evariste is ever the law-abiding enchanter," Clovicus said.

"With all too much of a streak of justice that *you* taught him," Tristisim grumbled.

Enchanter Crest scratched his jaw. "It is probable he never would have requested Angelique as his apprentice if not for your tutelage."

A newfound fondness for Clovicus surged through Angelique with that epiphany. *I am so glad he's Evariste's master. And not just because he seems like he would be an unpleasant opponent!*

Tristisim clenched his right hand into a fist and lightly rapped the surface of his desk. "It is apparent this conversation isn't going to produce anything fruitful. You are free to go, Apprentice Angelique, but be aware you are on thin ice. Next time, the Council will not be so understanding."

Angelique bit her tongue to hold in the sharp words that wanted to burst from her, but she managed a curtsey before she trooped down the few steps of the dais and followed Clovicus into the hallway.

Angelique smiled and nodded at the enthusiastic war mage who bowed to her. "Thank you, Enchanter Clovicus, for your help."

Clovicus shrugged as he sauntered down the hallway. "You're doing all the heavy lifting in the search for Evariste. The least I can do is keep the Council from sealing you out of spite. You know, if you threw Evariste's name around a bit more, they wouldn't drag you in here so often. They summon you because they *know* you fear them."

"I doubt that," Angelique said dourly. "They feel too sanctified in their actions."

Clovicus shrugged. "It's your choice, I suppose. What will you do now that the conflict in Arcainia is resolved?"

"I need to return to Torrens to check in on Evariste's house," Angelique said. "But I'm back to combing the continent in search of him. I'll do some research before I pick the next country I mean to visit."

"Very well, keep in touch. Let me know if you find anything—or plan to break more magical laws," he said.

Angelique's smile lessened to a frown. "I don't mean to break them out of a desire to make havoc."

Enchanter Clovicus rested a brief hand on her shoulder. "I know," he said. "You have acted with honor. I meant for it to be a joke—obviously one that is poor in taste if you could not tell that. Don't let them make you doubt yourself, Angelique. You'll be an excellent enchantress if you can manage that." He winked and set off, beckoning her to follow. "Come, I'll walk you to Evariste's office."

Finally, Angelique thought as she glided after the Lord

Enchanter, *I can finally get back to focusing on my search for Evariste. If only I could do more.*

Winter passed, and in early spring, Angelique set out for Ringsted.

Unfortunately, the storms surrounding the shipping giant had only worsened over the winter, cutting the country off from all outside contact (its northern border that attached it to the continent was made up of the nearly impassable Chronos Mountains).

The mountain range was treacherous and impossible for armies or merchant caravans to pass through, but one determined Enchantress-in-Training with a starry steed could—and did—make it.

Unfortunately, she had very little to show for it.

Angelique had been hopeful that the country's isolated state meant Evariste was present, and the black mages were covering their tracks. She found no sign, however, of her instructor—or a magical mirror.

She couldn't even find a hint of black mages in the country, although she was convinced there had to be one hiding *somewhere* in the green land of Ringsted. (There was no explaining the storms, otherwise.)

Angelique tipped her head as she watched one of the storm lines. Though sunlight shone on land, out on the sea—in the deeper waters where boats would sail—angry black clouds dumped torrential rains and spat lightning strikes at an alarming rate.

I should see if the Veneno Conclave has sent any weather mages to investigate the storms, Angelique thought. The wind tugged on a lock of her hair—today she had settled it into a copper hue—and the ocean lulled her with the steady crash of waves and salty scent.

Ringsted—with its green lands, rocky sea cliffs, and plentiful beaches—was the kind of country that carved a spot in one's soul.

"Another time." She opened her eyes and squared her shoulders. "I need to continue my search for Evariste...and these storms bear investigating."

Angelique turned her back on the blue ocean accented with frothy white lines of cresting waves and made her way to Pegasus.

The constellation stood at the tree line, sniffing greenery though he made no move to taste it. When he saw Angelique approaching, he tossed his head, making his bridle—one of his new accessories—jingle.

The bridle was made of leather dyed blue and accented with tiny glittering gems that reminded Angelique of stars. His other new accessory was a saddle—one Angelique felt hesitant to sit on given that the seat of the saddle displayed a silvery moon that *changed* with respect to the real moon that hung in the sky. He had...Angelique hesitated to say it, but...*created* them after Angelique asked if he could get her across the Chronos Mountains that spring. (One moment he was bareback, the next he wore a saddle.)

"I think I'm ready to go. Evariste clearly isn't here, though there is black magic at work in those storms." She lifted her nose, as if she could scent out the perpetrator. "*Twisted* black magic, though I suppose all kinds are." She held in a shudder as she leaned into the constellation for comfort. "If I'm not mistaken, and there's a large chance that I am, this one has a hint of blood magic in it."

Of all dark magic, blood magic was among the worst, for it required the sacrifice and blood of the innocent to manufacture power for its wielder.

Angelique shivered, until Pegasus dropped his head over her shoulder in the horse-y version of a hug.

She rested her head against his neck, then made herself pull away and swing onto his back.

Pegasus started heading northwest, angling towards the mountain range they would spend the next few terrible weeks crossing.

As his hooves trod in a steady beat, Angelique continued to mull over recent events.

There's something going on. In the span of a few years, Evariste has been taken, Prince Severin was cursed, Arcainia was briefly taken over by a witch, and now these storms?

The world always had a history of fights and skirmishes with black mages. But this seemed like a lot in a very short span of time.

And to top it off, this year Princess Rosalinda of Sole turns eighteen. Her modified curse will make her fall asleep. The timing of it seems very... providential given everything else.

She needed to return to Sole. In the latest report Angelique had received from Firra—before she left for Ringsted—the fire mage said Carabosso was slowly closing in on the woods where Princess Rosalinda—unaware of her birthright and raised as a commoner—lived.

If Carabosso killed Rosalinda instead of merely setting off her curse, the results would be catastrophic for Sole given she was the heir to a throne that prized—above all else—its lineage to a queen of the distant past.

Angelique ducked a branch and frowned deeply. *So much is going wrong. How am I supposed to decide what to do first?*

It was moments like this when Angelique missed Evariste.

Four years had passed since Evariste was taken. Acceptance had finally settled in—Angelique was now more used to traveling alone and acting without looking to her mentor.

But, in a terrible twist, she seemed to feel his absence even more keenly. Early on, she had missed him because she worried she couldn't do it alone, that she wasn't skilled enough and possibly was too dangerous.

Now, I've learned that doesn't matter at all, as often times, I'm the only available option, she thought wryly.

Now, with every bow she received and every smile of thanks she was given, Angelique missed his hidden jokes, easy warmth, and general presence.

Angelique snapped out of her pity party when Pegasus came to an abrupt halt.

He pricked his ears, listening. She kept quiet and also tried to listen for whatever had made him stop but heard nothing.

Pegasus, however, must have heard more.

He tossed his head and pranced, taking a few steps south rather than north.

Angelique held the reins of the bridle loosely so the constellation was still the navigator in any situation, but it seemed like he wasn't going to go back on course without some semblance of a discussion.

And I thought my life with Evariste was strange.

Angelique cleared her throat. "Is something wrong, Pegasus?"

Pegasus snorted, then started through the underbrush at a brisk walk.

Eventually, Angelique heard a voice—playful-sounding but lost and mournful in pitch. "They said he was with the mage—the sea witch," this new voice said. "And I am my clan's best singer."

The voice whispered something Angelique couldn't make out and was followed by a dull thump.

CHAPTER 23

Pegasus barged his way between trees, then shifted slightly so he and Angelique could together peer down at the young lady slumped on the ground.

Her skin was a warm shade of olive, and she had lovely hair of tight curls that were a dark brown color, though the top layer was a burnished gold—bleached by the sun. Even from this angle, it was obvious the girl was taller than Angelique.

Angelique blinked as she struggled to process this. *Golden skin, tall, curls in her hair...what does that mean?* She looked at Pegasus, who jerked his head in an eastern direction, and even this far inland, Angelique could hear the call of sea birds.

Angelique brightened. *Aha-ha! Of course!* Feeling surer of herself, Angelique spoke. "Strange, I didn't think I would find someone who looks even worse for wear than I do. What is wrong, selkie lass? Why are you out of the sea and away from your colony?"

Selkies were a rare race of magical people who could shift between a human form and seal form. They were able to transform by putting on their seal pelts and were, in general, considered the guardians of the oceans.

Though Ringsted was the location of their only colony, they were rarely seen inland—and certainly never far from their family.

Slowly, the selkie raised her gaze, revealing mesmerizing sea green eyes swirled with hints of ocean blue. "You're a magic user," she whispered, her eyes glowing with renewed hope.

Angelique slid off Pegasus' back, banging herself in the kneecap with a saddle stirrup on the way down. "I am an Enchantress-in-Training. My name is Angelique. Can I help you?"

Tears welled up in the selkie's eyes. "I'm Dylan, youngest daughter of King Murron and Queen Gwenllian of the selkies."

Angelique successfully managed to keep her jaw from dropping at this tidbit, and her sense of concern for the selkie lass was now linked to a desire to groan.

If Selkie royalty is on land, this is worse than I thought.

"A sea witch has been plaguing Ringsted's shores," the selkie princess continued, unaware of Angelique's new dread. "She is responsible for the storms that tear through the ocean. We selkies have been tracking her for months, and it has been a stain on our pride that she has avoided capture for so long."

Well, I suppose that solves the mystery of the storms—though it's probably the worst possible outcome. A sea witch—it will take a squad of weather mages and water mages to take her down.

Dylan scowled, making her lovely eyes stormy. "We have set so many traps and launched many an attempt to capture her, but she's evaded us, and sometimes the landers unknowingly muck up our traps and ruin our plans." She smacked an open hand on the ground in her frustration.

Angelique nodded in encouragement when the selkie glanced her way.

"Today, my family set up another trap for the sea witch. We would have caught her—we *should* have—but she was wielding some sort of sword, and we were in our seal bodies..." She trailed off and mashed her lips together. Her eyes once again welled with tears, though her furrowed brow spoke more of vexation than sadness.

Angelique strained her memory for more selkie lore. "If a selkie pelt is damaged, the selkie can no longer take up the form of a seal, yes?" she asked gently.

Dylan wordlessly nodded. "I chased her onto land," she finally said. "Against my Da's wishes. I *had* her! My selkie magic had her trapped! But she's allied herself with some shady humans and they snuck up behind me!"

Though Angelique was inclined to feel sorry for the selkie princess, Dylan's ire only seemed to grow. *This one is a handful, that much is for certain.*

Dylan finally snapped her gaze up. "They took my pelt, and now I can't go back to my selkie form."

Angelique's heart broke for her.

She had seen princes taken to their knees, a duchess desperate in her desire to mend two feuding countries together, and Puss unconscious and injured, but the grief in Dylan's eyes, her consuming fear made Angelique's chest wrench.

Dylan had been backed into a dark corner, and there was no curse to break, no spell to modify that would return the pelt—part of her very being—to her.

Angelique paused when she noticed a very key word in Dylan's explanation. "You said *they* took it?"

"Yes, the sea witch and some prancing man she's working with have it. Or so say the men in the encampment that held me imprisoned until I broke out," Dylan darkly said.

"Were they all mages—or magic users?"

The selkie shook her head. "Just the sea witch. The rest of them are all landers."

Humans—regular men—are working with a sea witch? That is grave and dangerous news indeed.

"But I am my clan's strongest singer, which means I have the strongest magic because we channel it through our singing," the selkie princess continued, oblivious to Angelique's horrible epiphany. "The sea witch and her cronies have my pelt; they will threaten me to use my voice and do their bidding. But I can't, I have to refuse, and then they'll destroy my pelt." A few hot tears finally escaped Dylan's eyes and rolled down her cheek.

Angelique cringed at the idea of the sea witch controlling Dylan. It was bad enough she was a selkie princess, but if she really was the best in her clan at magic...the witch could cause great devastation.

Dylan crouched in front of a tree, a more ashen hue settling into her bronze skin. "I am ruined, Lady Enchantress."

Angelique tapped her lower lip. *Magic can't help her here, and all of this is dangerous if it means black magic users have found human allies. What damage could a sea witch and humans working with her do while Ringsted is cut off from this? How can we change this?*

She forcibly ignored her desire to puzzle through *why* such a thing was occurring—there was nothing she could do about that at the moment but take it to someone wiser—like Enchanter Clovicus.

Perhaps for now it would be best to turn the matter over to the selkies until I can get to the Conclave and send for help? Angelique folded her arms across her chest, then quickly corrected her posture and stood straight again. "Couldn't you return to your people and tell them what happened? Surely they would storm the camp."

"Yes, and my pelt would be destroyed in retribution. Although perhaps I have earned it for my careless actions," Dylan said in a dry and scratchy voice. "It seems it is the only course available to me, for I cannot remain near my pelt. They'll use my voice. Unless..." She leaned forward and smiled eagerly at Angelique.

"Yes?" Angelique cautiously sat down on a log across from Dylan's resting spot.

"Could you...*take* my voice?" Dylan asked.

Angelique blinked. "I beg your pardon?"

"Could you separate my voice from my body and take it?"

Why is it that everyone I meet wants me to break magical laws that will cause trouble? Such a thing like taking a voice is undoubtedly among the blackest sort of magic there is! A voice is a means of expression, protection, and a declaration of being. I can't just take *it!* Angelique squared her shoulders. "No, definitely not. It doesn't work like that."

"Oh," Dylan drooped.

Angelique watched her sag with discouragement. *I can't leave her like this. But I need to start north given crossing the mountains takes time, even with Pegasus. What could I do?*

Angelique racked her brain for a moment, until she finally recalled the collar she had made for Roland that sealed his voice. She knew the more advanced version—which didn't require a collar of any sort. It just needed conditions to break the seal on her voice, since it wouldn't slide off like a collar could.

Reluctantly, Angelique said, "But…I could seal your voice."

Dylan looked afraid to hope as she pushed her hair over her shoulder. "Seal it?"

"Lock it up, essentially. Make it so you are unable to utter a noise."

"Yes! Oh, please," Dylan said, sliding forward on her knees. "I'll pay any price, just please, silence me!"

It took all of Angelique's self-control to keep from rubbing her eyes. *This selkie seems impulsive.* She kept her expression tranquil as she suggested, "Are you sure it is the wisest course of action? Shouldn't you tell your kinsmen first?"

"This is my mistake, and I know I can make it right—as long as I am swift. If my voice is gone, I will be as useful as a rock to the sea witch and can wait for her and her minions to lower their guard. When they do, I will take back what is mine," Dylan promised. "And *then* I will tell my clan. And tell them that the sea witch has human allies."

Oh yes, she is dangerously *impulsive.* Angelique pursed her lips. "I don't think it is wise to do this alone."

Dylan shook her head. "I don't need help. Besides you locking up my voice, I mean."

"*Sealing* it," Angelique stressed. (Locking sounded a little too final for the fuss-budgets in the Conclave. Sealing, at least, meant the spell could be broken.)

Dylan nodded eagerly. "Yes, that."

I know it was my suggestion, but I'm still not sure about this. It seems to be a bit too fast. But how much trouble can she get into if I ride north and send word to the Conclave before heading to Sole to check in on Princess Rosalinda? Angelique held in a grimace. "Are you certain? Making a decision that will have an immense consequence on all of your kinsmen without their knowledge seems unfair."

Up went Dylan's chin in the continental sign of stubbornness. "This is the only way."

Angelique sighed. "As you wish—although I will not pretend to agree with your methods. I would like to help you more, but I am needed in Sole. I can seal your voice, but I haven't much time to do anything beyond that. I'm sorry."

Dylan shook her head. "If you seal my voice, you will have done more than I could ever repay you for, Lady Enchantress. I am strong. I can handle this alone."

Angelique squinted, already second-guessing the decision, for Dylan sounded dangerously similar to Angelique when she fought with Evariste before he was captured. "It has been my experience that when we believe we are capable of handling it ourselves, it becomes a situation that is so very much bigger than we are. I will seal your voice, though I hope you won't regret it."

"I would much rather be able to swim as a sea lion in the ocean than sing," Dylan assured her.

Angelique relaxed slightly. "Oh, I won't seal your voice forever."

"What?"

"I can work a counter spell into it, so your voice will return to you when you fulfill the requirements."

"Oh. What will the requirements be?" Dylan asked.

That made Angelique wince. *In a situation like this, it's the more powerful counters that are best—the same way it is for curse modification. And of course I'm terribly limited in my abilities in this area. It is a failing of my schooling—though in all fairness, curses are not very common, and the rate at which they've popped up over the past few years is alarmingly unusual.*

Angelique cleared her throat and kept her expression calm. "True love's first kiss."

Dylan blinked. "*What?*"

Angelique smiled at Dylan, although she was unable to contain all the bitterness she felt about the subject, and the smile felt a little flat. "I apologize, but it is the most powerful counter spell I know. In something as powerful as this, love is the only key I can use."

Dylan shrugged, unbothered by the requirement. "As you say."

"You agree so swiftly?"

"It is my mess. Getting my voice back is more than I deserve," Dylan shrugged. "Someday I'll find someone to break the curse. The bigger threat is that sea witch."

I don't know whether to be horrified she impulsively decided that giving up her voice forever was a good idea, or admire her for seeing the bigger threats at play and moving to stop them. Angelique stared at Dylan for a moment. "You are...unusual."

"My father says that all the time. I think it is merely that most folk don't know how to take responsibility for themselves," Dylan scoffed.

Angelique managed another weak smile. "There's a difference between being responsible and being brash."

"So I have heard. Is there anything I must do for you to seal my voice? Do you need ingredients?" Dylan asked.

"No," Angelique said. "It's an easy enough spell. It is the results that are potent and dangerous." She hesitated. "Are you *certain* you do not wish to tell your family?"

"Yes. Please, seal my voice, Lady Enchantress."

Angelique pressed her hands together. *What else can I do? This is too big for me to handle alone. If Dylan's voice is sealed, the sea witch can't use her, and she might be able to uncover more information.*

Lacking any other idea, Angelique stood. She started to gather up her magic, molding it into the necessary form. She checked her work twice, grimly ignoring her silvery magic as it brushed around her and tugged at her clothes. But when she couldn't delay it any longer, Angelique looked at Dylan.

"Dylan, daughter of King Murron and Queen Gwenllian, guardians of the seas, I bind your voice and seal it from now until the day that a kiss of true love touches your lips," Angelique said, her voice deeper and sharp from the magic filling her voice. "You shall not speak; you shall not sing. You will be *silent*."

Light laced with twirls of pale blue and green encircled Dylan, swirling closer and closer to her. The light encased the base of her neck in a thin ribbon, encircling it like a necklace.

Angelique could see the faint glyphs and symbols of the spell settling into place with her magic. She held her breath, but Dylan's eyes were bright and unafraid as Angelique's sharp, cool magic tightened around the selkie's throat before soaking into her skin.

Her magic hummed when the seal settled in, and Angelique could feel the moment the spell took, sealing Dylan's voice. (It was a gentle tug at the pit of her stomach, followed by a ringing feeling in her chest.)

A deep thrum—similar to the slam of a great door closing—and the last bits of the spell disappeared.

Angelique exhaled, relieved the spell had worked. "I will carry your message of the sea witch to other mages and magic users." She rejoined Pegasus, dropping his reins over his neck so they wouldn't droop onto the ground. "And if I hear no news from Ringsted by next spring, I will return and see if I cannot help you. Don't worry; if you reclaim your pelt but not your voice, I have associates who can break off my magic." Angelique smiled. It dimmed when she realized it would have to be Enchanter Clovicus rather than Evariste.

She slightly shook her head, then swung up into the saddle, reclaiming her perch on Pegasus. "You are certain you will be all right?"

Dylan opened her mouth, but nothing came out. The selkie princess brightened and smiled at Angelique before she folded over in a deep bow.

I hope this all works out for the best.

"Take care, Dylan of the selkies." Angelique clung to the saddle when Pegasus turned and started to walk off through the trees.

A flick of his tail, and he rocked into a gallop, going faster and faster.

Thankful for the saddle, Angelique clung to his back, trusting him to avoid trees and low-hanging branches.

Mentally, she started down the checklist of spells she needed to activate once they hit the mountains: a heat charm, a wind charm to possibly help clear paths for Pegasus—for even this late in spring, the mountains were topped with snow—and perhaps anything she could think of that would invigorate a person. (Even though he was a constellation, climbing mountains at the pace Pegasus liked to adopt was taxing for him.)

Once we're over the mountains, I need to send word to the Veneno Conclave of what's happening in Ringsted: of the sea witch, the humans that help her, and that faint whiff of blood magic.

ANGELIQUE PULLED the hood of her cloak tighter as she huddled on Pegasus' back.

Pegasus snorted with effort as he made his way across the rocky mountainside. Steam rose off his body even as snowflakes pelted them, and snow melted into water and hissed as he plowed through snowbanks.

No regular mount would be able to keep their footing in such icy and rocky conditions. But Pegasus made his way with ease. (Though Angelique's heart nearly stopped when the tiny game trail they followed that wound around the mountain grew too thin and the constellation stepped into *thin air* for several panic-inducing moments. However he stayed aloft, Angelique wasn't going to dwell upon it, for only shapeshifting mages who took on bird forms had ever achieved flight.)

They were treading on the top third of the mountain. Above them was only gray rock and snow caps, but they were traveling above the tree line where only the most daring vegetation grew. (The only forests in these terrible mountains were in sheltered crevasses and the occasional slope that wasn't covered in shadows by its brethren.)

Angelique would have happily ridden at a lower elevation, but given the unusual abilities of her traveling companion, the higher elevation let them cover a greater distance in this stretch of the mountains, where several peaks were huddled together in an almost conjoined formation.

The wind screamed, and the snow raged, cold and unforgiving.

Angelique pushed more power into her heat charm and again used bits of her magic to tweak the weather around them, lowering the wind from painful gusts to an icy breeze.

Weather patterns this extreme were difficult to manipulate, but given that they were slogging along at a quick walk, Angelique had plenty of time to practice.

Angelique sniffed her numb nose and peered over Pegasus' shoulder, looking down into the heart of the Chronos Mountains—an almost cradle-like valley, surrounded on all sides by dangerously high mountains.

If one looked on a map, it was a place where three borders met—the northern most bit of Ringsted, the southeast corner of Erlauf, and the southwest edge of Baris. In reality, the Chronos Mountains were no man's land. Very little vegetation could survive the mountains' harsh climate, and only a limited number of creatures called it home. No humans whatsoever lived in its peaks on any side. Between the avalanches, extreme weather, and occasional rumblings of the earth, it was uninhabitable.

As the range extended north between Baris and Erlauf, it turned into the Arkane Mountains, which were more habitable; but here, in the heart of the Chronos Mountains, it was devoid of life.

I was crazy to ever ask Pegasus if he could get me to Ringsted. Though in my defense, I didn't think he'd actually say yes.

Angelique rethreaded her gloved hands through Pegasus' flaming mane, keeping her fingers warm as the horse pawed another snowbank, melting it on contact with his hooves—which temporarily sported blue flames similar to his mane and tail.

But at least this time, it's easier going than our initial cross in early spring. The only nice part in that entire ride was when we crossed a glacier.

"Thanks, Pegasus," Angelique meekly said as he carried her on, his muscles taut with effort.

He snorted again and stopped his forward progression long enough to turn and flex his neck so he could bump her foot—hidden behind a cloak Stil had enchanted for her.

Angelique smiled and leaned over to fix the edge of her cloak, pausing when she realized she saw movement farther down the mountain side.

She squinted and was able to make out a line of green smudges. "Are those...goblins?"

Pegasus also looked down the mountainside, halting when he saw where she pointed.

Angelique dug into the saddlebag attached to Pegasus' saddle. It was another one of Stil's creations, so it had nearly unlimited space in it, though that made it a little hard for her to blindly feel through her bag for her telescope.

When she finally found it, she pulled it out, fitted it to her eye, and fussed until it reached the proper focus, magnifying the green smudges so Angelique could clearly make out twelve green-skinned goblins.

They appeared to be half frozen as they trekked across the mountains, wearing crudely sewn capes of patchwork furs as ice formed around the edges of their giant, bat-like ears. They carried blocky spears, crude swords, and clubs—though Angelique also spotted the occasional shield and even a few bows.

"Those are *forest* goblins. What in the blazes are they doing here in the mountains?" Angelique wondered. "They can't survive up here; even mountain goblins would have a difficult go of it."

Pegasus rested his muzzle on her foot as she carefully stowed her telescope. "Do you feel like going on a goblin hunt, Pegasus?"

As soon as she gripped his mane, Pegasus abandoned his horizonal path and began picking his way down the mountain—a slightly terrifying experience as occasionally his hind end folded down, and Angelique had to cling with a white-knuckle grip to stay on.

When they were just above the pack, Angelique slipped off Pegasus' back, scrambling in a rather ungainly manner to keep her feet under her.

She flexed her fingers as she juggled trying to hold her heat spell and ready an attack spell. She paused, met Pegasus' gaze, then nodded before she went hurtling down the steep embankment.

She collided with a goblin, and though she skidded to a stop, her target was not nearly as lucky. He went hurtling down the side of the mountain, screaming.

Angelique flicked a spell at the goblin in front of her, who had turned around to watch his companion fall to his death and now raised his sword above his head.

A gust of wind barraged the goblin, knocking him over the mountainside as well.

Pegasus raised turmoil at the front of the line, trampling goblins—who fell over the mountain in their effort to escape him.

Angelique threw a ball of fire at the next goblin in front of her. He ducked, but it only took a tickle of magic to encase him in ice with the weather as temperamental as it was.

An arrow whistled as it narrowly missed Angelique's head. She threw up a defensive shield and dosed the archer goblin in a wave of water in short succession.

The goblin squawked, but his skin turned blue-ish green as the frigid temperatures instantly froze the liquid to his skin.

A kick, and he went tumbling down the side of the mountain with the rest of his fellows.

The one remaining goblin—for Pegasus had already taken care of the rest at the front of the line—tried to rush Angelique. She threw up an ice wall in front of her, but it was unnecessary.

Pegasus lunged, grabbing the goblin by the neck, and snapped his head, flinging the goblin down the mountainside.

He then reared and shouted his fury—a bugling call that echoed through the mountain range. When he slammed his hooves back down, the entire mountain rumbled.

"I'm excited too." Angelique staggered and had to grab the iced-over goblin for support. "But could we maybe not celebrate quite so much?"

Pegasus twitched his ears and stepped forward as she dismantled the ice wall so he could nose her.

"I'm getting faster." She patted his cheek as she edged around his side, sticking close to him due to the narrow path. "Did you see how quickly I threw some of my spells?"

Pegasus swished his tail and looked unimpressed.

Angelique rolled her eyes. "We can't all be powerful star constellations. Some of us must be satisfied with being a mere Enchantress-in-Training."

Pegasus snorted but braced himself as Angelique swung onto his back.

Angelique shivered and had to pour more power into her heat charm. (She'd nearly lost it in the fight as she concentrated on the goblins, something she was not going to tell her already-unimpressed traveling companion.) It took longer than she wanted before the numb feeling left her fingers and she could curl them easily.

As Pegasus started to pick his way along the mountainside, restarting their trip, Angelique twisted so she could glance back at the site of the fight.

Already snow was blowing in, covering signs of the altercation. *I don't understand what the goblins were doing up here. But is this why Erlauf is so plagued by them? It seems unlikely; nothing can live on this side of the mountains.*

Angelique tucked the thought away to ponder later. For now, she had greater worries—specifically the Princess Rosalinda's curse and the sea witch in Ringsted. And, above all else, Evariste.

CHAPTER 24

By the time Angelique and Pegasus popped out of the Chronos Mountains over two weeks later, Angelique would have happily baked in the golden deserts of Baris for at least a month. Unfortunately, Ringsted's situation was dire, and she needed to report it before hurrying on to Sole.

So after giving Pegasus a few days' rest in the skies, they pressed on to the Veneno Conclave fortress, reaching it just before mid-summer.

Angelique very carefully avoided the part of the fortress that held Hallowed Hall, and instead stuck to the administration building.

For the first time since Evariste was captured, she entered the Assignment and Appointments Department, which was responsible for arranging mage assignments and approving requests for magical aid throughout the continent.

Two mages were at the desk, a young man and a young lady. The man wore thick robes despite the warmth of summer, bronze-framed spectacles, and had a slight hunch to his shoulders even though he appeared to be in his early twenties.

The female mage was pretty with shiny, copper-colored hair

that she twirled around her finger as she smiled brightly at her co-worker. "You look so handsome when you're concentrating on work."

The man muttered something under his breath.

"What was that? I couldn't hear what you said, Alfonso." The woman practically purred as she leaned closer to him.

The man's face turned bright red, and he made a show of scooting his chair away, making his co-worker chuckle.

The woman noticed Angelique's entrance and winked at her, holding up a finger to request her to wait a moment. She watched the man—Alfonso—finish scratching out a sentence on a small slate. "Shall I transcribe that for you? Though I do so *love* watching you write."

Alfonso pushed his glasses farther up his nose, but they dropped down again immediately. "Someone is waiting to speak with you."

"Can't you speak to her? It's so attractive when you take charge."

"*Sinèad*," he huffed in exasperation.

The woman smiled like a smug cat, then finally swiveled to face Angelique. "Thank you for waiting, Apprentice Angelique. Welcome to the Assignments and Appointments Department. How can we help you this day?"

Angelique blinked, surprised. "You know who I am?"

"Of course! Everyone knows of Enchanter Evariste's loyal apprentice who searches diligently for him!" The woman, Sinèad, breezily flung an arm into the air with a smile. She almost smacked Alfonso with the gesture, but he ducked her hand without taking his eyes off his slate. "So, how can we help you?" Sinèad propped her chin on her hands and smiled invitingly at Angelique.

Angelique glanced between the two before continuing cautiously. "I have just come back from Ringsted."

That got Alfonso's attention. He put his chalkboard down and frowned at her. "You made it through the storms?"

Angelique shook her head. "No. I crossed the Chronos Mountains."

Sinèad whistled. "And how did you manage that? It takes more than guts and magic to get through that forsaken range."

"I rode a magical mount," Angelique said. "But I'm afraid I have dire news of Ringsted."

Alfonso narrowed his eyes. "What is it?"

"I encountered a selkie princess. She said the storms are the work of a sea witch. The selkies have tried capturing her, but she keeps giving them the slip."

Sinèad frowned. "That *is* bad news."

"Unfortunately, it only gets worse." Angelique rested a hand on the desk. "The sea witch is working with some humans—I am not sure to what end, but I assume it can't be for the betterment of the country."

"Given its forced isolation from those storms, I'd say that's a safe assumption," Alfonso dryly said.

"Do you know which selkie princess it was that you spoke to?" Sinèad pulled out a scroll of white paper and several different parchments, then retrieved an inkwell and a quill.

"The youngest, Dylan." Angelique hesitated. *This is going to get me hauled before the Council for certain, but it's important information.* "Her pelt was stolen by the humans working with the sea witch. She requested that I seal her voice so the sea witch would not be able to use her pelt against her and force her to use her singing magic. She planned to find the humans that have her pelt and stay with them until she can reclaim it."

Alfonso made a strangled noise, but Sinèad was all business, nodding as she started to write out several missives. "Understood. Will you submit a formal report before you leave the Veneno Conclave?"

"I can," Angelique said. "Though there isn't much else to say—

unless you want my observations of the storms." She hesitated. "How soon will a mage be sent, do you think?"

Alfonso frowned. "That's difficult to say. We're getting an influx of requests for help right now."

"Yes, but this is an *entire* country in duress," Angelique said.

"I agree with you that it is an important matter," Sinèad said. "In fact, I'll take the matter before the department chair myself. But paperwork slows down progress. It will likely be the end of the summer before a weather mage is free to look into the matter *and* is willing to do so."

"Thanks for that complimentary picture of us," said a voice from behind.

Angelique turned so she could face the two mages loitering in the doorway—a male mage with bright blue hair the color of the ocean, and a slim female mage with cornflower blonde hair.

Angelique recognized them as Rein and Blanche—powerful master weather mages and acquaintances of Evariste's she had met on occasion.

"Why if it isn't the Weather Wizards!" Sinèad's posture relaxed, and she grinned as she again leaned in Alfonso's direction. "Coming to check on us love birds?"

Alfonso sputtered and almost fell out of his chair.

"We're seeking clarification on our new assignment before we leave," the woman, Blanche, said. She looked a little older than the youthful Rein, but while her companion strode towards the desk in a heavy stomp, she glided like a spring breeze swirled at her heels.

They stopped next to Angelique at the desk, briefly inclining their heads in nods to her.

"'ello, Apprentice Angelique." Rein grinned, a pearl earring dangling from one of his ear lobes.

"Hello," Angelique said.

Alfonso scratched an ear as he frowned at the pair. "You two have an assignment together?"

"Yep." Sinèad made a popping sound when she drawled the word. "There's a big storm heading for Carabas Harbor in Arcainia. The place was nearly razed to the ground last year in some terrible storms, and the royals raised a ruckus about it, especially since our dear Angelique is the only mage who helped them during that season."

"I'm aware of the assignment," Alfonso said. "It came in only last night."

"I knew you would remember it! You have such an admirable work ethic. It's one of the many things I adore about you!" Sinèad batted her eyelashes at her coworker until he turned pink and looked away. Then, she continued, "Higher-ups wanted our best weather mages sent out immediately to disassemble the storm before it reaches Carabas."

Rein leaned against the desk. "It's surprising. I thought the department would have claimed it's a sign of political favoritism."

"There was talk of it," Alfonso said. "But if I recall, the message that relayed the request threatened to use the inaction from last summer as proof that the Veneno Conclave isn't impartial, but rather picking and choosing the royals it helps, then proceeded to call the Council a bunch of unscrupulous brutes."

Puss definitely drafted that message. Probably with Steffen.

Angelique wisely kept her mouth shut as the weather mages exchanged shrugs.

"We heard your update on Ringsted," Blanche said in her quiet voice. "If the assignment is approved by the time we return, I will ask to be placed on it."

Rein nodded, making his earring jingle. "I will, too. We can't leave Ringsted in such a dangerous position."

It's not as soon as I would like, but at least it means they intend to act on it. And if anyone could take on a sea witch, it would be Blanche and Rein. Angelique relaxed slightly. As the pair were both master weather mages, they were far more skilled than the average weather mage. "Thank you. Knowing both of you will look into the Ringsted matter would be greatly appreciated."

Cautiously optimistic of her thus far non-disdainful reception, Angelique ventured so far as to speak again. "Between the Ringsted storms this year and the curses on the princes of Arcainia, Prince Severin, Princess Rosalinda, and even the Farset princesses...is it possible that this is more than sheer coincidence?"

Sinèad tapped her cheek. "What do you mean?"

"I'm not entirely certain," Angelique confessed. "It's just...I don't recall curses being tossed around so frequently when I was a student. And there are undoubtedly strong black mages at work."

"Not likely," Rein said. "The Conclave stamps 'em out before they can get very powerful."

Angelique stared at the weather mage. "It took several *very* strong mages to kidnap Evariste."

Rein blinked in surprise then winced. "Ah. Yes. That's true, sorry."

"Perhaps you are right, Apprentice Angelique," Sinèad said. "For I agree that there has been an unusual amount of dark activity. But is that not why the committee was created—the one charged with hunting down the black mages who took Lord Enchanter Evariste?"

"Yes," Angelique hesitantly agreed.

"They'll find those responsible," Alfonso said. "And that will be the end of it."

If it's really that easy, then why haven't they found Evariste? And why all the dark magic? But arguing about it wouldn't further her cause, and Angelique wasn't certain she was desperately trying to see connections where there was none, so she held her peace. "Perhaps," she said.

Sinèad slightly tilted her head as she finished writing out another sentence with a flourish. "You'll still hand in a report about Ringsted, Apprentice Angelique?"

Angelique shifted slightly. "If you feel it will make the department take matters more seriously, I can. But I'm not sure if many would look favorably at my report."

Alfonso squinted at her. "Why not?"

Sinèad smiled sadly at her co-worker. "That is another attractive trait of yours. You don't care for mage politics." She waggled her eyebrows at Alfonso, who turned his back to her and busied himself with his paperwork.

Blanche smiled, but Rein made a face and shook his head. "Are you trying to get yourself disciplined for verbally ravishing your husband during work hours?"

Angelique held her calm expression only because she was too surprised to move a muscle. *They're married?*

"And here I thought," Rein continued, "as an office supervisor, you're supposed to set a good example."

Sinèad arched an eyebrow, and her smile turned into a smirk. "If you are so concerned with my work abilities, it seems now would be the *perfect* time to remind you I'm still missing three reports from your last mission."

Rein groaned, and Blanche patted his shoulder.

Alfonso merely shrugged. "You all but requested this dressing down," he told the weather mage.

A chuckle finally escaped Angelique, and all four mages swung their gazes in her direction, staring openly. Though their gazes weren't hostile—they appeared curious more than anything—there was still a certain edge to them that made Angelique clear her throat.

She shifted slightly. "That was all I had to say. I'll hand in my report soon. Thank you."

All four mages slightly dipped their head to her as she left the room. *At least they didn't treat me with scorn.*

Angelique made her way to Evariste's office, intending to use his gateway to get home to Torrens. That would put her far closer to Sole, greatly shortening the time it would take to get there.

Perhaps I could even take a day or two to rest? I ought to tell Clovicus about the sea witch, too. Particularly given there's a fairly good chance the Council will summon me for a meeting to berate me for sealing Dylan's voice, and I'll need his aid in defending myself.

She hesitated, several minutes later, when she passed the hallway that contained Clovicus' office, before continuing on to Evariste's office.

After the difficult trip over the mountains—and knowing she would soon face the Sole royal family alone—home was a siren song Angelique could not resist.

She practically sagged against the door to Evariste's office when she reached it and started to crack it open.

When she could see Evariste's desk, she paused.

Several letters were stacked on its surface, and one of them glowed gold with magic.

They weren't for the missing enchanter—after four years of being gone, no one tried to send him notes or mail anymore.

Which means they're for me. And what are the chances one of them is a summons to report into the Council for one bogus reason or another?

She knew she'd have to face them again—sealing Dylan's voice made it impossible to avoid. But perhaps...she could delay it just a bit longer.

Angelique shut the door and started back the way she had come. "I guess I'll file my report." *And then sneak outside and call Pegasus back as soon as I finish. It seems I'll be taking the long way to Sole. I'll cut back through Loire.*

Angelique made a face and vowed to avoid Noyers—and the smarmy Prince Lucien. But perhaps she could stop at Chanceux Chateau, home of Prince Severin and Princess Elle.

And maybe, she thought dimly, *maybe the prince will hear me out about everything that's happened. Perhaps he can make sense of it. He's no mage, but he's a military genius, and I suspect he and Elle see things most people miss.*

When the road Angelique and Pegasus were taking through Loire split—one part branching off towards Noyers while the rest continued to the large wood that contained Chanceux Chateau—Angelique tugged the constellation from his ground-eating gallop to a slow walk.

"I think this is the right way?" She squinted as Pegasus approached the forest.

He pranced for a few steps, demonstrating his approval.

Angelique shifted on her saddle—Pegasus had arrived still wearing it—and was about to nudge him forward again when she heard a scream.

She froze, straining her ears for a sign of where the noise had come from.

Another scream.

"Pegasus—" she started.

He moved before she could ask, lunging into a fast canter that traveled parallel to the forest.

He stopped abruptly—Angelique would have tumbled over his shoulder if not for the saddle—and she saw ahead a peasant woman in a brown dress, struggling with a stout and piggish-faced man.

"You are trying to cheat an honest woman!" said the peasant woman, her black hair barely contained by a dirt-brown kerchief. "This is black magic!"

Angelique sprang from Pegasus' back, twisting her powers in the blink of an eye.

But before she could throw her spell, the peasant woman abruptly stopped flailing. Instead, she jabbed her thumbs into the man's eyes. When he automatically raised his hands to his eyes, she slugged him in the gut, slumping him over.

The peasant woman backed up, then delivered a brutal kick to the man's head, hitting him in the left side of his face, up and down his jawline.

His head kicked back before he collapsed with a moan.

The peasant woman dusted off her hands in satisfaction, and Angelique could only stare.

What did I just witness?

The peasant woman yanked her dress straight and glanced in Angelique's direction. She cocked her head and said—in markedly more cultured tones, "Lady Enchantress Angelique?"

Angelique gaped. "*Princess Elle?*"

The Loire Princess was barely recognizable—she had somehow stuffed her dress to give her a plump figure, and the way she had smeared her face with dirt gave the suggestion of wrinkles, aging her prematurely.

Elle smiled and gave Angelique a curtsey that was at odds with her sack-like dress. "I am so glad to see you—what brings you to Loire?"

"I—I'm traveling to Sole." Angelique tried to collect her thoughts as she stared at the man Elle had just beaten into submission.

"It is a great time to be traveling," Elle breezily said. "The weather is so nice."

Are we just going to ignore him? Angelique wondered as she stared at the crumpled body. "I suppose so." She finally succeeded in yanking her gaze back to Elle and offered her a smile. *I'd like to compliment that kick of hers—it was a thing of beauty—but that seems like it would very much* not *be something an enchantress would comment on.* "You are doing well, I hope?"

"Very well indeed," Elle assured her. "Severin is in high spirits during the growing season, and he hasn't banned me from the rose gardens yet for touching his precious flowers."

"I see," Angelique said.

Her gaze had just started to creep back to the man, when a body abruptly fell from a tree branch overhead, hitting the ground with a painful smack.

Angelique and Elle stared at the newcomer—an unconscious woman dressed in orange whose face was already starting to bear the marks of a black-and-blue bruise.

Elle's smile grew even wider, and she released a small peal of lady-like laughter before patting her kerchief. "Did I say the weather was nice? I meant it was unusual, for Loire seems to be experiencing the strange phenomena of people falling from the sky."

Angelique laughed quietly. "Elle."

Elle cast her false pleasantry off and scrunched her nose. "I'd appreciate it if you didn't tell Severin about this."

"How did you drag that woman into a *tree?*" Angelique asked.

"It was a lot of work," Elle groused. She grabbed the woman by the arms and dragged her off the still-unconscious male. "You said you're going to Sole? Why don't you stay with us tonight at Chanceux?"

She dug through both the man's and woman's pockets, making a triumphant "ah-hah!" when she found the man's skein of water.

"Thank you for the invitation," Angelique distractedly said. "Might I ask what you are doing?"

"Leaving a message." Elle dumped the water out on a patch of dirt and used her fingers to massage the hard dirt until it softened from the water into a mud consistency. "The soldiers Severin sent to shadow me will figure out where I am soon. We'll be gone by then, of course, but at least they can clean up this mess."

Using her muddy fingers, Elle spelled out the word "BAD" on the forehead of first the man, then the woman. She wiped her fingers off on her dress and nodded in satisfaction. "There! They'll recognize my handiwork and take them in. Shall we be off?"

"If you are satisfied." Angelique twisted briefly to glance back at Pegasus. "Would you like to ride with me?"

"No—good heavens, *no!*" Elle shivered at the thought, then marched into the forest, rustling through underbrush. "It's all very good for a lady enchantress to ride the stars, but I'm just a merchant's daughter. No, thank you!"

"You're a princess, Elle. And please, just call me Angelique. I don't have a title yet." Angelique slowly made her way back to Pegasus, who lipped her hair as they waited.

"Regardless, Rosemerry suits me just fine." Elle emerged from the forest, holding the reins to a round pony with bright eyes, a reddish chestnut coat, and a white star on his forehead.

Seeing Pegasus, the pony pricked his ears and nickered in greeting. Elle kissed the pony's muzzle before she scrambled onto his back. "Don't mind him. Ever since Severin befriended him in his beast form, he thinks unusual magical beings means treats. He just about ran down a unicorn last week."

Angelique swung up onto Pegasus' back. "There was a unicorn in Loire? They don't often leave the woods of Farset."

"No, we were in Farset. Please don't tell Severin about that either—though that one he might know about, as he sent an annoyingly determined squad of soldiers after me." Elle grinned winningly. "Shall we be off?"

Angelique nodded, and Pegasus started for the road they had left behind, moving at a steady walk that Rosemerry trotted to keep pace with.

"If I am interpreting you correctly, it seems that Severin frequently sends soldiers after you?" Angelique asked.

Elle laughed. "Yes. He needlessly worries I'm going to run off and get myself in trouble."

Given that Angelique had just watched Elle beat a man senseless, she wasn't sure the prince's concerns were unjustified.

"But it's unfair because now the soldiers see it as some kind of badge of courage if they manage to follow me when I'm off on...*errands*. It makes them irritatingly resolute and much harder to shake." Elle morosely shook her head and sighed.

"What sort of *errand* brought you to encounter peddlers of black magic?" Angelique glanced back—she could still see the lumps where Elle's victims were plopped—before Pegasus and Rosemerry turned down the forest lane, stepping into the dappled shadows of leafy trees.

"Heard that, did you?" Elle glanced up at Angelique—who was a great deal higher given Pegasus' height compared to the chubby pony's. "I unearthed rumors that someone was peddling harmful spells around Noyers and tracked it down to those two. I've heard of this pattern—peddlers doling out gray-but-not-fully-illegal magic sniffing around a city to test its receptivity, and then opening up a shop for black magic."

Angelique raised her eyebrows. *King Solon of Baris spoke of a similar model when Evariste and I visited him years ago. It seems he was correct in thinking Baris was not their only target.* She carefully measured her words before venturing to ask, "Have you seen this happen often in Loire?"

"This is the first time I witnessed it myself. I heard of a few other cases in other countries, though," Elle said.

"I did not know royals shared such information—though it is encouraging."

"I'm afraid to say they don't," Elle said. "I just *happened* upon it."

Given Elle's history as an excessively talented intelligencer Ranger, it was safe to say she had "happened upon it" probably while rifling through several monarchs' personal belongings.

At least this is not necessarily a new model the black mages have recently adopted, given that King Solon was already aware of it. I know the committee charged with finding the black mages who took Evariste has been searching for similar patterns.

"You don't seem surprised," Elle said.

"I heard similar reports some years ago," Angelique said. "Though it's still not welcome, particularly given the unusual number of curses and black magic activity that has popped up."

Elle ripped the kerchief off her head, freeing her ink-black hair, and abruptly changed conversation topics. "You never responded to my earlier invitation. Please say you'll join Severin and me this evening at Chanceux."

Angelique was about to agree, but she paused and glanced at the princess. "You intend to use me as a diversion when we arrive, so you can slip off before Severin sees the garb you are dressed in, don't you?"

Elle smirked, utterly unrepentant. "Yes, but if you come, you'll also be able to point out to Severin what you just said to me. And isn't that more important?"

Angelique wanted to smile, but the princess' observation struck too close to the truth. "It is."

"Then it's settled," Elle declared. "Stay with us—because frankly we've made some worrisome observations as well, and we would very much appreciate the input of a Lady Enchantress."

When Elle and Angelique arrived at Chanceux Chateau, Severin was waiting in the front courtyard, his arms folded against his broad chest. At his side, unfortunately, was Lucien, turned out in puffed petticoat breeches of a deep burgundy color that matched his doublet.

When Angelique first saw the crown prince, she and Elle were only halfway down the long, green drive. The crown prince hadn't noticed them, so while Severin stood firm, Lucien slouched and yawned before digging his pinky finger into his ear.

When he saw Angelique, however, he effortlessly switched into a preening posture and smiled dazzlingly.

What a puffed-up little toadstool, Angelique wryly thought.

"Severin!" Elle said—all brightness and good cheer. "Hello, darling! Look who I ran into—I have convinced her to stay with us for a night or two."

Severin gravely bowed his head. "Lady Enchantress." He

offered her a smile—which was barely more than the slight upturn of his lips. "Welcome to Chanceux Chateau."

"Thank you, Your Highness."

"I hope your journey was a pleasant one?" he asked.

"It was, thank you."

Severin nodded slightly. "And where do you think you're going, Elle?" he asked, his voice flat as he addressed his wife—without looking away from Angelique.

Elle, already off her pony and halfway to the chateau entrance, laughed airily. "I thought I might freshen up."

"And change out of your disguise?" Severin asked.

"Yes, well, I might want to use it again, but if your men catch sight of me in it, it will be of no use." Elle walked backwards towards the door and winked at her husband's back.

Severin finally shifted so he could stare at his wife.

Elle blew him a kiss. "I'll just be a few moments."

"We're going to talk about this later," he called after her.

"Of course! I have an update to share!" Elle slipped inside the gorgeous chateau before her husband could say more.

Severin growled under his breath, but no one seemed bothered by it.

Instead, a lad in a white shirt grinned at the prince as he passed by to collect Elle's pony.

It took Angelique a few moments to place the stable boy—for he had grown a great deal since she had last seen him. "Oliver?"

Oliver smiled sweetly and bowed, making the mussed mess of his hair flop over his face. "Welcome to Chanceux Chateau, Mademoiselle Angelique!"

Angelique gaped for another moment longer before she slid off Pegasus.

Pegasus, at least, seemed to share her surprise, for he cautiously sniffed Oliver and flicked his tail.

It's only been two years—how has he grown so much? Two years is nothing!

"Do you mean to let Pegasus run the skies tonight?" Oliver asked, interrupting Angelique's shock.

"Er, possibly? What do you want, Pegasus?" Angelique gratefully turned back to her companion.

Pegasus pressed a muzzle to her temple, then walked off, heading for the stable.

"It seems he intends to stay here," Angelique said, slightly bewildered.

"I'll see to him, Mademoiselle!" Oliver and the pony set off after Pegasus, trotting to catch up.

Angelique watched them, still marveling over Oliver, when Lucien decided to inflict himself on her.

"Lady Enchantress Angelique, you look *ravishing*." The crown prince plucked up Angelique's hand and started to bend over it.

But Angelique was too familiar with his ways, so instead she clasped her free hand around his then firmly shook their hands, pumping them up and down so she almost smacked him in the face.

"Lucien, you seem to be doing quite well." She yanked her hands free before he could recover, then started to glide for the front doors, deciding for everyone it was time to enter the chateau. "And thank you, Severin, for allowing me to intrude upon your home."

"It is our honor," Severin said. "What brings you to Loire?" He nodded his thanks to a footman, who flung the chateau front doors open so they could pass through.

"I am actually only passing through." Angelique spared the entrance hall a quick glance, admiring the damask wallpaper and turquoise carpets spread across the stone floors. "I am traveling to Sole."

"Surely you must stay with my family in Noyers for a week or so before you move on to Sole," Lucien strolled at her right side, walking unnecessarily close so occasionally their elbows brushed.

Angelique shifted so she clasped her hands at the bottom of

her ribcage and angled her elbows out. The next time Lucien tried to brush her, her elbow jabbed him. "I'm afraid I must decline your generous invitation, Your Highness," she said. "I must get to Sole in a timely manner, for Princess Rosalinda's eighteenth birthday approaches, and a dark mage has been tracking her for months."

"That's right; it was you who modified the princess' curse when she was just a babe so it didn't kill her, but made her sleep." Elle called from the top of a marble staircase.

She was a bit breathless—from sprinting through the castle, Angelique suspected. She had, however, transformed in a short amount of time.

Gone was the ragamuffin look, exchanged for demure order between the artful braid of her silky hair and the once-again youthful appearance of her face. The final touch was her gauzy, red gown that exposed the tops of her shoulders and had tiny, pale pink flowers embroidered into the neckline. It perfectly showed off Elle's artless yet graceful beauty.

"I've already called for refreshments in the rose garden," Elle continued.

When Severin, Angelique, and Lucien climbed the stairs to join her on the second story of the chateau, Elle stood on her tip toes to kiss Severin's cheek, then pushed her way between Angelique and Lucien so she could take her brother-in-law's arm and smack it harder than necessary. "So we ought to retire there."

A smile that actually briefly showed a flash of his white teeth skidded across Severin's lips. "A good idea."

"But it's almost dark," Lucien complained. "There will be bugs!"

"That, my dear brother-in-law, is what the frog pond is for. Come! We must get out there before the sun sets so we can properly admire it!"

The rose garden was a wash of green bushes and roses of varying sizes and colors—there were brilliant yellow and orange roses, tiny red roses the size of a fingernail, huge pink roses bigger than Angelique's palm, and wild white roses blushed with purple.

The garden smelled heavenly, and at the center of it was a fountain that trickled water in jeweled tones.

Surrounded by beauty and in the golden light of the dimming sun, Angelique was able to discuss her concerns with the prince and princess, who listened without interrupting her as she listed off the grievances the continent had endured—from the cursed princesses of Farset to Clotilde in Arcainia.

"Individually, these issues would not be unexpected. They would still be a trial, and terrible to experience, but..." Angelique trailed on, not certain how to proceed.

I sound insane—or anxiety stricken, like I am seeing a black mage under every rock. But those storms in Ringsted...that's not by chance—that's a deliberate action.

"With so many wrong-doings, it's difficult to believe they are all happenstance," Severin said, finally.

"And it's been my experience as a Ranger that often things can *appear* to be natural, but someone unseen is moving," Elle added.

Angelique almost collapsed in her chair. *They believe me. Thank goodness, someone finally believes me!* She nodded and glanced over at Lucien, who was poking around the edge of the fountain. (He had grown bored about five minutes into the talk and had taken to wandering around the garden.)

"Thank you for speaking to us, Angelique," Severin said. "Though the Conclave seems reluctant to move, they are undoubtedly better informed."

I hope we would be—we're supposed to know everything involving magic! Angelique adjusted her hold on the stem of her chalice and stared at the red wine within it. "What, then, do we do now?"

"Elle and I were considering attempting to talk to royalty of other countries to see if they were also having similar problems," Severin said.

"We were starting with Erlauf as they are a major military power, and because Queen Freja is stepping down and Princess Cinderella will be crowned queen in early winter," Elle said.

Angelique's edginess thawed slightly with the recollection of the one-time destitute Trieux duchess. *It seems Cinderella is achieving her desire to unite Erlauf and Trieux with far more success than she initially planned.*

"And also because we are aware they've been harassed by goblins," Severin added. "It seems like they would be more aware of it—and willing to address the possibility—than, perhaps, other nations."

"Given what I have shared with you, will you change that plan?" Angelique asked.

Severin frowned at his chalice and tapped the side of it. "Perhaps we ought to push ahead with it—not just with Erlauf but all the countries."

"I am not certain that it means anything," Angelique said. "But I will offer whatever help I can."

Elle smiled. "Thank you, Angelique. It is to your credit that you are proactive in this matter, even though the Veneno Conclave hasn't been the most supportive."

Angelique ruefully smiled. "Thank you." *Heaven please do not strike me down for refraining from admitting that I am determined in this because the Conclave does not make an effort.*

"Will you stay with us a second night, Lady Enchantress, so we can further discuss this?" Severin asked.

Angelique eyed Lucien. "That depends; is Prince Lucien staying?"

Elle burst into laughter. "No, he is to return to Noyers tomorrow morning. King Rèmy makes him attend lectures and classes—yes, even at his age—and if he skips too many there are consequences."

"Then I believe I will accept your offer." Angelique smiled at the couple, feeling a little uncertain but peaceful. For once, her heart warmed. She wouldn't have to watch the continent alone.

Yes, the Veneno Conclave was failing in its duty to mind magic, but if the countries could take up the slack, all would not be lost.

For once, things look brighter.

CHAPTER 25

Angelique's two-night stay turned into a week. Combined with dodging summons from the Council and stopping in Trieux—now Erlauf—for a few weeks to subdue a goblin attack and help rebuild a ruined village, Angelique arrived at Sole in early fall and with high spirits.

With Princess Rosalinda's birthday in winter, she was still reasonably early!

Pegasus seemed to catch onto her mood, for he flared with his power, shining brightly as he galloped across the open field, bearing down on Ciane—the capital of Sole. He stopped right outside the city gates with his usual cracks of thunder, and it seemed Angelique's rare streak of luck was more potent than she could have hoped, for Mage Firra and Mage Donaigh stood just outside the city, a young knight standing with them.

Angelique beamed. "I have arrived early!" It was all she could do to keep from laughing triumphantly. "Hello Donaigh, Firra! For once I have beaten calamity and come before—what happened?" She cut herself off when she noticed the mages' expressions.

Donaigh had dark circles under his eyes, and his usual straw hat seemed flat. Firra held blue fire with shaking fingers, and the slant of her brows spoke of sadness. The pair looked older than when she last saw them, but she suspected it wasn't just because time passed slower for her, but rather that recent events had added to their weariness.

"Lady Enchantress Angelique." Donaigh went down on his knees. "I fear I have terrible news."

Oh, no. Not here, too. Angelique slumped forward until she rested her forehead on the crest of Pegasus' neck. *Why are these attacks suddenly so prevalent, and why am I always late? I am so tired of running around. I'm tired of endlessly searching for—*

Angelique forced herself to sit upright again. She took a deep breath, then pushed her sense of despair behind her as she slid off Pegasus. She waited to speak until certain her voice was steady. "What is it? I have arrived before Princess Rosalinda's birthday—Pegasus got us over the Chronos Mountains so quickly, I even had time to stop at the Veneno Conclave before coming here."

Firra shook her hands, and her fire went out. "The princess has already been struck by her curse. She has fallen asleep."

That's not so bad, in the bigger scheme of things. She has her modifier, after all. Why, then, is their expression so grim? Angelique frowned. "That is terrible news. Have they summoned her true love?"

Donaigh adjusted his straw hat. "The king has trooped every eligible—*noble*—male through her chambers to kiss her."

What. Angelique's frown grew sharper. "And he thinks that will break the curse?"

"It won't?" asked the young knight.

Angelique shifted her gaze to him, taking in his white-gold armor with accents of sky blue. Between the Magic Knight crest cut into his chestplate, his fancy blue cape, and the beautiful feathers etched into his pauldrons and layered over the ears of his helm, it was easy to place him as one of the Magic Knights of Sole —an elite force of knights trained with magic-based weapons and anti-magic armor. They were the pride of Sole, and the only fighting force in the continent to possess armor and weapons blessed by ancient elves.

To be a Magic Knight at such an age, the young man had to be very talented indeed. *And if his reaction to the news is anything to go by, he is close to Princess Rosalinda.*

"No," she said, answering his question. "I didn't use true love's first kiss because I am a romantic fool. I used it because it is a powerful emotion that can be harnessed to shatter Carabosso's magic. Taking a group of men and using Briar to search for the one will never work—it makes it into a task, not the act of love needed to break the curse." She refrained from rubbing her forehead, though her head was starting to ache. "Doesn't she have a true love?"

Firra sighed, which sounded like a groan of the heart. "She might, but King Giuseppe is shouting down anyone who dares to suggest she might already be in love—particularly if they imply it is with someone outside her social caste."

"Firra and I estimated that if Briar's curse would be finished off, the country would be fine," Donaigh said. "Neither the nobles nor the government officials are against letting an extra heir be named just in case—nor are they against allowing foreign gentry to approach Briar." A frown settled on his normally curved lips. "Unfortunately, though the rest of the country is amiable, King Giuseppe appears to be falling apart. Forgive me, Isaia, but it is true."

The young knight—Isaia, it seemed—shifted at Donaigh's bluntness and insult to the knight's liege. But he didn't grab for his weapon or glare; instead, he looked to Angelique. "Princess Alessia and Prince Consort Filippo will wish to speak to you."

"King Giuseppe will as well," Firra said. "But I wouldn't expect tears of happiness when he sees you."

What a shock. All my life I've been so beloved and popular. Angelique shrugged. "He wasn't particularly happy with me when I modified the curse, so I'm not surprised."

Donaigh's gaze darkened. "If he lays a hand on you..."

Angelique, warmed by his reaction, let a quick grin flash on her face. "Peace, Donaigh. I'm still in disgrace from using magic in Arcainia last year. Baiting royalty will not ease my situation. Come, let us find the royal family and get it over with. I will have to explain to the king that his system won't work, anyway. Pegasus!"

Donaigh fell in step behind Angelique, and Pegasus behind him. She heard Firra's voice behind them, speaking to the young magic knight, but no one moved to join Angelique at the front of the line.

She wished they would.

Foremostly, because I don't know where I'm going, she joked to herself. Even in the privacy of her mind, the joke didn't fully ring true.

Yes, she would rather have someone lead the way so she didn't take them in the wrong direction like an idiot, but more than that, it would be nice to walk shoulder-to-shoulder with someone again, instead of being ever aware of the hole where Evariste once stood.

THE ROYAL RESPONSE was about what Angelique expected. The princess and prince consort—Princess Rosalinda's parents—were grateful to see her, but King Giuseppe scowled.

I cannot blame him for his poor countenance. His granddaughter has just had her curse go off. It's understandable. Mostly. Except Rosalinda is just sleeping—a far better position than the seven princes of Arcainia were in when they were swans. And worlds better than Severin when he was first cursed.

Angelique idly wondered if it was a bad sign for her soul that she was starting to grow less horrified by curses and now measured them by the pain they dealt.

"It is your fault we are in this situation," King Giuseppe said in a voice of ice and darkness. (He'd been railing at her for a good fifteen minutes already. But he had nothing on the Council in terms of intimidation, and thus was a bit of a bore.) "If you had just broken the curse off—if Lord Enchanter Evariste had bothered to work the spell himself!"

Angelique's polite smile slipped for a moment, and she felt her magic brush invitingly against her fingers. "Yes, you've mentioned that several times, Your Majesty. So, in the interests of using my time wisely, I will go see to the sleeping princess myself." She curtseyed, then turned and started to make her way from the room.

"We are in this situation because of your inability to properly use magic." King Giuseppe stayed on his throne, but Angelique didn't need to see his face to hear the disdain that lined his voice. "If the country unravels, the guilt will rest on your head. You are a failure of an enchantress."

Angelique stopped in the doorway.

It's not fair, she thought. *I've rescued princes and princesses, fought goblins, modified curses, and it's still not enough. I don't think it ever will be.*

Her polite smile fell from her lips, leaving her expression blank or perhaps even a little dark.

Why does everyone try to make me take responsibility for whatever darkness it is that pollutes these lands?

Her magic was a feather-soft touch on the back of her hand, and for a moment, Angelique tapped it.

She tapped her war magic, and the heat of her anger faded, unable to remain hot under the cool surge of her powers.

Abruptly, Angelique remembered herself. She released her magic and snapped her eyes shut.

Breathe. She told herself. *You have a duty. Even if it's to an ungrateful king—who is really just heartbroken and scared.* When she opened her eyes, the tenseness in her body was gone, and she was able to replace her serene smile.

She took a breath then glided into the hallway. Though she didn't glance back, she could still feel the presence of the young knight who had stood with Firra and Donaigh at the gates of Ciane. "Sir Isaia, was it?" she asked. "Would you be so kind as to show me to the princess' quarters?"

The magic knight bowed. "This way, Lady Enchantress."

Angelique brushed the fabric of her skirts—which were turning from sunrise red to wine red—as they strolled down the hallway. "The title isn't necessary. I'm only an Enchantress-in-Training."

She was not surprised to hear a scuffle and a few thuds as Firra dragged Donaigh out of the throne room—though it was amusing to hear the guards eagerly shut the doors behind them. (*Someone* knew just how strong a war mage Donaigh was, it seemed.)

Firra yanked Donaigh along and quickly caught up with them. "Well," Firra said. "That might have gone worse."

"He's more emotional about this than I predicted," Angelique said. Worry made fine lines crease on her forehead. "I thought he was sensible—but he's locking everything out of his heart right now."

Donaigh glanced coldly over his shoulder, but when he faced forward again, his easy-going smile was back. "Briar has not brought out the best in King Giuseppe."

Firra chuckled darkly. "He is offended by her headstrong ways—which is a hoot, as she's a great deal like him."

Angelique furrowed her brow even deeper as she thought. "His iciness is a bigger threat than the princess' curse," she said, "for he could drag his country down if this continues."

"But what if Briar never awakes?" Sir Isaia asked.

Oh, yes. He's at the very least a friend, if not a close companion. That's an interesting position to be in, given Rosalinda's need for true love's kiss. Angelique kept her expression even as she twitched her skirts a little. "I must inspect the curse before I make any observations."

Between Firra attempting to keep Donaigh calm and Isaia...

who seemed about as talkative as an exceptionally well-made sculpture, they were silent as they made their way to Princess Rosalinda's room.

When they reached the right hall, Angelique was irked to see several young men loitering about the passageway—undoubtedly waiting for their chance to kiss Rosalinda—or Briar, as Firra and Donaigh had referred to her in their reports.

This is ridiculous. I am as jaded toward romance as a person could be, and even I can see this would never work! Someone needs to smack that old badger king upside the head and knock some sense into him!

"Away with you lads," Donaigh decreed. When the men gave him dirty looks, he offered them a half-smile. "The Lady Enchantress wishes to inspect the princess' curse. You'll have plenty of time to make your fruitless attempt later. Now, off with you!"

The men exchanged looks and grumbled, but Donaigh's reputation as a war mage must have proceeded him, for they grudgingly ambled off.

Sir Isaia knocked on the door, then opened it for her.

A muscle in Angelique's cheek twitched in irritation when she saw Briar—laid out on a giant bed in an ornate and most assuredly uncomfortable dress. *He really is trying to get her married in this insane fashion.* Angelique held her sourness in and murmured, "Please pardon the intrusion." She smiled at a pretty, young lady in a velvet gown and a young man—another magic knight, if his armor was any indication—who were stationed in the princess' room.

The knight almost dropped his weapon, and his eyes widened when he saw Angelique. For a moment she worried her reputation of ill repute might have proceeded her, but he recovered as the lady curtsied, though he kept his eyes on Angelique as he bowed.

Strange. Angelique nodded to the pair as she approached Rosalinda's bed. She could see strains of her magic swirling over the princess, and at a glance, it appeared normal.

She sat on the edge of the bed, then wriggled her fingers at her magic. The rest of the spell blazed to life, creeping down Rosalinda's body to pool at the areas closest to Angelique.

Angelique held in a scowl at her magic, then raised her gaze to address the room. "This may take a few minutes," she warned, then returned her attention to Briar.

She was vaguely aware when Firra leaned against the doorframe—able to peer down the hallway and watch for the badger king—while Donaigh flopped into a chair with a yawn.

As she tugged on her magic, studying the silvery script and symbols of her modification, the young lady joined Firra at the door.

She murmured to the mage, and there was some conversation, but Angelique paid no mind to it. Instead, she carefully combed through the spell, going so far as to even brush some of her magic entrenched in it to be certain it felt right.

I was terribly green when I made this modification. I have to be certain it is correct, or I'll need to return to the Veneno Conclave and ask Clovicus for help.

Thus far, everything appeared fine. Perhaps she had put a little too much magic into the spell, but as it directly combatted the angry red swell of Carabosso's curse, she wasn't too inclined to be sorry about it.

Angelique stood and moved around the bed, studying her magic critically from a different angle.

Time passed, and she was reluctantly forced to admit it seemed like she had done it correctly. Everything looked spot-on.

She blinked, restoring moisture to her dried eyes, and rose when Princess Alessia, Prince Consort Filippo, and a legendary magic knight entered the chamber.

"Lady Enchantress, might I introduce you to Sir Artemio." Princess Alessia spoke in a thin, worn voice. "He is a Legendary Knight, and trusted by my father."

Legendary Knights were a step above Magic Knights—though

they were incredibly rare because in order to be made a Legendary Knight, one was chosen by one of the ancient, magical and uncomfortably close-to-sentient weapons that were considered treasures of the country.

If Angelique recalled correctly, there were only four Legendary Knights active at the moment. Though the royal family possessed more of the rare weapons, it was somewhat dangerous to make a knight because they could only be made by a direct descendant of the royal d'Avalas family, and if the royal chose the wrong person, the weapon could kill both the royal and the potential knight.

Angelique bowed her head in respect to the honored Legendary Knight. "It is a pleasure—though I wish the circumstances were different."

The Legendary Knight bowed. "Thank you for coming, Lady Enchantress—and for your aid."

Angelique barely registered the title with more than an internal sigh. She stood, brushing the skirts of her iridescent dress as it shifted from a deep blue to a plum color. "The curse modification is working perfectly. It seems I might have put a little too much power in my spell—the inexperience of youth—but the only thing it has done is make the reactions slightly more...explosive. There is nothing wrong with the spell itself. When Briar's true love kisses her, she will wake up."

Prince Consort Filippo crouched by his daughter's bedside, his eyes crinkled with worry. "Yes, but *can* she awake? What if she hasn't met her true love?"

At least the prince consort grasps how this works. Angelique eyed Briar, taking in the spell one last time. "Based on the weaving of the spell, I can confidently say she has a true love and is primed to wake. The only other necessary part of the equation needed is for him—whoever he is—to kiss her. The princess will be fine."

The prince consort exhaled deeply. When he stood, a smile returned to his face.

(Angelique was very interested to see that the young, stone-faced Sir Isaia relaxed minutely as well.)

"In that case," Princess Alessia's face was grave as she clasped her hands together. "I ask you, Lady Enchantress, what we are to do with the rest of the country?"

What?

Angelique smiled blandly and hoped in vain Princess Alessia would say something more, but she didn't.

What, what, what? I'm an apprentice—not a ruddy monarch! What, do they expect me to do, pop next year's budget out of the skirts of my dress? How am I supposed to know what to do with a country?

Angelique kept her voice light when she responded. "I fear I cannot give you any advice. I am but a magic user; I know nothing of running a country."

"But we need your help," Princess Alessia said.

And what does that mean? Is this some kind of trap from the Council so they can finally get rid of me if I muck around in politics too much? Angelique stiffened. "According to Veneno Conclave laws, magic users are strictly forbidden from meddling with governmental affairs."

Sir Artemio eyed Angelique with an edge to his gaze that Angelique didn't like. "You helped Prince Severin when he was cursed, and you saved the princes of Arcainia," he said.

Yep, they definitely have something in mind, and whatever it is, I'm not going to like it. Angelique hastily stepped back, anxious to distance herself from whatever task it was that would clearly get her in *more* trouble. "Not in the least," she said. "It was Elle who broke Severin's curse, and Elise saved her foster brothers. I only modified their curses—as I modified Princess Rosalinda's."

"That's not entirely true," Firra said. "In Arcainia, you tried to kill Clotilde with Gabrielle, then helped the princes get back to Arcainia and fought a basilisk."

Angelique broke her charade of pleasant politeness and glared at Firra. *Traitor! What are you trying to accomplish?*

Firra shrugged. "Sole is my homeland, and it's going to crumble if we don't do something."

Now that is definitely illegal—from the Conclave's perspective.

Mages were taught *not* to favor any one country—specifically their homeland—in order to keep the Conclave neutral.

Angelique flicked her gaze to Donaigh, who was still splayed in his chair. When he caught her eyes, he nodded slightly.

Angelique pressed her lips together. *Donaigh is a war mage, the only type of mage who takes any sort of pride in me. He wouldn't let Firra lure me into a trap, which means this is more serious than I thought.* She sighed. "I will hear you out, but I make no promises to act."

"The specific problem is my father," Princess Alessia said. "He's lost his way."

Angelique interrupted before she could utter anything potentially blasphemous. "I am not doing *anything* to affect his thinking or his mind. Such magic is only used by black mages or sorcerers."

"We thought as much," Prince Consort Filippo said. "But if things continue as they are, King Giuseppe will have to be removed from the throne."

"Princess Alessia would become queen, but it would not be a peaceful transition," Sir Artemio said. "There will be bloodshed, and our allies will likely be displeased with us, as King Giuseppe was previously an exemplary monarch."

"Then leave the king on the throne," Angelique said.

"We cannot," Princess Alessia said. "I love my father, but I know he will ruin this country and bring civil war to us if we let him continue." She stood straight and proud as she set her true-blue eyes on Angelique. "Can the continent survive the chaos it would bring?"

The question took the fight out of Angelique because Alessia was right.

The continent likely couldn't survive the chaos. Not because Sole was more important than any other country but because of the way the continent teetered. Already they had avoided disaster in other instances, but how many more curses would be laid? How many more royal families would be attacked?

For a moment, grief cracked Angelique's façade. She was so *tired*. Why was all of this being laid at her feet?

Because it's my duty as an enchantress—even one in training—to see it through. Angelique took a deep breath. "It survived Erlauf's takeover of Trieux," she pointed out—more because she wasn't going to play so easily into their hands than out of any true belief.

"I beg your pardon, Lady Enchantress, but that was several years ago. The world is in a different mess now," Sir Artemio said.

"So what would you have me do?" Angelique asked.

Princess Alessia took a deep breath and glanced at her husband—who nodded encouragingly. "We ask that you tie all of Ciane to Rosalinda's curse."

Angelique stared at her, dumbstruck. *What the—are they mad? They want to purposely inflict a curse on the capital of Sole?* A short bark of laughter escaped her, then she took another step away from them. *If they make one more potentially explosive suggestion, I'm leaving.* "You are serious?"

The princess bowed her head.

Sir Artemio gazed at the slumbering Princess Rosalinda, wrinkles carving deep crevasses in his forehead. "If the seat of the government sleeps with the princess, it will forcibly smother all conflicts," he said. "We have a number of knights and government officials standing by, ready to leave Ciane. While the rest of us sleep, they will keep the country running and circulate through the countryside and cities. Already, the ambassadors who had returned home to celebrate Princess Rosalinda's arrival have left and returned to their posts."

Angelique blinked. "You want me to put your royal family and the majority of your government under a spell so they *sleep* until Princess Rosalinda wakes up?" *They want me to make an entire* city *slumber? And the capital, no less! How many people live here? Forget* lectures—*the Council will seal me, and that's only if I have enough power to pull it off!*

She glanced at Firra and Donaigh feeling a slight sting of betrayal. Firra oozed worry and concern, and Donaigh was scowling. Firra was throwing her to the dogs, but it appeared she felt they had no other option.

"Some of us Magic Knights would remain in Ciane and sleep as well," Sir Artemio said. "If we all left, King Giuseppe would suspect something."

Yeah, you better bet the badger king would!

Sir Isaia also looked to the sleeping princess. "What of Carabosso? He is still at large and will pose a danger to Ciane."

Donaigh made a noise of approval.

"We have been assured that we will receive more help from the Veneno Conclave," Sir Artemio said.

"As loyal as I am to the Conclave," Donaigh said, "I must warn you it is not known for acting with haste."

Firra raised her black eyebrows and glanced meaningfully at Angelique.

Ahhh, that is why she supports this plan. She doesn't think help will arrive soon enough.

Sir Artemio nodded. "Perhaps, but I am confident those knights who remain awake will be able to manage while we wait."

Angelique sighed. "If the princess does not swiftly wake up, things could go very badly very quickly."

"Then, in that case, we will remain sleeping until the continent is more peaceful and enough enchanters can visit to remove the spell," Princess Alessia said.

Sure, just wait it out until the worst is over. I'm sure Severin would LOVE to hear that plan! Angelique narrowed her eyes. "Some believe things are going to grow worse."

"I agree. This does not seem right," Donaigh said. "In fact, it smacks of what Carabosso sought all along—keeping Sole preoccupied with its own problems."

"Be that as it may, what other choice do we have?" Sir Artemio asked, a chord of anger in his voice.

Princess Alessia smiled sadly at the war mage. "If we leave things as they are...my father will ruin us all."

Silence reigned for several tense moments.

"I have heard that Princess Cinderella and Prince Cristoph of Erlauf are to visit Prince Severin and Princess Elle of Loire. I assume they are among those who believe things will grow worse?" Prince Consort Filippo asked. "If that is the case, it is even more important that we quiet Ciane. If the chaos continues, Sole will only degenerate faster."

Angelique had to keep her jaw from dropping. *I dally for a few weeks in Trieux, and they know Severin's movements already? Gossip flies faster than magic!*

She shook the thought from her mind and turned to study the princess, prince consort, and Sir Artemio. She tilted her head as she took in the creases in Princess Alessia's gown and the redness of her eyes. She saw the sorrow present in the furrowing of Sir Artemio's brow and in the downward slant of his chin, and she could practically feel the despair that radiated off Prince Consort Filippo as he stared at his daughter, looking lost.

This isn't something they're bringing before me on an impulse. They believe it's necessary, and they're scared what will happen if I don't do it.

Angelique turned to Firra and Donaigh. "The Veneno Conclave will be very upset," she bleakly said.

"I know as mages we're supposed to stay out of governmental matters, but I am reasonable enough to admit my bias for Sole," Firra said. "If we attempt to wait it out, it might thwart Carabosso in some manner, but I fear it will be at the cost of Sole itself. I, for one, would rather minimize our losses with the proposed plan." She hesitated. "If Lord Enchanter Evariste were here, perhaps we could do something differently, but he's not. Please, Angelique."

Heartfelt, but an expected reaction. Angelique shifted her gaze to Donaigh.

He scratched his chin, then smiled with his eyes. "I will respect whatever decision you make, for I understand that your path is a hard one to walk."

In other words, he's aware of what I've experienced already and isn't going to ask me to endure more, even if it's the right thing to do.

Angelique shut her eyes and raised her hand to cover them.

What do I do? Fall in line with the Veneno Conclave and risk Sole's downward spiral, tripping off other catastrophes, or sacrifice myself? But if I get kicked out of the Veneno Conclave...I won't be able to search for Evariste anymore.

It was an impossible situation, and Angelique felt like she had been plunged into darkness with no sign of light.

What would Evariste say? The thought came unbidden to her, but it made her lower lip tremble for a moment before she reined in her emotions.

She knew without a doubt Evariste would gently tell her not to worry, that she was an amazing student, and then he'd probably hug her for good measure before telling her to run off...and then he would cast the necessary magic in her place.

If the worst happens and I'm sealed, maybe I could go to Severin and Elle. Perhaps they would help me find Evariste.

Angelique felt like she had aged a century in a moment. "Very well." She dropped her hand and opened her eyes again. "Send those you wish to remain awake outside of Ciane. I will set up the spell and add some natural defenses so Ciane cannot easily be broken into." *IF I have the power to pull this off.*

Tears gathered in Princess Alessia's eyes. "Thank you, Lady Enchantress. You have saved us."

Sir Artemio tipped forward in a bow. "If you will excuse me. Isaia, come with me."

Angelique waved him off. "Of course," she said, distracted.

"Thank you, Angelique." Firra smiled fiercely, then bowed.

Donaigh adjusted his straw hat and offered her a slight smile. "Sole will be in your debt, Lady Enchantress. I don't think many have the power to succeed in this."

"We'll see," Angelique said. "For now, we should begin preparations."

"Of course!" Prince Consort Filippo said. "Please, tell us whatever you need."

Angelique started for the doorway, but she paused and looked back at the sleeping princess. *I hope this works. All of it. Or there are going to be irreversible repercussions.*

CHAPTER 26

Angelique licked her lips as she watched the small clusters of horses and riders that ebbed away from Ciane.
I hope this works.
Pegasus, sensing her anxiety, swatted his tail. He twisted his neck so he could bump her shoulder, ignoring Sir Isaia's horse—who snorted and pranced sideways, trying to put more distance between them.
"It's not your fault, Pegasus," Angelique murmured. She stood on the ground next to him and patted his neck—more for her comfort than his. Her magic roared within her—ready, even though she hadn't begun to tap it yet.
I suppose that's one good thing that came out of facing the basilisk. This task is daunting, but I wouldn't even dream of attempting it if I hadn't seen that little display from my magic.
Donaigh and Firra's argument finally broke through the haze of worry that gnawed at Angelique.
"All right, I have something in mind," Donaigh said.
Firra grumbled and sat deeper in the saddle. "I don't care about that stupid word game. I should have burned Rumpelstiltskin to a cinder for teaching it to you."

"Aren't you going to ask questions to try and figure out what it is?"

"No, because you *cheat*!"

"I never!"

"Then why haven't I ever won?"

"Because you are excessively poor at games that require deep thinking?"

"*What?*"

A wry smile finally bloomed on Angelique's lips at the mages' antics. She was grateful for the distraction, especially as she saw the last group of horses and riders trot out of Ciane's gates.

If Princess Alessia and Prince Consort Filippo succeeded on their end, they were taking afternoon coffee with King Giuseppe, who was still ignorant to the sleeping spell about to settle on Ciane.

Pegasus peered at Sir Isaia's horse when she snorted at him again. The constellation turned in a tight circle, dragging Angelique with him as she held onto his reins. "I believe everyone is clear. Prepare yourself, Sir Isaia. Your mount might spook."

Isaia nodded and drew his war horse farther back.

Angelique made herself release Pegasus and took a few steps closer to the city.

Reluctantly, she started to loosen up her magic.

It flooded her like a tsunami, and for a moment Angelique couldn't tell which way was up and which way was down. It was a cold, terrifying experience, overwhelming in all the worst ways.

Just as quickly as her magic released, her senses returned to her with a jolt. She felt different—weirdly aware of the massive amounts of magic that rolled within her. Angelique slightly shook her head, then started speaking the lolling tongue of magic. (A short, wordless cast wouldn't do for magic of this magnitude.)

Please work, please work!

She carefully built up the spell, casting layer upon layer of thin, sparkling magic. She tried not to let her worry show as she pulled more and more magic through her fingers, twisting it into the sleeping charm. Her palms itched from the sheer amount of power she balanced, but she tried not to think about it too much.

(The last time she had held such a huge amount of magic was during her pre-evaluation on the plateau in Baris. Granted, that had involved even greater amounts, but it had ended rather poorly.)

She stretched the layers, making the spell big enough to encompass the city. She swallowed thickly as she started to tie the spell off. *If I bungle this part, the whole thing could violently collapse.* Carefully, she searched for the faint chime of her magic deep in the palace where Rosalinda slept.

She held her breath until she felt it, a barely noticeable jingle in the mass of activity that was Ciane. Angelique extended her hands and twitched her fingers, knitting the spells together.

A silver mist crawled over Ciane, cloaking it with fog so thick it obscured parts of the city from sight.

The magic felt right—it perfectly echoed the bit she had tied around Rosalinda—but it wasn't until the guards standing on the walls drooped, then plopped down on the walkways, that Angelique relaxed slightly.

At least that part is correct, thank goodness.

Birds that circled above the city abruptly banked and landed on the walls, tucking their heads under their wings.

Silence stole across the meadow. The only noises were the muted hoofbeats of the mounted, fleeing parties.

But she wasn't done. Ciane would turn to ruin and rust quickly if she left the city as it was. She needed to add in a preservation spell.

The preservation spell would be the top coat of her magic, and it needed to touch everything. Sweat beaded at Angelique's temple as she dusted the preservation spell on top. Every flicker her magic gave made her heart jump with fear.

Stay stable; stay strong. I cannot mess this up, or the city residents will end up hurt.

Her throat was scratchy and dry as she carefully painted every human, building, animal, and item with her cold, sharp magic. But as the spell stretched over the city, eeking across every inch, it sucked her dry of the magic she had pulled loose, so she had to doll out more.

How fun.

Angelique broke out in goosebumps as she nervously turned inward to pull more magic from herself.

It seemed to stretch endlessly around her in a sea of potentially smothering and sharp power.

Again, she held her breath as she gathered up more. The magic listened, moving through her with enough power to make her toes curl. But it twisted into the proper spell and fell into place over the sleep charm without raising a stir.

Angelique didn't relax, though, for she could mentally feel *every* weapon and sharpened edge her fog touched while the preservation spell settled.

When the spell covered the last inch on the city wall, Angelique shakily exhaled.

That's it. It's stabilized now. As much as it surprises me to think it, it is safe. But I need to add some kind of defense so the city isn't pillaged and plundered in this state.

Already the afternoon sun began to burn away the mist, making everything less foreboding.

Angelique smiled slightly as she recalled a brisk afternoon with Roland and Evariste before she again started gathering her magic up.

It took a few moments to build the right amount of power—given Ciane's size, this was also going to be a massive power-suck—before she could start twisting it. Once she had the foundation laid, encircling the city perimeter, Angelique again spoke in the twisty language of magic.

The ground rumbled, and massive brambles and thorns burst out of the earth, forming a tall and thick protective hedge that surrounded all of Ciane.

Angelique kept twisting her magic, pushing more power into the spell until the thorns grew almost as high as the city walls and were as thick as some of the saplings Angelique had seen in Alabaster Forest.

She was shaky from adrenaline and the release of her nerves, but looking at the city she felt a brief moment of pride.

The spells—all of them—were strong and had a clear ringing feeling that echoed into the deepest parts of the city. They would hold, and they would protect Ciane.

This is why I want to make enchantress, why I will keep trying even if nearly every mage is against me. I want to use my terrible powers for good things and stand where others cannot.

A slight smile threatened to settle on her lips until her stomach rebelled, and nausea hit her like a wild boar.

She toddled back to Pegasus, pushing her head into his neck so she wouldn't groan at the sick feeling in her stomach.

Yep. Roland is right. This is definitely my price.

"There," she croaked. "Everything is asleep—including all animals—and there's a preservation spell layered in. It will preserve the moment in time so nothing in the city will spoil or rust, and the weather shouldn't change."

"Are you all right, Lady Enchantress?" Sir Isaia asked.

Angelique meant to wave a hand at him, but when she started to let go of Pegasus, she almost sagged to the ground. "Yes, I'm fine. Just feeling a little ill."

Firra finally chose this moment to disengage from her fight with Donaigh. "Are you certain?" She nudged her mount closer to Pegasus so she could peer at Angelique. "That was a much more complex—and powerful—spell than I was expecting."

Angelique managed to pull herself on top of Pegasus, slumping over his neck. "I'm fine. It just used quite a bit of magic." She snapped her mouth shut when her stomach churned and threatened to make her revisit her lunch, but the feeling passed after a moment. Remaining draped over Pegasus' neck, Angelique pointed her head in Sir Isaia's direction. "You'll need to hack your way through the thorns, Sir Isaia, to re-enter Ciane. They will replace themselves after a time, so have no fear of cutting them back too much."

Isaia bowed while mounted. "Thank you, Lady Enchantress."

Angelique tried to sit up, but that made the world spin, so she settled for waving at him. "Happy to help. What next, Firra, Donaigh?"

"We planned to look for Carabosso next," Donaigh said, "as we're not too anxious to return to the Conclave and get a lecture. Also, King Giuseppe put a bounty on Carabosso's head, and I never say no to money."

"If you will excuse me," Isaia said. "I shall begin making my way to Ciane."

"Of course." Firra smiled at him. "Donaigh and I will try to drop by frequently to share intelligence. I hope the princes arrive swiftly!"

"Take care of Little Rose," Donaigh said.

Isaia nodded and wheeled his horse towards the wall of thorns.

Angelique watched him go with narrowed eyes. She wasn't sure if it was her upset stomach or just general tiredness that made her say it, but she blurted out, "Is Sir Isaia Princess Rosalinda's true love?"

"What?" Firra asked.

"Nothing." Angelique made herself sit up, though she pressed a hand into her gut. "I wish you both well on your hunt."

"Do you want to come with us?" Donaigh asked. Though he tried to nonchalantly adjust his straw hat, his grin was deeper than usual.

"I'd like to, but I think I'm going to outmaneuver the Veneno

Conclave and go there before the Council can send me a summons," Angelique said.

Firra winced. "I'm sorry."

Angelique sighed. "As am I."

Donaigh squinted at the sky. "Any news on Lord Enchanter Evariste?"

"Not since I've uncovered that he's somewhere in a mirror, no." Angelique twisted uncomfortably so she could look east. *No sense putting it off. I might as well face my doom. And if I get there fast enough, I can ask Clovicus for help.*

"Is there any way we could help, Lady Enchantress?" Firra asked.

"We could come with you before we begin our hunt for Carabosso and speak on your behalf," Donaigh said.

Angelique tried to smile at the pair, but it was tough given her stomach flopped in her insides like a fish. "Thank you. I am grateful, but I don't think it will make a difference to the Council. Only Evariste could..." She stopped herself before she could say anything that sounded too much like self-pity or would flood her with another wave of bitterness.

She shook her head. "It doesn't matter, but thank you for the support."

"We stand with you—if not physically, then in the heart," Firra called after her.

Angelique waved, but when Pegasus chose a path between grass fields surrounding Ciane, she let herself wilt again.

All this meddling with magic. I only hope it pays off. But even if I did the spells right, in a way it still feels like a failure that we had to resort to such a measure. I've been casting so much magic, but it seems like nothing is truly resolved, and I'm just waiting for the next fire that I have to put out.

CHAPTER 27

Though Angelique chose to face her bleak future head-on, she couldn't bring herself to go to Torrens and use Evariste's office portal to reach the Conclave quickly. Pegasus gladly carried her to the Conclave fortress, but as she expected, while riding through Loire and on her way north to Mullberg, a black crow dropped a letter in Angelique's lap, ordering her to present herself immediately before the Council, or they would put a warrant out for her.

Which is why, in mid-fall, Angelique trooped down the long hallway that led into Hallowed Hall, Clovicus strolling with her.

"Relax, Angelique," Clovicus said.

Angelique snorted. "Relax. Yes. That seems perfectly easy to do when I know they will punish me for this."

"They can't punish you for anything without Evariste unless you do something terrible—like black magic," Clovicus reminded her.

"That's not going to stop them from trying," Angelique grimly said.

"Yes, well, we need to work on your tendency to self-judge,"

Clovicus said. "You cower quite a bit whenever they put you on the stand, which is what makes them think they can bully you."

Angelique shot the lord enchanter a glare when they paused outside the door and waited for the war mage on guard to open the doors for them.

Clovicus rolled his eyes. "Looking at me like that doesn't mean it's not true."

Angelique smiled at the war mage. "Thank you," she said before she hurried into Hallowed Hall.

Clovicus, however, wasn't done. "Do you think Evariste would be happy watching you troop before them every few months? Let me answer in case you doubt him: no." He spoke in a whispering hiss as he trailed Angelique.

Angelique stopped several steps short of the hateful, lit dais that was waiting for her and turned her back to the waiting Council so she could address Clovicus. "I'm trying to do what Evariste taught me to—I'm trying to be a valiant enchantress!"

"And you are!" Clovicus said. "You're the best blazing enchantress alive even though you're still an apprentice—and not just because you're powerful but because you're *good*. But it seems you haven't figured it out yet, so I'm going to tell you straight: the Veneno Conclave doesn't want outstanding mages that the populace adores and celebrates as heroes. They want an organized machine that they can count on to fall in line and follow the rules."

"Lord Enchanter Clovicus," Lord Enchanter Crest called, sounding amused. "Why do I get the feeling that whatever you're whispering into Apprentice Angelique's ear, it isn't complimentary to us?"

Clovicus met Angelique's gaze and nodded, then backed up. "Surely you're joking, Crest. Everyone knows I have the *highest* regard for the law."

Lord Enchanter Tristisim scowled. "Only so you can figure out how to get around it. Apprentice, step onto the dais sometime this century, if it pleases you," he growled.

Angelique scurried up the steps, climbing onto the dais that was almost washed out due to the brilliance of the light that shone above it.

Five enchanters and enchantresses stared Angelique down. (The sixth, Lazare, was still snoring on his desk.)

Primrose was the first to speak. "Ciane, Angelique? An entire city?" She sighed and looked sorrowful.

"I was directly appealed to by Princess Alessia and Prince Consort Filippo, as well as the Magic Knights of Sole," Angelique said. "They were concerned about the mental state of King Giuseppe and the upheaval effect Princess Rosalinda's slumber was having on the country."

"You put an entire city to sleep—the *capital* of Sole, no less," Enchanter Crest said. "You should have appealed to us before doing anything so drastic."

"There wasn't time," Angelique said. *Which has seemingly become a theme in my life.* "There was no way I could return here and make the trip back to Sole. If I hadn't arrived when I had, there's no telling what King Giuseppe would have done."

"We don't entrench ourselves in politics, Apprentice," Enchantress Galendra said in a lecturing tone.

"Even to save a *country*?" Angelique asked.

"You stomped all over rules and traditions long held by the Veneno Conclave," Enchantress Primrose gently said.

"Something you've done with aplomb in your master's absence," Tristisim added dryly.

"Because I've had no other choice," Angelique said.

"There is always a choice, Apprentice," Felicienne said.

Crest sighed. "I have tried to support you, but you grow more and more bold in your actions."

"Because the tragedies striking our lands are growing," Angelique said. "I did not seek to enchant Ciane for the *fun* of it!"

"Be careful with your words, apprentice," Tristisim warned.

Angelique sucked in a breath of air and gritted her teeth. She forced herself to take out the sting and sarcasm she so wanted to use. "Ciane was in a state of emergency." Her voice was admirably calm, not betraying the frustration that rocked in her. "If I followed Veneno Conclave law, the entire country might have fallen."

"I understand you meant well," Primrose said. "But can't you see how dangerous it would be if we let all mages run around, using their power however they like?"

"We have rules and regulations to keep the continent safe," Tristisim said. "They have withstood for centuries. Do you really think you are wiser than all those who passed before you?" He slammed his fist down on his desk, waking Lazare.

"Arrest them!" Lazare shouted. He blinked owlishly down his long nose and smacked his lips. "Hmm? What's Evariste's apprentice doing here?"

"She was ordered to appear before us," Primrose loudly said so the elderly enchanter could hear her. "For putting all of Ciane under a sleeping enchantment."

"What a terrible idea." Lazare yawned and scratched his beard. "Would have been far easier to sink it underwater."

Tristisim shifted a disturbed gaze to Lazare, but Primrose merely patted the old man's hands. "She's here because she broke our core belief and involved herself with country politics."

Lazare squinted in the light. "I thought we called her here because she scares us with her sheer amount of power, and we have to keep her in line."

Hallowed Hall was silent for several long and uncomfortable moments.

Angelique curled her hands into fists. *Don't cry*, she told herself. *I knew they feared me. It was inescapable.* And yet, Lazare's words were a dagger to her heart.

They, the Council of the Veneno Conclave—some of the most

respected magic users in the community—feared her. It was something she had long known, but to hear a Council Member *voice* it was a different thing.

"Don't be silly, Lazare," Primrose finally said. "She's a sweet girl."

"One who throws around enough power to put an entire capital to sleep," Tristisim muttered.

Felicienne shook her head. "I said she was dangerous," she said with enough fire to show she'd been holding back for a while. "To be able to use such power on a whim?"

"Having power isn't dangerous," Clovicus said. "Evariste or myself would be capable of putting Ciane to sleep as well."

"Perhaps," Felicienne said stiffly. "But you don't have war magic as your core."

"This is the trouble that happens when one breaks the laws of nature," Tristisim growled.

"War mages are not against the law of nature—they're respected members of the Conclave," Clovicus snapped.

"Yes, as *mages*, not enchantresses," Tristisim said.

Angelique stared at the railing of the dais and wondered if Lazare's blundering admittance was kinder than these false pretenses they tried to feed her about *tradition* and what was *natural*.

It wasn't a nice feeling, knowing she was beheld in terror like a wild animal. In fact, it was soul-crushing. But at least she now knew straight out it was her power they feared. She could understand that.

Their insistence on pretending otherwise, however, was a blade between the shoulders and a wound that wouldn't heal because it gave her false hope that if she said the right thing, looked the right way, did all they asked, she would eventually be accepted.

But they won't. Angelique finally knew this. *In the end, all I can do is embrace my purpose as an enchantress and find my worth in that—in helping those who need it and protecting the continent from harmful magic. Because I will never win them over.*

Not ever.

"Your conduct is unacceptable," Tristisim continued. "You've made it clear you will act out as you see fit."

Clovicus snorted and scratched his jaw. "Angelique has acted to avert crises; you can hardly punish her for that. And if someone was dense enough to punish her for such a thing, it would be Evariste's responsibility to do so."

"She should be reprimanded," Galendra squeaked.

"And you've done so again and again," Clovicus said. "And you'll continue hauling her here to yell at her every few months when you should be *thanking* her for her actions—when you would laud anyone else who has done what she has."

"We would do no such thing," Primrose protested.

Angelique shut her eyes as she listened to the argument.

Clovicus was right. The Council would forever be summoning her for everything she did. They would never leave her be.

Peace. All I want is just a little peace.

"I said it before—our rules and laws have kept us safe for centuries," Tristisim rumbled. "We must continue to observe them."

"The rules and laws you love so dearly didn't save Evariste, and they haven't found him either." The words were out of Angelique's mouth before she realized she was speaking, but she didn't regret them.

"You are young, Apprentice. You know little of the world. It's understandable that you cannot see the wisdom in them," Primrose said.

Her placating smile was Angelique's undoing.

She was sick of having to face judgement with a bowed head and listen as they spoke down to her, failing to recognize that the peace the continent enjoyed was going up in flames.

I'm done. I will not apologize for what I do. I will cower no more about the magic I have used to save others.

Angelique's power churned around her, but she impatiently pushed it off. "The folly is not with me, but the laws," she hotly said. "I have broken the rules and laws you so venerate because we are living in a time they were not meant for. The continent is *not* at peace! Royals are getting attacked; black mages are trying to get holds in each country; catastrophes abound. I will do whatever it takes to save lives and spare innocent people, even if it means crossing lines we previously stayed out of. Because if we don't, whatever chaos boiling right now is only going to get worse!"

The Council was silent.

Primrose covered her mouth with a hand and glanced at her fellow members. Tristisim scowled, making deep, ugly wrinkles around his mouth and eyes. Felicienne held a hand to her heart—as if Angelique's hot response frightened her, and it likely did—but Lazare merely scratched his beard and jutted out his lower lip.

Crest tapped his pointer finger on his desk. "Apprentice," he said soothingly.

He's going to pacify me. He thinks he can, after all the questions they've shouted at me and the vague threats they've made. He thinks he can cow me because every time, I do bow to them and apologize for doing what's right.

Angelique raised her chin. *But not today—and not ever again.*

"Don't bother to send for me again—for I won't come," she said.

Gasps rippled through the council, and even Clovicus swiveled so he could peer up at her.

"The continent is in danger, and I don't have time for your lectures and suspicions. Deliver it in writing if you must, but I will not pause my work to give you a chance to soothe your fears that I am a monster under your control," Angelique continued.

Felicienne shook with anger. "We will send mages after you!"

Angelique smiled—not her polite one, but the amused smirk she usually hid. "Of course. When you can find Evariste so you can formally charge me, I will happily return. But until then, you'll have to forcibly remove me from whatever palace and royal family I am working with at the moment. I'm *sure* they won't mind you ripping away the only mage who is actively addressing their concerns and trials."

Tristisim slammed his fist on his desk again. "This is an outrage!"

"I don't care," Angelique said.

"Angelique, I understand your frustration, but you cannot ignore laws and rules," Primrose said.

"Can't I? You six seem to enjoy doing so," Angelique blandly said.

Clovicus whistled and then lowly chuckled.

Felicienne sent him a poisonous look, but he only smiled benignly at her.

"I am finished with these sessions." Angelique's voice was hard as she glared up at the Council. "What will you charge me with?"

The Council was silent.

Clovicus casually fixed a fold in his robe. "Seems to me that since you haven't been charged with black magic—only with breaking the rules—nothing can be done without Evariste."

Tristisim glared at him.

"Good day, Council Members." Angelique curtsied to them before she stormed down the dais steps.

None of them called for her—though Clovicus ambled after her—as she swept from the room.

"That was quite the display," Clovicus said after the door to Hallowed Hall shut behind them.

Angelique paused long enough so he could catch up to her. "I'm tired of these games. Something is going on, and I no longer have the energy to waste on...this."

Clovicus shrugged. "Perhaps, but I'm mostly glad you stood up for yourself. It bodes well for Evariste."

Angelique frowned. "Why would that have anything to do with Evariste?"

Clovicus raised an eyebrow. "I wonder."

More puzzles that I frankly don't have the energy to wonder over. Angelique shook her head. "Regardless, it's finished." She started down the hallway again, moving a little quicker than was acceptable.

"What will you do next?" Clovicus asked.

Angelique straightened her shoulders as she felt for the first time in years—perhaps even the first time since the magnitude of her magic was discovered—*free*.

"Now," Angelique said, "I see if we can make any sense out of these 'incidences.'"

Evariste watched Liliane through half-lowered eyelids as she set to work painting a troll.

He tried to stand up, but every muscle in his body protested, having just survived another draining in which Liliane funneled his magic for use of another dark spell. He licked his cracked lips and swallowed, cringing when it sent a spike of pain down his spine.

Get up. Go insult her poor spells or something. Be an irritant. Don't get placid! Though his thoughts railed at him, his body wouldn't cooperate.

He was exhausted from the gray that invaded his sleep and waking hours, and he was in a lot of pain from being drained. The fight in him wasn't quite enough to prod him to his feet.

Acri—standing in attendance near his mother—smirked at Evariste, as if he could sense the pathetic nature of his thoughts.

Evariste narrowed his eyes. *The first thing I'm going to do when I get out of here is clean this brat's face. Then I'm going to break a hole in this cave so I can see the sun again.* It was one of the things he missed most—the warm caress of the sun, the fresh smell of dampened soil, teasing Angel—*don't think of Angelique.*

Heavy footsteps pounded down the hallway that led into Evariste's chamber.

"Liliane!" Suzu rushed into the room so quickly, her black skirts were askew.

Liliane set her paintbrush aside. "Is something wrong?" She pointedly looked at Suzu's windblown appearance.

Suzu glared angrily. "*Yes*," she snapped. "Something is most certainly *wrong*! We just received word: Apprentice Angelique placed *all* of Ciane under a spell—including the royal family."

Liliane stiffened. "What?"

Suzu shook her head, tossing her mussed black hair out of her face. "Apparently she showed up after the princess set off her own curse. The whole capital is asleep—from the nobles to the maids to the chickens."

Acri frowned. "But it was going perfectly. King Giuseppe was acting irrationally and well on his way to starting a civil war!"

"She—or someone else—must have noticed, because she stopped that! Many of the Legendary Knights made it out of the city before she shut it down—they're forcibly holding the country together." Suzu snarled like an angry cat and stalked back and forth.

Evariste peered in Liliane's direction, trying to gauge her reaction.

She was frowning sharply but remained seated on her stool, her hands in her lap.

"She's getting to be dangerous," Suzu said. "I received a report from some of our contacts. Apparently when the Council called her in to take her to task for putting an entire city under, she shouted at them and informed them she wasn't going to listen to their summons anymore."

Acri cursed. "I thought she was supposed to be docile and fragile!"

"She was," Suzu snapped.

"Then what happened? You said the loss of Evariste alone would be enough to mentally cripple her! Funus said we didn't have to worry about leaving her loose." Acri flicked his hands, and one of his black daggers appeared.

"Indeed," Liliane said. "I, too, would like to know how we came to so badly underestimate a single mage."

Evariste straightened, but he didn't dare stand. He didn't want to draw their attention to him and distract them.

"All our observations about her said she would self-destruct without support. She is the pariah of the Veneno Conclave," Suzu said. "By all our predictions, she *should* be trampled underfoot by now."

"Then *find out* whatever is keeping her afloat and destroy it!" Liliane shouted. For a moment she looked frightening, her sweet features twisted in an ugly sneer. "I will not have centuries of planning ruined by one inexperienced mage!"

Acri played with his dagger. "She's more powerful than we thought to be able to put all of Ciane under a spell."

"I don't care if she's as strong as the *Snow Queen*!" Liliane's voice wasn't musical, but hot and crackling like the ravenous roar of a forest fire. "She is afraid of her power and won't use it—we cannot lose to such a pathetic example of a mage! We are stronger and have been preparing for centuries. This failure is on *you*!"

Suzu shrank back, and even Acri backed up a few steps and looked down. "Yes, Liliane," Suzu murmured.

Liliane cleared her throat, and some of the savagery left her, though her voice was still growly, and a sharp scowl bent her lips. "We can no longer afford to let her languish in our belief that she will self-destruct. *Acri*."

"Yes, Mother?"

Liliane's expression turned cold. "Kill her. I don't want her alive or taken captive; I want her in the ground. End it."

"NO!" Evariste lunged at the mirror, smacking against the glass as he pounded on it.

Acri ignored him and bowed. "Yes, Mother. I will enjoy this mission." He smirked and glanced mockingly at Evariste.

"Do *not* fail me," Liliane warned him. "She has war magic—even if she's clumsy with it. Take her out fast—no playing around. Do you understand?"

Acri bowed. "Yes, Mother."

"Then go," Liliane snapped.

Acri sauntered off, calling a sword forged of shadows as he disappeared through the door.

Liliane took a breath, and the darkness fled from her expression. When she opened her eyes, the ugly twist to her pretty features were gone. "You had best hope the rider succeeds in taking out Rumpelstiltskin." She started after her son—though at a much slower and more sedate glide.

"He has him trapped in Verglas," Suzu said.

"Trapped is *not* the same as slain."

"Perhaps, but we've received positive news from Mullberg and Farset…"

The ladies' voices faded from hearing range.

Evariste fell to his knees, simultaneously shocked, proud, and concerned.

That Angelique had not only the power, but the ability to craft and stabilize a spell powerful enough to affect the entire capital was surprising. She must have come far in her abilities since Evariste had been taken, for such a thing was normally only possible for more experienced enchanters and enchantresses.

But even if she had grown, Evariste knew she'd be no match for Acri.

Unless…she used her war magic.

And that was not something Evariste could guarantee.

He shouted and punched the unbreakable glass pane, making his bones crunch painfully.

She has to fight. She has to win.

The End

For free Curse of Magic extras and short stories, visit kmshea.com!

THE LOVE POTION

This short story takes place during the events of Apprentice of Magic.

Angelique sat in the safety of Evariste's workshop, shivering as she stared at the blank paper on her desk.

She was *supposed* to be writing up the report for the sentient-puppet-assignment/fiasco they had just returned from solving the day prior.

A diligent student would have begun their report last night. Or after breakfast. Or before cleaning the entire workshop from top to bottom.

She suppressed another shudder. *But I can't bring myself to write about it.*

"You still haven't started your paper?" Roland, Angelique's magical kitten, mewled from his velvet cushion. He was bigger now, but still a little clumsy as he tried to majestically get off his cushion and instead slipped and faceplanted.

Angelique rubbed her pointer finger in the fuzzy black fur on the top of his head. "I can't help it. It was a traumatizing event."

"It was a *puppet*."

"A very *rude* puppet!"

Faintly, Angelique heard a knock.

Roland opened his mouth—probably with an insult in mind—but Angelique lightly tapped his nose to distract him.

There, another knock.

"Ruffian!" Roland sputtered.

"Sorry." Angelique marched across the workroom, aiming for the stairs.

"Where are you going?" Roland called after her.

Angelique paused at the top step. "Someone's at the door, I need to answer it."

Roland hopped off the desk and made his way towards her. "You're just trying to get out of your report."

"No, I'm not," Angelique fibbed. "Evariste is gone visiting with King Channing and Queen Lisheva. He told me to look after the Thicket in his absence."

"It does not mean you aren't purposely delaying your work. Now pick me up." Roland batted at her skirts with a paw.

Angelique grumbled as she scooped the kitten up, carrying him downstairs where she plopped him on an end table in the hallway.

He protested, but she turned away too quickly for him to make a jump for her.

"Be good," Angelique said as she put a smile on her face.

"I am *intrinsically* good!" Roland complained.

"I wasn't talking to you." Angelique took a deep breath, rolled her shoulders back, then threw the door open. "Hello, can I help you?"

A young woman stood at the house entrance, a pleasant smile on her lips though her eyes were wide with awe as she yanked her stare from the house to Angelique. Her green gown was clean and serviceable, and though her undershirt had only a touch of embroidery at the neckline, the cloth was a bright white.

Middle class, then. Her hands say she does some work—a royal servant, perhaps? Or maybe a merchant's daughter?

"Ah, yes," the young woman said. (In truth she looked about seventeen or eighteen, which made Angelique more disposed to think of her as a young girl, but she was fairly certain if she called the young lady that she would protest the youthful idea.) "Is Lord Enchanter Evariste available?"

Angelique shifted slightly so she wouldn't lean against the doorframe as she wanted to. "I'm afraid not."

The girl's expression drooped. "Oh, I see," she said in a voice heavy with disappointment.

Angelique gave the girl another lookover. "But I am his apprentice and an Enchantress-in-Training. Perhaps I may be of service?"

She brightened, her eyes shining again. "Oh, would you, Lady Enchantress?"

"Enchantress-in-Training."

"I do *so* need your help," she continued without registering the correction.

Angelique briefly pressed her lips together as she weighed out her options. *I'm not keen to invite her inside as I don't know exactly what the situation is. Staying outside the Thicket would be wisest.* Angelique stepped through the doorway, pulling it shut behind her—ignoring Roland's protests as she did so. "Why don't we take a stroll through the yard, and you can tell me why you are in need of aid."

The girl nervously clasped her hands together and bit her lower lip. "Thank you, Lady Enchantress! Thank you."

"I'm afraid—as I said earlier—it's only Enchantress-in-Training, miss...?"

"Amice, My Lady."

Angelique nodded as they approached the pond—keeping an eye on the swans that paddled on its clear surface. (The birds, though beautiful, occasionally got it in their cracked knobs to act more like attack dogs than swans.) "What seems to be the problem, Miss Amice?"

Amice blushed and wrung her hands. "I am in love," she declared.

Angelique waited a moment or two for more information, but it seemed none was forthcoming. *How am I supposed to react to that?* "...Congratulations?" she asked more than stated.

Amice slapped her palms to her cheeks. "Pate is so handsome and strong. If I meet his gaze it sends a thrill through me! I steal away whenever I get the chance to watch him work the forge—he's a blacksmith's apprentice you know."

Angelique squinted in the bright light, more than a little confused. *Why would being in love bring her to an enchanter's doorstep?* "I see?"

Amice giggled as they followed the curve of the pond to the far shore. Abruptly her cheer leaked from her, and her lower lip trembled. "There is just one problem."

Ah, here we go.

"Pate does not love me in return."

Angelique blinked. "Pardon?"

"Pate does not love me in return—he is sweet on another girl. And so, I am in need of a love potion—the strongest you have!" Amice held her hands in front of her, in an almost prayerful gesture as she scrambled to stand in front of Angelique. "Please, Lady Enchantress, make one for me!"

Angelique hadn't stopped blinking as she struggled to process the girl's rather jumbled words. "You love a man who doesn't love you, so you want me to brew you a love potion that will *force* him to love you?"

"Yes!"

Is she insane? At the very least she is stupidly infatuated—someone in love would never *make such a selfish request!* Angelique inhaled deeply, forcing herself to remain calm. "I'm afraid that's not possible, for love potions don't exist."

"They don't exist? Surely not!" Amice protested. "You must mean they are only frowned upon?"

"No," Angelique said through clenched teeth. "I mean *they do not exist*. Love is a powerful emotion that plays an important role in various magics. It is *impossible* for magic to twist love in the manner you desire—not even black magic is capable of such a thing!"

This was correct—mostly. Of course, there were short term potions that could make a person infatuated, but they didn't last for more than a day, or at most a week, but even those potions created more of a puppy-like infatuation than true love.

Love is far too powerful for even enchanters and black mages to muddle with. We can use it with *our magic, but we cannot use our magic to* make *it. It would be like a single ant attempting to carry a horse—impossible.*

The tremble of Amice's lower lip became more pronounced as they rounded another bend in the pond, taking them back to the entrance of the house. "T-truly?"

"Truly," Angelique said with some wryness. "No, I'm afraid Miss Amice that if you want this Pate's heart, you'll have to go about it the old-fashioned way and *earn* his admiration. There are no short cuts when it comes to love."

"I see...but maybe there is a potion that will make him think well of me?" the young girl tried.

(*Definitely* a girl now, because only someone childish would make a request like this.)

"There is not," Angelique said firmly. "Good day, Miss Amice." She opened the door to the house and stepped inside.

"Oh, but maybe—"

"Have a safe journey home." Angelique shut the door on the young girl's request, shaking her head in dismay.

Roland, who was curled up in a fluffy ball, cracked an eye open. "You look like someone plucked your feathers. What happened?"

"Nothing," Angelique said. "It's just *shocking* how people don't stop to ponder the ways their personal desires might affect others."

"Humans are selfish," Roland yawned. "Now pick me up and take me to the kitchen. I desire a snack."

"And *that's* not selfish?"

"It is, but I am a magnificent creature worthy of such treatment—not an ugly, mostly bald being like you humans."

"I see. Well if you're so *magnificent* surely you can manage a small thing like getting to the kitchen yourself."

"No, for I am—where are you going? Angelique—I say!"

THE FOLLOWING DAY, when Angelique was pushing a unicorn foal from the kitchens, there was another knock on the door.

"It sounds like we have company," Evariste said. He also left the kitchens, sandwiching Angelique between himself and the unicorn foal.

"Yes, I will answer the door." Angelique wriggled, trying to free herself.

"We could answer it together," Evariste brightly suggested.

"No, it's fine." She grabbed the unicorn by the neck when he started nibbling on a leaf of a rare orchid, dragging the foal in her wake.

She stopped at the door just long enough to smooth her skirts and twitch her hair into place, then fixed a polite smile on as she threw the door open. "May I help you?"

Standing outside was a brawny young man. Though his appearance was neat and clean, the faint smell of smoke and hot metals wafted from him.

A smith of some sort, Angelique decided as she glanced at his muscled forearms.

"Good day," the blacksmith said rather nervously. "Is this the house of Enchanter Evariste?"

"It is," Angelique said. "I am his apprentice and an Enchantress-in-Training. How can I help you, master...?"

"Hudde," the young man provided.

Angelique nodded, then grabbed the unicorn when it leaned forward to sniff Hudde and narrowly missed stabbing him with its pearly horn.

Hudde rolled his shoulders back. "I'm here for a love potion."

Angelique almost released the unicorn in her surprise. *Another one of these? Why?* Angelique opened her mouth to give the young boy his answer (He, too, would now be relegated to boy due to the nature of his selfish request) but he held up his hand to forestall her.

"I'm in love with a beautiful woman, Amice," Hudde said, shocking her a second time.

What are the chances that he wants a love potion for the girl who wanted a love potion for someone else?

He continued, "She is kind, gentle, and unselfish."

"I wouldn't be so sure about that," Angelique muttered.

"But she is sweet on my fellow apprentice, Pate," Hudde explained. "Even though everyone knows Pate is a goner for Rohese."

"The plot thickens," Angelique dryly said.

"To protect her from heartbreak, I would like a love potion that I might use on Amice, so she would come to fall in love with me instead," Hudde said. "For I do love her, and I would do anything to keep her from pain."

"Yes, I can tell by your *genuine* request for a love potion that is not *at all* self-serving," Angelique said.

"Exactly!" Hudde said brightly.

Angelique sighed and clenched her eyes shut to stifle her desire to thump her head against the doorframe in her irritation.

"So, you will make one for me, then?"

"I'm afraid not." Angelique opened her eyes again and stood tall, forcing herself to slant her eyebrows in an expression of slight sympathy. "Love potions exist only in stories. They are not real, and they cannot be made."

Thank goodness. As exemplified by this, humans are already terrible at love. We don't need more help bungling our attempts at romance.

"But can't you—"

"So sorry, but I'm afraid not. Safe travels!" Angelique cheerfully bid.

She firmly shut the door and sighed, sagging slightly.

"That was an unusual request," Evariste said from directly behind her.

Angelique grudgingly turned around to face him. "I had one yesterday as well."

Evariste winked and briefly squeezed her hand. "You handled it perfectly."

"Thank you. It's a *silly* desire."

"Yes. Unfortunately, such things seem to come and go in fashion. I remember when I was an apprentice, Clovicus and I were sent to investigate a swindler who was posing as a mage and selling fake love potions. He had the whole region in an uproar."

Angelique covered her mouth with her fingers in a show of dismay. "How unfortunate."

"Yes, though it was outrageously funny when he revealed he was only giving them water with juice from crushed berries. Shall we return to our tea?"

A DAY PASSED, and Angelique thought the strange influx of love-potion-seekers was over.

She thought wrong.

In the late afternoon, just at the edge of dusk, there was a knock at the door. Given that Evariste was reviewing the report she had *finally* written for the sentient puppet incident, Angelique slipped downstairs to answer the knock.

She swung it open and was surprised to find a middle-aged man on the doorstop.

He stood with quiet confidence that perhaps bordered on arrogance given the slant of his chin, and wore clothes that were carefully pressed and meticulously in place. His blonde hair was threaded with silver and gave him an air of competence, but his smile seemed a little brittle.

"Good evening." One of his eyebrows flicked up when he studied Angelique. "I have come to discuss a business transaction with Lord Enchanter Evariste."

Her hackles raised, Angelique frowned. "Enchanter Evariste is occupied at the moment. I am his apprentice and an Enchantress-in-Training. How can I help you?"

"Very good," the man said. "You may be allowed to help me, then, for I am seeking a love potion.

Angelique's smile turned feral. "*Are you?*"

"Not for myself, but my daughter, Rohese. She has a suitor, a blacksmith."

"Pate?" Angelique guessed.

The man blinked. "Are you skilled in the magic of foresight?"

"Maybe. Why do you need the potion?"

"Because I want her to marry wealth. My brother-in-law has connections with a rich merchant with a single son who agreed to marry Rohese. But my wife refuses to make the girl marry for something other than love, so I'd like to manufacture that connection."

"Can't be done," Angelique said. "*So* sorry."

The man bullishly shook his head. "Money is no object."

"It has nothing to do with money. Love potions aren't real. They are fables. Made up."

The man pursed his lips. "Let me talk to Lord Enchanter Evariste."

"He'll tell you the same thing. Love potions don't exist, and even if they did no mage would make one as it *coerces* a human being. Good luck with your daughter, and good evening."

Angelique slammed the door on the objecting man and smiled smugly for a moment. *Well. That made me feel a bit better. Though if I ever find out who started this love potion craze I would appreciate being given three minutes alone with them and a heavy, thickly bound book of morals.*

She shook her head as she started down the hallway, hoping that was the end of it.

BRIGHT and early the following morning, Angelique held her breath as she made a tiny twist in the spell she was working on.

Using her magic, water from a porcelain teacup rose into the air in individual droplets, glowing with a rainbow haze. The water flowed together, forming the liquid shape of a galloping horse.

"Excellent, Angel. That's just the right amount of control you need," Evariste said, his voice barely above a murmur. He stood beside her, his head slightly tilted as he watched her work.

Angelique gave him the smallest of nods and licked her lips, almost afraid that too much movement would break her concentration and destroy the shape. Slowly, carefully, she pushed a tiny amount of her magic into the water, and the misty horse began to gallop in place.

"Making shapes out of water, ice, fire, or any element, is a great way to perfect your grasp on that particular element. It's tiring, but the more you do it, the easier it will become." Evariste was silent for several moments, then added. "And don't be afraid to interact with your exercises."

Angelique swallowed, her eyes pinned on the horse as she made it toss its head, sending tiny flecks of water into the air. "What do you mean?"

"Here."

Out of her peripheral vision, Angelique saw Evariste reach for her right hand. Sliding his palm along the back of her hand, he pulled her fingers forward until Angelique reached out in front of her, and the water horse settled on her pointer finger.

Angelique blinked at the wet, dappled sensation of the horse prancing the length of her finger.

Evariste lightly squeezed her palm. "Now—"

A knock at the door interrupted the Lord Enchanter and startled Angelique, breaking her concentration.

The water lost its shape and fell to the ground with a splat, splashing droplets everywhere.

"I'm sorry! So sorry, I'll clean it up right away." Angelique took a few steps backwards, looking for a rag to wipe up the liquid.

"Nonsense. You get the door, I can handle this," Evariste said.

Angelique bit her lip. "But I made the mess."

Evariste grinned as he flexed his hand, and blue magic twirled around his fingertips. "What mess?" he innocently asked as the water rose from the ground.

Angelique watched with admiration as he dexterously pulled the water into the air, then returned it to the cup Angelique had originally pulled it from.

He really is amazing.

Another knock at the door.

"I'm coming!" Angelique exited the kitchen and hurried down the hallway. She smiled as she flung open the door. "Good morning…" Her good cheer dropped, replaced with a wave of suspicion as she peered at the young lady on the house stoop.

With her brown eyes and brown hair she perhaps would have been common, except her smile—tentative as it was—was warm and bright.

And yet, given the past few days, what are the chances she wants a love potion?

"Can I help you?" Angelique asked with precise politeness.

"I hope so. Is this the home of Lord Enchanter Evariste?" the young lady—possibly girl—asked.

Angelique slightly narrowed her eyes. "...Yes."

"Would it be possible, then, to purchase an invisibility charm here?"

Angelique relaxed, her relief making her usually polite and kind smile a little more enthusiastic than necessary. "Of course! Please come in!"

After showing the girl to the front sitting room, Angelique turned to join Evariste in the kitchen to inform him of the situation, but paused at the threshold of the room. "Do you mind explaining why you need an invisibility charm? They can be *quite* expensive, but depending upon what you want we might be able to come up with a different charm that is more cost efficient."

"Yes, but, I'm afraid you're going to find my reason for wanting one to be rather silly," the young lady laughed self-consciously.

"Never, miss..."

"Rohese," the young lady said.

Rohese? Why does that sound familiar? WAIT. "You're Rohese—the Rohese, Pate the blacksmith's apprentice is sweet on?"

Rohese's brown eyes widened. "How did you know?"

"I have had some...*interesting* interactions with some folks from your hometown the past few days," Angelique dryly said. "So tell me, why do you want an invisibility charm? Given your fellows, I'll admit I'm surprised you're not asking after a love potion."

Rohese flinched, and Angelique stiffened, like a wolf scenting blood.

"No, I have no desire for a love potion," Rohese said. "No use for one either. I'd much rather go unnoticed."

"What do you mean?"

Rohese stared at her hands for several long moments. "I just want to live in peace. I like my life as it is now. I don't want to think about marriage yet. And I don't want to be hated."

Angelique narrowed her eyes. "Are they *troubling* you?"

"No, no! Nothing like that!" Rohese shook her head. "But, I hear the whispers. Amice has feelings for Pate, and sometimes it makes her a bit upset that Pate likes...someone else. And I know that Papa has been talking to a merchant. But I don't *want* to get married yet." Rohese pressed her lips tight together. "I work in the royal stables. I care for Queen Lisheva's mounts, and the mounts of her friend, Lady Vorah. It's extra special because before Lisheva was queen, girls weren't allowed to work in the stables. And she hired *me*! I don't *want* to give my work up yet. I just want to live in peace." She bit her lip, but Angelique could see the faint sheen of tears that glazed her eyes.

Angelique crossed the sitting room and crouched down in front of Rohese, taking her hands into her own. "Your desire is not silly, nor is it outrageous. You have a right to peace."

Rohese nodded, but pressed her lips together even tighter in an effort to keep tears from falling.

Angelique released Rohese's hands and leaned back on her heels as she considered the situation. "You live in Mersey, then?"

"No, in Upper Swell. A tiny village just a short walk north."

Angelique's smile grew. "Perfect. Go home, Rohese. I'll come visit you in a day or two with a spell that will help you live this life you want."

"What about payment?" Rohese asked.

Angelique darkly chuckled. "Don't worry about that. This situation strikes me as *needing* a moral lesson. And who better to deliver one than an Enchantress-in-Training?"

ANGELIQUE COULD HARDLY KEEP herself from gleefully rubbing

her hands. She stood in the center square of Upper Swell, dressed in a drab cloak with a hood.

Evariste's smile bordered on doting as he stood at her side, clothed in a far more extravagant cape. "I'm glad you are excited about today's outing. It's unusual for you to volunteer yourself for a task."

"Yes, but after Rohese's visit yesterday I realized that it wasn't enough just to turn away those seeking a love potion," Angelique piously said. "I need to teach them a lesson. With magic *and* words, of course!" She laughed airily and patted her hand over her heart.

"Naturally," Evariste agreed—though his grin seemed a bit lopsided and he loudly cleared his throat. "I'll just leave you to it, then. You're my cute little apprentice—you'll handle everything just fine." With a wink and a swirl of his cape he was gone, leaving Angelique alone in the bustling center square.

Dusk was settling in the sky, staining it shades of violet and scarlet red as the villagers headed for their homes.

Angelique grinned mischievously, then forcibly smoothed her lips and cleared her throat. "Attention, residents of Upper Swell!" she shouted. "I am Angelique, an Enchantress-in-Training and apprentice to Lord Enchanter Evariste. I have come to your fine town so that I might ask, who, here, would like a love potion?"

The bustle of movement slowed, then stopped as more and more residents paused to look in Angelique's direction.

"Come now, don't be shy!" Angelique coaxed. "Who would like a love potion?"

"Me! I want one!" Amice—the young *girl* who had first inquired after the potion—elbowed her way through to the center. "I *knew* you were lying when you said you couldn't make one!" She stormed up to Angelique and clicked her tongue in displeasure.

"Then I'll take one as well!" Hudde declared.

A middle-aged woman came after him, followed by several more villagers.

Eventually, Rohese's father joined the growing crowd. "I don't know why you felt the farce was necessary, but I see you have come to your senses," he scoffed.

"Uh-huh, yes," Angelique vaguely said. She caught sight of Rohese standing with another young lady, watching from under the awning of a shop. Angelique held a finger to her lips and winked at her, then returned her attention to the crowd.

It had grown beyond what Angelique had planned for—though her plan was still feasible even with the increase in size. *I didn't know this many people would be so selfish.*

"Is this everyone?" she asked. "I'm afraid I'll only be able to do this once..."

Several of the villagers murmured, and two more joined the crowd.

Of the sixty or so people gathered in the square, Angelique estimated about thirty—maybe forty tops—stood before her, self-seeking in their desires.

"No one else? Truly?" Angelique turned in a circle, scanning the crowd, then nodded. "Very well."

She spun around so she faced the horde of potion-seekers, then flung her right hand at them, throwing out the spell she had spent the day practicing and preparing. Her smile grew as she watched her silvery magic loop around the crowd.

"Thank you for joining me this *delightful* evening, and for giving me the chance to bestow upon you all a very important lesson," Angelique started. "It's funny, but it seems none of you standing before me stopped to think of what a love potion entails."

The potion-seekers glanced at one another, and the quiet hum of whispers settled in the square.

Angelique started to prowl the perimeter of the crowd around her huddled victims. "By definition, a love potion forces a person to feel a powerful emotion for someone else, *against their own will.* At its bones, a love potion is a spell of coercion. It's despotic in that it robs a person of their free choice, and puts them under the control of someone else."

She reached the head of the circle again and twisted on her heels, taking great pains to meet the potion-seekers' gazes. "It has become apparent to me that those of you who are standing before me are well aware of this, and yet *you don't care.* So." Angelique's smile turned predatory. "To help you understand why it's such a poor idea, I have just cast a spell to put you all under someone else's will: *mine.*"

The hushed whispers became frenzied murmurs, and judging by the panicked expressions on some of the potion-seekers' faces, they had figured out what spell she had cast.

"And my will is this: you will not move. You may stand, sit, or lie down, but you cannot step, scoot, or roll from the spot you stand in right now. No matter how you pull or struggle, you will not budge from this spot." Angelique's voice was loud and clear, piercing through the hubbub that ate away at the center square.

Several members of the crowd tried to walk away, panic flashing across their faces when they pulled at their feet and discovered they couldn't move.

"That's not fair!"

"This is monstrous!"

"A misuse of magic!"

"*Is it?*" Angelique was unable to keep the hiss from her voice. "Then what, pray tell, do you think *forcing* your affection upon someone is?"

Silence struck Upper Swell, and those whom Angelique had cast her freeze charm on gulped and stared at their feet.

"A drafty night outside is a grace you don't deserve," Angelique said. "Compared to the terrible things you would have me do, all for your personal exploit." She tilted her head back so she studied the crowd with half-lidded eyes. "Next time you feel the desire to force a person into something they don't want, or to twist their will against them, remember this night. Remember how powerless you felt, and how terrible it was to be unable to control your own body."

Abruptly, she turned so she addressed the villagers who had *not* taken the bait. "And as for you who did not compromise for the sake of a potion, you have my admiration and respect. But tell everyone of this night in Upper Swell, so that *all* might learn through this unfortunate but necessary trial."

Feeling rather dramatic, Angelique snapped her cloak, then glided off into the elongated shadows of the village.

When she reached a darkened street she almost hopped in her joy.

It worked! That lesson should stick for at least a few decades!

"Thank you, Lady Enchantress!"

Angelique quickly recovered from her glee and stood straight so she could offer Rohese a benevolent smile when she approached. "For?"

"That." Rohese gestured back in the direction of the town square. "For teaching them—all of us, really—a lesson."

"It was one that needed to be taught," Angelique dryly said. "I have no idea where the sudden interest in love potions came from, but it is *most* inappropriate."

"Oh, I can tell you who started it," Rohese chuckled. "It was Lady Vorah—Queen Lisheva's friend and companion."

Angelique—who was acquainted with the fiery Lady Vorah given that Evariste took pains to be on good terms with the Torrens King, Queen, and royal family—frowned. "*Vorah?* I would have thought she would lambast anyone who would dwell on such a thing."

Rohese laughed. "She meant it as a joke—she dropped by Upper Swell last week to thank me for training her favorite warhorse to bow whenever Queen Lisheva approached it. When I met her in the village square she jokingly said I must be feeding her horses love potions to get them to obey me so well."

Angelique cracked a smile. *Ahh yes, that does sound like Vorah.*

"I cannot thank you enough for your help, Lady Enchantress," Rohese continued, unaware of Angelique's thoughts. "I do think this will end my difficulties. It seems like it was a great deal of work, though. I apologize you had to go to such lengths."

She looked like she was contemplating curtsying, so Angelique rushed to respond.

"Great lengths? Not at all! *Teaching* is one of my great joys in life. Being able to impart such...wisdom upon folk is so invigorating."

"If you say so, Lady Enchantress."

"I do. Good evening, Rohese. Let me know if any trouble over this matter ever surfaces again."

Rohese did curtsey this time, but she grinned. "Somehow, I don't think there will be any requests for love potions for some time, Lady Enchantress. Good evening."

Angelique smiled and watched the young lady leave. Just before Rohese re-entered the village square, she called after her. "Rohese...do you even *like* Pate?"

Rohese blinked in surprise. "Of course. I'm in love with him—though I'm not ashamed to admit I fell in love with the horseshoes he makes first. They are of great quality."

Angelique blinked in surprise. "You love him, and yet...?"

"I love my work, Lady Enchantress," Rohese said simply. "Pate is willing to wait for me. So, I'd like to keep on working. For now."

Angelique watched in shock as the young lady marched off.

All of this drama, for that?

"Well done, Angelique."

Evariste would have surprised her with his sudden arrival, but after Rohese's revelation, Angelique didn't have it in her to be startled.

"Thank you," she numbly said.

Evariste's shoulders were shaking suspiciously—with laughter, perhaps?—and he had to cough twice before he managed to ask, "will you really leave the villagers outside all night?"

"No," Angelique said. "The spell will wear off around three in the morning. But I'm counting on them being too placid to realize it—which will further hit my point home when they finally *do* figure it out."

Evariste rubbed his chin, then pushed back the fringe of his bangs (magicked for the day given that the previous night his hair had been shorn close to the scalp.) "You don't sound as satisfied as you usually do after properly completing an assignment."

"I'm a bit in shock, actually," Angelique confessed.

"Over that young lady's parting comment?" he asked.

She nodded.

"Why?"

"I don't know entirely," Angelique confessed. "Maybe it just seems...surprising that this Pate of hers is willing to wait."

Evariste's smile turned soft and gentle. "Any man worth his salt would be willing to wait until the end of time for the right woman."

Angelique snorted. "If the wait is that long I question his intelligence because obviously there must be something wrong with the woman if she's not ready after *that* amount of time."

"Maybe she just needs to grow a little," Evariste gently suggested.

"Grow? *Flowers* grow." Angelique scoffed. "But what really gets me about this entire ordeal is that if people like Amice and Hudde were just more *honest* with each other and themselves, things might work out. Considering how easy communication can make life, it seems most people are morally opposed to it."

"Perhaps it's not as easy as you think," Evariste said.

"In what way? You open your mouth and the truth comes out. That sounds a lot easier than facing the Council."

Evariste smiled, though he shook his head. "That's hardly romantic."

"Bother romance. I'd much rather have a rare book of spells." Angelique rolled her eyes. "The way folk carry on you would think romantic love is the only thing that makes life worth living."

"One day I think—and hope—my dear apprentice, that you will discover the joys of love."

Angelique wanted to snort again, but she held it in and instead eyed her master as he gazed warmly upon her.

She *wanted* to tell him that she'd willingly seal her magic first (what was *she* going to do with romantic love? Her greatest concern in life was retaining her powers and avoiding becoming the Veneno Conclave's chained monster!) but there was something about the soft light in Evariste's eyes that kept her lips glued shut.

Evariste's smile grew as he stepped closer to her so his cloak brushed hers. "Now, shall we go home? Or do you wish to observe and watch your spell play out?"

"I'd like to go home, if that's all right. I have some assignments I would like to practice."

"I am yours to command, Angelique."

"Evariste," Angelique said in a slightly scolding tone. "I just spent the night impressing upon the folk of Upper Swell that it's *not* good to try and control another!"

"Even if they willingly surrender?"

"*Especially* then!"

"Well then, you'll just have to be extra diligent in what you want me to do!"

"*Evariste.*"

THE END

OTHER SERIES BY K. M. SHEA

The Snow Queen
Timeless Fairy Tales
The Fairy Tale Enchantress
The Elves of Lessa
Hall of Blood and Mercy
Court of Midnight and Deception
Pack of Dawn and Destiny
King Arthur and Her Knights
Robyn Hood
The Magical Beings' Rehabilitation Center
Second Age of Retha: Written under pen name A. M. Sohma

ADDITIONAL NOVELS

Life Reader
Princess Ahira
A Goose Girl

ABOUT THE AUTHOR

K. M. Shea is a fantasy-romance author who never quite grew out of adventure books or fairy tales, and still searches closets in hopes of stumbling into Narnia. She is addicted to sweet romances, witty characters, and happy endings. She also writes LitRPG and GameLit under the pen name, A. M. Sohma.

Hang out with the K. M. Shea Community at...
kmshea.com

Made in the USA
Middletown, DE
29 December 2024

68357627R00210